PRAISE FOR

THE

GOOD
LIAR

"With twists and turns, the lives of three women intersect in the most unexpected ways during the aftermath of a tragedy. Thought-provoking, suspenseful, and mysterious, *The Good Liar* is a true page-turner that explores the ways stories are connected and created, and what can be hidden underneath. This is a book you won't be able to put down!"

MEGAN MIRANDA, *New York Times* bestselling author
of *All the Missing Girls* and *The Perfect Stranger*

"A riveting story . . . The twists are shocking, the characters are well drawn but unpredictable, and the conclusion is as poignant as it is surprising. *The Good Liar* is thrilling, captivating, and not to be missed!"

KATE MORETTI, *New York Times* bestselling author of
The Vanishing Year and *The Blackbird Season*

"Lines will be crossed and secrets revealed when tragedy intersects three women in *The Good Liar*, a guilty pleasure you won't be able to put down until the very last page. A must read!"

LIZ FENTON and LISA STEINKE, authors of *The Good Widow*

"For many years, Catherine McKenzie has been writing some of the best thrillers around. She's outdone herself with *The Good Liar*, the powerful and heartbreaking story of the painful aftermath of a national tragedy. It's sharply written with engaging characters and twists and surprises up until the very last page. A smart, fast-paced, and riveting thriller!"

DAVID BELL, author of *Bring Her Home*

"In her latest, Catherine McKenzie continues to prove she's a master at crafting psychological thrillers. . . . The story is layered with superb twists and expert pacing, deftly building in suspense until its stunner of an ending. A compulsive read that kept me guessing!"

KERRY LONSDALE, *Wall Street Journal* bestselling author of *Everything We Left Behind* and *Everything We Keep*

"With her compelling characters, whip-smart dialogue, and edge-of-your-seat pacing, McKenzie asks how well we know those around us—even the people we love the most."

PAULA TREICK DeBOARD, author of *Here We Lie* and *The Drowning Girls*

"Catherine McKenzie isn't just a talented storyteller; she has a knack for asking the questions every woman secretly asks, and answering with a story that expresses our collective dreams and fears. . . . Far more than a first-rate page-turner, it's an exploration of the cost of keeping secrets, how the bonds between women both chafe and comfort, and how in the midst of the terror and beauty that is life, we find grace."

ALLISON LEOTTA, author of *The Last Good Girl*

"Catherine McKenzie has done it again . . . In yet another page-turner, three women, linked by trauma, transform from images seen through the camera's lens into human and relatable characters as their layered lives come into focus. As you settle in for this tense and compelling ride, you'll start to question who 'the good liar' really is—Cecily, Kate, witnesses, the media, friends, family, or maybe even Catherine McKenzie herself."

EMILY BLEEKER, bestselling author of
Wreckage and *When I'm Gone*

THE
GOOD
LIAR

CATHERINE McKENZIE

PUBLISHED BY SIMON & SCHUSTER

NEW YORK LONDON TORONTO SYDNEY NEW DELHI

Simon & Schuster Canada
A Division of Simon & Schuster, Inc.
166 King Street East, Suite 300
Toronto, Ontario M5A 1J3

This Simon & Schuster Canada edition April 2018

SIMON & SCHUSTER CANADA and colophon are
trademarks of Simon & Schuster, Inc.

For information about special discounts for bulk purchases,
please contact Simon & Schuster Special Sales at 1-800-268-3216
or CustomerService@simonandschuster.ca.

Library and Archives Canada Cataloguing in Publication
    McKenzie, Catherine, author The good liar / by Catherine McKenzie.
Issued in print and electronic formats. ISBN 978-1-5011-7856-6 (softcover).
—ISBN 978-1-5011-7858-0 (ebook)
    I. Title.
    PS8625.K4395G66 2018 C813'.6 C2017-904195-9 C2017-904196-7

Manufactured in the United States of America

10 9 8 7 6 5 4 3 2 1

ISBN 978-1-5011-7856-6
ISBN 978-1-5011-7858-0 (ebook)

For Sara—

For making it through.

CECILY

I was late. That's why I wasn't there when it happened.

Not in the building, not even that close.

I lost track of time that morning trying to get the kids organized and out the door. It happens sometimes. I'll have everything under control and then—*poof!*—an hour will have gone by and we've missed whatever deadline we were supposed to hit. School drop-off, a kid's birthday party, even an airplane once, despite the fact that we were in the terminal with plenty of time to get to our gate before pushback.

None of those misses ever made a permanent difference in my life. Not that I knew of, anyway. Just consternation and an eye roll from the kids. *Mo-om* being Mom.

Usually, it seemed beyond my control. I could've sworn I'd done everything possible to finish whatever needed to get done for me to arrive on time. That day, though . . . that day, I might've been late on purpose.

I can admit that now.

But then, my foot tapped at the sticky floor of the train car as if that might make it go faster. I counted down the stops from ten to one, like I was counting down to a rocket launch. And when the "L" finally pulled into the right station, I pushed past the slow, slow crowd and ran for the stairs.

Like *Alice in Wonderland's* White Rabbit, I was late, late, *late*.

My heart throbbed as I ran up the concrete stairs. That's probably why I didn't notice the first tremor or the panicked looks on the faces of the people I sprinted past. I was too focused on getting to my destination. When I was finally outside, I had to stop to catch my breath.

What I saw stopped me from breathing at all.

The building I was trying so desperately to get to was two blocks away. The October sun should've been glinting off its glass panels. Instead, they were engulfed in flames. Before I could process what was happening, screams swallowed me. It felt like being caught in that noise at the beginning of "Sgt. Pepper's Lonely Hearts Club Band"—that discordant, reverse sound that has a basis in something melodic, and yet not.

I remember only bits and pieces after that.

People running past me, my nose filling with the awful stench of burned plastic, the crushing heat. A feeling like the building was sucking in its breath, pulling me toward it, before it blew apart, the heat slamming into me. The ringing in my ears that reminded me of the bell on my son's bike when he was a child. Paper and debris and things I can't think about raining down around me, burning holes in the belted coat I'd picked out so carefully the night before, back when it felt like it mattered what I wore that day.

Then I lost the thread of time again. It's probably only minutes I can't account for, but if you told me it was hours, I'd have no basis to disprove you.

Through it all, I couldn't move. I was the lamppost more than one person rammed up against. I stood there, stuck, as the fire licked the building clean. And then a man's hand was in mine, tugging, tugging, and I could finally hear the instructions he was shouting and had the power to obey.

Run!

We ran.

PART

I

ONE YEAR LATER

I

POSTER CHILD

CECILY

I'm late again.

That's rarer today than it was a year ago, because now, when I feel the tick of time, my body starts to prickle with an anxiety I can't shake without medication, and I feel each second pass as if I'm one of the gears in a clock. As a result, more often than not, I'm early, my foot tapping with impatience as I wait for others as they used to wait for me.

After what happened, I can't believe anymore that being late has no consequence. I'm proof to the contrary. Yet, my changing personality isn't rationally connected to what happened. I'm alive today because I *wasn't* in the building. I wasn't sitting on the fifteenth floor in a conference room with a river view, trying to remain calm. Because I was late, I was safe. Close by. Marked, scarred, even, but alive.

Five hundred and thirteen other people weren't so lucky.

So I don't want to tempt fate again or rely on not being where I'm supposed to be to save me from my destiny. Like the man who escaped the Twin Towers, only to die in an airplane crash a few years later. Death had plans for that man; it would not be denied.

But despite my efforts, I *am* late today, my racing pulse reminds me. I check my watch for the twentieth time. It's only five minutes past when I'm due, not enough to matter, I tell myself, breathing in and out slowly as I've been taught to do in these situations.

My pulse slows. It will be all right. Death will give me a reprieve; even it can't punish me for my lateness today of all days, the day before the first anniversary of my husband's death.

"Cecily Grayson?" the receptionist for the Compensation Initiative asks. I try not to notice as every head in the room snaps toward me with a collective *so that's who she is*. It would be wrong to notice. Immodest. Selfish. Ungrateful.

I'm not allowed to be any of these things.

Instead, I raise my hand as if I've been called on in class, follow the receptionist to my meeting with Teo Jackson, and try not to think about the fact that this building also has a fifteenth floor and I'm on it.

The Initiative said they chose the floor deliberately when they rented the space and announced their intention via press release. They did it to remember—memorialize—the fifteen-floor build-ing that had come crashing down a year ago. Remembering. That's their purpose, they repeat loudly and often in ads you can't skip at the beginning of YouTube videos or those pop-ups that follow you around the Internet like a basset hound.

Remembering's important, but the Initiative's real purpose is compensation. Weighing up a life lost and assigning it a value, then paying it out to the victim's family, changing their lives forever, though they've already been changed forever. There's big money in this, I've learned, as the furnishings on this floor attest. I'm surrounded by plush gray carpet, newly painted cream walls, and expensive pieces by up-and-coming Chicago artists hanging under directed lighting. People might leave here millionaires or paupers, but they'll all be treated to the experience.

As if love or loss has a price. As if being denied access to the funds set aside to ease their way through life after suffering this tragedy can be softened by a glass of ice water with a perfect lemon wedge floating in it.

I push these ungrateful thoughts aside. The Initiative has done a lot of good for a lot of people, myself included. I shouldn't be so critical.

Teo Jackson's waiting for me in a boardroom lined with corkboards. They're covered in multicolored cue cards arranged in columns. Above each one is a white card with one word on it. *Street*, reads one. *Unidentified*, reads another.

"Cecily," Teo says. "Great to see you again."

"Is it?"

Teo rubs at his close-cut beard. His skin is a dark amber, and he's wearing his trademark gray-blue T-shirt under a well-cut corduroy jacket. Inky jeans. Converse shoes. He's worn some variation of this outfit every time I've seen him. I imagine his closet divided into four neat sections, his day eased by a lack of decisions.

"Why would you even question that?" he asks, smiling with his eyes. I avoid eye contact. Teo's far too handsome for my current level of self-esteem.

"My therapist says I need to be more . . . definite."

"Does he?"

"She. Yes."

I wasn't in therapy before, but it's the only place I can unburden myself. Now I use the fact that I have a therapist as a measure of someone's merit—if they flinch or look embarrassed when I mention it, then I know they're not worth bothering over.

Teo doesn't flinch or look embarrassed. He does, however, say, "Wait."

He picks up a pink card, writes *Poster Child?* on it in thick marker, then tacks it into place beneath the *Street* column.

"What's all this?"

"It's my storyboard. My map of the day."

He smiles again. It's the first thing I remember about him, how he smiled and told me it was going to be all right when he had no way of knowing if that was true. But there was something about him that made me want to believe him, and so I did.

"It's what I do for every film," he says. "It's a way to set out the narrative."

"But it's a documentary."

"It still has to tell a story. Have a beginning, middle, and end. A protagonist and an antagonist." His hand shifts from one column to the next, tapping the cards so they pop. "A hero."

His hand comes to land on the card he just wrote on.

"I'm not the hero, Teo."

"Why don't you let me be the judge of that?"

A year ago, Teo had been scouting locations with his assistant for a commercial he'd agreed to shoot to pay his bills. He was photographing some of the homeless who hang out at Quincy Station when the world turned sideways. He was another person who stood still that day, photographing Chicago as it changed irrevocably, taking a more careful catalog than the crowds who captured what they could on their cell phones. When the fire started to spread up Adams Street, he knew they had to get out of there. But first he decided to take one last shot.

He caught me in a whirlwind of debris with the river glinting in the background. When I look at it now, the image seems staged, like a scene in a movie where the heroine's been through hell and is waiting for her final showdown with a bad man who's almost impossible to kill. My clothes are covered in grime, but my face is unmarred, and I'm staring fixedly at the building. If you look closely enough, the fireball it's become is reflected in my eyes.

He got his shots—*click, click, click*—and then he grabbed my hand and pulled me to safety.

While we waited in Washington Station like Londoners during the Blitz, Teo uploaded that picture to a website freelance photographers use to sell their photos. It became the shot of the day, the image everyone associated with October tenth, and for the next month, two, three, wherever I went, my own face stared back at me.

Somehow, I'd become the poster child for a tragedy that killed 513 people and injured more than 2,000, including Teo's assistant, who ended up with second-degree burns on his arms and torso.

I didn't want the recognition, the notoriety, the fame. When Teo asked for my permission to upload the picture as we waited for the "all clear" in the station, I didn't think of the consequences; I just said yes to the man who'd saved my life. By the time I thought to revoke my consent, it was too late. So instead, I've tried to pass it off, to play it down, to let it pass me by.

But I've learned that you don't get to choose what becomes an enduring image, even when you're the subject of it.

A couple of months ago, Teo was hired by the Initiative to make a documentary about what's become known as Triple Ten, because the explosion occurred at precisely 10:00 a.m. on October tenth. His approach, he told me in the series of e-mails he used to persuade me to participate in his film, is to follow three families a year later.

My family—the Graysons—is the "lucky" family. Though my husband, Tom, was killed instantly in the blast (one hopes, and one will never tell our children otherwise), we were able to recover his body; bury him; and, ostensibly, through the generous support of the Initiative, move on. One of the "unlucky" families—the Rings, who are fighting for their compensation—is the flip side of the coin. And then there's Franny Maycombe.

But more about her later.

"I'm not sure I want to do this," I tell Teo as his hand rests on the index card that's supposed to represent me. His nails are short but neat, in contrast to my own, chewed down by my worry.

"Why not?"

"Isn't it someone else's turn in the spotlight? We aren't the only family who's been compensated. Why not use one of the others?"

I turn from him and catch my reflection in the bank of floor-to-ceiling windows. I'm wearing black slacks and a simple gray sweater. My blond hair's two months past a cut, but I've been told to leave it as is till we finish filming, "For continuity," Teo's production assistant told me. As if a couple of inches of hair could make me unrecognizable from the woman in that photograph. If only.

"I understand how you feel," Teo says. "But we need you in this film."

I inch over to the glass, getting as close as I can to see if panic sets in. Another side effect: ever since I missed that meeting, whenever I'm at any height above a few feet, I feel as if I'm standing on a cliff and there's a hand on my shoulder waiting for an opportune moment to shove me off. And sometimes, even, as if I might jump.

"Why, exactly? And don't say because I'm the face of this tragedy. Please."

I touch the pane. It's cold today, and the glass burns my fingers. I pull my hand away. My fingers have marred its clear surface, which now holds a perfect print of my index and middle finger. If I jumped, floating down like the lazy flakes that have started to fall from the dark clouds gathering above, they'd have something to identify me by.

Teo moves behind me.

"Because you're the heart of this story, Lily. I can't imagine telling it without you."

Lily. It's what Tom used to call me. Had I told Teo that, or did I just look like a Lily to him? A placid flower floating in a pond, providing a counterpoint to the bullfrogs?

"I'm not the heart of anything," I say. My voice is wavering, unconvincing.

I need to work on that, too, my therapist says. I shouldn't live with so much uncertainty, or project it, either.

"I wish you could see what I see," Teo says, resting his hand on my shoulder.

I lean against it, letting him hold my weight for a moment.

"Ahem."

His hand's gone so suddenly I almost fall.

"Yes, Maggie?"

Maggie is Teo's production assistant. Twenty-five, slender, and dressed in an outfit my fourteen-year-old daughter, Cassie, would beg me for if she saw it, she looks at Teo territorially, even though, at forty-two, he's technically old enough to be her father. I wonder, not for the first time, whether something's going on between them or if he's just the object of her fantasies.

"Franny Maycombe's arrived," she says.

I guess we're getting to Franny faster than I'd planned.

I catch Teo's eye and shake my head.

"Can you ask her to wait?" he says. "We're not quite done here."

"Of course," Maggie says. "I'll let her know."

"I thought you were close with Franny?" Teo says when Maggie's out of earshot. "What's up?"

"I'm just tired. It's a lot right now with the memorial and everything, and Franny . . ."

"Can be needy?"

"Yes, frankly. Not that I blame her."

I turn back to the window. Teo lets me take a minute. A beat.

"Are you still okay to do your first interview tomorrow? After the memorial?"

"I suppose you'll be filming all that, too?"

"I will."

My eyes meet his in the glass. What does he see when he looks at me? I don't feel like the woman on the cover of all those magazines.

What's that song? "Pretty on the Inside." I used to feel that way.
Now . . .

"And after," I say, "you'll come to the house?"

"Yes."

I guess there's nothing left to do but face it.

I nod my agreement. "Is there a back way out of here?"

2

A FARTHER SHORE

KATE

A country away, Kate Lynch lay in a bed in Montreal that still felt alien to her, staring at the patterns on the ceiling cast by the light from the street lamp. The clock next to her glowed brightly. A minute ago, the time had changed to twelve o'clock. And so there it was. October tenth. The day she'd been dreading for months was finally here.

She knew it would be a day full of memories. Some unbidden, some forced upon her. Five hundred people don't die in America without incessant news coverage. All the anniversaries would be marked. But this anniversary, the first anniversary, would be the subject of special attention. As would anyone connected to it.

Kate had done her best to block out information about Triple Ten over the last year. That was part of the reason she'd chosen Montreal. She'd guessed that French Canada would be less obsessed with the gory details than everywhere else. She'd been right. It wasn't that they didn't cover the event; the world had done so. But the reporting was more like what she'd experienced when she'd been in Europe during Hurricane Katrina. There was a detached cadence to the news announcers. This wasn't happening to them but to someone else. And that was exactly the amount of remove Kate needed. A buffer that would wall her off from the worst of it.

It had worked for the most part. There'd be stretches where it felt as if she'd forgotten who she was. Why she was there. What she'd left behind. As the daily thrum of life slipped by, she concentrated on the small moments in front of her rather than the larger world. Not that she had much time to watch the news or read the paper that still, almost quaintly, struck the front door each morning. That was part of the point of this new life, too. But as the countdown clock to the anniversary unwound, Kate knew that even here, a thousand miles away, there'd be no escaping it. The images. The tributes. Maybe even some direct reference to her former life.

This next week, maybe two, would be a nightmare. Because even something as simple as that word—"nightmare"—was enough to trigger what she wanted to avoid.

A memory.

• • •

This time a year ago, almost to the minute, Kate's daughter had a bad dream. This wasn't an infrequent occurrence. Her daughter was sensitive, fragile. Her brain seemed to sift together every negative thing that happened to her during the school day and assault her with it at night. It had taken years for them to get her to sleep in her own bed. More years still before the night-light in the hall and the half-cracked-open closet door were enough to keep her there on all but the worst nights.

A year ago, a familiar scream tore Kate from sleep. She pried herself from the cocoon of blankets they'd put on the bed that week in anticipation of cooler weather and scurried down the hall before the shrieks woke more than her.

When she got there, her daughter's hands were grabbing the blanket, her eyes wide open, her mouth moving without any sound emerging. Kate had placed her hand on her daughter's damp forehead and crouched down, her knees popping like corn.

"It's okay, baby. Hush now. I'm here."

"Mommy?"

"I'm here. I'm right here."

"Is the bad man still here?"

"There wasn't any bad man, sweetheart."

She turned her head toward Kate. Her limbs were thin and stretched out—no baby fat left on her five-year-old frame. Her eyes looked black. "There *was*."

Even after years of being a mother, Kate hadn't figured out the right approach to this kind of situation. Should she humor her daughter? If she told her she was wrong, was she calling her a liar? There were so many questions to which she could never find any satisfactory answers. And when she tried to ask *the others*, as she thought of them, the competent mothers, the ones who lined her block and the park and Gymboree—everywhere—they'd give her this funny look, as if she'd asked how to tie her shoes. Or worse, breathe.

"What did he look like?"

"It was too dark to see him. But I could hear him. He was *breathing*."

Her daughter's chest rattled, a heavy yogic exhale that made Kate go cold. Perhaps there had been someone in her room? Home invasions happened. He could be hiding in the closet. Or in the linen cupboard down the hall. So many scary possibilities.

She'd searched the gloomy room with her eyes and listened carefully. The window was closed. The light in the closet was on. The house was silent. She would've felt it if she'd passed someone in the hall. They were alone.

She'd gathered her daughter in her arms. "I'm sorry, baby. I'm sorry you're so scared."

"It's not your fault the bad man came."

She was right, but it felt to Kate as if it were. It felt to Kate—always—as if she should've figured out a way to keep the bad men at bay. Even from her daughter's imagination, even from her dreams.

"I love you, baby. I love you so much."

Kate let her down against her pillows gently and stroked her damp hair. It was silky and thin. No one had told her, before she had children, that being a mother would be like reliving her own childhood, only worse. That she'd have to re-feel all the slights and worries a hundredfold.

When her daughter's breathing finally went soft, and Kate had dragged herself back to bed, she thought about that failing and felt defeated.

Now, a year later, as she lay in a new bed, in a foreign city, with everything changed so irreversibly, she had a different idea of what "defeat" meant and a whole other set of regrets. And as she waited with increasing resignation for sleep to come, she wondered.

Would she survive tomorrow, or would it finally be her undoing?

INTERVIEW TRANSCRIPT

Subject: Franny Maycombe (FM). Conducted by: Teo Jackson (TJ).

TJ: I wanted to begin by thanking you for agreeing to participate in the documentary.

FM: Of course! I think it's so important, what you're doing. This film is going to contribute to our efforts—I can tell.

TJ: So, we'll be doing a series of interviews over the next couple weeks, covering a broad range of topics, with the tragedy and its impact being the central focus.

FM: I understand.

TJ: Good. Let's begin with some background questions. What's your full name?

FM: My name is Franny Susan Maycombe.

TJ: And how old are you?

FM: I'm twenty-four years old.

TJ: Where were you born?

FM: Right here in Chicago.

TJ: Did you grow up here?

FM: No, in Madison. I was adopted when I was a baby, and that's where my adoptive parents brought me.

TJ: Madison, Wisconsin?

FM: That's right.

TJ: What was growing up there like?

FM: It was all right. Nothing special. Just life in a smallish city. I'm sure you can imagine.

TJ: Did you go to college?

FM: Only high school for me. I wanted to go, you know, and I had the grades, but we couldn't afford it. Maybe I'll go someday.

TJ: Did you work after you finished high school?

FM: Yeah, I did a lot of things. I was a receptionist in a dentist's office. And I worked in a hardware store. Then as a waitress. You know, the whole nine yards.

TJ: But now you work for the Triple Ten victims' fund?

FM: I do.

TJ: In fact, you're the chair?

FM: *Co*chair . . . Mrs. Grayson is the chair, too. She was the chair first. But yes, I do.

TJ: How did that come about?

FM: I got involved because of my connection to Triple Ten.

TJ: So, let's talk about that. Where were you on October tenth?

[Pause]

TJ: Everything all right? I know talking about it can be hard.

FM: I'm fine. It wasn't that; it was just, wow, I had this flash. Like déjà vu or something, but not, you know? And it feels like a million years ago, right? Another lifetime.

TJ: What was that lifetime like?

FM: I was in the diner I was waitressing in, getting crappy tips. Wearing that uniform, you know, the apron, this yellow shirt and skirt that was too short. Anyway, it was just after the breakfast rush finished, right when we can usually take a bit of a break, but then this tour bus stopped in, and so we were superbusy, running around, trying to get everyone's order right. Then the news came on, took over the TV station, you know, the way it does when there's breaking news, and we all stopped what we were doing and watched. I stood there for an hour without moving. We all did.

TJ: This was in Madison?

FM: Yes.

TJ: Was there anything else that happened that day? Something that stands out?

FM: There sure was. We had the TV on for hours and hours. We all sat in the booths and kept our eyes glued to the screen. Everyone thought it was another attack at first, like a terrorist attack, and that tour bus never did leave. And then it was dark, night, and they started releasing the names of some of the victims. I began to get this feeling, this shaky feeling, you know, like my life was about to change.

TJ: Why did you feel that way?

FM: I'm not sure. But I had this connection to Chicago, right, and then there it was, a huge tragedy there, and I felt like I knew. I just knew.

TJ: What did you know?

FM: I know it sounds crazy, but I swear—I knew my mother was dead even before they said her name.

3

OUR HOUSE

CECILY

I don't need any alarms to wake me the next morning, even though I set three and asked my mother to give me a wake-up call, fearful I'd be up every hour on the hour, then fall into a deep sleep around four and miss the allotted time. But instead, I went to sleep easily and dreamed I was skiing—Tom and I used to take yearly trips to Jackson Hole with the kids—and the powder was fantastic and I was laughing the way you do sometimes when you're having pure *fun*.

And then I skied off a cliff.

Normally, in one of those horrible falling dreams, you wake with a start, your heart shuddering. Instead, as I was tumbling into a white oblivion, I told myself: *This is a dream*. It's a trick I learned long ago, a way to wake up without a flood of fear, to somehow remain conscious enough to push away the panic. *This is a dream,* I thought again, and pulled myself back from the edge.

I open my eyes.

I'm safe in my bedroom—our bedroom—sleeping on my side of the bed as if Tom's body is still a barrier to stretching out. The last book he was reading—a thriller by Mary Kubica he took from my bookshelf—is cracked open on the nightstand, its spine broken. I remember how mad I was when I saw him do that. He knew I loved keeping my books pristine, never folding the pages or bending them open, keeping my place with a tissue, or memory, because breaking the spine on a treasured book is a sin, isn't it?

I used to think so before real sins became everyday currency.

But he'd done it, and we'd had a fight, a stupid fight. We'd gone to bed in angry silence, the air thick with our words. We lay with our backs to each other, two opposing forces in the bed, our anger a reverse magnet neither of us had the strength to match. But then the next morning, *that* morning, Tom apologized and said things would be different going forward. He kissed me on the forehead and said he'd see me later. *Don't be late . . .* I couldn't quite tell if he was being serious or trying to tease me. I gave him the benefit of the doubt and did my best to move past it.

And maybe things would've been different if death hadn't intervened. It's one of the things that drive you crazy, the *what-if*s of unexpected loss, even though life is full of them, too.

But he's gone now, and I still take a shower every morning in a stall filled with his shampoo and favorite soap and the last razor he used sitting in its niche. I pull my clothes from a closet full of his—business suits and pressed shirts and his "good shoes" and his "comfortable shoes" lined up like soldiers across the floor because Tom had a thing about his clothes and how they had to be arranged just so. Our grocery delivery still contains the same amount of low-fat milk, even though the kids and I don't drink it. Every week, I place the containers in the fridge and vow I'll call and amend the order, then drain them into the sink a week later, untouched, right before they turn sour.

I'd meant to change all this. I had a plan, even, that involved a few close girlfriends and wine and doing something symbolic like rearranging the furniture or getting rid of the chair that didn't match the rest of our living room that Tom insisted on keeping because it was a comfortable place for him to fall asleep in after a long, hard day.

That never happened, either.

My friend Sara has said more than once that it's like I live in a shrine. She's even taken to calling me "The Widow Grayson" in moments of levity. I get mad at her sometimes for that, though I know it comes from love, but she's not wrong. I will forevermore be Cecily Grayson, stuck with a last name that still doesn't feel like my own but that I took for the sake of our children. "So we can be a real family," Tom said, though I never understood what my last name had to do with whether we were a family or not.

Whether asleep or awake, I'm stuck. I have no idea how to move forward or even where I want to go. Someday soon I'm going to have to do something. I can't go on living in stasis, trapped under the glass of the public's glare and unceasing sympathy. But today's not about moving on, it's about remembering, so I'll play my role and smile through the worst of it, and tomorrow, *tomorrow*, I'll make a plan.

"Why'd you agree to the documentary, then?" Sara asked me the night before, when I was circling the rim of a glass of Chablis, my complaints nothing new, her advice still unheeded.

"I didn't at first. It took a while for Teo to convince me."

"Ah," she said, reaching for the half-empty bottle. "Teo."

"It's not like that . . . It was easier to agree than to fight."

"You always take the path of least resistance."

If it were anyone else, I might've been upset at this bald assessment of my character. But Sara was Sara, and Sara was right. "That's a pattern I need to break, too."

"Easier said than done, though, right?"

I agreed with her. If things had been like they were two years ago, Tom and I would sit down at the kitchen table while the kids were asleep and make a list. What are the pros of being involved in Teo's film? (*Remembering, helping others deal with their grief, raising money for the Initiative.*) What are the cons? (*I miss my privacy, I feel like a fraud, what if Teo finds out?*) And then we'd decide, together, what was best.

But it's too late to do that now. I can't back out without raising questions, so I'll have to take it like I have everything else. One day at a time.

My cell phone buzzes on the nightstand. It's my mother, my wake-up insurance.

"Hi, Mom. Thanks for calling."

"You sound awake."

I flip onto my back as anxiety gathers. The crack in the ceiling seems larger than the last time I looked. Another thing to take care of tomorrow, tomorrow.

"I am awake."

"I'm sorry, honey."

"It's okay. It was bound to happen."

"Are you sure you don't want me to come with you?"

"They've only given us three seats together. You might not even be able to get in."

My mother gives one of her patented *humphs*. "You let me take care of that."

"No, truly. I promise. We'll be all right. I feel horrible saying this, but . . ."

"It might be easier without me?"

"Is that terrible?"

"Perhaps a little. But I understand."

"Thanks, Mom. Are *you* okay?"

"I'm thinking about your father."

"I know."

My father died six years ago. He was the love of her life, and his death hit her hard. She'd been doing better before Triple Ten, making new friends and joining a walking group, playing bridge. But having her own daughter become a widow set her back, and in some ways, this last year has been harder for her than for me.

"I'll be thinking of Dad today," I say. "Thinking of both of you."

"I love you, Cecily."

"I love you, too."

The clock radio turns on as I hang up. It's playing one of those Justin Bieber songs all my girlfriends love for some reason. I slap the "Off" button and track through the list of what I need to accomplish to get us to the ceremony on time.

I cannot be late today.

I cannot.

• • •

The memorial takes place on the exhibition floor of McCormick Place, which is big enough to hold all of us and our noise, the thousands of people who make up the families, the living monuments to the victims, not to mention the dignitaries—the mayor, the governor, the senators, and the members of Congress dressed in somber suits, glad-handing around our tragedy.

If he were here, Tom would be singing Dylan lyrics about standing in doorways and blocking up halls, because that's exactly what they're doing.

I have a child on either side of me—Cassie, fifteen, on my left, and Henry, thirteen, on my right. Their hands are firmly in mine, and they're dressed in matching black outfits—their decision, not mine, one that kind of breaks my heart. They used to do that when they were little—Cassie was small for her age then, and Henry was tall, so they used to pretend they were twins and dress the same to play up their similarities.

They haven't done that in forever, but when they told me of their plan a few days ago, I let them choose something for me, too. And so here we are, looking at the line of important men in front of us, a trio of blond, pale-skinned grief.

We look like a family a candidate might use in a campaign ad in the Middle West.

Henry strains against my hand. He loves sports, and violent video games I don't want to know the name of, and history books about World War II. He's still tall for his age, passing me in height a year ago. Of all of us, he's been the hardest hit by this. He and Tom were close, closer than Cassie and me, much to my dismay. Tom was a great father, and I'm at a loss to know how to fill the hole he's left behind.

It's very loud inside, the noise jump-starting the headache I knew I'd have today. The air's both stale and full of too much after-shave and the perfume coming off the bank of white flowers behind the stage. The kernel of unease in my stomach has grown to fist size, like a punch; I wish I still had some of the medication my doctor prescribed to deal with the first month after Tom died, when I couldn't sleep without it and going outside seemed impossible. But I didn't think to keep any for emergencies, so we stand there for a few minutes, not saying anything, taking it all in, while I remember how to breathe.

Then one of the senators notices us and nudges his colleagues out of the way. The First Family of Grief, we've been given special status with seats in the front row, small *Reserved* signs holding our spaces on the foldout chairs draped in white fabric. Like so many things, I didn't ask for this, but I couldn't turn it down. I've let myself be photographed in an endless cascade of black dresses, and now there will be more time on camera, more exploitation of us for the "common good," that eternal excuse that has led me to agree, time and again, to interviews, appearances, and even a few sweaty-palmed speeches.

There's a thick book on each of the seats, professionally produced. For once, my face is not on the cover. Instead, it's another shot of Teo's, taken in the minutes before the explosion, when the building was highlighted by a sunbeam and the puffy blue clouds above held no sense of foreboding.

It's 513 pages long, one page for every person lost. Those who were simply injured, or scarred in other ways, have their own book, their own groups, and though they were invited today, they're seated in the back, out of the line of sight of the cameras. For some reason their injuries, their very real, physical ones, don't seem as important as ours, the psychological remnants of those who are gone. As a result, many of the survivors are angry, disillusioned, fighting for recognition. I don't blame them, and I should help them with that fight, but I don't have the energy.

The hour grinds on. The room is overflowing and hot. There are big screens behind the stage projecting a stream of family shots, a photo collage of memories. When it's our family's turn, Henry starts shaking next to me. I pull his towhead to my shoulder, making soothing sounds. Cassie stares straight ahead, watching as her father splashes her with a garden hose while she giggles, as he stands proudly next to her when she dressed up for her first formal, as she unwraps a Christmas present while Tom laughs. We chose these photos together a few weeks ago, picking randomly among the digital files I'd never managed to get into physical albums. We had a good cry and a good laugh, too, and I thought about all the progress we'd made since I finally got home on October tenth, and in the days after when it became clear that Tom wouldn't.

Cassie's been harder to read since then, withdrawing into herself instead of acting out. Will I learn later that she's been sneaking off in the dead of night to meet the wrong kind of boy and numb herself with alcohol, pills, or meaningless sex? There's no sign of this, though more than one person has suggested I should be on the watch for it. *Do you know something I don't?* I always ask. *No, no, of course not. Only . . . I've heard stories about some of the other girls . . .* And then they shrug. *You know girls . . .*

These stories—and their casual acceptance as inevitable for my daughter—make me so, so angry. As if the only way women can deal with their grief is some form of self-injury.

The din cuts out suddenly. Teo's assistant—the scars from the burns he got that day on his arms still visible—scurries across the stage and tweaks the flags behind the podium. Several tall men in black suits with earpieces surround it. It's 9:59 a.m.

And while a year ago, I might not have even noticed, now I know what this means.

The president's coming.

"Where do you want to begin?" I ask Teo four hours later, when the speeches are done and we've been allowed to return to our everyday lives that do not involve bear hugs from presidents and crudités passed on silver platters.

Despite the abundance that surrounded me, I'm hungry. I never eat any of the funeral fare; the food they serve at the parade of events I've been to all tastes the same to me, high quality or low. It's like the meals that still show up at my door on a regular basis, so much so that I no longer need to cook for my family. I still do; I've always loved to cook, and I cannot eat another slice of frozen lasagna, ever, but there's security in knowing that if I disappear, too, my children will have provisions for several months.

This is how I think now. I don't know how to stop it.

Teo gets me to give my basic details: name, age, occupation. And then: "Why don't you tell me about that day?" Teo says. "From the beginning."

He wore a suit for the event, but now he's changed back into his trademark T-shirt and jeans. How many versions of this outfit does he have?

"It was an ordinary day," I say, trying to focus on the now. "Nothing about it stands out."

Teo raises an eyebrow. "Nothing?"

"I mean before the explosion. It was the usual getting the kids ready for school and getting myself ready, and . . . I know that probably doesn't help you."

"It's fine. I'm just surprised because the other people I've talked to, well, most of them seem to remember everything that happened that day."

We're sitting in the solarium off the kitchen. It smells like slightly rotted rosemary; the plant it was Tom's job to water barely survived this year without him, putting up with Henry's imperfect memory as best it could. Beyond it lies the backyard—a cedar hedge, a covered barbecue that hasn't been used since last summer, burnished gold mums in a set of planters my mother gave me years ago.

"I think people enjoy saying stuff like that," I say. "Like, if they missed a flight that ended up crashing, they'll say: *Something was bugging me all day. I just knew from the moment I woke up I shouldn't get on that airplane. I think that's why I was late*, et cetera. But think of all the times you feel that way and nothing happens."

A shiver runs through me, because that *is* how I feel now all the time, that nervous feeling like something bad's about to happen, something I could avoid if I knew which event to skip, which route not to take, which call not to answer. Sometimes it's overwhelming, trapping me in the house because if I don't leave, then I can't make a bad decision. Most of the time, like now, it's simply a companion, a new part of me I have to carry around, like weight I can't shed.

"What is it?" Teo asks. "Have you remembered something?"

"Nothing, really . . ."

"Tell me."

"This is probably ironic given what I just said, but I *was* late that day. I got behind with the kids and . . . I was late. Nothing unusual for me, but that's why I wasn't in the building."

"Did you have a bad feeling? Is that what made you late?"

"No . . . I was annoyed with myself, but it wasn't a premonition or anything. I used to be late all the time. If you asked Tom, it was my main character flaw."

"You were going to meet Tom that day, right?"

"Yes, that's right."

"An early lunch?"

"Pardon me?"

"It was ten in the morning. Seems like an odd time to meet your husband at his office."

I look out the window. The grass is longer than Tom kept it, and it hasn't received the final mowing he used to give it before the snow flew. We have a service that comes now, but they close up in September. A burst of Indian summer a week ago pushed a few inches out of the ground. What would Tom think if he came back? Would he find things to complain about, or would he just be so happy to be alive everything else would pale by comparison?

"We did that sometimes. Met up when he had a break in his schedule. We were going to go look at some furniture. At CORT, I think, that discount place on Lake Shore."

Teo looks around. "Seems like you have all the furniture you could use here."

"I know, right?" I bring my attention back to him, looking right into his brown eyes. "There are so many things—after—that seem silly in retrospect."

Even though he's filming this, Teo's taking notes. He's got his questions typed up on pieces of paper with spaces below for my answers. I don't feel anything as I watch him write down my lies.

After a year of telling them, it's become second nature.

4

DREAMS

KATE

In Montreal, Kate was dreaming. A few hours before, she thought she'd have a sleepless night, a "white night," she used to call them, back in her old life, when it still seemed as if a night without sleep could be benign. But sometime soon after two, she'd gone under, and her brain, like her daughter's, was torturing her.

In the dream, she was in her old house. She'd forgotten to pull the shades on her bedroom windows tightly closed. They hadn't wound the clocks back yet, so the light that pushed her awake wasn't the sun but the street lamp on their front lawn that her children would decorate in a few weeks for Halloween. Kate knew without looking that her alarm would sound soon. That she'd have to pry herself away from the warmth embracing her and face another morning of getting the kids ready for school and herself ready for work.

She could feel her husband sleeping next to her. When she thought of him, Kate was always split in two. Sometimes even being married seemed weird, like a word you repeat so many times it loses its meaning. Other times Kate wondered how they'd ended up together. Had it simply been a case of musical chairs? That he was the one she was sitting next to when it was time for the music to stop? She knew she was being unfair to him, forgetting all the great things that were the reasons she was lying next to him in the first place. But instead, often, all she could focus on were things like the fact that he'd become a great father against his will.

When they'd discussed having children, it had never occurred to Kate to ask whether he wanted to be involved. Weren't all fathers involved these days? They both worked equivalent jobs. Surely he wouldn't expect her to give all that up and become the kids' primary caregiver?

But he had. In those first months after they came home from the hospital, he'd refused to do diapers. He never offered to get up for a night feeding, or any feeding at all. Kate was at first amused, and then, slowly, furious. What was happening? She was too tired to understand. Too worn out to have the conversation she knew she should before this pattern became set in stone. They'd both come home from the hospital with the same amount of information. How had she become the expert and he the helpless?

And then things had shifted, she'd shifted, and he'd come to the rescue. He learned all the things they should've been learning together, and he'd done it so seamlessly, so easily, she often thought she'd made up the time before. Regardless, now he was in the trenches right along with her, maybe more than that, even. The cavalry, while she was the rear guard. A bad analogy. Of course, she was dreaming. She hadn't thought all that, that morning a year ago. She'd just waited for the clock to click over. The music to start playing. The day to start up.

Time passed. Maybe she fell asleep again. Maybe it had been earlier than she thought. All she knew was that when she finally woke up, she was running.

Now, a year into her new life, Kate felt as if that was all she was doing—running. The direct result of her job as a nanny to a pair of three-year-old twins.

That was a laugh.

In fact, Kate did laugh when she accepted the job and realized what it would mean. She laughed again her first night in the basement apartment that came along with it. Lying in a brand-new bed (her employer, Andrea, had a *horror* of used mattresses and insisted on buying a new one for Kate, along with two pairs of Frette sheets and a set of the softest bath towels she'd ever used). Listening unaccustomed to the groans of the old building. Kate had stuffed a (organic) pillow into her mouth to keep the sound from flowing upstairs to the family she was now bound to.

"I can't believe how lucky I am," Andrea said the first time Kate met her, when she'd gone to an interview a week after she'd arrived in Montreal.

"Lucky?" Kate asked, but they both knew what Andrea meant. Of course Andrea was lucky. Look at where she lived—a sprawling brick house on a street in Westmount called Roslyn "on the flat," as

Kate would learn to call it, as if she were selling real estate. Everything on the property was neat as a pin. Even the leftover leaves from the big maple that dominated the front yard, yellowed and spotted with black nickel-size marks, had been bagged with more precision than anything she'd ever been able to accomplish.

"To find *you*," Andrea said. Her hair was an ash-blond color most of the women in the neighborhood wore. Andrea was personal-trainer, low-carb-diet skinny, and though it was October, her skin had a glow to it that was a shade too orange.

"My French is not very good, though." Excellent French had been listed as a job requirement.

Andrea frowned. From the moment Kate had shown up in the chino slacks and argyle sweater she'd bought on sale the day before at the Gap, she'd been able to read the thought bubble over Andrea's head. Kate was *white*. She was *educated*. She *had the job*.

But now there was a hesitation. Kate had revealed something about herself that was less than ideal. Were there other things to worry about?

"Oh, I don't care about that," Andrea said, her laugh tinkling. "They'll be going to French school starting when they're four. No." Andrea leaned in. Kate could see the black hollows under her eyes that even a thick layer of foundation couldn't hide. "I just need help *getting them* to four, if you know what I mean?"

Kate glanced over her shoulder at the photograph of Andrea's boys that sat on the granite counter in the gleaming all-white kitchen. They looked harmless, with their milk teeth showing and their matching coveralls. But Kate knew that was likely deceptive. Two two-year-old boys. They'd be full of energy and questions. She wouldn't have time for herself. It sounded . . . perfect.

"I do," Kate said. "I know exactly what you mean."

Kate's dream shifted again. A tumble of images from the last year. The boys. The house. Her small moments alone. The picture she tried not to look at too often. The people she'd left behind. She felt herself sink deeper, even as it lightened outside. And perhaps that's what this last year had been, a dream within a dream.

But it was time to wake up now.

So wake up, Kate. Wake up.

INTERVIEW TRANSCRIPT

TJ: Your mother . . . You mean your biological mother?

FM: That's right.

TJ: When did you first learn you were adopted?

FM: I know this'll sound like a cliché, but I think I always knew.

TJ: Why do you say that?

FM: I never belonged in my family, you know? I mean, my adoptive
      parents, I think they tried to love me like my sister, but biology.
      Biology is something that can't be denied. It can't be faked.

TJ: Did they treat you differently?

FM: Not deliberately. If you could ask them, they wouldn't think
      they'd done anything wrong. But it's the little things, you know?
      Like how people were always saying that my sister looked like

my mom, my adoptive mom, and then they'd look at me and be all puzzled. "Does she look like her father?" they'd ask. And Mom would always say, "Yes, I think so." But there was this hesitation, right? This moment before she'd actually answer when the word "adopted" sort of hung there. Like, if I wasn't there, then she might tell them the truth.

TJ: That must've been tough.

FM: It was. Those kinds of things work on a child. They wear them *down*.

TJ: But they did tell you eventually?

FM: Yeah, when I was eight. They sat me down in the living room and said they had something to tell me. And I know, because I've read all the literature, okay, that there are lots of different theories about how to do this, when to do this. Some say do it from the beginning, don't make it a big thing. Others say it's better to do it later when the child can understand. There's even some who think you should never tell. But it *is* a thing. Whether it's said or not. Like if I were gay, I would've known. I wouldn't need my parents to confirm it, right?

TJ: What did they tell you?

FM: They said they loved me, and part of me thought they were getting divorced, because that had just happened to my friend. But then I thought if they were getting divorced, they'd tell my sister and me together, because they were always careful about treating us equally. My mom even had this book where she wrote that kind of stuff down. *Gave Sherrie a toy at the supermarket*, with the date, et cetera, et cetera. Weird, right? Anyway, so I knew I was going to hear my dad say I was adopted. And that's what he said. And then they tried to put this positive spin on it, like, "We picked you. You are our special chosen baby," or whatever. But I started asking, "Who is my mother? Who is my mother?" I think that upset my mom, you know?

TJ: Do you think . . . I know you were eight, but was that when you started thinking about looking for her?

FM: Oh, absolutely. That's when I became a little Nancy Drew.

5

LOOK AT THIS PHOTOGRAPH

CECILY

I suppose there's a time in everyone's life where you discover you're a fool. Sometimes, maybe, it's a slow revelation. For others, there's a moment when it becomes obvious. In my case, I can tell you the precise date and time. I even have a text to prove it. It arrived at 2:22 p.m. on my twentieth wedding anniversary.

I'd been running around frantically all day trying to find the perfect outfit for the trip to New York Tom and I were taking to celebrate. Making sure my mother had the list of all the things Henry couldn't eat because of his allergies, arranging for carpooling for Cassie's and Henry's activities throughout the weekend, and ticking items off the long list I'd been working on for weeks, as if making my family function for a weekend without me required the same level of planning as a minor invasion. It all sounds so stupid now, like that point Teo made about the furniture in our house.

None of it was necessary, but it felt like it was at the time.

After two hours of questions, I ask Teo if we can take a break.

"Could we stop for the day, actually? My head is splitting."

"Of course." Teo turns off the camera and starts to efficiently pack it away.

I like that about him. He's compact. His equipment fits into a reasonably sized bag and consists of his camera, a tripod, and a boom mic that folds out like the protractor set I had in high school. His body is compact, too, no extra flesh but not any extra muscle, either. Proportional. He seems to take up less space than Tom, who was always the center of attention in any room he occupied.

"I should've noticed the time," he says. "It's almost six."

I noticed every minute going by, counting down until I could reasonably say "enough" for today. I haven't felt this anxious in months. I wanted to jump out of my body and land somewhere soft, white—oblivion. But now that the interview's over, the feeling falls away.

"It's fine." I stand stiffly.

"You all right?"

"Just stiff. I'm a casualty of a lifetime of running. I shouldn't do it anymore." In fact, I haven't run in a year, but that hasn't helped the problem, only exacerbated it.

"I couldn't ever do it."

"You look like a runner."

"Do I?"

I smile, then lower my eyes. Our interactions are often like this, full of undercurrents. Not flirting, exactly, but not strictly professional, either. Sometimes he looks at me like he's looking at me now, and it feels like a caress, one I want to prolong.

It's been so long, you see, since I've been touched.

"You're probably one of those men who stays slim no matter what you eat."

"That's possible."

He tucks his camera into his bag and zippers it closed. Whatever part of myself I gave up today is safe inside there, too.

"I've noticed, you know," I say.

"Noticed what?"

"You don't like it when I ask you personal questions. Which is . . . I don't know . . . ironic?"

"You're probably right."

Cassie wanders in. She's changed out of her funeral clothes and into a tight-jeans-and-T-shirt combination I would never have had the confidence to wear at her age. Part of me wants to shield her from the attention dressing that way might bring, and another part is proud that she feels comfortable enough to do so.

She's had a crush on Teo ever since she met him a couple of months ago when he started coming to the house for preinterviews. A teacher crush, or perhaps it's a my-dad-is-gone-forever crush, nothing sexual despite the provocative clothing, but a gap that needs to be filled. Though she's not as vocal about it as Henry, she misses Tom, misses how he used to watch her soccer games with intensity but never embarrassed her by yelling like some of the other dads. How he went over her essays for English with a special red pen he bought for that purpose, and how proud he was when she brought home an A. The horror movies they used to love to watch together on Saturday nights while they made fun of how I screamed at every squeak of the floorboards.

"What's ironic?" Cassie asks.

"The expression of one's meaning by using language that normally signifies the opposite, typically for humorous or emphatic effect," Teo says. "See also: 'A state of affairs or an event that seems deliberately contrary to what one expects and is often amusing as a result.'"

"What?"

"It's the definition of irony."

Cassie hugs herself, her thin arms pale against her dark shirt. "Oh, ha. But that's not what you were talking about."

"You're right," I say. "But it's none of your beeswax."

"Jeez, Mom. Where do you get these expressions?"

"Your grandmother."

"My mom said that, too," Teo says. "So the question is, why aren't the kids today using it?"

Cassie laughs and asks him if his mom's still alive. He says that she is. She starts to poke around his equipment, asking questions. I'm glad to see that whether or not he's aware of her interest, Teo treats Cassie appropriately, telling her how his camera works and then what the boom mic is for.

"Are Henry and I going to be in the documentary?"

"No," I say quickly.

"Good. Hey, can Teo stay for dinner? I'm making my special spaghetti." She lifts up her hair, a slippery, straight length I've never been able to get into any hairstyle since she was little, and loops a hair tie from her wrist around it so it stands up straight from the top of her head like a question mark. "Please, Mom?"

"You're cooking?"

"I cook. You taught me enough times."

"Well, in that case . . . Will you stay, Teo?"

"I'd love to."

At dinner, my kids ask Teo all the questions I've wanted to without any prompting.

"How did you get into filmmaking?" Cassie says.

"I wanted to be an actor when I was a kid. I got a few small roles and realized sitting around, waiting for the action to start, was boring. It's better to be in charge."

"Why documentaries?" Henry says.

"The first job I got out of film school was on a documentary, and there was something about it, the stories I could uncover, how life was more complicated and surprising than anything you could make up. It grabbed hold of me."

"Why are you making a documentary about my mom?"

"It's not about her, exactly. Not only, anyway."

"It's about Triple Ten, right?" Cassie says. "Like, one year later and how everything's changed but kind of stayed the same?"

"That's a great way of putting it. I like to think of it as my love letter to Chicago and everything we went through that day. And your mom, and a few others, have been nice enough to agree to help me tell that story."

"That's cool."

"Thank you. This dinner's cool, too."

Cassie flushes. She's done an admirable job. She defrosted several portions of the lasagna I swore I'd never eat again, chopped them up, and heated them in a skillet, simmering it all in a can of crushed tomatoes and fresh basil she made into a chiffonade, wielding the knife expertly. She even created a passable Caesar salad and got Henry to make garlic toast, the one thing he knows how to reliably cook, despite the years of lessons I've given to both of them.

"Where did you grow up?" Henry asks.

"Chicago. My mother still lives in the same apartment in the Loop. But the Loop wasn't the Loop back then. We were comfortable but not rich."

"We're rich," Henry says.

"Henry! That is so embarrassing." Cassie lifts the hem of the apron she'd found hanging in the pantry and covers her face. She always does that when she watches a TV show or a movie if a character does something that makes her uncomfortable. She lifts her shirt and shields her eyes, as if she could cover up their awkward behavior with a bit of cloth.

"Why?" Henry says. "It's obvious, isn't it? Look at this house."

Henry waves his hand around. We're in the formal dining room, with its white wainscoting that goes up a third of the wall and the robin's-egg-blue paint above it. The table's a shiny mahogany, not an heirloom but made to look like one. The chairs are mahogany, too, and their seats match the paint and the rug on the floor with its variations on an oriental pattern it took us months to find.

The rest of the house is to the same standard; Tom and I spent enough of our lives making sure that was the case. We both contributed our time and money to the project. Neither of us had much when we started out other than our degrees, which were paid for by scholarships and odd jobs. We both worked hard to make something of ourselves, to have nice things. Tom building up his software company, me managing Knife & Fork, one of the more successful restaurants in the city, where I worked for fifteen years before it closed.

"It's a nice house," Teo says.

"We're lucky to live here," I say.

"Have you asked everything you wanted to, kids?"

Cassie giggles.

"This is so interesting to me," I say.

"Oh?"

"Normally, I can't get so much as a detail. He must like you guys."

I'd tried to find out everything I could about Teo before agreeing to the documentary. His take, his intentions, the research he was doing. Teo was polite but evasive. "Trust me," he'd said, and I decided to do so, which meant there were important things about Teo I didn't know.

Was he a storyteller or a man looking for a story?

I was betting on the first, but I was preparing myself for the second.

6

RUNAROUND

KATE

Kate forced herself awake at six thirty as her alarm switched on to Mix 96. Today was the day. One more day, and she'd be past the worst of it. She had a plan for how to do that, even. Written down on a scrap of paper and then burned in the backyard in the outdoor fireplace. Get up. Act like everything's normal. Avoid screens. How hard could that be?

Her morning routine was quick. She had no one to dress up for. The twins would mar anything nice she wore in minutes. She preferred these new, easy clothes anyway. The casualness she had toward her appearance. Before, she'd looked at the stay-at-home mothers in their perpetual yoga outfits and thought uncharitable thoughts. Now she understood the practicality of it. Spending the day with children required flexibility. Fabric that would stretch with you.

Upstairs in the kitchen, Kate made sure the espresso maker was brewing Andrea's and Rick's separate coffee orders. If—when—she left this job, Kate could easily get a job as a barista. She pulled ingredients from the freezer for the breakfast smoothies they all drank so she'd be ready to pop them into the blender the moment the first of the Millers appeared. Then she set about making sandwiches for the boys. Part of her plan for the day was to take them to Westmount Park. Out of the house and away from the temptation of the TV on the wall.

The sun shone through the wide windows that looked out over the backyard. It was a bit barren now that the leaves had tumbled from the trees. The wind tossed a forgotten balloon around. The large rubber swing on the play set was swaying back and forth as if a child's legs were propelling it.

She glanced at the clock on the microwave, wondering if she had time to divert Rick's latte order for one of her own. It wasn't even seven yet, and Kate was already tired.

Back in Chicago, being a mother had been part of Kate's identity. There wasn't a day that went by that wasn't shaped by her children. Their needs and wants elevated above her own. But now she wasn't a mother; she was a mother's helper. A nanny. The *babysitter*, as Andrea called her because she thought it sounded less pretentious. Less like she was dependent on Kate for attending to the basic needs of her children. A babysitter was someone more temporary. Someone you called in when you had somewhere else to be. Not *the help*. Only, Kate wasn't someone who was called on in an emergency. She was always there. She was upstairs every day by seven—earlier if she heard the twins clattering around the kitchen. She crawled under her expensive sheets some twelve to fourteen hours later—later still if Andrea and Rick, a lawyer who wasn't home much, had an evening event.

Kate wasn't complaining. This was what she'd signed up for. She'd seen enough from some of the more affluent mothers in her old neighborhood to know what it would be like. She had no illusions that the two hours she was supposed to have off every day would be respected. And she was fine with that. Scrambling after the twins kept her from having time to think. When she fell into bed at night, she was so exhausted she usually went right to sleep.

It was ideal in a lot of ways. The job came with a comfortable bed and food. She never had time to spend the money she was making. It was accumulating nicely in the box she kept tucked away behind one of the ceiling tiles. But the thing she hadn't counted on, the thing she'd known on some level but had never accounted for, was how being with the twins would enhance her memory of her children rather than help it fade.

"Aunt Kwait," Willie said, skipping into the kitchen in his cow-covered footie pajamas. This was what he called her, a vestige of the babysitter thing or perhaps the white thing. She didn't look like the other nannies, so she'd been passed off as an aunt of sorts. "I am so happy to see you."

"I am so happy to see you, too, Willie. Did you have a good sleep?"

"Good, I think."

They had the same conversation every morning.

Willie climbed up onto one of the bar stools, being careful to reach up and place his favorite stuffed bear on the counter first. Kate watched him closely, ready to spring into action if needed. A few weeks ago, when Willie had added this independent move to his morning routine, he'd lost his grip and hit the hardwood floor with a sickening *thunk*. "I okay," he'd said before Kate could get the words out. "I not mean to do that."

Willie made it up safely this morning. Kate tucked his chair in as he recovered his bear and held it to his chest.

"What would you like for breakfast?"

"Pancakes?" he asked hopefully.

"Sorry, muffin. It's not the weekend."

He looked momentarily defeated, then said with more resignation than Kate thought a three-year-old should, "Green smoothie."

"Correct!"

Willie giggled. He knew Kate would put as little of the "nasty" green parts into the smoothie as she could get away with and add an extra splash or two of organic apple juice.

"You know what, Aunt Kwait?"

"What's that?"

Willie beckoned her closer. She bent over his silken head.

"You are my bestest friend."

"What about Steven?" Kate asked, referring to his twin. "I think he's your bestest friend."

"No, uh-uh. He not share his LEGO." Willie's water-blue eyes turned dark and serious. "Don't you want to be?"

Kate wrapped her arms around him. She was assaulted by his little-kid smell—organic children's shampoo and warm blankets.

That was all it took to kick her back. Flash after flash, like a sped-up montage in a movie of her life. Playing in leaves in the fall. Bath time. Pulling sweaters over their heads and pretending they were stuck. The way their little hands curled around hers.

"Are you crywing, Aunt Kwait?"

INTERVIEW TRANSCRIPT

TJ: What do you mean by "a little Nancy Drew" exactly?

FM: I was always looking for evidence. Curious. Like her. I read all those books. I bet you read the Hardy Boys or something.

TJ: Nope.

FM: Well, my parents got all these old Nancy Drew books at a garage sale when we were small. I think we had a hundred of them.

TJ: So you started looking for your mother when you were eight?

FM: Basically. There wasn't much I could do then, but yeah, that's when I started looking. I had this book, like a journal? I hid it under my bed so my parents couldn't find it. I called it my book of clues.

TJ: What kind of clues did you put in there?

FM: Hints my mother would drop sometimes. Like what the hospital had been like where they went to pick me up, though she wouldn't tell me where it was. And she had a picture of me that was taken in the hospital, before, you know. Before my mother gave me up. I stared and stared at that picture. I even went over it with a magnifying glass.

TJ: So you didn't have any other information about your mother? Only that you were born in Chicago?

FM: No. The adoption system . . . Well, I know there's been some changes over the years because of all the advocacy groups, but when she gave me up? It was closed adoption all the way. I mean, I guess those records are somewhere, right, they'd have to be. But sure as shit they weren't going to let me look at them. And once my parents died, I couldn't even count on them to help me.

TJ: How old were you when they passed away?

FM: Eighteen. A stupid accident. My dad fell asleep at the wheel.

TJ: I'm so sorry.

FM: Thank you. It was . . . a blow. I was an orphan, but yet not, you know? It felt very . . . strange.

TJ: But you did end up finding your mother? Despite the closed adoption?

FM: Yeah, through one of the advocacy groups I belonged to. I can't say much more than that . . . I want to protect their anonymity.

TJ: Is that because the way you found her was illegal?

FM: I don't know about that. Is what Anonymous does illegal? Information should be free, right? I mean, look at it this way— should it be illegal to find out who your real parents are?

TJ: No, I don't believe it should. But I am curious about how it all worked . . .

FM: Like I said, I can't say. I found out; that was the point. And it's one of the reasons I wanted to be involved in the Compensation Initiative.

TJ: How does one lead to the other?

FM: It's all about advocacy. People think they know best, right? Like how everyone told my mother, my biological mother, that it would be a great thing for me for her to give me up. She was what, eighteen when she had me? That's too young to have a baby; that's what they said. And they'd find me a good family and all that other crap. And look, I'm not complaining. I get it. Taking all of that on when you're that young, that's a lot. And I did have a good home. My adoptive parents tried as hard as they could. But it wasn't my family, you know? Not before I knew and especially not after.

TJ: So where does the advocacy come in?

FM: At these adoption support groups I used to go to, that was one of the themes. We'd had all these people make these major decisions for us—our biological parents—and then we weren't even allowed to know who they were. I didn't want that happening to the families of Triple Ten. Especially not the kids. Let the victims decide what they want, what they need. Not the government. Not the church. Not the celebrities falling all over themselves to appear on TV looking like they're doing something to help.

TJ: That sounds like a worthy goal. But there's been some controversy, hasn't there? About who is allowed to receive compensation?

FM: You're talking about the Identification Protocol?

TJ: Yes.

FM: Well, that was my idea, actually.

TJ: Why did you think it was important?

FM: Because people could lie, couldn't they? There were all the
       people who worked there who died, sure, but there were also
       tons of folks going in and out of that building all day. And then
       those who were just around the building . . . Anyone could claim
       they were there, and no one would know for sure. Take Cecily
       Grayson.

TJ: What about her?

FM: She says she was on her way there, right? And we all know that's
       true because we have the photographic evidence. You took it. But
       if she'd actually been in the building, what proof would we have?

TJ: Aren't there entry logs?

FM: Not for guests. Not electronic ones. They were still using a paper
       system. That got lost, obviously. And you've heard about the
       cameras, right? Totally unreliable.

TJ: Are you suggesting that someone might make a false claim in
       order to get compensation?

FM: Don't look so shocked. That sort of stuff happens all the time.

TJ: So the Identification Protocol . . .

FM: Requires irrefutable evidence that their family member actually
       died there that day in order for them to get compensation.

TJ: And I understand that your own . . . um, your biological mother's
       family's claim was refused?

FM: That's right.

TJ: How did that happen?

FM: I can't make special exceptions. We can't, I mean.

TJ: Sure. But there's some irony there, that the rule could affect your family in particular. You, even, I suppose.

FM: Yeah, but that claim is under review. You never know what might turn up.

7

HERE WE GO LOOP-DE-LOOP

CECILY

This is how I found out I was a fool.

It was six months before Tom died, as I was running around trying to make everything perfect for our upcoming wedding anniversary extravaganza weekend away! (I thought in exclamation marks back then, more often than I'd like to admit.) I received a text from Tom that said: *I can't stop thinking about last night.*

Nothing so unusual in that. In fact, he'd texted me something similar a few years before, after we'd had a particularly steamy evening when both the kids were out with friends and we'd had a few glasses of wine and ended up having sex on the kitchen counter. I'd texted an emoticon back to that one (probably a smiley face, knowing me at the time), and we'd engaged in mild sexting for about an hour until it petered out.

But not this time, because this time—as far as I knew up until that moment—Tom was supposed to have been on the flip side of an all-nighter at work to get the bugs out of the product they were about to launch so we could leave for the weekend. He was supposed to be surrounded by bad pizza and sour coffee and people in need of showers, not something he couldn't stop thinking about. Not someone.

I knew the text was bad news the minute I read it. Stomach-churning, gut-twisting bad. And then my phone chimed again. *Ding! Ding!*

I got the texts while I was in Victoria's Secret. That's right. I was actually in the middle of buying sexy lingerie for that fucker when I received the announcement that my husband had slept with another woman. Because that's what it was, what it meant. There wasn't any other way to read it. Or maybe there would've been if he hadn't followed it up with: *I love how you suck my cock.*

A classy guy, my husband. Also generally very careful, but I guess he was so taken away with his memories of the night before, the world-class cock-sucking he'd received, that he'd tapped the wrong text thread—was her name similar to mine or were we the only two people he texted with? One of a million questions leaping through my mind—and sent the message to me instead of whoever he intended it for.

When I received the alert for the second text, I tried to look away. But in my innocent life as it existed then, I'd enabled the floating preview bar on my phone so I could see the first lines of whatever anyone sent me. I had nothing to hide, you see, nothing to fear. I couldn't avoid the words as they appeared on the screen that was grasped in my shaking hand, warm to the touch. I read them and felt frozen to the floor, my other hand still stuck in the 50-percent-off silk underwear bin I'd been riffling through to find my size.

My mind was whirling as fast as my gut. I had no idea how to react. Should I write back or allow him to sit and wonder why the cock-sucking genius was letting him twist in the wind without a response until he figured out who he'd actually texted? Should I simply pretend the whole thing never happened?

I admit: I kind of wished I could do the last one. My finger actually swiped to delete the texts, but I couldn't bring myself to do it. I didn't want that filth on my phone, but I couldn't put it in the trash and pretend I'd never read it, either.

Oh, Tom, you stupid asshole.

Why couldn't you have been more careful?

"So," my therapist, Linda, says. "You made it through the memorial."

We're in her office, the place I've been coming to once a week for nine months. A friend of a friend suggested her without my having to ask for a referral. When your husband dies suddenly, it's assumed you'll need some kind of mental health assistance to recover.

"I did."

"I saw you on TV."

I pull a face. "Maybe now it will stop."

"Perhaps."

Linda's a pragmatist, and she doesn't believe in feeding me false hope. Better to accept the things I cannot change and all that, like an addict, even though I'm the substance being consumed.

"You were feeling anxious about the interview with Teo. How did it go?"

"Okay, I think."

"I'm going to need more than that."

I pull my feet under me on the couch; Linda's across from me on a matching one. One of the things I like about Linda, she doesn't believe in creating distinctions between us. Our sessions are often like highly effective conversations with my girlfriends, sans alcohol. I don't know what I expected therapy to be; I only know that when I got out of the car before my first session, I started crying, and the first thing I said to her was, "I don't want this to be a lifetime relationship." She'd agreed, and we'd gone on from there.

"You always say that."

Linda's eyes crinkle. A natural beauty in her midforties, she has few lines that mar her dark-brown skin. "That is what you pay me for, after all."

"True. Well, I got through it. He asked all the questions I expected, and I gave the best answers I could. If I had to guess, I told two outright lies and six lies by omission, but I wasn't keeping strict count."

"You don't have to keep a tally of lies."

I shift my eyes away from hers. Linda's office is a palette of taupe. I keep meaning to bring a colorful throw with me someday to brighten up the place, but it always slips my mind.

"Don't I?"

"We've discussed this. You could simply unburden yourself. Or, alternatively, make peace with the fact that you're entitled to certain secrets."

"I feel like a fraud."

"You're not a fraud. Your husband died. You did what you had to do to protect your children's future. To protect your future."

"But I hated him. I hated him when he died, and everyone thinks I'm this grieving widow, that I'm missing him, that I wish he was still here. Still with me and our family."

"Who cares what anyone thinks? And you are grieving him. Maybe not in the way you think others assume you are, but you are. Do you think you're the only person who wasn't happy with their spouse that day?"

"It's not the same. I wanted him dead. I'd even fantasized about how I'd do it."

"Did your fantasies involve rigging the gas pipes beneath his building so they'd explode and kill five hundred and twelve other people?"

"No. Well, maybe just him and her. I didn't care how it happened. But I thought it, and then it came true."

Linda frowns. "You don't believe your fantasies played a role in what happened that day, do you? Because it was a terrible accident, one that could've been avoided with better inspections, perhaps, but nothing more than that."

"No . . ."

"This is important, Cecily."

"It is strange, isn't it?"

"Coincidences aren't strange or the evidence of anything; they're a part of life."

I pluck at a loose thread on the couch, then stop when I feel Linda watching me.

"You aren't to blame for what happened."

"I know that rationally, but I wish there was a way I could get some resolution."

"About what? With Tom?"

"Her. I wish she'd died that day, too, and she probably did, but I don't know for sure."

"What makes you think that?"

"I've been over it and over it. She had to be someone he worked with. Or someone in the building, maybe someone who worked at another company, because he was at work the night before we went to New York—at least part of the time. Will Blass told me so."

Will was Tom's business partner. He'd hemmed and hawed when I'd asked him impulsively at the reception at our house after the funeral where Tom was the night before they launched SecretKeeper, their new privacy software. He'd pretended at first that he didn't remember, but when I told him I knew Tom was seeing someone, he'd relented and told me Tom had been there until about midnight, if he could remember correctly, and then left for several hours. He didn't know for sure that Tom was with another woman, though he'd suspected it. "I'm sorry," he said. "I don't know who it was." I was almost certain that was a lie, but when I'd pressed, he said to leave it and walked away. I haven't spoken to him since.

"Even if that's true, that doesn't mean she was there that day," Linda says.

"The not knowing is driving me crazy."

"Why?"

"Because how could I be so stupid? How could I not know what was going on in my own life?"

"Your husband was an accomplished liar and very, very careful. It's not a failing of yours that you didn't figure out he was cheating on you or who he was cheating on you with. As for the other woman, if she's alive, she's most likely suffering from loss herself."

"Am I supposed to care about that?"

"No, but I expect the last thing she'd do is seek you out, so you're probably never going to know what happened between them or who she is. You have to find a way to be okay with that."

"So she gets away with it? With destroying my life?"

"This isn't about her. It's about you. About you finding a way to get past this. To get closure."

"How can I get closure when I have to play a role all the time and listen to everyone talk about what a great guy Tom was? When I have to preserve this lie for my kids and our friends? It's not fair. It's not fair."

"Will you be stamping your feet anytime soon?"

"No," I say, pouting. I know I'm being childish, but it isn't fair. It really isn't.

"You can do whatever you want in here, Cecily. And I can agree with all those things. But unless you find a way to forgive yourself, and to forgive Tom, too, we are going to end up having a lifelong relationship because you're going to be stuck in the same place you are today."

"So what do I do? How do I get unstuck?"

"You do the work."

"That sounds . . . tiring."

"I never said it was going to be easy."

• • •

After Linda, I pull myself together and make it to my Compensation Committee meeting early. There wasn't any traffic for once, but also, perhaps things can change. It would be nice to think so, if even for a moment.

The Compensation Committee meets as needed to reconsider the cases the retired judge we've hired to make the initial determination rejects. Given the importance of our decisions, these meetings are always a challenge, and I know already that today's meeting is going to be harder than most.

"Shall we discuss the Ring case?" Franny asks when we've assembled around the table. She speaks in a Midwestern twang, an accent she tries to cover up, though I've told her time and again she doesn't need to. She's wearing a gray wool blazer I helped her pick out a few weeks ago from the sale rack at J.Crew. It strikes me how different the Franny of today is from the one I met so many months ago. Better hair, better clothes, twenty pounds shed, but also, she has much more confidence and assurance. She's found her purpose and her sense of place. She's more at home here than I am. "Okay with you, Cecily?"

"Of course."

We're sitting at opposite ends of a long glass table in the second conference room in the Initiative's offices. The others on the committee—two men whose wives died in the building, a twenty-three-year-old girl who lost her father and whose mother is long dead of cancer, and Tanya Simpson, the committee's secretary—fill up the space between us.

"I know this will be difficult for some of you," Franny says, meaning mostly me, I suppose, and her. "But it's an important part of the process."

I voted against Franny's "process" when she proposed it six months ago, when we first gathered to set out the guidelines we wanted to follow. Her idea was that for a family to get compensation, they'd generally need a DNA match to something—nobody liked to use the words "flesh," "blood," "bone"—found in the wreckage that's still being sifted through, even now. I understood why she proposed it, but I couldn't bring myself to support a measure that would leave some people without the help I'd received. Especially because I'd gotten my check before the process was in place.

In the beginning, when the money was rolling in from the celebrity fund-raisers and they wanted a photo op to keep it coming, they'd turned to me, my family, put us on a dais, and handed us a big check with more zeros on it than I could believe. Donate today, and every family can have this future . . . But when the donations slowed down and the complaints started, the judge had been brought in and the committee was created above him to hear appeals and special cases. I owed it to all the people who didn't get the opportunity I did to do my best to make sure that if their claim was denied, it was for a valid reason.

When the Rings' claim was turned down because they couldn't match Franny or the girls' DNA to anything in the wreckage, I'd been the one to console Franny when she wept about what she'd done. It was a *stupid rule, stupid. So stupid,* she said over and over until I was worried she'd gone into some sort of autistic trance. I had to hand it to Franny, though: when she'd pulled herself together—a shot of whiskey had done it—she hadn't given up on the idea that the decision could be reversed. And here we are today, with that possibility.

"What's the new evidence?" Jenny, the twenty-three-year-old, asks. Her thin limbs concern me. I didn't know her before, so it's possible that she's naturally this skinny, this almost-see-through. But she doesn't have anyone looking out for her anymore, so I feel responsible, as if I should paint her back in, make sure she's visible.

"It's the mug," Franny says, her voice wavering.

A few weeks ago, the search team found a coffee mug in pristine condition. It seemed impossible that the explosion and the fire and everything else hadn't shattered it into a million pieces, but like the pottery that survived Pompeii, there it was, covered in dust but intact.

It wasn't only its survival that was so arresting. Other whole things had been found—a desk, phones, paintings, many bodies, including Tom's. It was the fact that it was a mug that obviously belonged to someone, one of those mugs kids make for their mothers at school, with *We Heart Mom* on one side and her picture on the other. And on the rim, the thing that made it eligible for consideration: lipstick that had been left—presumably—by its last user. The media had become obsessed with this mug, debating its provenance, wondering what we were going to do with it, and while they weren't allowed in this meeting, it wouldn't be long before the results of it became known, analyzed, dissected.

Franny puts a white square box on the table. It looks like a cake box, something that generally houses something delicious, something perfectly frosted rather than tragic. None of us has seen the mug in person, only photographs, though it still was a blow when I caught sight of it on the nightly news. I remember when her children gave her this mug, almost two years ago, on Valentine's Day.

Franny opens the box, then puts on a pair of surgeon's gloves, snapping them into place with practiced ease.

"Is that necessary?" one of the men asks. Robert's always been hostile to Franny and only slightly less so to me. He's not used to being anything other than in charge is my take on the matter, so he has to lash out whenever he feels someone else's authority. "It's already been through testing."

"It belonged to my mother," Franny says. "I want to treat it with the appropriate respect."

This logic is hard to argue with, and Robert keeps any further thoughts to himself. I watch Franny lift the mug from the box. She unwraps it and places it on the table in front of her, turning it so we can see the imprint of someone's lips left like a kiss along its rim.

And then I couldn't speak even if I wanted to, because I know that shade of lipstick. She wore it every day, a deep cranberry that would've looked awful on anyone else but fit her perfectly.

I'm not sure why it's this thing rather than all the others that breaks me, but it does. As the rest of the room watches the cup like it might spit out the entrants to this year's Triwizard Tournament, I lay my head down on the cold glass table and weep.

8

MORNING NEWS

KATE

"What's going on here?" Andrea asked as she walked into the kitchen. She was wearing her standard day uniform: lululemon yoga pants and a thin cotton hoodie that showed off her toned arms. Although her hair was on its third day after her weekly blowout, it was still as beach-wavy as when she'd left the salon.

Kate straightened up. She kept her back to Andrea as she wiped her tears away with the sleeve of the dark-blue sweatshirt she'd bought on sale for $12.99. It itched where it met her collarbone, but beggars couldn't be choosers.

"Willie was just being the sweet little boy he always is," Kate said, ruffling his head. "That's all."

Andrea sighed, then tapped a finger against the touch screen in the wall to turn it on. Perhaps this was what Kate's tears were about. An advance reaction to the fact that Andrea always had the television on when she was at home, usually the news. The morning news was how Andrea stayed "connected to the world," she always said, "now that I'm not in the paid workforce." Then she'd get this wistful look on her face. Remembering back, Kate supposed, to her job as the CFO of a magazine distribution company, which she'd given up a month after she found out she was having twins.

The television sprang to life with a loud chime. Kate didn't have to look to know what the day's banner would be: "A Year Later. Remembering Chicago," or something similar. She tried to block out the low murmur of the announcer speaking in a somber tone about the upcoming memorial.

Kate walked to the sink. She should've told Andrea where she came from and why. Some version of it, anyway. Enough. Andrea wouldn't foist the coverage on her if she knew the toll it was already taking. She wasn't cruel. Perhaps she'd even have given her a day off. Allowed her to hide in the dark basement all day rather than face the cold sunshine. The darkened orange leaves as they fell from the trees. Her memories.

Kate filled up the sink with hot water and added the Andrea-approved amount of nontoxic dishwashing liquid, which she measured out with a shot glass. She made the water scalding hot. She'd forgotten to line the pan she made last night's pork ribs in. There was a hard coat of sauce baked to the bottom of it. She'd let it soak overnight to tackle that morning. Perhaps the scrubbing would do her some good.

"This is so sad," Andrea said in a tone that expected an answer. "It is."

"What's sad, Mommy?" Steven asked as he entered the kitchen.

Kate turned to watch him. Steven was a more cautious copy of his brother. It was always interesting to see how he'd adapt to a situation. His eyes moved from where his brother was sitting, to Kate at the sink, to his mother, whose own eyes never left the screen. Satisfied that everyone was where they should be, he put his blanket down carefully and walked to Kate.

"Up," he said, holding his arms above his head.

She took off her rubber gloves and did as he commanded. Lifting him up and then lowering him into his high chair. Then strapping him in tightly as he nodded in approval.

"What's 'sad' mean, Mommy?" he asked again.

"It's what you feel when bad things happen to people you love."

"On the TV?" Steven asked, pointing.

Kate followed his finger. McCormick Place, Chicago's convention center, was on-screen. It would be a convention of grief.

Kate felt feverish. She was going to fly into a million pieces. She was sure of it.

"Yes, Stevie. The TV's showing the sad people."

Steven cocked his head to the side, trying to puzzle it out. Kate refrained from suggesting that it would be better for the children if Andrea turned it off. Andrea wouldn't comply. She didn't believe in shielding her kids from harsh realities. Or, at least, not any more than the shield that came from living in the rich, mostly white enclave of Westmount.

"Why is TV showing sad people?" Willie asked. He picked a

spoon up off the counter and started drumming it against the quartz. His spoon was in time with the quick cuts flashing by. A car. A picture. A wreath of bright flowers. *Tap, tap, tap.*

Andrea assumed the most serious expression she could on her newly Botoxed face. (She was "trying it out for fun," she'd told Kate in confidence a week ago. Kate doubted that highly.)

"What city do we live in?" Andrea asked.

"Montreal!" the twins said together.

"Correct. And there are lots of other cities in the world, right?"

"New Work!" Willie said, looking to Andrea for approval.

Andrea smiled back. She and Rick had taken the twins there for a long weekend a few months ago. Andrea had been upset when Kate told her she wouldn't be able to travel with them when she'd realized too late that her passport was expired. She'd offered to reimburse her plane ticket, but Andrea swept that suggestion away as if she were shooing a fly. "It's not about the money . . ." The unfinished part of that sentence being that it was about the fact that she and Rick would be without childcare for a weekend. But she couldn't admit that out loud.

"Correct!" Andrea said. "And there's another city called Chicago."

"Chi-cag-wo?"

"Very good."

"What happened there?"

Kate felt light-headed. She forced herself to breathe. She picked up a glass, meaning to fill it with water.

"There was a terrible accident. A building blew up."

Willie looked puzzled, but Steven looked upset.

"People dwied?"

"Yes, honey. Many people. A year ago. And today we're remembering them."

"Mommies and daddies?"

"Yes," Andrea said. "Mommies and daddies. And also . . . some little kids—"

Kate dropped the glass she was holding. It shattered against the floor like a bomb.

"Oh, I'm so sorry, I . . . Nobody move."

She rushed to the cupboard where the wall vacuum was kept. She turned it on and scooted back to where the glass shards were thickest. Sucking up as many as she could along the way as the vacuum's engine whirred, blocking out the television.

"Don't move, boys," Kate said. She caught Andrea's eye. "I'm sorry."

"It's only a glass."

Kate bent her head again, searching carefully for each tiny shard. She'd have to make sure the boys wore shoes for the next couple of days. From experience, glass would continue to show up for a while despite her efforts.

"Hey!" Willie said. "It's Aunt Kwait."

"I'm right here." Kate smiled at him, waving from the floor.

"Not here . . . there!"

His little finger rose and pointed at the screen.

INTERVIEW TRANSCRIPT

TJ: Getting back to your biological mother. You obtained your birth
records when, exactly?

FM: Two years ago. I stepped up the search after my parents died. It
took a few years, but as I said, as a result of some help I got, I
was able to get a copy of the hospital record of my birth. After all
those years of trying and wondering and . . . I had this piece of
paper in my hand that was filled out the day I was born. That said
who I was. It had my footprints on it, too.

TJ: What was that like for you? To see that?

FM: It was surreal. I mean, I cried. I had a name. She didn't call me
Franny. She called me Marigold. And that's another thing, because

Franny never felt like my name to me, and Marigold did the moment I read it, but it also felt like it would be too weird to change my name back to that, you know? Like I didn't own either name.

TJ: What happened next?

FM: It took me another six months to find her. It wasn't easy. She'd gotten married, changed her last name. She had a whole family, you know? I had another whole family.

[Sounds of crying]

TJ: Do you need a minute?

FM: I'm all right. Let's continue.

TJ: Did you learn anything about your father?

FM: My biological father? She left his name blank on the birth record. She wouldn't tell me who he was.

TJ: Did she say why?

FM: She didn't want to talk about it. The whole thing was quite a shock to her, me contacting her.

TJ: I can imagine it must've been.

FM: But she was happy I did it. Happy I found her.

TJ: I'm sure she was. She must've wondered what had happened to you. Where you were.

FM: She told me she did. That she thought about me often. That she'd thought about finding me but . . . I wish we'd had more time together. It seems cruel, doesn't it? That she died so soon after we finally found each other again?

TJ: It does. Have you tried to locate your biological father?

FM: No . . . Mr. Ring has been . . . I guess you could call him my stepfather, right?

TJ: Is that what you call him?

FM: Well, no . . . I mean, he's been amazing and so welcoming, but I don't look at him as a father figure.

TJ: Has he discouraged you from looking for your father?

FM: Not at all. He doesn't know anything that can help me, though, and my mother's parents died a long time ago, and she was an only child, so it's kind of hard to find something to go on to track him down. I have some ideas, though, from talking to a few of her friends who knew her in high school.

TJ: She had you in high school?

FM: No, after. She took a year off between high school and college, like a gap year, you know, how they do in England? That's when she got pregnant.

TJ: Did Mr. Ring know she'd had another child?

FM: No, can you believe it? *[Pause]* That hurt, you know? Like, I wasn't even worth mentioning to the man she decided to spend her life with. And her girls, my half sisters, they didn't know, either. I feel kind of bad about that . . . Like she abandoned all of us, in a way.

TJ: How do you mean?

FM: If I found out something like that about my mother, I mean the one who raised me, after she'd died, I'd feel like I didn't know her at all. Like I had to revisit every moment I had with her. Was she missing this other kid the whole time she was with me? Was I only a replacement for the one she gave up? Shit like that. Oh, sorry, I shouldn't swear.

TJ: It's fine. We can edit it out if we need to.

FM: Right. That's what you do. Splice and dice people's stories together. Making them into good people and bad people. Turning people into villains. Like on *The Bachelor*.

TJ: That's not my intention.

FM: We'll see, I guess. But I'm not the villain, you know.

TJ: Who said you were?

FM: Lots of people. But it's not my fault. I didn't mean for everyone to find out like that. I didn't.

9

EARTHQUAKE WEATHER

CECILY

I have this theory about cheating.

I don't think it's inbred, necessarily, that some people are programmed that way and some aren't. I think, often, it's born out of circumstance.

Take Tom. When I met Tom in college, he was an average guy. A "nice guy," my friends called him, as opposed to the assholes I'd dated before, but not too nice. Not some geeky guy who was grateful I was going out with him, which would make him a boring guy and not enough protection against the bad guys I was trying to stay away from. Tom was his own man. He had plans. He'd had a serious girlfriend before me, and they'd drifted apart. They were still friendly without being friends, which seemed like the right balance. He even had a few women friends, which I liked, too. Women were people to him. He'd played the field a bit, but he was always someone who was happier with a home base. He wanted to get married, to be settled, to start his business and build something with me. He didn't want a wife who stayed at home with the kids—he liked that I worked, that I had passions outside of us. He didn't want to be the sun and the moon and the stars: just the stars would do.

That's what he used to say to me: *just the stars would do.* It was kind of our thing, our motto, our secret exchange that would make us smile and my heart flutter. Back then, it felt like a nice sentiment. It's what I wanted, also. I'd had that stomach-churning, crying-in-the-shower-when-a-guy-canceled-plans-for-the-third-day-in-a-row love. That sucked. I wanted a partner, a man, someone who understood I might need to disappear inside my work for a while and we'd see each other on the other side. We'd be each other's touchstones, our lodestars.

And we were. Through the end of college, Tom starting his business, me my career, and buying our first house, we kept true to what we'd promised—we were together but apart when we needed to be. Secure. When we felt ready for kids, we started trying, and it happened right away. Tom was ecstatic, calling his friends and family and telling everyone he met even as I shushed him because it was too soon.

Having kids changes a lot of couples, and we weren't an exception, but we weren't changed in any fundamental way. We were still Lily and Tom, a team. He changed diapers. He did pediatrician runs when the kids needed shots or had a fever. He knew the bedtime routine as well as I did. We both cooked and cleaned. I don't think it's possible to be exactly fifty-fifty at anything, but we did our best. We came close.

I'll admit—we were complacent. We looked down, sometimes, at our friends who didn't have the same kind of balance. We were self-satisfied with our life, which had turned out mostly as we'd planned when snuggled up in my single college bed. We had this thing figured out, we thought, dialed in. We were doing it. It wasn't perfect, it got messy sometimes, but we had each other. We'd make it through.

Here's what I didn't factor in: because we were just the stars, one of us might start to miss the moon or long for the sun. We'd packed those things away as unattainable, unnecessary in the grand scheme of things, but they weren't. I'd forgotten to account for the fact that even the brightest of stars may dim as the years tick by because of compromise, because of time, because of life.

And if you're used to the stars, however clear they may be in a country sky, how can you even see them if the moon is full? What chance do they have in the face of the sun? If you looked at the sun for the first time, really looked, after all that stargazing, you'd be blinded. And then sunlight begins to feel essential in a way it never did before; starlight pales by comparison.

That's what I think happened with Tom. Now, with all this distance between the receipt of those horrible texts and the last memorial I'll attend for him, I feel like I might get why he did it. Maybe a little, maybe enough. Or then again, maybe not.

Because you can turn away from the sun. You can shield your eyes.

You can be more fucking careful with your texts.

I've tried to forgive him, and to hate him, too, but the Tom I met on campus at a stupid mixer my dorm was throwing who pushed his glasses up his nose and then up on top of his head, that Tom who never let me treat him like I was his mother and who was perfectly capable of doing his own laundry, who stayed up all night with the kids when they had croup, who held first Cassie then Henry in his arms as if they were the best present I could ever give him . . . I still love that guy. Most of the time, I still think I made the right choice. Many days I'd probably make that choice again. But in this new life, post–texts and death and anger and grief, if ever faced with the possibility again?

This time I might go for the moon.

This time I might bask in the sun.

The committee waits for me to compose myself. Jenny hands me a Kleenex and someone else offers me water, but *I'm fine*, I say, *fine*.

"Go ahead, Franny."

"So we know this is her mug," Franny says, fighting back her own tears. "We know my mother worked there and that she logged in to the building that morning."

While the building's paper entry records were lost, there was a computerized system for those who worked in the building—they had to swipe their pass in order to get through security or exit the building. Unfortunately, the program that tracked departures had a glitch in it that was discovered only after the explosion. So we knew who'd gone into the building—Tom had entered at 8:22 that day, a bit early for him—but not who'd left before ten o'clock.

"And she sent an e-mail from her work computer at nine fifty," Franny continued. "To Cecily, actually."

I still had that e-mail. It said simply: *Good luck. Call me after.* I'd seen it only days later, when I finally had the energy to look through the hundreds of e-mails that had gathered in my in-box. I'd felt so tired, so crushed, after I read it—one of her last thoughts had been about me. Not that she knew what was coming, but my wish for my friend was that she was at peace in those final minutes, not worried, and certainly not worried about my stupid problems.

She was Tom's head programmer, but we'd known her for years before she joined the business. The Rings lived in Evanston like us, and she and I were in a book club together for a while. But it was after the birth of her second daughter, Julia, four years ago (her third, I guess, a fact that still took me by surprise even though I was sitting down the table from the evidence, the person, Franny), when she was hit with a bout of postpartum depression, that we became close friends.

Depression's a funny thing. We don't know what to do about it—as a society—unless we've been there ourselves. The person before us is not someone we know, and their unhappiness is often not something we can understand. So we downplay it, and we make the afflicted somehow to blame. No one would ever tell someone with cancer that if they tried a bit harder, if they got out of bed and took a shower, everything would be better, but people told her all those things. That and more, worse.

Her husband, Joshua, hadn't known how to handle it, but I'd been there in college—clinically depressed for much of my sophomore year—so I knew what it felt like. I knew what had worked for me, what had pulled me through and brought me out the other side. I made myself as available to her as I could, and we became close.

When she was on her feet and feeling ready to go back to work, I suggested she apply for a job at Tom's company. Tom agreed—they'd always gotten along—and several months after she started working for him, he told me how happy he was that he'd taken her on.

"Yes," I say to the committee in the here and now, "she wrote to me that day."

I can feel their curious stares. They've read the e-mail. What was she wishing me luck for? Why did she want me to call her after? After what? I've been asked more than once. It isn't anybody's business, and I'd made up some answer, some inside joke between us about how we wished each other luck on ordinary days. Just for fun. Ha.

"You've all seen the e-mail," I add. "Nothing relevant there."

Jenny looks as if she wants to ask more but turns to Franny instead. The others follow suit. The fact that anyone read her e-mails feels like the worst invasion of privacy. Which it is, but privacy gives way to compensation.

"Did someone check the IP address?" one of the men asks. "She could've sent it from her phone."

"We checked," Franny says. "All this information is in your packets."

There's a slim white folder sitting on the table in front of each of us. It has the shadowy label of the Initiative on it. I open it up. It's full of the usual application materials. Financial information, the details of the deceased's job, how many family members are seeking compensation. A photo.

I touch its matte surface. It's been a long time since I held a real picture rather than simply scrolling through memories on my phone. It's a happy photo taken at a backyard barbecue. There's a date stamped on the back. Two years ago, almost to the day.

"The judge had all this information," Jenny says.

"Correct," Franny answers. "But he didn't have the mug, and her DNA is clearly on it. It was matched to the DNA we have on file for her."

"But it's the mug she used every day, right?"

"Your point being?"

"It isn't any better evidence she was there than anything else we have. Not based on the criteria you insisted we put in place."

Everyone waits for Franny to respond. She takes a moment, possibly counting to ten in her head before proceeding as we'd discussed when we'd prepped for the meeting on the phone last night.

"I agree with you. It alone doesn't prove anything."

"Then why are we here?"

"Hush, Jenny," I say. "Let her make her case."

Jenny slouches down and thrusts out her bottom lip. I can count the ridges in her spine through her cream linen shirt.

Franny gives me a grateful smile. "I think if you turn to the last page of the packet, you might feel differently." We do as she asks. There's a grainy photograph of a woman standing at the elevators. It is time-stamped 9:56 a.m. "They found this in a cache of backups on the cloud," Franny says.

She explains. The company that owned the building used a cloud service to back up its security camera footage. But since all the passwords and people with authorization were blown apart in the blast—their offices were located on the first floor, next to the day care—access had proven difficult. We'd get packets of information at a time without, it seemed, any rhyme or reason.

"Look at the time stamp," Franny says. "It's her. She's in the building right before it happened. The lipstick on the cup matches her DNA, the cup she washed meticulously every day, according to anyone who knew her. I think there's sufficient evidence to bring this to a vote. Do I have a second?"

"I second," Jenny says, perhaps to make up for her former criticism.

"The vote has been seconded. I call the vote."

The voices ring around the room, and I don't have to count to know.

The ayes have it.

"Thanks for the support in there," Franny says at the coffee shop where we go after our meetings to grab a coffee and decompress. "What's gotten into Jenny?"

I poke my finger at the foam in my latte. The server's made a smiley-face pattern in it, perhaps sensing we have something to celebrate but don't quite know how to do it.

"It's hard, all of this. It gets to all of us sometimes."

"I know." Franny picks up and then discards the cookie she bought. Though she's thinner than she was, she still struggles with her weight, something I've tried to get her not to care about. "Why don't I feel happier?"

"About what happened today?"

"Yeah. I mean, I got what I wanted . . . for the family."

"For your family."

"It's hard for me to think of them like that sometimes."

"Has something happened?"

"What? Oh, no. They've been so kind, especially Mr. Ring."

"I'm sure you can call him Joshua."

She nods. There's something about the gesture that reminds me of her mother, and I'm struck again at how her face has changed since I first met her. She looks younger now, freer, though she wasn't old to begin with. "He's told me that many times, and I do mostly. Emily and Julia call me Auntie Franny, even though that's not right."

"It does rhyme, though."

"You're trying to cheer me up."

"Is it working?"

"You don't have to do that."

"I want to."

"But you have to take care of yourself, too. That's one of the things I learned in group. It feels good to help other people, but you can't give all of yourself to them. You have to reserve something for yourself. There was this woman . . . kind of like the group leader, you know, but unofficially? Her name was Erika. Anyway, she called it boundaries. 'You need to boundary up.' That's what she'd always say."

I put my hand on her forearm. The hair on it is thick for a woman, like I've seen on some anorexics, though Franny has enough meat on her bones. "You're wise beyond your years. And your mother would've been very proud of you."

"You think so?" Franny's eyes are brimming with tears.

And even though I actually have no idea, because what do I know about her mother now, if she'd keep something like Franny from me, I smile and say, "Of course I do. Now eat your cookie."

10

THROUGH THE LOOKING GLASS

KATE

If Kate hadn't already shattered her glass, it would've dropped to the ground as surely as gravity. Instead, her eyes moved reflexively to the television, where she saw not herself but images of her children. Her husband. Her best friend. Photographs she didn't remember taking but that showed them all at their best. Missing front teeth and dress-up clothes and toys scattered under a Christmas tree. Ghosts, all of them. She was looking at ghosts.

"Aren't kids funny?" Andrea said, half to herself and half to Kate. "Sometimes people look like other people, Willie. It happens."

Willie frowned and looked at Kate. "Not Kwait?"

"No, honey," Kate said. "I'm right here, see?"

She stuck out her tongue, catching a disapproving glance from Andrea but a laugh from the boys. She walked to the television—the announcer was focusing on another broken family now—and tapped it twice to snap it off.

"Who wants to go to the park?"

Although it had been her suggestion, an hour later, bundled up and with a cold wind whipping against her that made her cheeks feel raw, almost bruised, Kate regretted her mention of the park. The boys loved it, their small hands red against the wood-and-metal play structure, their whoops of delight carried away on the breeze. But Kate's hatred of time spent with children in parks was long-standing. It was a penance for her, something she started counting down the minute she arrived. Setting a deadline like she used to do when she was working out. If she could keep going for two more minutes, then maybe she could stop.

Kate checked on the boys, then went to the big-kid swings and sat down. She gripped the metal chains with her mittened hands. Unusually, they were alone. Although she could hear the constant traffic on Sherbrooke Street, it still felt as if she were in a bubble of silence penetrated only by the boys' shouts of glee.

Where was everyone else? Where were the other nannies she typically passed the time with, the women from the Philippines who made up most of the nanny class in Westmount? The occasional mother there with her own children like a normal mom? Probably all watching television, their children distracted by iPads while they relived their distant grief at the horrors of October tenth.

She checked her watch for the umpteenth time. Though it felt like forever, it hadn't been enough time. She should keep them there for another thirty minutes at least. With the plastic swing cutting into the back of her knees, Kate broke up the minutes like she had a year ago on the bus from Chicago to Montreal.

That Greyhound bus ride takes one day, seven hours, and fifty minutes.

Kate registered that information when she bought her ticket—a bargain at $120 because she was paying for only one way—but it was one thing to know a detail and another to live through it. Chicago to Kalamazoo. Then Detroit. Then over the bridge to Windsor, Ontario. Then on to Toronto, where they switched buses. Another switch in Ottawa. And finally they pulled in to Montreal.

Nineteen hundred and ten minutes in all. Like that song from *Rent* where the minutes were counted out in a hopeful melody. Only it wasn't an upbeat show tune. But that was the number of minutes it took to change her life. No, that was wrong. It had taken a lot less than that. The minutes on the bus were the minutes it had taken to change her location. Her life had changed before that, much faster and much more slowly than those two days.

She watched Willie and Steven throw a stick into the dead grass and run after it like puppies. They were content for the moment, but she knew from experience that this could change in an instant. Happy laughter replaced by tears or screams. Arms flying, bruises raised.

She tried to concentrate on them. But now that she'd started thinking about the bus, it was hard to shake it. The dead-air smell. The way she'd become familiar with the odor of her fellow passengers. The way her own body's smell had changed, even the scent of her pee. How she hadn't had anything left to read. She'd refrained from asking the woman across from her, who seemed to have a small mobile library, for a book because that might lead to conversation, questions. Everything Kate wanted to avoid.

The worst part was the border crossing between Detroit and Windsor, Ontario. She'd sat with her nose pressed up against the dirty glass as the bus got closer and closer to Canada, her thoughts racing. Even on this bus full of oddballs, she stood out. Her clothes a mix of what she'd been able to buy at the bus station and what she'd been wearing when she made the decision to leave. She needed something new before they got to the border. A backpack full of the things people usually had when traveling, not the weird amalgam she was carrying. But with her money already dwindling, she settled for a new sweatshirt.

She washed her hair in the bathroom sink of one of the roadside gas stations they stopped at with hand soap. Then changed and transferred everything she cared about into the pouch of the new sweatshirt. Her money. Her passport. A picture of her family. She should've left it behind, but she couldn't bring herself to do it. She couldn't bring herself to look at it, either. But she knew, someday, she'd want this piece of comfort. Even if it came with pain. So she touched it like a talisman, and that was good enough for then.

For all her worry, the border was a breeze. Her Canadian passport was scanned, her photo checked. The customs officer asked her where she lived and what she'd been doing in Chicago. Montreal, she said, making sure to pronounce it as Canadians do, with the O replaced by a U. She'd been visiting friends in Chicago when everything happened.

"Bad luck," said the officer.

"Bad luck," she'd agreed.

And then, right when she couldn't stand being on the bus

anymore, when she thought she might be sick if she had to breathe in any more of the terrible antiseptic smell or the stench wafting from the bathroom, the bus driver announced that they were arriving at their final destination.

And all she could think was: *Now what?*

In the park, Kate checked the time again. Finally, enough seconds had passed, and it was coming up on noon. She looked around. She'd lost track of the boys for a moment, and her heart started to battle panic.

"Willie! Steven!"

She roamed through the play structure, thinking they might be hiding from her. They weren't. The swing set blocked the way to the street; they couldn't have gotten past her without her noticing. They must've gone deeper into the park. She started to run down one of the paths. The pond! The boys loved the pond, where ducks paddled in the summer. They drained it every fall, but there was always an accumulation of rain in the bottom that would be deep enough for a three-year-old to drown in.

"Willie! Steven! Where are you?"

She caught a hint of laughter on the wind. She pushed herself harder, turning the corner to bring her to the pond. She stopped, trying to breathe, searching for any sign of them. The pond circled an island of land planted with several trees. She heard a giggle.

"Willie! Come out, come out!"

Willie popped out from behind a tree with his arms wide. "Taadaa!"

Kate wasn't sure she'd ever felt such relief in her life. If something happened to these boys, she didn't think she could live with herself.

She jumped over a large puddle in the bottom of the drained-out pond.

"Steven!"

"I here."

"Let me see you."

Willie reached behind the tree and pulled his brother out. Their hands were muddy, as were the knees of their jeans. She rushed up to them, pulling them in close for a hug.

"Boys! You can't run away from me like that."

"Sorrryyy."

"You scared me."

Willie's lip started to tremble.

"Oh no, don't cry."

"We wanted to see the ducks. But they not here."

"They've flown away for winter. Next time, ask me first."

"We will."

Kate hugged them again. They smelled as if they'd been rolling around in the bottom of a bog. Andrea was going to be pissed. But they were okay. And with some luck, she'd convince them to keep this escape to themselves.

"How about lunch?"

"Yeah!"

INTERVIEW TRANSCRIPT

TJ: Perhaps we could circle back to how people found out about you later. Why don't you tell me what it was like when you met your mother for the first time?

FM: It's hard to describe. I'd dreamed about her my whole life, you know? Wondering things like, do I bite my nails because of her, or . . . You know that song from *Annie*? "Maybe"?

TJ: I'm not familiar with it.

FM: She's an orphan, right? Only, she doesn't think she's an orphan, she thinks her parents will be back for her. And she sings this song where she imagines where they are, what they're doing. Maybe they're in a house nearby, hidden by a hill. Or maybe he's reading a book while she's playing the piano. Simple things. You get the idea. She imagines them perfect, their one mistake being that they gave her up. Anyway, that's what I felt like my whole childhood was like, and then we met.

TJ: So you found the record of your birth, and then what?

FM: Once I realized she'd changed her name when she'd gotten married, I was able to track her down at the company where she worked. There was a picture of her on the website, and I knew right away it was her. Her e-mail wasn't listed, but I figured it out by using all these different combinations. It wasn't that hard. I think I got it right on, like, the third try.

TJ: What did you write to her?

FM: It was basically, if you gave a daughter up for adoption twenty-two years ago, I'm her, and I'd love to meet you. I included the picture I had from when I was a baby, because I thought she might recognize that more than me as a grown-up. Because we don't look much alike, except I think I have her eyes. That's why I recognized her in the photo on her work site. I take more after my dad, she told me.

TJ: That must've been a nerve-racking e-mail to send.

FM: Yeah, it was. I spent a week writing it and rewriting it. And then right after I sent it, I realized there was a typo. I'd spelled "adoption" "option." [Laughter] Like she'd optioned me for film or something. I felt kind of stupid.

TJ: I'm sure she wasn't focusing on that.

FM: You're probably right. She never mentioned it.

TJ: Did she answer you right away?

FM: It took a couple days. I don't think I slept, waiting for that answer. I was working at the diner, and I think I dropped, like, five plates every day because I couldn't concentrate. I got this talking-to from my boss and everything. But then she wrote me back, and she was super-apologetic about how long she'd taken. She needed time to process, you know? She'd tucked me away, she said, into this place in her heart where she didn't let herself go. And she thought, I'm not sure why, but she thought that when I turned eighteen I'd come looking for her, and when I didn't, she assumed I wouldn't ever do it. And she kind of mourned that and then put it all away again. So I was a shock.

TJ: Had she ever looked for you?

FM: She said she hadn't.

TJ: Did she say why not?

FM: She felt like it wasn't her place. She'd given me up. She made this decision about my life that she thought was the best decision at the time, but since she'd done that, she didn't think it was right to choose for me again. To interfere with my life. She hoped I was happy and healthy. I think she had to convince herself that I was in a good place, you know, to live with the guilt, and so if she went looking for me and found me, she might be bringing up all kinds of things she shouldn't. Like, what if my parents hadn't even told me I was adopted? Or what if I hated her? Or what if my life sucked? So many what-ifs.

TJ: Did she write all that to you in her first e-mail?

FM: Some of it. It was long. A real emotional punch in the gut in so many ways. And before you ask, no, you can't see it. That's private between her and me.

TJ: I understand. And then you met?

FM: Not right away. We e-mailed for a while, getting to know each other. It was kind of like dating in a way . . . I know that sounds weird.

TJ: It's okay; I get it.

FM: Do you? You have a strange job, don't you?

TJ: How so?

FM: Your whole life is about other people's stories.

TJ: I hadn't thought about it like that. Anyway, we're here to talk about you, not me. Let's get back to it, shall we?

FM: Sure.

TJ: You mentioned before that she hadn't told her husband and children about you. Did she do so once you'd made contact?

FM: She said she was going to find a way to tell them. The first time we met for real, that's what she said. "I'm going to have to tell them now." I told her it was okay, that she didn't have to do that, not if she wasn't ready, but she said she would. She shouldn't have kept it from them in the first place. She was ashamed she had.

TJ: She said she'd told them?

FM: When I saw her the next time—we'd meet about once a month for lunch, each of us would drive halfway, and we'd meet in this diner that was kind of like the place I worked, actually—she said she'd told them, though she didn't want to discuss it. She said I couldn't meet them, not yet, because they were still processing. I got the impression that her husband was upset. Which makes sense. That's a big secret to keep between a husband and wife, don't you think?

TJ: It could be. When was this? When did you reconnect with her?

FM: I sent the e-mail about two years ago. We corresponded for about six months before we met in person. Triple Ten happened six months later.

TJ: So you saw her six or seven times before she died?

FM: That's right.

TJ: How do you feel about how little time you had with her?

FM: Part of me is sad about that, but the other part . . . At least I got to know her, right? And she got to see me before she died. I feel good about that. If I'd found out who she was after everything happened, that would've been worse, I think.

TJ: Better to have loved and lost than never to have loved at all?

FM: What's that?

TJ: It's part of a poem by Tennyson.

FM: I've never heard that. But, yeah. It is like that. Because I did love her, you know? And she loved me, too. That's the one thing I know for sure.

11

BETTER TO HAVE LOVED?

CECILY

The first time I spoke to Teo again after he saved my life, I almost slapped him.

That's dramatic to say, but I was that mad. Furious.

It was two months after the explosion. I hadn't slept properly since. Between my own guilt and sadness and taking care of the kids, I felt like I did in those hazy days after their births. Day and night had ceased to matter; personal hygiene was no longer a priority. Everywhere I turned it felt as if I were discovering things I should've known but didn't. The fact that Tom had taken a new line of credit a year before because of business losses he never told me about, for instance. Had I signed those papers? The bank said I had, but I had no memory of it. And then there was the credit card I didn't know about with a hotel room charge at the Langham. I didn't want to know these things. And I was constantly worried about money, how I was going to pay the bills or eat when the free meals stopped showing up. There was money coming, I kept getting told, but it hadn't arrived yet. In the meantime, what was I supposed to do? Put the house on the market? Sell my children's childhood out from under them? How could I do that after all they'd suffered, what they were still suffering daily?

Then there was my face on all those magazines. I hated it but felt like a chump for complaining. What was my discomfort next to my children's pain and the pain of all the other families who'd lost someone that day? So what if it felt weird to be pushing a cart through the checkout line in the grocery store past a raft of publications with my shocked face on them? Big deal if some of the other shoppers looked at me funny. What did any of it matter compared to everything else? But then the calls started, the requests. Could I come to this event? Could I do this interview? Could I give more and more and more of myself, be more and more and more visible, when all I wanted to do was hide?

I said yes to all of it, tucking my anxieties away as best I could, but I didn't feel as if I had a choice. And that made me resent it. Resent him. Teo.

It was the inauguration event for the Compensation Initiative. I'd borrowed $5,000 from my mother that week so I could pay our mortgage and the electric bill, pay off the credit cards, buy groceries and a dress that would hide the desperateness I felt. Cassie helped me do my hair and makeup, and when I looked at myself in the mirror, I looked like her, the woman on the cover. The Poster Child, the part I was playing. I felt as if the woman I used to be was stolen from me, taken by his camera, and I could never get her back.

Sara drove me to the event, making sure I got there on time, or at all. We got caught in traffic, and she went to park the car, letting me off in front of the building with promises to return soon, reminding me to breathe. It was a blasted winter day, that lake-effect wind that cuts through everything and grips your bones. My feet pushed me inside, but I didn't want to go. I didn't want to ride the elevator or know I was going to be that high up. It was the first time I felt that vertigo, even before I left the ground, but it wouldn't be the last.

I stopped short in the lobby, right past the revolving door. Someone bumped into me from behind. I spun around, and there was Teo.

"Sorry, I—"

"You!"

He stepped back. His head was covered with a black watch cap, but I knew immediately who he was.

"Mrs. Grayson—"

"What are you doing here?"

"I was invited. I thought . . . I can go if you want."

That's when I almost slapped him. I don't know what it was that made me feel so violent, but as we stood there in the lobby of a building that was going to occupy too much of my life, surrounded by Christmas ornaments while the wind beat against the windows, I wanted that shock of contact. I could even hear the hard *crack* my hand would make.

"Mrs. Grayson," Teo said. "I'm going to leave, okay? I'm leaving."

The anger fled my body as quickly as it arrived.

"No, stay."

"Are you sure?"

"You have as much right to be here as I do."

He pulled the cap from his head and shuffled it between his hands. "I've been meaning to reach out to you."

"You have?"

"When I took that photograph, I didn't know . . ."

"You didn't know what?"

"What would happen. I shouldn't have asked you for your permission then. I should've waited."

A blast of cold air struck us. Sara twirled through the revolving door, the ends of her scarf flying.

"I had to park six blocks away," she said, panting.

"Why are you out of breath?"

"I ran from the car."

I felt Teo shift away, but I concentrated on Sara. "Why did you do that, silly?"

"I didn't want to leave you alone for too long."

"That's sweet, but I was okay."

And as I said it, I knew it was true. I'd felt okay talking to Teo, once that flash of murderous rage passed. Even at that very moment, something was tugging me toward him, some thread of connection that had been forged a few blocks away.

I just wasn't ready to have it pulled on yet.

After coffee with Franny, I go back to the Initiative to find Teo. He's in his boardroom down the hall from where our compensation meeting was, working on his wall of plot. Maggie's taking notes. She's sitting on the edge of the table, her short skirt riding up her toned thighs. Part of me wants to warn her—this is not the way to start out your life. The other part of me wants her to leave so I can have Teo to myself.

Which is interesting right there, to say the least.

"Cecily," he says, his face breaking into a grin when he sees me.

"Hey, Teo. Maggie."

Maggie hops down off the table. "Coffee, Teo?"

"I'm good. You, Cecily?"

"If I have any more coffee, I might levitate off the floor."

Maggie rolls her eyes in a way she means for me to see, then leaves.

"Alone at last," Teo says.

"Um, what?"

"Sorry . . . I didn't mean . . ." He shuffles some of the cue cards on the table, a kaleidoscope that flashes pink, blue, green, yellow. "How did the vote go?"

"All in favor."

"That's good, isn't it?"

"Off the record?"

"Anything you say to me when the camera isn't rolling is off the record."

I walk to the wall of plot. The *Poster Child* card is still front and center. I want to believe him when he says this, but I can't.

"I'm super-happy for the Rings."

The Rings are on here, too. Joshua, forty-five, Emily, six, and Julia, four. There are fewer cards below them, as if Teo hasn't quite figured out what their story is yet. Today's decision will help up the drama quotient in his film, though. *Family denied compensation gets it in stunning reversal,* if I were writing the headline. He'd asked to film our meeting, but they're closed-door, confidential sessions. No exceptions. Perhaps he'll reenact it. I wonder who will play me?

"And Franny?" he asks.

I search the board for Franny's card. There it is in pink, off to the left. Beneath it are more cards with the words: *Adopted, Outsider, Motivation?*

"Of course," I say.

"I never asked—how did you two become friends?"

"Maybe I'm standing in for her mother."

"Perhaps."

"You think I feel sorry for her?"

"Do you?"

I turn around. Teo's only inches away. I can smell his soap and the mint of his toothpaste.

"Are you one of those people who brushes his teeth after every meal?"

"Busted."

"Ha. See. You're not the only one who can figure things out."

"Your kids are good at that, too."

"They are."

"That was fun the other night."

"It was?"

"Why are you surprised?"

"Bachelor like yourself, dinner with two teenagers . . . Doesn't sound like the kind of thing you'd be into."

"I like kids in general, and your kids especially."

"That's sweet."

"It's true."

"How come you don't have kids? You don't have them, do you? I never asked. And that question was kind of aggressive. I don't usually ask things like that. Sorry."

Teo takes a step back, as if my stream of words pushed him. "It's fine. And no. I was married once, in my twenties—I guess you'd call it a starter marriage now—but no kids."

"That's too bad."

"It's fine. Besides, I still have time."

Teo's forty-two. "Men have all the time in the world, it seems."

I slap my hand across my mouth, the way I often did in the first days after October tenth when it seemed as if I'd lost control over the link between my brain and my mouth, like I was a kid again who didn't understand social cues. What a terrible thing to say. No one has all the time in the world. Tom certainly didn't, but I don't need to be saying that out loud. What's wrong with me today? Is it the vote? The lingering aftereffects of the memorial? I thought I was past all this.

Teo pulls my hand away, his fingers warm on my cold skin. "It's fine. Don't be embarrassed."

"I hate when that happens. I used to have better control of myself. I thought I did again."

"That's life. And you're right. Barring unforeseen events, I still have time to have kids, if I want. Which is good. Life is good."

Teo turns and splays the cue cards out over the table, like he's dealing a hand. We both look at them, seeing different things, I'm sure.

"So, what happens now?" Teo asks. "With the compensation?"

"It has to get approved by the Supra Board, but I'm sure it will go through."

"Supra Board?"

"That's what I call the muckety-mucks who administer the fund. We're only the recommending body. They make the final decision."

"Seems complicated."

"You ever watch that film about the guy who was in charge of the 9/11 compensation?"

"I have, in fact."

"Of course you have. Stupid question. Oh wait—you didn't make that film, did you?"

"Don't worry. Wish I had."

I watch him continue to move the cards around. I can't figure out what the colors mean. Where the peaks and valleys in the action are. Whether there will be surprise twists and turns.

"How's this all shaping up?" I ask.

"Too soon to tell, I think."

My phone beeps. It's a text from Cassie. She's having dinner at a friend's and will be home by curfew. Henry texted me something similar earlier. After all the togetherness of the memorial, we're now scattering to the four winds—or three. Ugh. Is this the beginning of a pattern? As our grief shifts, will we find there isn't anything holding us together anymore? Was Tom, despite everything, our glue?

"I should go."

Teo looks up. He has an expression on his face I haven't seen before. Shyness, maybe. Uncertainty. "What about you get dinner with me instead? Or do you have to get home to the kids?"

"I . . . No, Cassie and Henry are both out tonight."

"Then you're free."

"I am, in fact."

"And you'll come?"

"Off the record?" I ask.

"Off the record," he says.

12

A STRANGER IN A STRANGE PLACE

KATE

As Kate walked the twins home from the park, she was struck, as she often was, by the contrast between the environment in which she'd spent her first week in Montreal and where she was living now. Westmount was full of large brick homes built in the early 1900s sheltered by mature trees. Some of them on the flat that lay at the base of the mountain. The rest, climbing in neat rows until the overlook that gave a perfect view of the city and the sparkling Saint Lawrence River. That fall, Kate had watched the colors march down the hill in brilliant reds and golds. In the spring, she'd watched the green creep up, knowing that when it reached the top, she'd feel better. Sherbrooke Street, a few blocks away, was full of expensive shops where you could buy imported artisanal cheeses. Coffee shops and places that sold expensive yoga clothes. Aspirational furniture stores and a large wine store. Enough restaurants to eat a different expensive meal in each night of the week.

In contrast, the Montreal bus terminal was more depressing than the one she'd left in Chicago. Sad-looking people. Decor from the seventies. When she'd gotten off the bus, the first thing she'd seen was a group of drunks sitting in the corner passing a large can of something in a brown paper bag.

This wasn't the Montreal Kate had dreamed about visiting. The cobblestone streets and old stone buildings that featured in the on-line postcards. Had she picked wrong? If the rest of the city was like this, how could she survive? But no, it couldn't be. No city should be judged by the state of its bus station. Kate was panicking because it was actually beginning now. Her new life. Whatever that meant.

She'd arrived in the midafternoon. She made sure to gather everything she had with her on the bus and thanked the driver as she left, then kicked herself for doing so. It wasn't natural to her to be anonymous, though she'd felt invisible for years.

Kate had gone into the bathroom and counted up her money in a stall that smelled of sharp detergent and urinal cakes. Of the original $1,200 she'd started with, she was down to $960. That was probably worth more in Canadian dollars. She might as well find out. There was a money exchange window in the station. She was pleasantly surprised to learn that she had more than $1,600. That should be enough for the next couple of weeks. Put a roof over her head. Buy a few more things to wear, purchase food. Get herself squared away until she could find a job.

She had asked a few people to direct her to the nearest Internet café, praying such things still existed. She missed her iPhone. She knew this was ridiculous, the least of her worries. But its easy access to everything she needed—everyone—had become so woven into the fabric of her life that its absence felt like a phantom limb.

The third person she'd approached told her where she could find one. It was located on a seedy street a few blocks away. Ten dollars got her an hour online. She didn't check her e-mail or search for news of her family. Instead, she set up a new Gmail account and spent the rest of her time looking for a place to stay and at job postings. She answered a few "looking for a sublet" ads and applied for the only positions she seemed qualified for. With her hour dwindling down, she found the cheapest hotel she could, a single room within walking distance.

She passed a corner store on the way, one that sold cigarettes and burner phones. She purchased a cheap prepaid phone that would allow her to check her e-mail. She bought enough food for dinner and breakfast. Crackers and cheese. A waxy apple. Some cereal and milk. Then she shoved her items into her backpack and went to the hotel.

The old man behind the counter wrote her passport number down with a blunt pencil in the large ledger that rested on the counter. He never fully took his eyes off the television that was still showing the Chicago coverage. He handed her an old-fashioned key to room number seven. As she held it, her thumb rubbed at the worn-down grooves. Would it bring her luck?

It was hard to think so when she got to her room. A dirt-caked window. A bed whose lumps were visible from the doorway. A listing dresser made of plywood. A desk fit for a school-age child. The predominant color was brown. Kate thought immediately of bedbugs, then reasoned that if she ended up infested, she had almost nothing to throw away.

Exhaustion took hold. She put her meager possessions away. And though she desperately wanted a shower, she couldn't muster the energy to take one. Instead, she lay down on the bed, pulled the covers up over her head, and slept.

A year later, on the other side of Montreal, that was what Kate wished she could do. She was tired, so tired. Both alert with adrenaline and weakened by the less and less sleep she'd had leading up to this day. But she got the boys home without another incident, fed them, and tucked them in for their afternoon naps. Autopilot. It had its uses.

She circled back to the kitchen, enjoying the silence. Andrea was out at one of her lady lunches from which she'd come home two-glass tipsy and wanting to talk to Kate about why Rick was working so much and did she think it meant anything.

Hell yes, Kate wanted to say. Maybe not cheating. But, at the very least, that he didn't want to come home. Instead, she always reassured Andrea. Told her she was imagining things, because what else could she do? But she couldn't stand another conversation about Andrea's insecurities. She had to be the least intuitive person on the planet.

Kate knew she hid things well. Her own husband had never asked her how she spent her time. Never voiced any suspicion. She knew better than to give him any reason to. But still, even if she was a rank sociopath, she put out enough odd vibes that Andrea should be asking questions. She should be suspicious. Not of her husband, who maybe was banging some pliant girl in his office but was probably simply trying to make enough money to keep paying for this lifestyle. But of the woman to whom she'd entrusted her children without so much as a background check.

Kate paced through the first floor, fear like she hadn't known in a year catapulting through her body. She wasn't sure what the trigger was, other than the obvious. And maybe that was the answer? Her stupid plan hadn't worked. The idea that she could forget what the day was by avoiding screens?

She didn't need a screen to remember.

INTERVIEW TRANSCRIPT

TJ: How are you doing today, Franny?

FM: I'm good.

TJ: Was that Mr. Ring who dropped you off?

FM: Yes, why?

TJ: I've been trying to schedule my next interview with him. If you have any influence there, I'd appreciate it if he'd get in touch.

FM: This is hard for Josh . . . Mr. Ring.

TJ: I get that.

FM: Is it a problem? If he drops out of the documentary?

TJ: Did he say he was going to?

FM: I'm just wondering.

TJ: Ask him to call me, all right?

FM: Sure, I can do that.

TJ: Thank you. So, I'd like to fill in a few holes from the other day.

FM: No problem.

TJ: Why don't we start with you telling me more about meeting your mother for the first time? What was that like?

FM: It was awkward at first, but we connected quickly. It kind of felt like . . . You know that feeling you get when you come back to your apartment after traveling? How it smells familiar? It felt like that. Like a place I couldn't believe I'd been away from for so long.

TJ: That's an interesting way of describing it.

FM: Thank you. I've been thinking about that poem, you know.

TJ: Which poem?

FM: That one by Tennyson you were quoting the other day. I looked it up.

TJ: Did you?

FM: *I envy not in any moods / The captive void of noble rage, / The linnet born within the cage, / That never knew the summer woods* . . . I love that.

TJ: It is lovely.

FM: And I get it, you know? That's what I was . . . A linnet born within the cage. A linnet is a kind of bird, right? Did you know that? Anyway, I was living in a prison, but finding my mother and all this happening . . .

TJ: It set you free?

FM: That sounds bad. I didn't mean that. Of course I'm not happy my mother's dead.

TJ: Of course not. I didn't mean to imply—

FM: Can you please cut that part out? I wouldn't want anyone to think that. Because it's not true. It's not.

TJ: It's all right, Franny. I won't use it if you don't want me to.

FM: I know you're going to, okay? Don't lie to me.

TJ: Whoa, hold up. I've never lied to you.

FM: Sure. Right. Do you think I was born yesterday?

TJ: Of course not. Look, here . . . *[Shuffling]* I'm erasing the last few
      minutes, all right?

FM: It's really erased?

TJ: Yes, I promise.

FM: *[Muttering]* Pull it together.

TJ: What's that?

FM: It's nothing. Are we back on?

TJ: Hold on. Now we are.

FM: So we're starting again?

TJ: When you're ready.

FM: Does my makeup look okay?

TJ: You look great, Franny. Ready?

FM: Yes.

TJ: I'll ask the same question again, okay?

FM: Okay.

TJ: Can you tell us more about meeting your mother for the first
      time?

FM: It was . . . It was perfect. Like the mother-daughter relationship I
      always wished I'd had.

13

HAPPY ANNIVERSARY

CECILY

We went to New York.

After I received Tom's texts with my hands stuffed into a display case full of sexy underwear, I still went with him to New York for our twentieth wedding anniversary.

When I got control of myself again, I bought whatever I was holding in Victoria's Secret, went home, and finished packing. I packed Tom's bag, too, because he'd texted me an hour later asking me if I could. I was fairly sure that text was a ploy, a tactic to make sure I hadn't seen the others, that somehow his phone was lying to him and he hadn't been discovered. Or maybe he was trying to push those texts into the background, hide them from view, which is why he sent a long, rambling one followed by several short ones. Perhaps he was hoping I thought it was some silly joke, something that would be revealed to me on our romantic weekend, and I was waiting for him to enlighten me. Have a *ha-ha* moment.

I've often wondered since then whether Tom thought I was stupid. I never would've believed that before, but after a lot of thought, it's the only explanation I can come up with. That he must've assumed I wouldn't know what the texts meant. That I was so in love with him I'd trust whatever lie he was preparing to spin. That because he'd behaved uncharacteristically—or so I thought, but what the fuck did I know?—he could convince me I was the one causing the problem by misinterpreting his obvious joke. That the problem wasn't the fact that he'd let some other woman suck his dick, but with me.

Stupid, stupid. I felt so stupid. How could I have let this happen? How could I not know? I needed something, more information, better information, something to keep me occupied. So, before I did the packing, I checked his personal e-mail to see if I could find any further evidence, but there was nothing there. He'd texted me from his work phone—the only phone he had, that I knew of, anyway—and he mostly used his work e-mail even for communicating with me. He was the president of the company, after all. He could do what he wanted, apparently. And I didn't know how to log on to his work e-mail—password protected, he always told me, for security reasons.

Who could it be? Who, who? I sat down on the edge of our bed, surrounded by the clothes I was supposed to be packing, and thought and thought, cycling through the women we knew like a child reciting the alphabet. Allison from down the street? No. I'd actually seen him wrinkle his nose at her once when she wore an unflattering dress to a party. Bea from the office? He didn't think she was very intelligent, and maybe that wasn't insulation against her prettiness, but it felt like it was. Carol from the kids' school? He might be interested in her, but I'd overheard her saying she found him annoying, and she hadn't even blushed when she realized I heard her, just gave me a challenging look like she knew I agreed with her, deep down.

And so on. I never had any instinct. No name stood out as likely. It was all unbelievable.

I know some people in my situation would've felt as if they were to blame, that it was some kind of reflection on them, but I didn't. I felt like an idiot for not knowing it was going on, but not that it was my fault. I was surprised, though. Not because of the act itself; I always knew cheating was a possibility. I'd had my own opportunities I'd turned away from, and so I knew, I *knew*, it was something that could happen to me.

No, it was the carelessness. Tom, who was always so, so meticulous, who never made mistakes, not ever, had made a major one. And because of this, I couldn't help but feel like he wanted me to know. That he wanted me to find out but couldn't find the words, couldn't bring himself to make a decision, and so let a thoughtless moment do it for him. I'd always made it clear to Tom that if I found out something like that, it was the end. There'd be no forgiveness, no going back. If you want to end things irrevocably, I'd said more than once—in a mocking tone, in a joking way, the way couples do sometimes, but he knew I was serious—then cheat on me. Cheat on me and tell me. Now he had, and there I was in the place in which I always said I'd know exactly what to do. And you know what took me by surprise?

My lack of certainty.

"These are pretty," Cassie had said, startling me.

She was holding the camisole and underwear I'd bought. She had a shy look on her face, as if she was thinking about the nice things she might wear for a man one day, someday soon.

"They are." I rubbed my hands across the silky fabric, then swept everything on the bed into my suitcase without taking the time to fold anything.

"Mom!"

"What?"

"It'll get all wrinkled like that."

"Probably."

"Are you okay?"

"Sure I am, honey."

I tugged on one of her braids, holding myself in check. I felt the first prick of hate for Tom, then, for making me lie to our daughter.

"I hope you have a stupendous time," she said.

"Word of the day? I like it."

Cassie smiled and gave me a quick hug, then darted out of the room, embarrassed.

I sat back on the edge of the bed and stared at the wall until Tom came home.

Before our date, I told Teo I needed to go home and change, but I also wanted time to do something I haven't been doing enough of in the last couple months—visit the Rings.

We've spent a lot of time together in the last year, our two broken families blending into something resembling one. Being together was simple because there didn't need to be any explanation.

If someone cried, they were comforted. If someone needed to be distracted, there were enough petty squabbles and video games and chores to accomplish the task. If Josh didn't feel like cooking or facing the freezer full of prepared guilt dinners the neighbors left, he knew they could always find a meal with us and vice versa. There were others who joined us, other families we knew from before who were also affected, but we were the core. For months and months and months.

Something shifted a while ago, slowly at first, then more rapidly. There were fewer dinners, fewer game nights or spontaneous drop-bys. Maybe it was a sign of healing, an inevitable change that meant things were improving. I'm not sure what started it, though things felt noticeably different during our last two evenings together, with Franny there. But that wasn't Franny's fault; it was us, our chemistry that wasn't working as well when we didn't need it so much. But when I saw their names hanging on the wall this afternoon, I realized I hadn't seen them in weeks.

They live a few blocks from us, their brick colonial built on a similar plan to ours, so there's always this moment of disorientation when I enter it. The colors are slightly off, the furniture not quite where I would've put it. But I don't end up inside the house today. Instead, as I park my car, I see Franny leaving the house, one of the girls' hands firmly in each of hers, like they belong there.

I reach for my seat belt to unclip it, but something stops me. Maybe it's the normalness of it all, but why should that bother me? Where else should Franny be right now? This is her family, and a woman should be with her family in times like these. Maybe it's as simple as the fact that, on some level, I blame her for being here instead of her mother, and thinking this makes me ashamed. It's not

Franny's fault her mother's gone, and, if anything, Franny's loss is greater than mine. I lost a friend—she lost a parent. A future.

So I don't get out of the car. Instead, I watch as the girls climb into the back seat of the minivan. Franny checks the girls' seat belts, doing all the things a mother should. Doing all the things their mother should be doing.

When it hurts too much to watch anymore, I drive away.

Teo takes me to The Angry Crab on North Lincoln, a deliciously messy eating experience I've always loved. I don't tell him it was one of the places Tom and I went with the kids. As the familiar bouquet of steamed shellfish and garlic fills my senses, I push those thoughts down, the memories that feel fresher than they have in a while, and decide to order something different from what I'd usually have, hoping the unfamiliar will make this evening less weird.

If this is a date, and I suppose it can't be anything other than that, it's the first I've been on in more than twenty years. Tom and I met in college, and I'm not sure we ever had a real first date. Does inviting me to his dorm room to watch a movie count? The last time I felt this awkward was a few months before that, when my roommate set me up with her boyfriend's roommate and we all went for beers at a pub. I'd been worried that night, too, about what I should wear, and how my body fit into my clothes, and whether I'd be able to keep up my end of the conversation. Only this was Teo. He'd already seen me at my worst. Shaken, terrified, covered in dust and God knows what else.

We find a table and each order Dungeness crab in "grumpy" garlic butter sauce, making sure to pile up on napkins. It's a BYOB restaurant, and Teo had the foresight to bring a six-pack of a great IPA I haven't tasted before.

"I'm glad I didn't get too dressed up," I say as we dig into our bags of crab. A trail of spicy steam rises from the food and tickles my nose. The acoustics are terrible, so I have to lean toward Teo to catch much of what he says.

"I should've brought you somewhere nicer."

"What? No. I love this place."

He grabs a cracker from the table. "Tell the truth, now, or I'll use this on you."

"You going to keep that for our next interview?"

"Now there's a thought. You are a tough nut to . . . crack. Ugh, that's terrible."

"It is."

He opens up the body of his crab and takes a pull from his beer. He's dressed in a slightly nicer version of his usual uniform—the blue-gray shirt is a button-down, and the jeans have a darker wash to them. The forest-green sweater he's wearing over his shirt complements the rest of it, which I almost tell him, then don't, because I have no idea how to do this, be casual with a man. Flirt with him.

"But seriously," Teo says. "Is this place okay? We can go somewhere else next time, if you want."

"Next time, huh?"

"I think you made me blush."

"I do love this place; I don't need anything fancier. And as to whether there'll be a 'next time,' why don't we see how this evening goes and then decide?"

"That sounds like a good plan."

"I am curious, though." I bite into my own crab claw and nearly moan in pleasure. It's been too long since I ate something this good, despite the best intentions of my neighbors. "What makes you think I like fancy restaurants?"

"Didn't you used to run a fancy restaurant?"

"I did."

I look down at the label on my beer. Brewed right here in Chicago, it says.

"Sorry. It was in your background info . . . I guess it's weird that I know all these things about you without even having to ask."

"No, it's fine. The restaurant's not a secret." I look up and smile. "I managed Knife & Fork for fifteen years, and I loved every minute of it."

"I ate there a couple times."

"You did?"

"Yup. Great food."

"Funny to think of us being there at the same time and not even knowing it."

"Life's often like that. It's closed now, isn't it? What happened?"

"We were shaky after the last recession and never quite recovered. The owners were getting close to retirement and had the opportunity to sell for a lot of money. For the location. The buyers didn't want the restaurant. There's some Italian franchise there now."

"You didn't want to stay on?"

"No. I . . . We'd actually tried to buy it ourselves, but it didn't work out."

We'd scraped together everything we had to put up the earnest money. And then I'd stupidly assumed that fifteen years of loyalty would win me the space, the chance to make it my own. I'd gotten way ahead of myself, commissioning architectural plans that cost the earth and signing a contract with an up-and-coming chef. When the owners "went another way," I was left holding the bag. Jobless, in debt, heartbroken.

I sincerely hope this information isn't in his file, or anyone else's, either.

"That must've been tough," Teo says.

"It was. But life moves on."

"When did all this happen?"

"A few years ago. I was sad for a while, but I'm over it."

Tom had never gotten over it. Not the betrayal by the Urbans, who we'd always thought of as family. Not the bad judgment he thought I'd shown in putting all that money down before things were a certainty, even though we'd decided to do it together. When I'd run into Seth Urban a couple weeks before Tom died and made the mistake of telling Tom about it, he flew into a rage, just as angry, angrier, even, as he'd been when it had all fallen apart.

"I like that about you," Teo says.

"What's that?"

"Your forgiving nature."

"Does it say that in your background info? Because that would be wrong."

"You sure? I'm usually a good judge of character."

I stuff some seafood in my mouth, then chase it down with beer. "So what do you think of Franny, then? You keep asking me about her, but you never say what you think."

"I think she's interesting."

"She talks about you a lot. I think she might have a crush."

"Oh?"

"'When I was speaking with Teo the other day,' or 'Teo was

asking me in our last interview.' Things like that. I shouldn't have said that."

"It's fine."

"No, I hate when I do that."

"What?"

"Rat other people out. Not that she's said anything, I wouldn't betray a confidence, but . . . God, I can't believe I'm telling you this."

"You don't have to."

"No, I do. I just . . . When I've figured something out about someone, I usually end up telling other people. It's this weird form of showing off. I hate it. But I can't seem to stop myself from doing it."

"I think you're making a bigger deal of it than it is."

"If you say so."

I watch him for a moment across the table. He's a careful eater, even with this messy food. Sometimes Tom would eat so quickly, his face would get covered with sauce like when the kids were little. But I should stop this, comparing these two. They have nothing in common but me, and maybe not even that.

"I am curious, though," I say. "What do you think of Franny?"

He winks at me. "I guess you'll have to watch the film to find out."

"Well, that's completely unfair."

"It is rather, isn't it?"

"So forget Franny, then; what's *your* story?"

"My story?"

"Yeah, the story of Teo Jackson. Illegitimate love child of Michael?"

He nearly spits out his beer. "What? The singer?"

"Sure."

"Um, no."

"Not a fan?"

"Elvis Costello's more my style."

"I never got him. But I do love his wife's stuff. Diana Krall."

Teo thinks about it for a moment. "The jazz singer?"

"Yep, she's great. My friend Kaitlyn met her once."

"When?"

"She used to go to Vancouver a lot for business. Anyway, she was in some store, not Target but something like it, and there was Diana Krall with her twins at the cash register. And Kaitlyn was this huge fan. She's the one who introduced me to her music."

"What did she do?"

"Stood there like an idiot until Diana came up and asked her if there was something wrong. She actually thought Kaitlyn was having a stroke or something because she was standing there with her mouth hanging open and she couldn't talk. I guess she's not used to having people react to her that way."

"That's refreshing."

"Right? Kaitlyn said she was super-nice and normal. They talked for a bit in the store and then Kaitlyn embarrassed herself by asking Diana Krall to go for coffee and . . ."

Teo has an odd look on his face.

"Have I been speaking very fast?" I ask.

"Kind of."

"I do that sometimes, get kind of manic in my speech. But I'm not actually manic—I just sound that way occasionally."

"When you're upset?"

"I guess that's why. I miss Kaitlyn." I push my plastic bag of food away.

"Tell me about her," Teo says.

"Just for us, right?"

"I'm not taking notes here."

"She's . . . Oh, I don't know. I could tell you all these things about her, what she looks like, or how she throws her head back when she laughs, or her weakness for cheese Pringles, or a million things, but that wouldn't explain her. You wouldn't know her. She's someone who got a famous person to talk to her because she was in awe."

"She sounds great."

"Yeah," I say. "But don't think I haven't noticed."

"What?"

"That you still haven't told me anything about you. I've got your number, buddy."

"I guess there'll have to be a next time, then. If you want to learn more about me."

I don't say anything, just finish my beer and wait for him to finish his. There's a line of people waiting for tables like there often is, so we don't linger. We clean ourselves up as best we can with wet wipes and get ready to go. I know from experience that my hands will still smell like seafood in the morning, no matter how thoroughly I wash them.

Teo helps me with my coat, and I catch a look from a couple in line. They're watching us. I hear one of them say distinctly, "It's her."

I duck my head. "Can we get out of here?"

"You bet," Teo says, taking me by the elbow and pulling me through the line and out into the frosty night. We stop half a block away on North Lincoln. The traffic's light, the sky a cloudy black. I can feel the cool breeze coming off the lake and taste a tang of it in the air.

"Sorry about that," Teo says.

"For what?"

"Those people in the restaurant. That's my fault. Because of the picture."

"You didn't know it would be like that. Everywhere."

"But I kind of did. You know that feeling you get when you're doing something and it's turning out great . . . I had it that entire day. I'd taken these amazing shots of the building before, and during, and when I saw you standing there, I could see right away what an incredible photograph it would be. And I stopped and I took it. I took it, and I sold it, and even though you agreed, I stole something from you. So I'm sorry. I've been wanting to say that for a while."

I reach a cold hand up and stroke his soft beard. "I forgive you."

He looks pleased. "You do?"

"You said I was a forgiving person. Maybe you were right. Maybe I am."

"See, I told you I was a good judge of character."

And maybe he is, but his timing and mine, it's always been skewed. Because he leans down to kiss me, and as his lips meet mine, I hear the *click* of a mechanical shutter.

I've been caught on film.

Again.

14

HOW A PERSON RUNS AWAY

KATE

Once she turned off the TV, Kate got through the rest of the day
without incident. After the twins' nap, she spent the requisite hour
teaching them the alphabet and working through their flip-book so
they'd be on track for the preschool they were already enrolled in
for January. Then they played with their LEGOs scattered on the
kitchen floor while Kate cooked. She ate dinner with the family—
Andrea and, surprisingly, Rick, who looked tired and distracted,
dark smudges emphasizing his light-blue eyes. She watched him
as Andrea talked brightly about what she'd been up to that day.
How the twins were progressing and, of course, Chicago. How sad
it all was, and what it must be like for the families who still didn't

know for sure if they'd lost someone because they hadn't found their r-e-m-a-i-n-s.

Rick nodded occasionally, not even always in the right places. He shoved the roasted chicken Kate had made into his mouth like he was starving. Maybe Andrea was right to worry. Rick had a look about him that Kate recognized. As if he was calculating the distance to the door. Whether he could simply get in his car and drive away.

Kate knew that look. She'd seen it on her own face more than once. Caught in the bathroom mirror in the morning or in her reflection in the glass behind the barista counter.

Could she escape? Was such a thing possible?

"And there was such a touching story about the people from that company," Andrea said. "Oh, you know, the one that lost so many employees. Anyway, what an amazing group of people they were . . ."

As Andrea droned on about the virtues of the dead, Kate couldn't help thinking that whenever more than five hundred people die together, odds are that at least some of them were assholes. It was the law of averages. And also: deep down, at least one person was probably glad when their wife, husband, lover, friend didn't come home that day.

That was the law of averages, too.

Kate thought she was that person for a long time. The person no one would mind was gone. The one whose kids would be happier without her. The one whose hassled husband would sigh in relief when he was alone. It wasn't that she blamed them. She'd done a lot of things she regretted over the course of her life, not the least of which was how she'd handled motherhood, her marriage—all the things that shouldn't have been so challenging but somehow were. They'd be better off if she disappeared. Wouldn't they?

Kate had fantasized about leaving off and on throughout her life. Whenever a tragedy occurred, she couldn't help but wonder if someone had used the event as cover to escape, to start over. She thought about how she'd do it. Where she'd go. What she'd call herself. What would her new life look like? Racked with guilt or set free?

There were so many endless possibilities. So many new beginnings to contemplate. It became a constant she returned to. When things were bleak, mostly during those black autumns, she'd pick it up again. Modifying her plan, updating the technology involved, working through the details until she felt calm again.

She had it all planned out. If an opportunity arose, she was ready. And yet, she still couldn't fully explain the way she'd acted on October tenth. How panicked she'd been feeling all morning. How she'd felt in the elevator as it raced toward the ground. The screech of the explosion, the sense of flying, then nothing. She'd woken moments later, thrown from the building as if it were as disgusted with her as her life. She'd stood on the shaking ground and then started jogging as fast as she could in her heels, joining the terrified crowd.

Two blocks later, she'd turned around and looked at the burning building. In an instant, she acknowledged the certain death of most of those within, though she was, somehow, alive. She loved some of those people; others she wished she'd never met. Some kind of miracle was at work here. Something that had let her walk away unscathed.

Because that's what she'd done. Walked away.

No, that wasn't quite right.

What she'd done was *run*.

INTERVIEW TRANSCRIPT

TJ: I'd like to discuss the Compensation Initiative. What made you get involved?

FM: It came up at one of the support groups I was attending. They were asking for volunteers.

TJ: But you do more than volunteer. You're the cochair.

FM: That's right.

TJ: You actually ran for the position.

FM: What are you getting at?

TJ: Nothing, Franny, I'm just asking questions.

FM: They feel a bit funny.

TJ: I'm sorry about that. Do you want to stop for today? I know talking about all this can be difficult.

FM: No, that's fine. Why did Cecily say she joined?

TJ: Why do you ask?

FM: Just curious.

TJ: Did something happen between you and Cecily?

FM: What makes you think that?

TJ: Your tone just now when you mentioned her.

FM: What about my tone?

TJ: I thought you were friends.

FM: We are, but sometimes I think . . . Well, I feel like she blames me.

TJ: Blames you for what?

FM: For my mother. And it's not my fault, you know.

TJ: What's not your fault?

FM: That my mother . . . that Kaitlyn never told her about me. That's not my fault at all.

PART

CECILY

One of the things I thought about on October tenth as paper and plastic and a wet, tacky substance I couldn't think about the origins of rained down around me like confetti was that I didn't know how to react.

Maybe that seems obvious. Who knows how to react to watching life evaporate before your eyes, particularly when you've loved that life? And yet, all around me, people were reacting. Running, crying, screaming. I did none of those things. It wasn't until Teo grabbed my hand and made me move that I did anything at all.

Then, hand in hand, we ran several blocks—from the "L" station I'd come out of to the stop before. There, a police officer held us up, directed us to the platform, and told us we'd be safer under-ground. It was chaos down there, medieval, but I wasn't making the decisions; Teo was making them for me, and he obeyed, pulling me this way and that but never letting me go. We walked through a sea of bodies, their legs pulled up to their chins, hugging, tearful, shaking, until he found us a patch of concrete that was big enough for me and him and the camera slung around his back.

Teo pulled me down to the ground. It was cold, that concrete. Colder still because the cuts in my coat and the dress underneath meant my skin was in direct contact with it. In any other circum-stance, I would've been horrified at the potential for a staph infec-tion, but that never crossed my mind. The floor was dirty. I was sitting on a dirty, cold floor surrounded by people I didn't know, still holding the hand of a strange man who hadn't said a word to me in the hour we'd been together.

And then he did.

"What's your name?"

I tried to speak, but my throat was full of dust.

"What's your name?" he asked again.

I pointed to my neck and made a slashing motion. He reached into his pocket and pulled out a pad and pen. I took them, finally breaking contact to hold the pad steady against my bloody knee. My left hand had a gash on it that was scabbed over with pebbles and grime. I wrote my name in block letters and handed the pad back to him.

"Cecily?"

I nodded.

"I'm Teo."

I reached for the hand he held out to me. It was the only warm thing in the cold, cold world.

"Do you want me to call anyone?"

I shook my head and put my free hand in my coat pocket. My phone was still there, and when I pulled it out, it had service. This surprised me, something normal in a world askew. How had it never occurred to me until then to reach out to my children? How long had it been since I stepped into the street? Where were they? Did they even know anything had happened? What—oh my God, what if this was happening everywhere?

I used my rattling thumb to text Cassie and Henry.

I'm okay! Go to Grandma's. I'll be there as soon as I can.

I listened to the text whoosh away from me. "Received" it said under it, and then, seconds later, "Read" by Cassie. "Read" by Henry. *Okay*, they wrote back almost simultaneously. *We R okay!*

I started to shake. They were safe. Whatever was happening, whatever this was, they were where I'd left them, at school, surrounded by responsible adults and counselors and—

My phone quivered with another text.

It was Cassie, who'd written, *Are you with Dad?*

15

MEMORIES

CECILY

"Why, Cecily," my mother says, opening the door in a dark-blue robe cinched tightly over her pajamas, "you're here late."

"I'm sorry. I can come back tomorrow."

"Nonsense. Come in. I was watching the Netflix."

"Anything in particular?"

"Oh, this and that. I'm not sure it's working properly. It keeps asking me if I'm still watching. Do you think it's judging me?"

I take my coat off, hanging it on the hook that's always waiting for me here. We go into the living room, where the television screen is frozen on an episode of season four of *Orange Is the New Black*. The room is actually overwhelmed by orange—my mother's

Halloween decoration box is open, much of its contents organized into piles on the thick beige carpet.

"What's all this?"

"I'm trying to cull." She looks down at the stuff on the floor. She's taller than me, five ten when she was at her tallest. It felt like I was looking up to her my whole life. "With the kids getting older, seems like I could get rid of some of this."

"You'll still give out candy, though?"

I feel uncharacteristically sad. My father always took Halloween so seriously, keeping statistics of how many kids came to the door each year and how much candy had been given out. Since he died, my mother's kept dutifully on, her messier handwriting following his in the log. The thought of no one writing in that book seems like the end of something I'm not ready to accept.

"Yes, dear, don't worry. Harry would never forgive me if I didn't give out the candy."

She looks up at the ceiling, as if that's where my dad's been hiding all this time. We named Henry after him but kept the more formal version of his name.

"Henry, either, I don't think."

"Probably not. It's a real pain in the ass, though."

My mother never said one bad word in my presence the entire time my father was alive. He wasn't in the ground twelve hours before I heard her use the word "asshole." That was because of the broken garbage disposal. Now that term often refers to anything she doesn't like, like she's a child who doesn't know how the word works or what it's meant for.

"We could take over," I say.

"It's all right. But you could take some of this off my hands."

I sit down on the floor. The gas fireplace is on, throwing off a nice flickering light and a good blast of heat. I pick up a paper skeleton, one that used to glow in the dark.

"Tom never liked decorating the house."

"I didn't know that."

My mother sits in a lotus position near another pile of Halloween debris. She's seventy-five but does yoga every day and has better knees than I do. She'll probably be the one who helps me up when we're done.

"So, what brings you by?"

"I went on a date tonight."

Her face lights up. She let her hair go its natural gray five years ago, and it suits her. "Oh, that's good! Do I know him?"

I untangle the skeleton's strings. One of its feet is missing. "Nope."

"Mmm. That means I do, and you don't want to tell me who it is."

"I don't want to tell anyone, Mom."

"And yet you're here at bedtime."

She looks at me, squinting. She always could see through me, even without her glasses.

"You're right. I guess I did want a buffer."

"From what?"

"From him to home."

My mother pops the lid on another plastic container. "Damn, Christmas ornaments."

"You know, I have no idea where Tom put ours. I had to buy new ones last year."

"Are you missing him?"

"Would it be pathetic if I was?"

"It would be normal, I think."

"It's been a year."

"And there were more than twenty behind that."

"Nineteen."

She frowns at my literalness.

"Nineteen years without another woman in the picture," I amend.

"Asshole," my mother says, and for once she's got the word right.

When I arrive home an hour later with two plastic containers full of Halloween decorations, Cassie's made sure Henry went to bed and is reading in her room.

I check the book she's holding. She's rereading one of the Hunger Games books for the umpteenth time. I read them along with her the first time, four years ago. I thought they were wonderful then, particularly the first book. But now that we live in our own dystopian future, I have trouble seeing their continued appeal.

"How's Katniss?"

Cassie doesn't lower her book. She's wearing a Mickey Mouse T-shirt we bought for her when she was ten. It was too big for her at that age. Now it's tight on her arms and doesn't quite cover her stomach.

"Henry's asleep."

"I saw that. Good job."

"Where were you?"

A lump forms in my throat. "I was out to dinner with a friend. Teo, actually."

The book slips from her fingers. "Teo?"

"We went to The Angry Crab. It was fun. We should go back there soon; it's been a while."

She picks up the end of one of her braids and flicks it into her mouth. "I don't know if I could."

"Because of Dad?"

She nods.

"Are you upset I went there?"

"No."

"Are you upset I went there with Teo?"

She starts to shake her head, then stops. I sit on the edge of her bed and remove the braid from her mouth. Her eyes are welling up.

"What is it, sweetheart?"

"I don't want to forget."

"Forget what?"

"Daddy. I don't want us to forget."

"Of course you'll never forget him, honey."

"I don't want you to, either."

I look at the picture of the four of us she has on her night table. The last official studio portrait we did in coordinated outfits. *Coordinated outfits!* My old life was a fantasy. Anyway, we're all laughing because Henry had belched loudly and the photographer looked horrified.

"How could I ever forget him?"

"You could. You could get married again or whatever. Or maybe have another baby, and then . . ."

She bursts into tears. I lie down next to her and hold her close. She's starting to smell different from how she used to—more like a grown-up than my little girl.

"Sweetie, what's going on? Where is this coming from?"

"That's what Kevin was saying at dinner."

"Who's Kevin?"

"He's . . ."

I hold her away from me. Her lip's trembling.

"Is Kevin your boyfriend?"

She shakes her head. When did my daughter become so tongue-tied?

"A friend?"

"Yes."

"Were you out with him tonight?"

"Yes."

I feel queasy. I'm not sure I'm ready for this. "So you weren't at Stacey's?"

"Don't be mad."

"I'm not mad. I want to know what's going on."

She pulls away and wipes at her nose. I have a mother's instinct to grab a Kleenex off her nightstand, hold it to her nose, and tell her to blow.

"I wanted to go to this movie with Kevin. He asked me, and I'm not sure I like him, and I didn't want it to be a big deal."

"I wouldn't have made it a big deal."

"Mom. Come on."

"Okay, so I would've made a big deal about my daughter's first date. Sue me. It is your first date, right? I didn't miss that?"

"It's the first."

"Phew. Your first date! Wow."

"I knew it."

"It's not like I would've insisted on pictures or anything. Well, maybe only a couple."

She starts to cry again.

"Oh, honey, I was kidding."

"It's not that. It's just . . . I miss Dad."

I hug her to me again, the queasiness having turned to sorrow. I thought I was done crying over Tom, but there are still so many firsts he's going to miss.

"He always said he couldn't wait to beat up my first boyfriend."

"He did say that."

"And now he can't."

"It's true. It's not fair. He should be here to beat up that Kevin guy. I can do it if you want."

She tilts her chin. "You're joking again, right?"

"Of course I am. Or not. Your choice."

I stroke the top of her head while she rests against me. Her room is in a transition phase, like her. Posters we put up years ago are half papered over with photos she's printed out on our color printer of her friends. Thick books with black covers are perched on top of a confetti of others about magic and twins in high school. It's like an archeological dig of her childhood.

"So, I get the hiding where you were going from me—not that it's okay—"

"I won't do it again."

"You probably will. I'm not saying it's allowed. I'm just being practical."

"I won't. I promise."

"Good. But what about that led you to think I'd be marrying someone else and—God forbid—having more children?"

"You don't want to have more kids?"

"Sweetheart, you know I love you and your brother to death, but no. I'm forty-three. I'm too old for that."

"Janet Jackson had a baby at fifty."

"Good for her! Come on, where's this coming from?"

Cassie squirms, then settles. "We were just talking . . . I don't know, about stupid stuff. How his brother was still obsessed with Pokémon and stuff like that. Anyway, then he kind of asked me about the memorial, and it felt good to talk about it because none of the kids at school ever ask me anything about Dad, like it's contagious or something and their dad will die if they mention it. So I talked about Dad for a bit and how it's been, and then he told me how he'd read this thing, or heard his dad talking about it, I guess, about how all these babies are being born now, like how there was this baby boom or whatever starting nine months after Triple Ten, and it's still going on, and even some of the survivors' families have new babies and . . ."

She pauses for breath.

"And then what?"

"And then he asked me if you had started dating 'yet.' And I just lost it, Mom. I ran out of the restaurant and all the way home. And now he's never going to talk to me again."

I can feel Cassie's heart thrumming against her ribs. I know that feeling all too well. "I'm sure he will. And if he doesn't, then he wasn't worth it."

"If you say so."

"Trust me."

She's quiet for a moment, and then, "Is that what you were on tonight with Teo? A date?"

"I'm not sure."

She pulls away.

"I know it might be upsetting to you and Henry to see me with another man, but that's not what's happening. Maybe it will someday and maybe it won't, but it was just dinner."

"But he likes you. I can tell."

"And I like him, too. We all do. But I don't know if I'm ready for that again or, even if I was, whether he's the right person. This is complicated. Does that make sense?"

"Yeah," she says, but she's not looking me in the eye.

I turn her head gently to me with my fingertips. "How about this? Why don't we agree that we'll both keep each other up to date on our, for lack of a better word, love lives?"

She wipes her nose again. "Like, in detail?"

"Um . . . no, I don't think that's a good idea. But if I go on a date with him or you with Kevin, we'll tell each other about it. Sound good?"

I smile bravely, because it doesn't sound good to me, and I can't imagine it sounds good to her, either.

None of this is how it should be, but it's all that we've got.

16

DOWNTOWN BY MYSELF

KATE

I have a secret, Kate typed into the dialogue box. *Last year, I ran away from my family.*

She stared at the words on the screen. How had she ended up here? After some nearly sleepless nights, and desperate for an outlet for the thoughts chasing her through her days, Kate had discovered IKnowWhatYouDidLastSummer.com, one of those secret-sharing websites, where users could spill their innermost shame in anonymity. *I cheated on my husband. I regret having children. I hate my best friend and I don't know how to tell her.* These were the easy secrets to absorb. Some were almost laughable, others criminal. Their combined effect was a white noise and a sense of relativity.

What she'd done wasn't so bad. Not truly. Especially not now that she'd written it down and the comments of support had started flowing in.

I've wanted to do that for years!

I think UR brave.

I left my kids when they were babies.

Kate knew she had to add more to the story. That, to actually unburden herself, this was only the beginning. But it had to come out in dribs and drabs. There was no point in setting it all out at once. Let them drag the details out of her, as she'd seen others do. That was part of the experience. The normalization of her immorality.

The wind rattled against the basement window. It was late, almost midnight. Kate should be asleep. Her alarm would sound too soon. But Andrea's house, once so spacious, was starting to feel claustrophobic. Kate was giving serious thought to running again.

It wouldn't be a frantic getaway this time. She could simply hand in her notice and scuttle away into the good night. She had some savings. She could last for a while. But where would she go? When she'd left her old life a year ago, that part of the decision had seemed easy. The location. How to get there. Those first steps.

It was frightening, how automatic it had been. The inventory she did of her situation, skipping past the fact that she was leaving her family behind. It was more like she was going through a checklist she didn't even know she'd been building. All those years of fantasizing, planning, coming to fruition.

First, money. She had $600 in cash in her purse to pay her nanny, the woman who took better care of her children than she did. The same miracle that had thrown her to safety left her cross-body bag in place. After a brief hesitation, she risked pulling another $600 out of their bank account when she passed an ATM twenty blocks past her building. Her husband never checked the bank statements; that was her job. Besides, all the statement would say, if he ever looked at it, was that the money had been taken out that day but not at what time. For that, he'd have to go looking. And why would he do that?

Second, walk away from the crowds that had gathered at a safe distance to watch the fire casually so you don't draw attention to yourself. Pay attention to where the cameras are and try to avoid them. Walk in a crowd with your head down, one of many. Do nothing to stand out.

Third, take the SIM card out of your cell phone and crush it under your shoe in an alley. Leave the phone in a garbage can. Make sure no one sees you do either of these things.

Fourth, get rid of your ID, but not where someone might pick it up and use it, leading to awkward questions. Think about leaving your wedding and engagement rings somewhere, too, but decide instead to keep them to sell later for cash.

When she'd stopped at the ATM, she thought briefly about wrapping her scarf around her head in case the footage was checked. Then realized that might bring more attention to herself. Besides, no one would be looking for her. Certainly not if she didn't do anything stupid. Didn't give anyone reason to believe she was anything other than a victim of the day's events.

Kate's borrowed iPad chimed with another comment.

Why did you leave? asked Anonymous4Life. He was one of the cheaters who seemed to form the majority of the website's users. Kate had the impression that many of them were simply looking for other like-minded people for further adventures. As if the site was a coy Ashley Madison. A4L had cheated on his wife twice with the same woman, three years apart, and claimed he'd joined the group as a way of avoiding telling her.

They were better off without me, Kate replied. And given how quickly she'd left them when she had the opportunity, that was clearly true.

Once she had the additional cash, she'd walked to the Greyhound station near the water. By the time she got there, fat blisters had formed on the soles of her feet. Her work shoes were not meant for walking or the running she'd done earlier. She checked her reflection in the glass of one of the stores she passed. She looked disheveled but not entirely out of place.

The bus station was in a bad area of town. But as she watched the weak sun glint off the black water of the lake, she didn't feel as if she was in danger. She'd survived. She felt insulated, wrapped in bubble wrap.

Lucky.

Inside the cavernous building, she checked the schedule. There was a bus headed to Canada in three hours. She waited in line with twenty others, an impatient group held back by nylon tape barriers. She'd been worried the bus station would be closed. But other than the intense way people were looking at their phones, everything seemed to be business as usual.

When she got to the counter and asked for a one-way ticket, the clerk told her the price and asked for her passport. She reached into her purse for the cash and thanked her continued luck that she had both her passports with her.

That was the key to her success, if she did succeed. Her two passports. Her American one, because that's where she lived and mostly who she thought of herself as being these days. And her Canadian one, because that was where she was born and where she still traveled to frequently for work. Since she was a citizen, Canada required her to enter on her Canadian passport. But were they linked? She'd never thought to ask. Would the fact that a dead person used a passport hours after she was supposed to be dead raise a red flag somewhere, someday? She'd have to take the risk.

Her passports were still in her purse from a trip to Toronto a few weeks earlier to attend a tech convention. And her Canadian passport still had her maiden name on it because she'd never bothered to make the change when she renewed it after she was married.

The woman at the bus station scanned her passport. She said something about how she'd move to Canada if she could, what with the way the world was these days. Kate smiled and nodded, holding her breath. Nothing happened other than the woman handed her a bus ticket tucked into the pages of her passport. She went to wait for her bus.

There were two hours until it left. She settled into an uncomfortable seat. She rested her purse on her lap and fixed her gaze on the television so she didn't make eye contact with anyone. She watched the breaking news about her former workplace, wondering what had happened to everyone. There were all kinds of theories. The CNN anchor reminded people to remain calm. Their sources were telling them it was a gas leak. But still, there were rumors of bombs in other buildings. Suspicious packages being left behind. Certain types of people to be rounded up. Civil liberties that needed to be violated.

She watched TV for a while. Then she went to the small store and bought a few things she would need. A toothbrush and tooth-paste. A backpack. A T-shirt and sweatshirt with the same logo on them. She needed clean underwear, but that wasn't available. In the bathroom, she took off her blouse and jacket, stuffing them into the bag. She washed the dirt and sweat off her face and neck. Then slipped the T-shirt over her head and then the sweatshirt, pulling the hood up so she'd have something to retreat inside of. Already she felt different. More like the woman she'd been before she got married. Before . . .

She went into a stall and sat down on the toilet and wept. Was she actually going to do this? Walk away from her children, her hus-band, her life? Let them think she was dead when she wasn't? Was the pull of something different so great that she had to take such a drastic step? There was divorce, surely. There were alternatives she hadn't considered.

She sat there for a long time. Her rear end turned numb, and she felt almost faint from the combination of emotion and shock and not having had anything to eat that morning because she hadn't been able to swallow her breakfast.

She'd almost talked herself into changing course when an an-nouncement sounded over the PA system, a robotic voice like the one used to make announcements on the "L."

All departures are canceled until further notice.

The city was on lockdown. And it was only then, with her plans most likely thwarted, that she knew she must press ahead. That the only way for her was forward.

That in order to live, she had no alternative but to die.

INTERVIEW TRANSCRIPT

TJ: Who didn't Kaitlyn tell about you?

FM: Her friends. Her family.

TJ: She didn't tell her husband? I thought you said she had?

FM: That's what she told me. But she hadn't.

TJ: How did you find that out?

FM: You've heard the story, haven't you?

TJ: I've heard a few things. Why don't you tell me what actually happened? I want to hear your side of the story.

FM: You don't care about my side of the story.

TJ: That's not true.

FM: I can just picture it, you know. You're going to do one of those reenactment things at this point, right? Like how they did in that Robert Durst thing? Like, you'll find some actress who kind of looks like me, and you'll restage the event. All those horrified women. And the music. The music will be terrible.

TJ: I'm not . . .

FM: I think . . . Can we stop for the day?

TJ: Of course we can, Franny. I'm sorry I've upset you.

FM: It doesn't matter.

TJ: Yes it does. I know it can be tough to sift through all this, but that's what makes it real. Do you understand?

FM: It's not real, though. It's not even close. Ted gets it, I think. He doesn't make me talk when I don't want to.

TJ: Who's Ted?

FM: Ted Borenstein. You know, the *Vanity Fair* writer?

TJ: You've been talking to Ted Borenstein?

FM: So what if I have?

17

INTRUDER

CECILY

There's someone trying to get into my house.

I lie in the inky dark, gripping the sheet beneath me, my heart shuddering.

There's a heavy tread on the deck beneath my open window. It's not one of the kids. It's not the sound of anyone I know, even if it made sense for someone I know to be creeping around my house in the middle of the night, which it most obviously does not.

I grope for my phone on the nightstand. It's not there. I left it downstairs on the counter where I placed it after I got a text from Teo asking me if I'd gotten home all right. We'd ditched our land-line two years ago—a decision I'd fought at the time because cell phones could die or not be within easy reach when you needed them. Tom had hushed my fears. We hadn't received any calls on our landline except for telemarketers for years, and what could possibly happen with us both there safe and snug? I'd agreed rather than fight him.

And now look. My life seems to be one long series of my worst fears being realized.

Two more heavy steps, and now it's the sound of someone rattling the handle on the sliding door. Barely breathing, adrenaline and anxiety fighting for prominence, I roll onto Tom's side of the bed, trying to keep my breathing regular, trying not to make the bed squeak. I slide my hand under the mattress. It's still there, the knife Tom kept in case of intruders, the one I was never happy about because what if the kids found it?

"There are plenty of knives in the kitchen," he'd always say in the tone he used when he thought I was being an irrational mother. And then I'd start to doubt myself, even though I knew that this knife, in its hunting sheath, hidden away, would have an attraction to the kids that all the ordinary, everyday knives sitting in the butcher block never would.

"At least it's not a gun," I hear Tom's voice saying now. But right at this moment, with my children asleep in their rooms down the hall, I wish for a gun. This knife I'm clutching is useless to me if whoever's trying to get in my house intends violence against the kids or me.

The kids.

The handle rattles again. I force myself to stand and pad quietly across the carpeted bedroom floor. The room's pitch-black because this is how I've always needed to sleep, and now that Tom's gone, I can shut the blinds and wait until my alarm wakes me rather than rising with the vagaries of the sun.

My hand reaches for the doorknob. I find its cool surface and ease open the door. Out in the hall, I think I can hear breathing, but that might be my own. I get to the door to Henry's room before I freeze in fear. I feel like I have Sophie's choice. How can I protect both my children at once? How could I ever choose between them?

Another click from downstairs, and I hear a muffled curse. Instinct drives me to Cassie's room. She's the easiest to wake. She's lying on her back, her arms splayed above her head, her phone still clutched in her hand. I shake her gently. Her eyes flutter open.

"What—?"

I place my hand across her mouth as I lean down and whisper into her ear. "I think there's someone trying to get in the house. Don't say anything. Follow me to Henry's room. Bring your phone."

Her eyes are wide with fear, but she nods. She looks so young and vulnerable in her too-small T-shirt and the matching bottoms that graze her calves. We hold hands as we cross the hall. We stop as we hear something tapping against the glass. Cassie's shaking so hard it feels like she's vibrating. I tug her hand, pulling her into Henry's room and locking the door behind us. I grab the chair from his desk and tilt it under the door. Cassie sits on the floor next to Henry's bed, huddled into the space between his nightstand and the bed frame. Henry couldn't be more oblivious, snoring gently, his covers pulled up to his chin the way he's always done ever since he was a tiny thing.

I sit next to Cassie on the floor and pry her phone from her hand. She tries to speak, but I shake my head. The battery's low, but there's enough to make a call. I can't help but notice the text on her screen from Kevin. *Sleep tight*, it says.

My fingers shake like they did a year ago when I texted the kids to let them know I was alive as I tap out 911. I press the phone against my ear, turning the volume low. The woman who answers asks me to state the nature of my emergency.

"Someone's trying to break into my house."

"I'll need you to speak louder, ma'am."

"Someone. Breaking in. My. House," I hiss. "Send the police."

"Ma'am . . . are you there, ma'am? Do you need the police?"

I call up the keypad and press the number one, loud and long.

"Is that one for yes, ma'am?"

I press again.

"Are you in danger?"

Another press.

She asks me if the GPS system is showing the correct address, and I confirm it.

"I'm dispatching a unit to your house immediately. Keep this line open."

I gather Cassie to me and lean her head against mine. Where earlier tonight her smell was foreign, adult, now it's an echo of her as a baby. The 911 woman speaks, reassuring me, but nothing will comfort me until I know my children are safe.

I can't hear anything now. Is he in the house? Does he have a weapon? What, what, what does he want?

Cassie and I stare into each other's eyes. I do my best to convey both the seriousness of what I'm feeling and the assurance I need to. *We're going to be okay. We're going to be okay.* If I think it a million times, can I implant the suggestion in my daughter's mind? Can I make it come true?

Cassie reaches down and takes the knife from where I've stashed it in the waistband of my pajamas. I shake my head as she removes the blade from its sheath. She nods back, makes a slight stabbing motion with it. It must be the nerves, but I want to laugh.

I put my hand around her wrist. We cannot do this. We cannot try to defend ourselves.

I speak into the phone. "Please hurry."

"Ma'am? Did you say something?"

I press one again.

"Hurry," I say as loud as I can without disclosing our location if he's in the house. "Please."

"They're two minutes away, ma'am."

I sound my acknowledgment as something flashes through the window. Is that a . . . ?

I spring to my feet and pull the chair out of the way.

"Mom! What are you doing?" Cassie says in a harsh whisper.

"It's okay. The police will be here in a moment."

I open the door as more lights flash. I can hear the whine of sirens approaching. I run down the stairs, suddenly unafraid, the adrenaline winning. In the kitchen, I find what I knew I would when I saw the lights: a man with a camera standing on the other side of the glass.

"What the hell is wrong with you?" I scream.

"Say cheese," he says loudly enough for me to hear him as his flash goes off once again.

· · ·

After the police have left without catching the guy, the kids have been soothed with cocoa and calming words and are back in bed, and the alarm is on, which I forgot to do earlier, I try to settle into my own bed without much success. What the hell was that all about? Why are people so interested in my life? It's not like I went around asking for any of it . . . The photograph, the publicity, the status as the poster child for a tragedy I wish I had nothing to do with. I tried to bat it away, and I hate how it makes me a target. Take last night at the restaurant with Teo. A simple moment that should've been private, between us, was fair game to some passerby.

I even wanted to turn down the money until my mom talked me out of it. But I've used it for the kids—paid off the mortgage and the debts from the restaurant that never was, topped up their college funds, created a trust. I work as hard as I can on the Compensation Committee to make sure that as many deserving families as possible get their due. And yet, it's never enough. I still feel like a fraud, a fake, a prop in my own life.

What the hell was that man doing? What was he hoping to find? Me with another man? Me with . . . Oh God. I'm so, so stupid.

I pick my phone up off the bedside table, where it will sleep forever now, and open a web browser. TMZ seems like the best bet. And yes, there it is.

TRIPLE TEN WIDOW MOVES ON?

Teo and me kissing is tonight's breaking news.

•   •   •

The dawn, when it finally comes, does not improve what happened in the night.

Though I need to tell Cassie and Henry about the kiss before they read about it online, I don't want to wake them again. I let them sleep in while I count the ways in which I'll kill the man who terrified us when they find him. I silently send curses to the man or woman—I wasn't able to tell which—who took the picture of Teo and me. I revive the litany of words I have for Tom, the betrayer, because if he hadn't done what he did, I'd be a real widow, too torn up with grief to even think about a man, even one as great as Teo. And then I think about *her*, that anonymous woman who tore my life open. Who is she? Where is she? If she's alive, does she lie awake at night full of regrets? Or did she slough off Tom's death, consider it a close call, and scurry back to the comfort of her family, her life?

I get up and go to Tom's study. I start to pull items from his desk and sort them into piles—keep, toss, donate. I try to tell myself I'm doing what I should've done long ago, sort through his things and start to make room for myself in here. But really, I'm looking for evidence, some sign or clue to point the way to her. I've been avoiding this forever, not asking the right questions when I had the chance, not searching my own house for further proof of his betrayal because I had enough to deal with.

But now, in the early morning after a night when my stitched-together life feels like it's falling back apart, it seems like the right time to look under corners and reach to the back of drawers to see if I can find the monster after all and slay it.

Instead, all I find are remnants of our life together. Old bills, the to-do lists he'd make, packs of photographs that never made it into albums or frames. Tom was old-fashioned about his photographs; he didn't want them to be only digital, so he'd dutifully take his camera chip into the pharmacy and return with an envelope full of carefully curated memories. The ones I find today are an amalgam from the year before he died—our last ski trip, the house we rented in Cape Cod with the Rings, Kaitlyn and I with our arms slung around each other after our first successful foray on the stand-up paddleboards we rented.

Kaitlyn's wearing the wide-brimmed hat she always wore to protect her delicate skin from the sun. I was more reckless and have the wrinkles to prove it. Kaitlyn looks happy that day, strong and smiling, halfway between the broken woman I'd befriended and the one she was in the months before she died. I didn't notice it so much then, as it was happening, like the changes in my own face that caught me up short when I finally looked at myself for the first time in a while. But examining this picture now, I recall clearly what she looked like the last time I saw her, when I met her for coffee before she went to work and we talked—I talked—about Tom.

She had dark circles under her eyes, and though she said all the right things, the things I needed, her eyes were downcast, and she kept stirring her coffee without drinking it. When she'd said she had to go, I'd stood up and hugged her. I'd asked her, finally, if she was okay. What was wrong?

"It's nothing. I haven't been sleeping well."

"Any reason in particular?"

She'd shaken her head. She had more than a few gray hairs mixed in with the honey brown she'd adopted as a hair color a few years before. I wondered if she'd noticed them the way I'd noticed my own, evident to me despite their being close enough to my natural blond to be invisible to most people.

"Don't worry," she said. "I'm not . . . It's not happening again."

"I wasn't thinking that. But it would be okay if it did. You can tell me. I want you to."

"I know . . . I just don't know how to talk about it."

"About what?"

She shook her head again. "Not today, okay? You have enough on your plate."

"Then when?"

"How about next week? When things have settled down."

We'd hugged again, and then she was gone, running to her car with her purse over her head to block the worst of a sudden pelt of rain.

Franny. It must've been Franny she was thinking about. She must've known the day was coming when she had to fess up to Joshua, to her kids, to us, and how that was probably going to rip her life to shreds, when she'd just gotten finished building it back up.

How I wish I'd known. How I wish I could've told her there was nothing to be ashamed of, nothing to fear in telling me, that it was keeping the secret that was painful.

Was it ever.

18

THE GORDIAN KNOT

KATE

In Montreal, Kate looked with curiosity at the photo of Cecily Grayson kissing a strange man. The photo was on TMZ, a site she was embarrassed to say she spent too much time on in the last year. There was something about the voyeurism of it all; she found it strangely soothing. That people who had everything anyone could want were caught in unflattering positions. Drunk after dinner. Or "canoodling"—such a ridiculous word—with someone they shouldn't be. It was an escape. Something she knew more than enough about.

It had started during that interminable wait in the bus station. She'd spent two days there once her bus's departure was canceled. Waiting for the all clear. For her bus's departure to be rescheduled.

She couldn't leave the building because if she did, she might miss her bus. And she couldn't leave for real because it was too dangerous. She might be recognized. Run into someone who thought she was dead. And even though she knew that was a possibility in the bus station, too, it seemed lower. She was pretty certain she didn't know anyone who still traveled by Greyhound. Which was awful, because what was wrong with traveling that way? But the people she knew now, the person she was, they drove to things or flew if it was too far away.

So she stayed inside and read the trashy magazine equivalents to TMZ that littered the building. When she ran out of reading material, she fed quarters into the arcade games, worrying she was wasting her precious stash of cash. But she had to do something other than watch the horrible images on the television. Especially when the commentators started talking about people she knew, and then her and her family. She kept the hood of her sweatshirt up at all times, her face in shadow. When the TV trucks had camped outside her house and her husband had come out to read a statement looking pale and drawn with the kids behind him holding her blown-up picture, she'd run to the bathroom and thrown up.

When she'd come back, she felt the stares of several of her fellow travelers. As if they could see through her hood. Like she was wearing a big red A on her breast. A for Abandonment. Despite her best efforts, she knew she'd be recognizable to them now. There was no helping it. The half dozen people in the bus station who had nowhere else to go were all becoming familiar to one another.

By the second day, Kate felt as if she were unraveling. Being pulled apart thread by thread. She thought again about leaving, but she didn't know where she could go. She couldn't book into a hotel, both for the money it would take and the ID they'd demand. It was one thing using her Canadian passport once at this poky bus station, and then again at the border crossing far from here. But she couldn't take up life as a new person in Chicago. Though she'd been lucky up until then, at some point she was sure to run into someone she knew. Despite the vastness of the city, it happened all the time. And as for going somewhere else in America, that, too, was impossible. Working would require her Social Security number. And given the attention this tragedy was getting, more chances to be recognized.

The only option was Canada. Nothing connected to her life now. Leaving without a trace.

She stayed put. The TV moved on to other families, other grief. She limited herself to two meals a day. Five dollars for a banana and a granola bar in the morning. Another five for a cheeseburger with as many condiments as she could get on it in the evening. Her dress pants already felt looser. *The Runaway Diet*, she thought. Perhaps she could market it someday. And then she hated herself even more for having the thought.

She'd spent a few more precious dollars on a travel pillow. Then a garish shawl that was the closest thing to a blanket the store sold. Soap, deodorant, and aspirin for the near-constant headache she couldn't seem to shake. The store didn't sell shoes or underwear— the two things she needed most. So she walked around in her socks and washed out her underwear in the sink, drying it with the hand dryer as best as she could.

On the afternoon of the third day, she shifted uncomfortably in her seat as she looked around from within the folds of her hood. Each of the permanent travelers, as she'd come to think of them, had their own section of the station. A space that was respected as if it had curtains around it. As night crept in, she placed her backpack on the floor with the pillow on top and wrapped herself in the shawl. The floor was uncomfortable and cold. She wasn't sure how much longer she could stand it, but eventually, she fell asleep.

She dreamed of her family. Not the way it was but the way it could've been if she hadn't screwed so many things up.

And then someone shook her awake.

"You're on that Montreal bus, right?" It was one of the older women who'd been there the whole time. She was missing a few teeth, and her hair was thinned out like a man's.

Kate sat up. "That's right. Why?"

"It's leaving in ten minutes."

Kate's heart accelerated. Her head spun to the television. There it was on the ticker. The travel ban had been lifted. There had been no other incidents. The explosion was definitely the result of a gas leak. They were safe. For now.

She hastily shoved her new belongings into her backpack. She had a brief moment of panic when she couldn't find her ticket. Then remembered she'd put it inside her sweatshirt pouch along with her money in order to keep it safe. The woman who'd woken her eyed the bills Kate was unable to hide when she pulled the ticket out.

She stuffed them away again. "Do you know what gate?"

"Twenty, I think." The woman pointed with a grizzled hand. She smelled vaguely of sweat and pee. But Kate likely smelled the same. Who was she to judge?

"Thank you for waking me."

"You'd better hurry."

Kate turned to rush to the exit, but something held her back. Did this woman actually know who she was? Was her next call going to be to the police? Or was she just starving? For attention, for food, for somewhere to go herself?

Kate reached into her pouch. She touched a bill, crisper than the others. One of the fifties she'd promised herself she wouldn't break until it was absolutely necessary. Before she could talk herself out of it, she handed it to the woman and pressed it into her scratchy hand.

"What's that for?"

"To thank you for waking me. I've got to go."

"Don't worry. I won't tell."

Kate thought about stopping, trying to extract some greater promise. But the bus driver was looking around to see if anyone else was coming. She turned to the woman and said, "Thank you," then crossed the station just in time to catch her bus.

The Triple-Tenner You've Never Heard Of

by TED BORENSTEIN

Special to VANITY FAIR

Published on OCTOBER 29

A fter a year of covering the Triple Ten tragedy, I thought I'd heard it all. That I knew it all. Every name. Every story. I'd literally helped write the (memorial) book, after all, and had spent the last six months of my life reliving each of their stories, cataloging the grief.

Then, shortly after the six-month anniversary, a new name began to circulate around the survivor community. That name was Franny Maycombe.

I first heard of her at a fund-raising event for the Compensation Initiative, the organization that was established to dole out the donations that poured in from around the world for the victims. Its goal is something they call "total compensation"—they want to make sure every victim's family receives the money they would have had but for the tragedy. A formal, legal way of saying they want to do right by everyone.

What that means in practical terms is that more money is always required.

"When you add everything up," says Jenny Chang to me one night, "we're talking about as many as twenty thousand people who've been affected. Not just those who died and their families but the thousands who were injured and their families. Total compensation means you make everyone whole again. Everyone."

Jenny Chang is a twenty-three-year-old whose life was already marked by tragedy before she lost her father on October 10. Jenny's mother died of breast cancer when she was sixteen. An only child, she and her father were close. Though she was accepted to several prestigious schools with a full scholarship, she decided to attend the University of Chicago to stay close to home.

Midterms were approaching in her senior year when her father died. Since then, Jenny has completed her degree in astrophysics and put off the many internships she's been offered to work full-time raising money for other victims' families. She's one of six people who sit on the Compensation Committee, an ultrasecret wing of the Initiative that has recommending power to the board regarding claims that have been turned down or held over by the adjudicator.

"It's a lot of responsibility," Jenny says while sipping on a glass of prosecco in the Initiative's stunning boardroom. "But it's important."

The Compensation Committee is celebrating surpassing another fundraising goal, and the room is thick with men in Brionis and women in Louboutins. Jenny, incredibly thin and wearing a spangled dress, is younger than most of those involved, but she's one of those who's been hardest hit by the tragedy, though she doesn't agree with that label.

"I think that honor goes to Franny. You must've heard of Franny? Her story is ah-mazing."

I haven't, and she gladly fills me in. Ten minutes later, my head is spinning—Franny's story *is* amazing, unique. Adopted twenty-four years ago, she'd recently met her birth mother, only to lose her soon after when the building fell. Initially reluctant to get involved, she's turned into a tireless advocate for the cause and is now the co-chair of the Compensation Committee.

"You must talk to Franny," Jenny says, looking around the room. "I thought she'd be here by now."

Jenny promises to bring her to me but returns with a fresh glass, a canapé, and no Franny.

"I'm sure she'll show up soon. I can't wait for you to meet her."

That proves more difficult than I could've imagined.

19

POSTER WHAT?

CECILY

Kaitlyn's funeral was a hard day for me. Joshua was a mess, and her daughters were inconsolable. I know, sometimes, Kaitlyn felt like the kids were closer to Joshua than to her, that they remembered the time when she was postpartum after they were born or the echoes she felt after that, and had never bonded with her properly, but it wasn't true. I often told Kaitlyn that she had a kind of dysmorphic disorder about motherhood. She saw herself in a completely different light than her children did, or anyone else who was watching. Those girls doted on her, emulated her, looked to her first when they said or did something they were unsure of. Joshua was a good father, patient and kind, but it was Kaitlyn who was the star of their everyday life.

Sitting on the hard church pew that was starting to feel too familiar, we clung to one another, Henry and Cassie and the girls and Joshua, as the service went on and on. We rode together in the limousine to the house, Kaitlyn's daughters shuddering on either side of me, Cassie and Henry still brittle from Tom's funeral two days before. A car full of broken people; how were we ever going to be made whole again?

Joshua's cousins had stayed behind to get the catering ready, to make sure the canapés were hot and the crudités were cold, that there was enough booze to go around. I heard someone remark, as I went in the front door, that she'd been subsisting on cheap wine and spanakopita for a week, that she'd lost two pounds already. Then they saw me, and one of them turned red and the other said, "Sorry," and I just shook my head because what did I care? They were right. If I hadn't lost Tom and Kaitlyn, I might be one of those women, annoyed that I had to wear black for weeks on end, tired of the sadness, the endless parade of receptions and sermons, and happy that my clothes were fitting looser than they had in years.

Hell, I *was* one of those women. I would've given anything to avoid it all, to throw out every black thing I owned and never wear anything but bright colors again. But I couldn't forget that if things had been different by a couple of inches, in the grand scheme of things, then I would've been on the other side of it and might not be there at all.

The cousins had forgotten to open the windows, so it was stuffy in the house. I settled the younger children in the basement with a video, then went to the kitchen to do just that. As I pried open the window over the sink, I noticed a group of women standing in the backyard, smoking cigarettes. It had been a while since I'd seen that.

It felt illicit even watching them, like my first hidden puffs taken in a clearing with my girlfriends up behind our high school, worried a teacher would find us.

Only these women weren't furtive; they weren't hiding their sins; they were shaking their heads as if they couldn't believe the story they were hearing. One of them kept glancing over her shoulder at the house. Something was off. People were acting strangely. Not just sad but upset.

No, that's not the right word. Disturbed.

I walked around the first floor. The furniture had been pushed back against the walls, and there must've been more than a hundred people in the house, pushed up against one another because the house wasn't that big. I'm not sure what I was looking for, but when I saw her, I approached with a sense of foreboding. She was at least fifteen years younger than the other women, early twenties, overweight, with dark-brown hair that had suffered a bad perm a few months earlier (did people still *get* perms?). I searched the brain tape, but I'd never seen her, though there was something familiar about her. She was wearing a black dress that didn't fit her very well, falling to an awkward place below her knee that made it difficult for her to walk.

She was the only person standing alone, and despite the lack of space, there was a clearing around her, as if it was dangerous to stand too close to her.

"Hi, I'm Cecily."

She held out her hand limply. We shook. Her hand was clammy, like a damp fish. It didn't feel as if it had the right number of bones in it.

"Nice to meet you, Cecily."

"Are you a friend of the family?"

"No."

I felt annoyed. I'd heard about this, strangers coming to the funerals of the Triple-Tenners so they could be in on the action, walk past the fence of media, feel a part of it all. Or maybe she was trolling for free booze and food, another person on the funeral diet those women out front were talking about, only this time, she's happy to be eating it because she doesn't have anywhere else to go. I'd heard about that, too.

"If you don't mind my asking, what are you doing here?"

She looked at me for a moment, sizing me up.

"Were you a friend of Kaitlyn's?" Her voice was strangely flat, as if she was masking an accent.

"She was one of my best friends."

"And she never mentioned me? Not even once?"

This woman whose name I didn't know started tearing up. I had an odd reflex to comfort her, even though I knew she was about to tell me something that would change my life again, like Tom's errant texts.

"I . . . Who are you?"

"I'm Franny. I'm Kaitlyn's daughter."

A small part of why I'm up so early sifting through the contents of Tom's office is so I can hear it when it happens, that *slap* of the newspaper as it hits our front door. Call me old-fashioned, but I still love the smell of newsprint in the morning. And since it was a family tradition, dividing up the paper into our individual interests, I still do it with the kids. It's usually Henry who collects it, my early riser, the way he's been since he was a baby, but I can't let that occur today.

When I hear it happen, I'm already waiting behind the front door, and I have it open to grab the paper before Henry can get to it.

I needn't have worried; there's nothing there. I must be getting full of myself, thinking I might be in the real paper because I kissed a man. I watch the kid who's delivered our newspapers for years ride away on his ten-speed, unsure of what to do. The photograph is on-line, and someone's sure to point it out to at least one of the kids. How will I explain this to them? Although Cassie knows something about the date, that's not enough. I didn't say enough last night to make this okay.

The pavement beneath my bare feet is cold, but I can't seem to make myself move. Then I hear the *click, click, click* of a camera, rapid-fire like the paparazzi use. It takes me a moment to spot him, because he's across the street, leaning up against the Hendersons' tree. I throw the paper down and run toward him.

"Stop it! Go away!"

He lowers his camera for a moment, then lifts it again. And even though I know this means that now he has even better shots of me coming after him like a madwoman in my pajamas, I don't care.

"What the fuck is wrong with you?"

He lowers his camera again. He's young, midtwenties, wearing an oversize hoodie with the words *Don't Criticize What You Can't Understand* written across it.

"Hey, lady. Calm down."

"Don't you tell me to calm down, Bob Dylan. I want you to erase those photos."

"No way."

"Yes way. What do you want, money? Is that what this is about?"

"I'm just doing my job."

"Bullshit. This isn't a story. Me in my bathrobe is not a story."

"Of course it is. You might not like it, but it is. Why else do you think they sent me here?"

"Were you here last night?"

"What?"

His surprise seems genuine. While his shape is similar to the man I saw through the window, jumping over my hedge as he ran away, I'm guessing he's not stupid enough to come back here after escaping the cops.

"Give me your card."

"Why?"

"I want to buy the photos."

He gives me that look again, the one that tells me I'm completely naive.

"Come on," I say. "What's the harm?"

He fumbles for a moment, then hands me a card. *Carl Hilton. Photography for All Occasions.*

"You should leave it," he says.

"We'll see. Now get, will you?"

"Mom!" Cassie calls from across the street. "What the hell?"

I turn around. Cassie's holding her phone straight out from her body like an accusation, a look of shock and hurt on her face.

Carl snaps another picture.

•　•　•

"Okay," I say twenty minutes later, after I've gotten Carl to delete the picture of Cassie after pointing out that she's underage and barely dressed. "Family meeting."

Henry groans. Cassie's still clutching her phone to her chest like she used to hold her special blanket.

"Why does it have to be a 'meeting'?" Cassie asks. "Why can't we just have a conversation like a normal family?"

Family meetings were always Tom's thing. I thought they were a bit corny, but he took them seriously, so eventually I did, too.

"Come on," I say. "You know the rule."

"If someone calls a family meeting, we all have to attend!" Henry says. His voice is on the verge of cracking, and I wonder if he'll end up sounding like Tom. He already stands and walks like him; from behind, he's a carbon copy except for his hair color. It's disconcerting, sometimes, when I see him suddenly, when I'm not concentrating. A bit of rage rises up without my being able to stop it. Another thing to hate Tom for, a list that's too long.

"That's right. Let's go."

They follow me into the living room. We each have our assigned seats. Henry's is the wingback chair Tom and I found on one of our first furniture outings. It's covered in a green chintz fabric whose hues match the modern striped rug we found several years later. Cassie's is the love seat I brought with me from college, re-covered in a dark gray. I take the sectional, making sure to place myself squarely in the middle, using my body to fill the void Tom left.

"So you've seen the picture," I say. "I went to dinner with Teo last night, Henry."

"Cassie told me."

"You said nothing happened," Cassie says.

"Nothing did."

"You kissed him."

"I did. He kissed me, and I didn't stop it."

"I like Teo," Henry says with a bit of defiance.

"We all like Teo," I say. "But this isn't about him. This is about us. And about what happened last night."

"This is such bullshit."

"Cassie. Enough."

"Who was that guy outside, Mom?" Henry asks. "Was he the same guy who tried to get in the house?"

"I don't think so."

"Why did he do that? Why do they care?" Cassie asks.

"It's because of that photograph. The one Teo took."

"That's right, Henry. The one Teo took. You know how much attention that photograph brought me. Us. People are interested in our family. I wish they weren't, but they are."

"It's so stupid," Cassie says. "Like we're these celebrities because our dad died."

"That's exactly right."

"Can't you make them stop?"

"It'll go away eventually—soon, probably, now that the memorial's over."

Cassie crosses her arms over her breasts. "How come you didn't try? I mean, you, like, *say* you don't like the attention, but you're on all these committees, and you're in that documentary, and if you wanted them to go away, why didn't you just say no to all that stuff?"

Cassie's words are crushing. She sounds exactly like my inner voice, the one I've only been able to respond to with *because, because, because.*

"I thought it was the best thing to do given the circumstances."

"What circumstances, Mom? We're not the only family who lost someone."

"There are things . . . I was worried that if I didn't go along, they might come looking."

"Who might come looking? For what?"

"The press. Journalists."

"Why? And who cares? You have the most boring life ever."

I smile. "I wish I did. I wish there was nothing to find."

"Do you do drugs, Mom?" Henry asks, looking serious, all those school assemblies having an impact.

"Mom doing drugs? That's a laugh."

Isn't it funny, how little your kids know you? Not that I do drugs now, but back in the day, in college and the years after? For a while, Tom grew pot in his closet.

"No, Henry. It's nothing like that."

"Then what?"

I look back and forth between my children. They have a view of me, of their father. It's like that photograph Teo took—true enough but not the whole truth. And like my initial decision to keep all this hidden, the idea of telling them, of changing that image for good, seems like the wrong choice. But they've learned enough about life from another source, so I take a deep breath, and then I confess.

20

LIFE AS A HOUSE

KATE

"Did you see this?" Andrea asked, pushing her iPad under Kate's nose later that morning as she was trying to cut up the twins' bananas into even circles. It was cold out, closer to winter than fall, and there was frost on the windows.

"I'm not sure. What is it?"

"It's about that woman. You know, the one they took that photo of? In Chicago? That blond one who looks a bit like the woman who dated Ellen. The one who went crazy?"

"Anne Heche?"

"Right. She was on *Another World*, the soap opera, wasn't she?"

"I think so."

"Can you believe it?"

"That Anne Heche went crazy?"

"No. About the Chicago woman . . . Cecily . . ."

"Grayson?"

"Yes, her. She was this picture-perfect widow, and now she's all over the place, kissing some other guy."

Kate put the knife down and scooped the banana circles into a bowl.

"Boys! Breakfast."

Kate watched Andrea. Her face was flushed as she stabbed at her iPad, scrolling from one news story to the next. She was dressed for a session with her trainer. A man who was good-looking enough to cause all kinds of trouble with the stay-at-home moms of Westmount. But Andrea seemed sexless, almost. Androgynous despite the long blond curls and fake semipermanent eyelashes.

"Who cares who she's dating?" Kate asked. "Her husband's been dead for a year."

"It takes two years to mourn properly."

"Really?"

"I had to read all this research once on the stages of grief. It takes two years to go through them."

"Okay, but still—"

Willie and Steven tottered into the kitchen. Kate helped them into their seats and fastened them tight. She put the bowl of bananas in front of them, admonishing them to share. Steven reached into the bowl and took out three circles, placing them in front of his brother.

"These are yours."

Willie gave him a thumbs-up.

"Just because she kissed a man doesn't mean she's through

grieving," Kate said, unsure of why she was arguing this point. "Besides, maybe it doesn't take that long for everyone. Maybe it's just an average? Or maybe he wasn't a very good husband."

Andrea's head rose. "Do you know something I don't?"

"Of course not."

"Well, then. It isn't right."

"Why do you care?"

Kate immediately regretted her tone. But who was Andrea to judge? She didn't know anything about grief. Sure, she had a husband who wasn't around much. She was bored and wished she could go back to work without actually having to do so. But she didn't know. She didn't know how it cut you in half. How even when you were past it, you were never over it. You were always in it. Always.

"It's just . . . wrong."

Andrea was clearly daring Kate to defy her. To give her an excuse to direct her anger somewhere. Kate turned away and went to the coffee machine. Maybe she needed to switch out Andrea's coffee for decaf.

Kate's own grief had hit her for real when she woke twenty-four hours after crashing out in her seedy hotel room, not sure where she was. Not sure *who* she was. Lying in a lumpy bed in clothes she'd worn for too long in a city where she knew no one after having run away from her life (her kids!)—that wasn't like her. The her she'd worked hard to become. She'd spent twenty years as one kind of person. Someone who did what was expected. Who showed up. Who had nothing mysterious about her. A good-enough mother. A good-enough wife and friend. And now she was another kind of person. A sneak. A thief. Someone who lied and deceived.

She'd risen and pulled back the curtain. It was dark outside.

The dirt-smudged window revealed only the broken bricks of the building next door. She craned her neck. The sky was black. The cheap clock radio on the rickety table next to the bed said it was five o'clock. It must be the morning, which meant she'd slept through an entire day.

Another day gone. Another day done.

She'd relieved her too-full bladder in the dingy bathroom down the hall. If there was anyone else staying in this place, she neither saw nor heard any sign of them. Back in her room, she ate some of the food she'd purchased at the corner store, then turned on the small TV that hung from the wall. Left over from the early nineties, it reminded her of her first television, its screen smaller than the computer screen at the office that was no more. Bulky in the back to account for the nodes or tubes or . . . Oh, who cared. It was a television. But easier to think about than what she'd left behind.

A few clicks of the dial brought her to CTV News Channel, a Canadian equivalent of CNN, but with a drier, newsier approach that she'd come to characterize later as Canadian. They were just as interested in the explosion as America was, but there was a certain remove. The empathy was there, but the . . . That was it. The fear was missing.

The funerals were starting that day. Or maybe they'd been going on for days, and she'd missed them. If past was prologue, she knew they wouldn't cover all of them. Only those of the people who'd become famous in their deaths. The public would feel invested for a time, as if it were their own loss. When everyone was buried, they'd move on to other things. The coverage would slow. The ticker would fill with other headlines. The only people who'd remember her would be those who knew her best.

Her children. They'd remember. And though they'd receded on her journey, they were front and center now. But no, they never went away. Not from the moment they'd been born. Even though she'd never felt as attached as she thought she would. As she thought she should. She loved her children. She was proud and happy and scared and nervous for them. Wanted the best for them, wanted their happiness. But she'd felt, for a long time, maybe from the beginning, as if she wasn't the person who was best equipped to give them that. It was hard to describe it other than that maybe it resembled the feeling you had when you gave a child up for adoption.

That they'd be better off without her.

Kate had pulled the picture from the pouch of the sweatshirt she still hadn't changed out of. A great weight was tugging at her chest. Trying to pull her back to what she'd fled. But she was on a path she couldn't turn back from. She did her best to push those feelings down. To concentrate on the television screen and its inferior picture quality. It worked after a while. When she returned from the quick shower she took under a lukewarm spray, she'd developed a morbid curiosity about whether her own funeral would rate a televised appearance.

She'd watched three before a familiar church appeared. Gray stone, a high steeple, a few brilliant maples surrounding it. It was the church she spent every Sunday in, bored, because that's what they did on Sundays. It's what they'd always done on Sundays. From time immemorial. That's what her husband always said, anyway. And then he'd laugh because everything was funny to him, even the mundane things, and JJ would shush him because JJ was the serious one of the bunch.

Kate felt sick at the thought of Em and JJ being in church

without her. Even if this funeral wasn't hers, this was where it would take place. And they'd probably be attending other funerals there, too. The dead they knew who worked in the building. Tom Grayson and Margo, his assistant. Or were they too young for that? Kate didn't know. Another thing to add to her list of motherhood failures. A long, long list.

Tom was dead. Kate had trouble absorbing that information. Because there was something about Tom. He'd seemed invincible, somehow. But as she watched the screen, she didn't have any choice but to accept it. There was Cecily, dressed in black, holding Cassie's and Henry's hands as they left a limousine and climbed the steps together.

And that's when she'd felt it for the first time. That wrench in her works. Watching a scene from her own life on a crappy television. There but not. Knowing she could never go back, no matter what happened.

"Did you hear what I said?" Andrea asked.

"Huh?"

Andrea looked exasperated. "The boys were asking for milk."

"Oh, sorry. Daydreaming."

Andrea frowned. Once again, Kate could read the thoughts in her head. Something was off. Kate was becoming . . . *unreliable*.

Kate took the milk from the fridge and filled the boys' cups. Because Andrea was watching, she added milk to the food diary next to the fridge, where she still had to record how often they pooped and peed each day as if they were babies.

"Wow," Andrea said. She was back to flicking through her iPad, her manicured fingers clicking against the glass.

"What's that?"

"Cecily lost both her husband and her best friend in the tragedy."

"That's terrible."

"Yeah. And here's something funny. Her best friend's name was Kaitlyn. Just like you."

INTERVIEW TRANSCRIPT

TJ: When did you start speaking to Ted Borenstein?

FM: Is that a problem?

TJ: Do you remember the agreement we signed before we started filming?

FM: The thing that was a zillion pages?

TJ: That's right. Lawyers. But, ah, as I explained to you at the time, it means you agreed to speak to me exclusively.

FM: I know I can't do another film or anything, but this is just a magazine profile. I mean, it might be a profile. I haven't decided yet.

TJ: What do you mean?

FM: I've talked to the guy—Ted—but it's been off the record, you know? So he can't use anything I say. That's how it works, isn't it? I have to give the go-ahead?

TJ: That's technically true, but . . . What sorts of things has he been asking you about?

FM: Sort of the same stuff you've been asking.

TJ: Has he mentioned anyone else he's been talking to?

FM: No . . . I mean, he's talking to Mr. Ring, of course, Joshua, and he asked me one time for my sister's phone number, but neither of them has anything to do with this.

TJ: Are you still in touch with your sister?

FM: Not . . . Not so much.

TJ: Have you spoken to her since you reconnected with your mother?

FM: Not really.

TJ: Does that mean no?

FM: Why are you cross-examining me?

TJ: I didn't think I was.

FM: "Does that mean no?" That's so totally from *The Good Wife* or whatever. You sound like a lawyer, not a filmmaker.

TJ: *[Laughter]* My parents would be so happy to hear that.

FM: They didn't want you to be a filmmaker?

TJ: Nope.

FM: But you've had so much success.

TJ: That's kind of you to say.

FM: But it's true! I mean, you get to do something amazing. Like that documentary you did about The Tragically Hip . . . And now with him dying and everything . . .

TJ: You know The Hip?

FM: Yeah.

TJ: Do you have some connection to Canada?

FM: Well, Kaitlyn's from there originally.

TJ: True, but . . . When did you learn that?

FM: She told me.

TJ: So you didn't know before you met her?

FM: No.

TJ: So that's not why you know about The Hip . . .

FM: There you go again.

TJ: Pardon?

FM: You're doing that lawyer thingy again. I'm telling you. Just show this tape to your parents, and they'll be super-proud of you.

TJ: Maybe I will. But you never answered my question.

FM: The Hip? My sister got into them in her first year of college. She was playing them when she was home for Christmas. Over and over . . . It grew on me. How did you know about them?

TJ: There were some Canadians in my film school class. And then later, a friend of a friend introduced me.

FM: It must've been cool to be out on the road with them.

TJ: It was. So your sister, Sherrie, introduced you to the band?

FM: Yes.

TJ: But you haven't been speaking?

FM: Not for a while.

TJ: Why not?

FM: I don't want to talk about it.

TJ: How come?

FM: None of your business. Besides, like I told Ted, it's not what this film's about, is it?

21

ORDER UP

CECILY

Though I made a confession of sorts, I didn't tell the kids everything. Cassie and Henry didn't need to know that their father cheated on me or how I found out. Telling them that we'd had some serious problems before he died was enough. And if I'm being honest— ha!—I've told so many lies about that time it's affected my memory.

Did I actually, for instance, spend the whole trip to New York with Tom and not mention the texts? Sit silently through the flight, where he took my hand in his and smiled into my eyes and sighed as if he was letting go of a great weight? Say nothing about it during our late dinner at Nobu, ordering ridiculously expensive sushi we couldn't afford and drinking sake until we were both giggling as we hadn't in years? Did I let him lace his fingers through mine on the walk to our hotel and agree when he suggested we take a detour through Central Park?

I think I did, but there was a riot in my mind that night. I searched for the words again and again to bring it up and couldn't get them past the lump in my throat. I caught him looking at me closely time and again, wondering, perhaps, whether I was going to say something. Convincing himself that I must've missed it, that he must've managed to escape detection. And when I asked him why he was staring at me, he simply said, "You."

"Me?"

"Yes, you. My wife. My amazing wife."

We were full of sushi and sake, and the lace on the dress I was wearing was itchy. Tom, on the other hand, looked completely comfortable in a checked chambray shirt and a newer pair of khakis he'd picked out, uncharacteristically, for himself. It was a nice night, though, to be in Central Park, a soft spring night, where the smells of the city were hidden by the scent of new grass and perennials.

"You're drunk," I said.

"That may be. Yes, I think that's true."

"You're talking funny."

"Am I?"

He tipped his head back, looking, I knew, for the constellations to steady himself. It was something he'd done since college. He told me once that if he could find Cassiopeia, he knew he'd remember what he'd done the next day. But it was New York, no stars visible, and I was the one hoping neither of us would remember that night.

"Tom?"

"Mmm?"

"What are you doing?"

"Looking for your star."

"My star?"

"Yeah. I . . ." He patted himself down, looking for something. He found it in his left pants pocket, a folded-up piece of bond paper. "Here. Sorry, I meant to wrap this, but the day got away from me."

I took the slightly damp paper and unfolded it. It was a certificate attesting to the fact that some distant star in the universe was now named after me. Lily's star was up there somewhere, apparently, though it wasn't bright enough to be seen in New York.

"You had a star named after me?"

He gave me a soft grin. His eyes were not quite focusing. He looked so harmless, standing there. Not like a bomb that had gone off in my life, and yet he was.

"I'd name them all after you if I could."

I started to laugh. A giggle at first, like we'd done at dinner, and then a full belly laugh, one that would hurt the next day if I kept at it too long.

"What's so funny?"

I shook my head and kept laughing; I couldn't control myself.

"Are you . . . Lily? What's going on?"

I wasn't making any sound anymore, but my body was shaking and tears were streaming down my face. I felt frantic, as if hysteria was setting in, but I didn't know how to stop it.

"Lily, you're kind of freaking me out."

I looked at him through my tears, and all I could think was that my husband, the man I thought was my partner in life, had paid fifty dollars for a bullshit certificate naming some star we couldn't even see after me while he was letting someone else . . . While he was touching someone else . . . While he was . . .

I punched him in the arm.

"What the hell?"

I hit him again.

I was still laughing, but I slugged him as hard as I could. Even though I was striking flesh, I felt the impact in my knuckles, my nails digging into my palms.

Tom recoiled, rubbing at his shoulder, getting out of harm's way.

"Lily, it's not—"

"Is everything okay here, folks?"

It was a beat cop. The buttons on his jacket sparkled under the street lamp.

"It's fine . . . We had a little too much to drink," Tom said. "My wife was teasing me."

The cop spoke directly to me. His eyes were almost black, from what I could see of them under the peak of his cap, but they seemed kind.

"Are you okay, ma'am?"

I caught my breath and forced myself to speak. "I'm fine. It's our anniversary. Twenty-two years! Since our first date, anyway. Only twenty married. Twenty."

The police officer looked from me to Tom. Tom was rubbing the spot where I'd hit him. I could feel the half-moon crescents I'd made in my palm.

"Violence isn't the answer, ma'am."

"We were only horsing around. Look," I said, retrieving the

certificate from the ground where I'd dropped it. "My husband named a star after me."

The officer took the paper. "I see."

"Do you?"

We locked eyes, and for a second, I felt like he got it. As if with everything he must see day in and day out, all the worst of humanity but sometimes the best, too, he could figure out what was going on. Not the details, maybe, though how hard were those to guess? Infidelity is pervasive. It's commonplace.

"Will you be okay?"

"I'll be fine."

"Yes," Tom said. "We'll be fine."

The police officer handed me back the paper. "You'll want to keep this safe." He turned to Tom. "And you should head home."

"Yes, of course. Thank you for your concern."

The officer tipped his cap to me and resumed his beat. We watched him go, the night full of all the things we were going to have to talk about now that it was out in the open.

Tom reached out his hand. I took it reflexively, like I'd done everything that night. Impulses. History.

After everything, my instinct was still to trust my husband, to take his hand, and to face the night together.

I was back to being late, which wasn't the best way to start a new job.

I'd been planning to go back to work for a while. Having spent my entire adulthood at the yoke of a restaurant, when Knife & Fork closed and our deal to buy it ourselves fell through, I found myself floating, aloft like a bud of pollen in the spring. I'd never had any other profession in mind, but it still felt too new, too raw, to start somewhere else, to learn a different menu and kitchen and staff and regulars.

The story Tom and I told each other was that I was taking a moment to figure out the next chapter. But really, I was sleeping, literally and figuratively, restoring the bank of energy I'd expended over the previous fifteen years. I'd tumble to bed minutes after the kids went up, only to be woken by the annoying Top 40 hits my clock radio blared nine hours later. In the afternoon, I'd often sneak away for a nap, though I was never sure what, or who, I was sneaking away from. The paintings on the walls? The judgmental flowers I clipped from the garden?

As our financial situation tightened, Tom encouraged me to put out some feelers. See what was out there, get back in the game, every cliché you can think of. I did, but my heart wasn't in it. I'd show up for an interview and blow it. Sometimes I didn't even go. Time and again I came away without the gig I should've had in an instant.

Then the texts happened. Then New York. The fallout from that robbed any energy I'd restored.

Then the world exploded.

But after a year of funerals and fund-raisers, I need a change, more, something of my own. When I saw the ad for a day manager at a newer restaurant on Noyes, I e-mailed my CV without taking too much time to think about it. I put on my game face for the interview, and if the owners knew who I was, they didn't let on. I got the job, and we set up a day for me to start.

Today.

"Cecily, hi," Kim says as I walk into the back office of Prato, which means "plate" in Portuguese. "So glad you could make it."

"I'm glad to be here. Sorry I'm a bit late. It won't happen again."

Kim leans back in her desk chair and stretches her arms above her head. About my age, Kim opened the restaurant two years ago. Her hands are callused and scarred like all chefs'. She's got a stack of orders in front of her, the day to day of the restaurant. Most of the restaurant has been given over to customers or the kitchen, but she's squared off a small space of her own.

"It's been a weird twenty-four hours," I add, wondering how much she knows about me or if she cares.

"You could start tomorrow, if you'd like."

"No. Please. I need the distraction."

Kim stands. She's tall and angular, her hair cut almost boy short.

"Great. So why don't we meet with the chef and go over the menu for the day?"

"That sounds perfect."

I work through lunch and the early dinner sittings without a break other than to answer my mother's anxious texts wanting to know how my first day is going. The deal I made with Kim is that I'll switch out with the night manager at six. The kids are older now, and they can handle themselves until I get home. Maybe dinner will even be on the table.

Hope springs eternal.

I like being in the restaurant, interacting with the staff, watching Kim in the kitchen, moving efficiently among the stations, hurrying everyone along gently, rhythmically, to get the plates out on time. The menu is a mix of Portuguese and Spanish—lots of grilled meat and flavorful paellas, and there are blue-and-gold ceramic plates on the walls. The air is spiced with saffron and lemon and garlic, and the grilled Portuguese chicken salad I had for lunch was fantastic. It feels good to be in the thick of things, to be interacting with strangers who have no expectations of me other than that I'll seat them at a good table and be attentive to their needs. If I get one or two odd glances, I ignore them.

Franny comes in with Joshua and the kids right as I'm finishing my shift.

"Is this where you're working now?" Franny asks. She's wearing a shift dress that suits her square frame, showing off the slimmer parts of her. She's also taken care with her makeup and hair. She looks poised, polished, secure. "I never made the connection."

"It's my first day."

"Hey, Cessy," Joshua says. He's wearing a suit, but he's taken off his tie. Not my type, Joshua, but forty-five looks good on him.

"Aunt Cecily!" the girls cry in unison, running around the podium I'm standing at to hug either side of me.

"We haven't seen you in forever!" Emily says reproachfully. The girls are wearing matching dresses I don't recognize. More appropriate for summer than fall, especially given the temperature outside.

"I'm so sorry, my darlings—things have been busy. But I'm very glad to see you now."

I give them each a close hug. Julia's is a little longer, since she's always needed the most affection. I miss when my own kids were this size. When I could hug them as long as I wanted without an eye roll.

When I stand up, Joshua and Franny are smiling at us. Joshua's gotten a haircut since the last time I saw him. His hair is thinning out on top, and I can see through to his skull. He looks relaxed, though, which he hasn't in a long time. In truth, Kaitlyn and Joshua were one of those couples I never quite got. Not because they fought or disliked each other but because they never seemed to have anything in common other than their kids. Though who am I to judge? Tom and I were the couple everyone always said was perfect for each other, and look what happened to us.

"I'm so happy for you!" Franny untucks her arm from Joshua's and gives me a hard hug. "Teo," she whispers in my ear, then giggles. I'm struck, as I've been the last couple times I've been near her, with how closely she smells like Kaitlyn. Maybe it's just that she's living in Kaitlyn's house now, using the same soap or shampoo, surrounded by Kaitlyn's things.

"What are you guys doing here?" I ask.

"We're celebrating."

"What?"

Franny laughs. "I guess you didn't hear with everything going on today . . . but the Supra Board decided to confirm our decision. Josh and the girls are getting their compensation."

"Oh, that's fantastic! I'm so happy to hear that."

I reach out and take Joshua's hand, giving it a squeeze. It makes sense that he's relaxed now. He wasn't desperate for money, like I was, but a future with one income and two girls was something that was wearing on him. Joshua's a planner—another divergence with Kaitlyn—and his spreadsheets weren't balancing.

"Do you have a reservation?" I ask.

"We do."

I check the computer, and there it is, a reservation for four for the Rings. I check them off and grab some menus.

"Do you have time to join us?" Joshua asks. "For a drink?"

"Let me call the kids and deal with a few things here. I'll be with you in a few minutes."

I seat them at their table and fill in the night manager on the transition issues. Then I call the kids to make sure they're home for the night. Henry answers and tells me that Cassie "has a boy over." I ask him to pass the phone to her.

"A boy?"

"It's just Kevin."

"Just Kevin the boy you had dinner with last night?"

"Yeah."

"You made up?"

"I guess?"

"He can't go into your bedroom."

"Mom!"

"I'm serious, Cass, or I'll call Grandma and have her chaperone you."

"You wouldn't!"

"Don't test me. Downstairs only, and you know Henry will rat you out. I'll be home in an hour."

"Okay, whatever."

I hang up and go to Joshua's table. I sat them at a six-top so there's plenty of room for me. The bottle of champagne I ordered arrives a moment later.

"What's this?" Joshua asks, smiling.

"It's on me."

Franny giggles again. The waiter pops the cork, an explosion that gets the attention of everyone around us. I make eye contact with one of the patrons who was eyeing me earlier. Seeing me sitting with Joshua, he's certain he knows who I am now. I turn pointedly away.

"Can we have some, Aunt Cecily?" Emily asks shyly.

"You can have the kids' version."

I signal for the waiter and order a bottle of nonalcoholic sparkling cider. When we all have our drinks, I propose a toast.

"To the Rings. My second-favorite family."

"Second?" Emily asks.

"After my family, honey."

"Right! Cassie and Henry and Uncle—" She stops and looks at Franny. Franny pats her on the head. Emily looks pleased.

"It's okay," I say. "I forget sometimes, too."

"I'd like to propose a toast as well," Franny says. She has a serious look on her face now, as if she has an important task to do.

"Please, go ahead," Joshua says, looking at her fondly. She touches his forearm, quickly, then pulls her hand back.

"I wanted to propose a toast to Kaitlyn."

The girls look grave, but I put a big smile on my face and raise my glass high. "To Kaitlyn."

And because it's been that kind of day, month, year, that's when the flash goes off.

22

FIRST, KNOW THYSELF

KATE

Though it came later than expected, Kate had spent a year getting ready for Andrea's question.

"Interesting coincidence," she said, her heart beating so loudly her own voice sounded odd to her, like something aquatic, swallowed by waves. "She even looks a bit like me, don't you think?"

Kate pretended to study the iPad for a moment, looking at the picture of herself with Cecily from two years ago. She was heavier then, carrying pregnancy weight she hadn't lost. She'd still had twenty pounds of it in her face and around her middle when she met Andrea. But that was before life robbed her of her appetite and she ran around after two little boys all day. The thirty pounds she'd lost in the last year had made a world of difference. Sometimes, when she caught a glimpse of her face in a mirror, she almost didn't recognize herself. And her hair in the photo was that sun-kissed color she'd been dyeing it then, not the dark-brown shot with gray it was now.

She handed the iPad back to Andrea. "See?"

Andrea gave the picture a cursory glance. She'd already discounted the possibility that it could be Kate.

"You're much more attractive than this woman."

"Thank you. They say everyone has a twin out there somewhere."

"I've heard that." Andrea flicked her finger, and the next news story loaded. "I don't think that's true. I mean, I've never seen anyone who looks enough like me to confuse someone. Though this one time, in the grocery store, a woman came up to me and was convinced I was Trisha Smith. Can you believe it?"

Trisha was a Westmount mommy who lived one block over. Her hair was the exact same shade as Andrea's, as was her spray tan, and since they shared a trainer, their bodies had the same emaciated shape. Kate had mistaken them from a distance more than once.

"That's crazy."

"Right? It's like all mothers look alike or something."

"Right. Anyway, I should get that laundry on . . ."

Andrea had already lost focus, peering at her iPad with a squint because she refused to accept that she needed reading glasses. Kate went down to the basement, the location of the laundry room, and promptly threw up in the bathroom. Then she washed her face and put on a load of laundry in case Andrea thought to check.

Kate spent the rest of the day until the boys went to bed on autopilot. She'd spent the last year with her head in the sand. She needed to correct that.

When the boys were firmly asleep, she asked Andrea if she could borrow the spare iPad and went to the basement. Her new friends on IKWYDLS.com were right. It was time to explore more than TMZ. Time to see what the rest of the world had seen since she'd stopped watching a year ago.

Back then, after three days of nonstop coverage, Kate had worked up the courage to leave her depressing hotel room. She'd spent a week getting to know her new city. Listening to its sounds. Reviving the French she'd learned more than twenty years ago. She still thought of herself as Kaitlyn Ring then. A persona she tried to shed as she walked. Up to Mount Royal. Down to the Old Port and the Saint Lawrence River. Along the Lachine Canal for hours. Letting the cold October wind whip against her skin until it felt baby soft.

Montreal was full of churches. At the end of the week, she lit a candle for the dead in one of the cathedrals. And then another for her family. She thought of them every day. Not less as time went by but more. As she walked and slept and spent time alone, certain things became clear. Everything that had happened since the fog of her second bout of postpartum had lifted was a lie. She wasn't better. The things she clung to as evidence that she was were just the gasoline she was dousing herself in. Waiting for it to spark, catch fire, and consume her.

So when she was faced with an actual fire, when her life had actually blown up, she'd taken the opportunity to run as far and as fast as she could. Thinking this would save her, finally, and for good. But it hadn't. She was still who she was. The things that had dragged her down were still inside her. Everywhere she went, there she was. And now, added on to that was the pile of lies and deceit and regret. So much of it she was afraid she'd be dragged fully under this time.

She had to live with her choices or end it all. And even that she couldn't do because it would lead to her being identified. Which would be even worse for her children. To learn that she'd run away, and then taken her life anyway? No. She'd built this prison, and she had to live in it. She had to make the best of it. Because she had no one to blame but herself.

She upped her efforts to get a job, to find a better place to live, to start eating three square meals a day. A list that felt more and more desperate as her money dwindled and none of the jobs she applied for ever showed any interest. And then one did.

It was, of course, the job she'd applied for thinking she could never do it. That she'd never have to. Because she couldn't be a nanny to someone else's children after having run away from her own. She just couldn't. But she had less than $600 left and no prospects. This position offered everything on her list: housing, income, food.

She spent two hours agonizing, then booked the interview. Then she went to the corner store and bought two cheap bottles of red wine that still cost more than she'd spent in the last three days. She drank them down like medicine until she could barely remember her own name. When she'd woken, groggy, her tongue thick, she said her new name out loud: Kate Lynch.

It was the name she'd grown up with. The person she'd been before Joshua and motherhood and the slow erosion of herself. Kate Lynch had started out as a carefree girl. Someone who laughed. Never planned. Was often irresponsible. She'd met Joshua after those traits had gotten her into trouble. Trouble she decided she'd never tell him about because he seemed the right mix of stability and love. And if Kate wasn't broken inside, he would've been. She became

Kaitlyn Ring willingly, soberly. She'd move forward without looking back. When second chances came around, you grabbed them.

This last year, it was, at times, as if she wasn't Kaitlyn Ring anymore. As if she'd never been. But that had been a mistake. She should've surveilled her old life. She should've kept up with the news. Today, with Andrea, perhaps that wasn't a close call. But next time, with someone less self-absorbed, it could be. Hell, even the twins had recognized her. She hadn't actually changed beyond all recognition.

She typed a few key words into Google and started reading from the beginning, the oldest post she could find. A year's worth of stories about her old city, her family, her friends. Her fingers were so slick with sweat she had to wipe them to get the iPad to swipe to the next story. But she didn't look away. She read and read and read, every word she could find.

It was late. Time to sleep. But first she hit the "Reload" button one last time, and a new story appeared. Cecily had been photographed again, out at a restaurant with Joshua and the girls.

She clicked on the link. And that's when she saw her.

Franny Maycombe.

The Triple-Tenner You've Never Heard Of

by TED BORENSTEIN

Special to VANITY FAIR

Published on OCTOBER 29

I start off by reading everything I can about Franny Maycombe. There had been scattered articles here and there when she'd surfaced soon after the tragedy. Her mother, Kaitlyn Ring, worked at a software company that lost twenty-three employees, including its cofounder, Tom Grayson. Mr. Grayson was Cecily Grayson's husband, the woman whose photograph became one of the enduring images of the day.

"Cecily and Kaitlyn were great friends," a neighbor and mutual friend tells me. "Cecily doesn't get enough credit for what she's had to go through. Losing her husband and close friend on the same day. And then having to learn about Franny. A lot of people would crack under the pressure, but not Cecily."

Franny's appearance at Kaitlyn Ring's funeral was the first story about her in print. It ran in the local paper and managed to capture the attention of a neighborhood already in shock. It was a distraction, perhaps, something to gossip over rather than the complexities of grief. Some secrets were expected to come out with so many dead, so many gone, but not something like this.

"That whole funeral was a . . . That's probably not fit to print. Let's just say it was dramatic. Kaitlyn hadn't told anyone about Franny. Not even her husband, Joshua." She wipes a tear away. "But I don't blame Franny. She had no idea. Kaitlyn told her she'd told her family about her, and can you imagine? Meeting your mother and then losing her like that?"

Was she mad at Kaitlyn for keeping Franny a secret?

"Oh, no. A lot of people did that then . . . still do it, I expect. Give a baby up for adoption and don't tell anyone. She must've felt so ashamed and sad and . . . And though I'm sure she was thrilled to meet Franny again, how do you tell your husband or your children about something like that?"

Not all of Kaitlyn Ring's neighbors and friends are so forgiving. One woman, who agreed to talk to me only on the condition of anonymity, spoke with some venom at the shock wave Franny produced at the funeral.

"Can you imagine? There we all are, another funeral, a young mother, Joshua left alone with those two girls, and then this woman none of us has ever heard of tells us she's Kaitlyn's daughter? It's just so selfish. It was making the day all about her. Why did she need to be at the funeral? She must've known people would ask who she was."

Then this forty-five-year-old mother of three asks, "You know who Chris Pender is, right? The lead singer of The Penderasts? Charming name for a band. Anyway, his sister's married to one of our neighbors. And when her father-in-law died, he came to the funeral dressed in his rock-star costume. He didn't put on a suit. So the moment he walked in, everyone knew who he was and started taking pictures. It was so disrespectful. And that's what Franny reminded me of."

Perhaps Chris Pender didn't mean to be disrespectful? Perhaps it was nice of him to come to the funeral in the first place?

"Sure, but if he was just trying to make a nice gesture, take off the costume. Dress like a normal person. I know this is controversial. I know what I sound like when I say this, but Franny was enjoying the attention that day. I'm sure of it."

Couldn't Franny have sought out all kinds of media attention? And yet she hadn't.

"But you're writing about her, aren't you? I rest my case."

23

HOPES DASHED

CECILY

When I get home from the restaurant I find the kids sitting together on the couch, each engrossed in an iPad. Henry's playing a game, and Cassie's texting with someone, her fingers flying around the screen, a flash of emojis I couldn't understand if I wanted to peppering her abbreviations. I used to be better at keeping up with this kind of stuff, the music they listened to, the cultural references they made. A year ago, I probably could've deciphered Cassie's texts, or certainly guessed at their meaning. Now they're like the grad note I wrote in my high school yearbook. Indecipherable.

"Hey, guys."

Cassie flaps a hand at me, but Henry doesn't move a muscle.

"Screens down, please."

"Not another family meeting," Cassie says.

I sit down on the coffee table that faces them. "Nope, just family time. It's been a long day."

Maybe hearing something in my tone they're not used to, they each lower their screens.

"You okay, Mom?" Henry asks. His hair's getting a bit long, but when I asked him this morning if he wanted a haircut, he said no, he was thinking of growing it.

"I'll survive. Though I'm thinking we should probably rethink this whole World Wide Web thing."

"Paparazzi suck."

"They do. But I don't want to talk about that. I want to talk about you guys. Tell me about your days. Leave nothing out. Not even the subtext."

"What?"

"The currents and undertows, I want to hear them all."

Cassie frowns, but Henry complies, telling me a story of something that happened in history class and how the class smart aleck got the best of their young teacher. Cassie, who was in his class in his first year of teaching, and who I always suspected had a crush on him, comes to his defense, and Henry and Cassie are soon squabbling in the way only siblings can.

This might sound strange, but I like listening to them bicker. It's all so innocent, so *before*, that I half expect Tom to walk into the room and ask them to keep it down because he's trying to watch golf in his study. When he used to do that, they'd turn to abusing him, making fun of his golf-watching habits, and soon they'd be tossing a baseball around in the yard or pulling out the Monopoly board so we could have a "real family fight, I mean moment," as Cassie often said.

But that's not what happens. Instead, I hear my phone ding with a text, and I realize I haven't checked my messages since lunch when I'd told my mother, probably more forcefully than I should have, to stop texting me. I let Cassie and Henry finish their argument, then tell them they can go back to their screens. They look surprised, but that doesn't keep them from diving back in.

I retrieve my phone and open my texts. I disabled the function that floats a preview across my screen after Tom's texts. I never wanted to be taken by surprise again. The universe laughs at me, it does.

I have more than a hundred texts I haven't responded to. A cascade of WTF and *you go, girl!* from my friends and pseudofriends and anyone who has my cell number, apparently. But buried in there are two texts from someone I shouldn't have been ignoring today.

Teo.

Call me, he says. And so I do.

Given how we ended up, it's easy to think badly of Tom. To forget all his best characteristics, the things I loved about him. The things I vowed to remind the children of, no matter what happened. After he died, I'd even started keeping a list, one that time and bitterness could not erase.

He was funny, and he wasn't showy about it. He'd just come up with the perfect hilarious summary of the conversation you were having at the exact right moment. And he'd take the joke one step further, like the best comedians, mining an ordinary situation for comedy gold.

He was generous, and again, he wasn't showy about it. I thought I knew about most of his charitable work, but after he died, I received notes from people I'd never met who told me how Tom had come through for their organization, or even them personally, right when they needed it. Even as my restaurant folly sunk us into debt, he still found the money to help pay the heating bill of an old friend long out of work so he could stay another cold winter in a house he couldn't afford but could not give up.

He didn't blame others for his faults, his mistakes . . .

I had to leave off there because, no matter what, I didn't want my children to know what their father also was. A liar, a cheater, a man who took his pleasure where he could find it rather than delay his own gratification. Not that I knew for certain that there had been others, but of course there could be. I didn't ask when I had the chance, so I'm left to wonder. How many? When? And who was she, goddammit, who?

He didn't deny it, though, when I finally confronted him in that New York hotel room, both of us still too drunk to have the conversation. He didn't deny it, and he didn't blame me, didn't make excuses or bring up our dwindling sex life or do anything but apologize abjectly. He'd "fucked up," and he was ashamed and mortified I had to find out at all, and especially that way. His hope had been that I thought it was a joke.

"A joke?"

He stepped toward where I was sitting on the edge of the bed and tried to take my hand.

"Don't touch me."

"I'm sorry. I'm so, so sorry."

"Why?"

"There's no excuse. No explanation."

"There has to be."

"Come on, Lil. Do you want to get into this? I made a terrible mistake, one I've regretted from the beginning."

"The beginning? That means there was a middle. How long—? No, stop. I don't want to know."

"It wasn't as bad as you think . . . Nothing actually happened."

"You expect me to believe that?"

"Maybe if you let me tell you—"

"No, shut up. I don't want to hear it. I don't. How could you?"

His chin trembled, and this made me angrier. How dare *he* cry at his mistake?

"I wish I could take it back," he said.

"Then why didn't you stop? Why did it happen in the first place?"

"It was . . . The only thing I can say is that it felt like an addiction. And I don't mean that as an excuse. It just felt like I couldn't stop. Not even when I wanted to."

"Do you love her?"

"No."

"How can you be so certain?"

"I don't expect you to believe me, but . . . no. No, I don't love her. I'm not in love with her."

"You're right."

"I am?"

"I don't believe you."

Round and round and round we went until I crawled into the soft sheets and told him I needed to sleep. Even though I knew I wouldn't, I needed that day to end.

He didn't try to press me; he just took a blanket from the closet and a pillow from the bed and set himself up on the floor.

It was a pitiful sight, and something about that, that I couldn't stand to have him near me even when I most needed comfort, broke my heart for good. I stuffed the end of the pillow in my mouth so he didn't hear my sobbing, but the bed shook around me. Tom rose and climbed into bed, wrapping his arms around me, and I let him. I needed comforting, and the only person there to do it was the source of my distress. I hated him for that, too, but it worked after a while.

"Lil?" he asked when I finally spat the soaked pillow from my mouth.

"Yes?"

"Have I fucked up our family for good?"

I pushed him from me and fled our room, those words chasing me, finally, away, because somehow, I hadn't factored the children into it yet, what this could mean for them. I felt the selfishness of that, and then reasoned it away. I was in shock, I told myself, blameless. But he'd forced the thought on me, like his texts, and now all I could think of, as I stood shaking at the end of the hall, was our children and our home and our life, and how I didn't want anything to end. How it would've been so much easier for me to remain in ignorance.

How could he have done this? How could he be so careless with our life, our children, our future, our family?

Why couldn't he have died instead?

In the end, the easiest thing was for Teo to come to me. I asked him to wait until the kids were in bed, till after lights-out, and to come through the backyard, climbing over the neighbor's fence, because there's a man sitting in his car across the street, the firefly wink of his cigarette giving him away. I can't tell if it's the same man from this morning or even if he's there for me, but I don't feel like taking any more chances.

Teo's punctual, his hand rapping on the patio door seconds before I start to listen for him. He's got a dark fleece on, zipped up to his chin. The cold night air follows him in.

"I feel like a criminal," he says, his white teeth flashing in the dimmed light.

"I feel like a zoo animal." I indicate the bottle of red wine sitting on the counter. "You want?"

"Sure."

I pour him some, listening to it glug into the stemless glasses I used to think it was so important to have. I'm nervous, and my hands are unsteady.

"Should we sit?"

He nods, and we go to the couches in the family room. I'm suddenly conscious of all the things I have, how this room is full of them. This couch, so comfortable and soft and six months sought after. The TV, large and flat and wall mounted. All the money in this room, all the things we wasted it on because we could, and even when we couldn't. And this lie I carry around, all the little lies it's spawned, it's because of the money, too.

"How are you?" Teo asks.

"I feel strange, to be honest."

"Strange?"

"Like I'm outside of myself. Like this one time in college when I took acid by accident and I thought I was floating around the room. Which is probably saying too much, as usual."

"It's fine. I wish you wouldn't worry about that."

"But it's not fine. I'm so sorry I didn't call you today or text. I should've checked in."

He takes a sip of his wine and puts the glass on the table.

"You already apologized."

"I know, but not face-to-face. A text. A text doesn't mean anything. Ha! You see, I don't mean that at all. A text can mean everything."

Teo puts a hand on my arm. I cover it with my own. His fingers are still cold from outside.

"You must think I'm nuts."

"It's been an odd day."

"Yes, very odd. Indeed. Good grief, we sound like characters in a Jane Austen novel."

He smiles. "No one's ever accused me of that before."

"I meant so stiff and formal and thinking things all the while . . ."

"You're going to have to help me out here."

"I would if I could."

I burst into tears. Teo's grip tightens.

"Don't," I say. "Don't worry, I'll be all right in a second."

I turn away from him, lifting my shirt up to wipe the tears away. What must he think of me? What am I thinking of myself?

"Perhaps a drink?"

"Yes. That might help."

He hands me my wineglass, and I take a large gulp. A sort of calm spreads through me, which must be a placebo effect—no wine could work this quickly—but I'll take it.

"I think I can control myself now." I give Teo a tentative smile. "Thank God you don't have your camera with you."

He frowns.

"Or, oh . . . Did you wish you were filming me falling apart? The ice queen cracks at last?"

"Of course not. It's . . . Why don't you tell me everything that's happened first."

I don't like the sound of the word "first," but I fill him in on the almost break-in, the guy across the road, my day at work, the Supra Board's decision, and the reappearance of the camera at drinks with Franny and Joshua. I speak quickly, but the note of crazy has left my voice. Teo listens, asks a few questions, sips his wine. I meet his eyes tentatively, trying to prolong I'm not sure what.

"So, in all the confusion, it didn't occur to me to call you. Which sounds like I forgot about you . . . But I don't want you to think that. I had a nice time last night, despite everything."

"I did, too, but . . ."

"Yes?"

"I feel bad about saying this, especially given the day you've had, but I think . . . I think we can't see each other again. Not like that, anyway. Not as more than friends."

There are two bright spots of color on his cheeks, as if he's embarrassed to be adding anything negative to my day. My own face feels hot.

"Why?"

"It's the film."

"The film?"

"It's wrong of me to get close to you. It hurts my objectivity." He looks at the floor. "I feel terrible. But . . . right now, no one knows who was in that picture with you, but if it came out . . ."

"The Initiative might cut your funding?"

"Maybe. I don't know. But that's not the point. It was . . . wrong of me to take advantage of you like that."

"I don't think you were."

"What I do, it makes people vulnerable. It creates a false intimacy. Kind of like therapy."

"Teo, what are you talking about? Where's this coming from?"

"I know it seems sudden. I know I was the one who suggested we go out."

"Yes, you did. But that doesn't mean you took advantage of me. If you're not interested, you can say so."

"I promise you that's not it."

"I'd almost rather it was," I say. "It's better than being passed over for the sake of a stupid documentary."

He grimaces. I've hurt him, but it feels justified.

"I'm sorry," he says.

"We seem to have spent a lot of time apologizing to each other today."

I pick up my wine and drain the rest of it. At this point, there's only one day that rivals this for awfulness, and that involved Teo, too.

"I hope this doesn't mean that you'll—"

"Pull out of the film? Honestly, Teo?"

He looks ashamed. "I should go."

"I—"

My front doorbell rings insistently.

"Mom?" Henry's voice calls down the stairs. "I think the police are here."

"What?"

I drop my glass as I stand. It bumps against the thick carpet. As

I pass through the hall to the front of the house, I can see the police lights rotating blue and red through the front windows.

I open the door. Two uniformed officers are standing there, looks of concern on their faces.

"Mrs. Grayson?"

"Yes?"

"We've had a report that there might be an intruder in your house."

"What? Who—?"

"On the ground. On the ground, now!"

24

A PICTURE WORTH A
THOUSAND WORDS

KATE

The next day, the twins woke from their nap the way they always did. Singing. Kate thought she was hearing things the first time one of their voices cracked through the baby monitor. "She'll Be Coming 'Round the Mountain" it was that time, perfectly on key with the words half pronounced. How had Andrea kept this from her? When she'd brought it up, Andrea had smiled and said she always left it as a surprise, because wasn't it "lovely"?

It was lovely. These two little boys who could sing One Direction songs in perfect harmony. That day, it was "Story of My Life," an apt choice if ever there was one. Kate got to their room as they were breaking into the chorus, standing up in their beds, swinging their hips.

"Sing, Aunt Kwait!"

Kate sang the rest of the song with them, but she still couldn't get the picture of her family out of her mind. She'd barely slept after she'd seen it. Something about it was getting to her in a way she couldn't explain. Franny was a part of it. That was for sure. The fact that she was sitting at a table with Joshua and the girls. How her hand was draped over Josh's arm as if it belonged there . . .

Why did she suddenly care? She'd left. Left all of them behind without so much as a backward glance. That was the truth. She'd run away from them to end up looking after someone else's children. To live on the fringes of someone else's life.

"What next?" Steven asked. "What song next?"

"How about . . . 'Little Things'?"

"I. Won't. Let. These. Little. Things . . ."

Willie swung his hips. "Slip out. Of my mouth . . ."

If she was done with that life, if she'd actually moved on, then she shouldn't care that Josh looked happy in the photo. That the camera had caught him with a soft expression on his face. An indulgent look, which Kate knew too well. She shouldn't care that Cecily appeared ferocious, as if she were protecting one of her own children. And she shouldn't care about Franny Maycombe. Certainly not about her, most of all.

"Kate? Where are you?"

Kate could've sworn that she actually saw Willie roll his eyes as Steven called, "Up here, Mommy. Having a dance party!"

Willie launched himself at Kate, landing half on her back and half on her head. And so went the next five hours. Being the boys' personal jungle gym, while she did her best to wipe that picture from her mind.

Kate didn't sleep that night. Instead, she watched a spider crawl across her ceiling. She counted a thousand sheep. She repeated all the reasons she'd left Chicago. She tallied up all the hurt she'd cause if she went back.

When her alarm pushed her from bed, she wasn't any closer to an answer. She'd made one fateful decision. One. But it seemed undoable. It seemed permanent.

Later, she was sitting at the kitchen table with the iPad when Steven padded in.

"Aunt Kwait!"

"What's up, muffin?"

He held his hands up over his head. Kate reached down and brought him onto her lap.

"You have an iPad."

"Mommy said I could use it."

"It's not iPad time."

"There are different rules for grown-ups."

Steven cocked his head to the side. "That not fair."

"Nope."

"You are funny, Aunt Kwait."

Kate put her face into his hair. How she loved that little-boy smell. These little boys.

"Those girls look sad," Steven said.

She'd been staring at the picture again. Franny with Josh and the girls. JJ and Em. Her special names for them. She wondered if anyone called them that anymore. She'd been so fixated on the adults that she hadn't spent as much time looking at them. Not in

the way she should've. She could see it now. JJ wasn't looking right
at the camera. Her eyes were cast sideways. And though it was hard
to tell, it seemed as if she was looking at Franny's fingers, gripping
Josh's arm. Her lip seemed to be quivering. There was a slight blur
to the photo on the lower part of her face.

"Maybe they're sad."

"I don't like being sad."

"Me, neither."

Steven looked at her, and then back at the iPad. "That other girl
looks like you."

His fat finger pointed at Em. No one ever said that she and
Emily looked alike, but that was back then. When her hair was a
different color and her face had a different shape. Now there was a
resemblance. It was like looking at a memory of herself as a child.

"She kind of does."

"Are you a mommy, Aunt Kwait?"

And that was the question, wasn't it?

The real question she'd been asking herself this whole time.

INTERVIEW TRANSCRIPT

TJ: Why would you say that, Franny? That this documentary isn't about your family?

FM: Because it's supposed to be about . . . You said it was about three families and how the compensation process affected them. Three families a year after October tenth.

TJ: That's right.

FM: So who's the third family? I mean, you've got the Graysons and the Rings, but who else are you talking to besides me?

TJ: That's it.

FM: I'm not part of a family?

TJ: I didn't say that. Of course you are.

FM: And that's why you keep asking me questions about my adopted family?

TJ: That's part of it, yes. It's also to get a better sense of who you are as a person.

FM: I don't want to talk about them.

TJ: I understand that, Franny, but I've explained to you how this works. We shoot several long interviews, and then the narrative will be shaped from that. We're asking these questions about all the participants.

FM: They're not my family.

TJ: I'm sorry you feel that way.

FM: I have a new family now.

TJ: Did you want to elaborate on that?

FM: Elaborate?

TJ: Expand. Tell me more about it.

FM: No, I don't think so. You'll see.

TJ: What am I going to see?

FM: Now that would be ruining the surprise, wouldn't it?

25

WHERE DOES THE TIME GO?

CECILY

Two years ago, there was a story floating around our neighborhood. A man—a *black man* or a *brown man*, some people would say, lowering their voices—was walking around at night, peering into windows. Someone's dog had kept him from entering a house, went one story. Two teenage lovers had scared him away another time. Other rumors had less detail, but the point was always the same—something had to be done about this before something bad happened. The police were called and the cameras were checked and nothing could be found. There were no fingerprints on the windowsill the dog had supposedly defended. No footprints beneath the window where the man had supposedly been seen.

"A ghost," Tom called him (if it was a him). "Our very own Halloween ghost."

"But Halloween's not for forever," Henry said.

"And Halloween is for losers," Cassie said.

"I've always loved Halloween," I said.

Cassie rolled her eyes, and Henry, who was on the cusp of maybe not trick-or-treating though I knew he wanted to, gave me a smile, and Tom shook his head at all of us.

"You're not scared?"

"Tom!"

"It's nothing, Lil. A bunch of overhyped, hysterical people who think too much."

"Are you speaking of me?"

"Of course not." He winked at me. "You know what they're like, that playground crowd. One black guy takes a walk and . . ."

"Tom."

"You know it's true."

"What's true, Dad? Are you talking about racists? We learned all about that during Black History Month."

Henry started hopping on one foot and patting the top of his head at the same time—a coordination exercise his baseball coach had introduced him to that he continued doing after the season was over because it drove Cassie nuts.

"Dad! He's doing it again."

"Henry, you know that makes your sister crazy."

Henry stopped jumping.

"So, is that what it is, Dad? Racism?" Henry was speaking as if he were in a museum. Like he was looking at a diorama meant to explain what it was. A kid in a hoodie, a man stopped for "driving while black," another senseless police shooting.

"Yes, son. That's exactly what it is."

"Why are people racist?"

"People are afraid," I said. "If something's different or they haven't experienced it before."

"But everyone's different," Henry said. "I'm different."

Tom and I smiled at each other. Our little blond boy who had every advantage in life was special and different, and how could we tell him otherwise? Once when he was seven, we tried to explain to him why the autistic boy in his class couldn't help it when he said "hi" twenty times a day. "Some people are different," I said. "I'm different," Henry responded. "Some people are special," Tom tried. "I'm special," Henry said emphatically.

"Everyone's different, and no one's better than anyone else," Tom said. "Some people are luckier, and some people have bad luck, and some people work hard and get things, and some people work very hard and don't get things. We're all entitled to the same respect."

Tom wasn't usually one to give speeches or lessons, but this was something he'd always felt passionate about. I was proud of him that day, knowing, as I looked at our children, that the force of his conviction would erase any doubts they might have in their minds, any hate they might have in their hearts.

Was he fucking her then? Was that moment false, too? Is it possible to be both a terrific father and a terrible man at the same time?

A man to admire and a man to hate?

• • •

I'm thinking of Tom now as the cops charge past me and shove Teo to the ground. Tom would know what to do. Tom would take charge.

Of course, if Tom were here, this wouldn't be happening in the first place.

"What the hell is going on?" I ask.

"Ma'am, step back, ma'am."

"This is my friend. This is my friend Teo."

"You know this man?" There are two cops in my house now, both white men in their midtwenties, stiff-necked. I can smell the scent of fear coming off the one closest to me, who looks too young to have this much responsibility. His gun's in his holster, but his hand is resting above it, twitching.

"Of course I do. Let him up. What the hell are you doing?"

The other cop has his knee in Teo's back.

"Shut that door!"

I reflexively kick it closed with my foot, nicking the side of it on the frame. My skin splits, and I can feel the blood start to flow.

"What's going on?"

It's Henry, eyes round and hair wild, standing in the stairwell.

"Get upstairs, Henry. Right now. Go to your sister's room, and close the door until I tell you it's okay. Now! Go now."

He turns and scampers up the stairs.

"Let him up. Why are you sitting on him like that? Teo, are you okay?"

"I'm okay," Teo says, his voice muffled.

"Get off him. Right this minute."

I'm using the same tone I used with Henry, my voice of authority, when I've had enough and they know I mean business. This twentysomething kid who hasn't been on the job that long responds to it like I'm his mother. He looks up with a guilty expression on his face and lets the pressure off Teo's back.

"Ma'am . . ."

"I mean it. I don't know why this is happening, but this needs to stop right now. Get up. Get up!"

The officer gets up. I race to Teo, my tears falling onto the back of his sweater. I help him turn over. There's a bruise forming under his right eye.

"Are you okay?"

"It's fine, Cecily. Just leave it, all right?"

He pushes my hand away.

"Let me at least get some ice."

Teo stands up slowly. The police officers back away, looking a bit confused, even though they're the cause of this scene.

"How did this happen?" Teo asks one of the officers. "What are you doing here?"

"We got a call from one of Mrs. Grayson's neighbors about a break-in."

"And you saw him in my house and assumed—"

"Please let me handle this."

I take a step back. I've done enough.

"I'm going to go check on my kids," I say. "I'll be right back."

I turn to the stairs. My feet feel like weights, exhaustion overcoming me. I learned a while ago that when you woke up in the morning, there was no accounting for how long the day would take, because not all days are created equal. The day I got Tom's texts, that day started out normally but then slowed down until it took up the space of a week. October tenth took no time to pass in comparison. Both changed my life irrevocably, and it feels like today will, too.

26

LIFE IN REVERSE

KATE

Growing up, Kate's father had an irrational hatred for the Kennedys. That's what her mother always called it, "Your father's irrational hatred." Kate never understood what it was that drove his ire, but it had the opposite effect than intended. Kate was secretly obsessed with Jackie Kennedy, Jackie O. She kept a scrapbook of images of her between her mattress and the box spring. Read the books she edited. Took the French option at school. When she was seventeen, she entered a contest run by *Vogue* to spend a year in their Paris office as an intern. Feeling petulant, Kate wrote her essay about her father. How his anger had taught her to look again. To look more closely. To see the flaws and the good parts, too. What it must've been like to be Jackie, starting out in the world. Full of ambition. Full of limits.

Kate sent off her manila envelope with no hope of winning anything. But she did win. She convinced her parents to let her postpone her entrance to college. She waved goodbye to them at the airport and landed a bad night's sleep later in the early morning of Paris.

How free she felt. How naive she'd been.

"What's that doggie, Aunt Kwait?" Willie asked as he climbed onto Kate's lap on the morning of October twenty-ninth. A few small flakes were floating down outside. The forecast was calling for a couple inches.

"It's a greyhound."

"Is that a real doggie?" Willie pointed to the image of a dog that scampered across his fleecy pajamas. "Like this one?"

"Well, not that one. That's a drawing. But yes, there are real greyhounds. Here, look." Kate opened a new browser window and Googled "images of greyhounds." "See?"

"That's a big doggie."

"It is. Sometimes they race them."

"Like horses?"

"No, not exactly. No one rides the dogs."

"I like riding doggies."

"Whose dog have you ridden?"

"Stu."

"Who's Stu?"

"He lives across the street! You know."

The door from the garage opened and closed.

"Mommy, Mommy, guess what?"

"What's up, Willie?"

"Aunt Kwait is going to ride a greyhound!"

"She is! That sounds fun."

Kate quickly closed the browsers and shut the iPad. There was no need for Andrea to see that she was looking up bus rides to Chicago.

"I think he misunderstood, didn't you, muffin?" Kate ruffled Willie's hair and put him down on the floor. "Aunt Kate is much too big to ride a greyhound."

"Clearly," Andrea said. She was sucking on a straw that was stuck into a plastic cup full of green goo. She turned on the TV. More all news, all the time.

"Did you see this?" she asked, nodding to the screen, which was reporting on a story that *Vogue* had broken. "What a crazy story."

Kate looked away. It was all anyone was talking about online that morning. The news wasn't going to tell her anything she didn't already know. It was the reason she was looking at Greyhound trips. Figuring out the logistics. Counting up her money and preparing herself to say goodbye to the only two people she cared about in this new life.

What she hadn't figured out yet was what she was going to do once she got there.

Was there a way for Kate to convince anyone that what she'd done was forgivable? Was there a cover story that could make her acceptable in her old life?

What would convince you?

If she told you Joshua was abusive? That it had started six months into their relationship. Just words, in the beginning. He didn't like her going out. He didn't like it when he didn't know where she was or who she was with. That it felt romantic at first. Then something she pushed against until, one day, he pushed back. But they were already engaged by then, everyone had been told, and the thought of telling them that he'd . . . What? Gotten a bit out of control during an argument, lost his temper after being provoked? Well, that happened. And he'd apologized so thoroughly that . . .

She'd tried that story out on IKnowWhatYouDidLastSummer .com. And while it had been satisfying to get anonymous encouragement for her decision, it was crap. Joshua wasn't abusive. He was cold sometimes. They didn't, in the end, see eye to eye on many things. A fundamental lack of compatibility that seemed exciting when she was twenty-four but wasn't good in the long run. And he hadn't understood what the postpartum depression was or the more general depression she'd had before that. How it alienated her from her children. How she never felt about them as she should've. But he was a good man. A good father. That most of all. Why else would she have left her children with him? Who else could she trust?

The truth was that there wasn't any reason Kate could offer up that could explain her behavior to anyone, even herself. Make it acceptable, wipe away what she'd done. And what was the point of trying anyway? If she went back, it wasn't going to be for her. It was going to be for the girls, for Joshua. She had to leave herself out of the equation.

But why was she even thinking about going back?

That had everything to do with Franny Maycombe.

The Triple-Tenner You've Never Heard Of

by TED BORENSTEIN

Special to VANITY FAIR

Published on OCTOBER 29

I finally caught up with Franny. She was elusive at first, reluctant to go on the record. She'd caused enough trouble, she said, she wasn't the story, and besides, she'd signed an agreement with the producers of a documentary, giving them exclusivity. But that movie wasn't going to be out for at least a year, and I could sense that she had some hesitation about the project. She'd talk to me on background, but I couldn't get her to commit. This happens sometimes in long-form journalism. You can spend a lot of time mining a story that doesn't work out. You have to learn to roll with the punches. Besides, perhaps I'd written enough about Triple Ten, and it was time to move on.

Then Franny calls.

"I'm ready to do it," she says. "Go on the record."

She sounds breathless, as if she's run to the phone to catch the call, though she's the one who called me.

I ask her if she's sure. She is, she says. Then what changed her mind?

"Don't you want to talk to me?"

I assure her that I do but remind her about her contract.

"Don't worry about that," she says. "I just have one condition."

She tells me what it is, and we set up a time and place to meet.

We meet two days later at Joshua Ring's house. She answers the door in a tan skirt and crisp white blouse, something she describes as "interview clothing." She's bubbly, almost dancing on her toes. This is in contrast to our previous meetings, where her tone was more marked and cautious.

Joshua Ring is here, too, but Franny's in charge. She shows me around the house, a typical suburban living room, dining room, kitchen. As in the other Triple Ten houses I've been in, there are photographs of the lost on the mantel—Joshua's wife, Kaitlyn. And there's a picture of Franny there, too, taken with her half sisters, two cute girls under ten.

"We never took a picture together," Franny says as she pauses to gaze at the picture of Kaitlyn on her wedding day. "Me and . . . Kaitlyn. I'm not sure why."

"She didn't like having her picture taken," Joshua says. "I'm not surprised."

"I'm not a picture taker, either," Franny says, then breaks into a funny impersonation of a young woman taking a series of selfies. "So silly."

"Rather," Joshua says, smiling. He's a slightly formal man. I suspect he was baffled after his wife died, as so many of the newly single fathers in his situation were. In my experience, the women always seem sadder but more in control—a stereotype, I know, but a truth I've observed.

Franny touches his arm. "Shall we sit?"

We move to the couch in the living room. Franny waits for Joshua to take a seat, then sits next to him. Close enough that I note it. Is this what Franny wants me to see? That she's stepped into her mother's shoes? Then Franny leans away from Joshua, and I banish the thought. Franny does seem different, though, from our earlier conversations. As if she's grown up overnight.

We discuss many things. How Joshua learned about Franny, how he'd processed the news. How helpful it had been to have Franny around since then, helping with the girls, distracting the family from their grief. That a part of Kaitlyn lives on in her and how she fits into the family.

Franny speaks very little. When the girls come in to ask for snacks, she leaves to attend to their needs.

Joshua watches her walk out of the room. "She's great with them, don't you think?" I agree. "She's so natural. Almost as if . . ." He trails off. I try to prompt an answer. "Nothing, nothing. I'm a bit nervous today, is all."

What did he have to be nervous about?

"This interview, for one."

Franny comes back and sits closer to Joshua. She's licking something sticky from her fingers. She doesn't seem nervous. She seems, if I had to use a word to summarize her, triumphant.

She pats Joshua on the knee. "Did you want to tell him or should I?"

"That's a lady's prerogative, I think."

Franny turns to me as she takes Joshua's hand in hers.

"It's all a bit sudden, but . . . we're getting married."

27

NEW ROUTINE

CECILY

The days flip by after the incident with Teo and the police.

When I got back downstairs from making sure the kids were okay, Teo had gone. He responded to my text asking him if he was okay with a terse explanation that he had to go. *I'm sorry*, he said in a text he sent the next day to which I didn't respond, because what am I going to do? Go back to being friends? Pretend his rejection doesn't sting more than I'd like to admit? Besides, I don't know what to say, so it's easier to say nothing at all.

I settle into a routine at the restaurant. It's good to have something to distract me, to pull my focus from myself. I skip my next interview with Teo and cancel coffee with Franny. I keep my therapy appointment, but I'm flirting with cutting that off, too. Linda can tell I'm distracted and asks me if I'd like to take a break. We've been over all the same ground, so maybe it would be good for me to see if I can make it through a few weeks on my own? I ask her if this is some kind of tough love, pushing me out so I can find my own bottom and admit the help I need, but no. She's serious, and when I get out into the parking lot, I feel a weight lifting from my soul. I'm not saying I'll never go back, but Linda was right. I needed to move on from her and the rut I'd created in her office, the deep depression in her couch that wouldn't go away no matter how much fluffing we both did.

In the days that follow, I can feel myself cutting ties as if I'm taking an actual pair of scissors to them, *snip, snip, snip.* The only ones I keep are the children, and Sara, and my mom. These people used to be enough for me, and they ought to be enough for me now. And now it's October twenty-ninth, a few days before Halloween, and it all seems flat. I hated the attention, but something about it made me feel alive in a way I don't now. As if the attention was what made me real, and now that it's gone, I'm like the photograph that made me famous in the first place. Artificial. A picture of someone I used to know.

"Cecily?"

"Yes?"

It's one of the waiters, Carlos or Carlitos, I haven't quite learned his name yet, much to my shame. I didn't use to forget details like that.

"There's someone on the phone for you. They say it's an emergency."

"The kids?"

My fear pushes him back on his heels.

"I don't think so. It's a man. I think his name is Joshua?"

I grab the phone from him. "Joshua? What is it? The girls? Franny?"

"No, not . . . I can't do this on the phone. Can you come over?"

I know that most people have never understood my friendship with Franny. There's the almost twenty-year age gap and our very different backgrounds, to start, and our very different personalities added to it. My mother thinks I'm trying to fill in for Kaitlyn, to be another mother to her, but that's not it. My feelings toward Franny aren't maternal.

My friend Sara's theory is that I'm close to her because she's wounded.

"You can't pass a hurt person by. It was the same with Kaitlyn," she said once when we'd gone for a drink last summer.

"Is that a bad thing?"

"Of course not. But you give too much of yourself. You need to leave room for you."

But leaving room for me wasn't working, it was giving me too much time to think, to regret, to ruminate. And I did feel bad for Franny. What a terrible position to be in, to have something you've wanted so badly ripped away from you. To know you were a secret that couldn't be revealed even once the secret was out. If I felt lost in my manicured house surrounded by my healthy children and my mom and my friends, how must she be feeling? I wondered and wondered for weeks after Kaitlyn's funeral, and then I started looking.

It wasn't hard to find her. She was living in Chicago and had already connected with the survivor community, joining one of the support groups for people who'd lost parents on October tenth. The woman who ran the group told me where I could find her. She was working in a diner on the east side of Chicago. One of those leftover places from the fifties where the menus are caked with grease and the women look older than they should. All the customers were men.

I sat at a table in her section. Her uniform looked newer than the other waitresses', as if she'd just cracked it out of the clear plastic wrap it surely came in. Her hair was pulled back tightly from her face, stretching it slightly. She looked tired and uncomfortable. I knew the feeling.

"What can I get you?"

"Hi, Franny."

"Do I know you?"

I searched her face for some sign of Kaitlyn. "We met about a month ago at . . . Kaitlyn's funeral."

Her pencil remained poised above her pad of paper. "You're one of her friends."

"Yes."

"What do you want?"

"Just to talk."

"I'm on shift."

"Maybe you could ask for a few minutes off? Don't you get a break?"

She glanced over her shoulder at the counter. I could see the half hulk of a man through the order window.

"Give me a minute?"

"Sure."

She disappeared. I pulled out my phone to check it, half expecting, still, a text or e-mail from Tom. That gentle flow of daily contact we'd always had, now a constant itch. Cassie had forgotten her homework at school, but there wasn't anything I could do about that.

Franny returned and sat down.

"You sure you don't want anything?" she asked.

"I'm fine. I'm trying to cut back on coffee."

"How come?"

"Can't sleep."

Her eyes traveled to my wedding ring. "I'm sorry for your loss."

"Thank you. How are you holding up?"

"Me?"

She laid her hands flat on the table. Her nails were painted a bright, festive red.

"I'm doing all right."

"Are you okay for money?"

Her chin rose. "Why are you asking me that? You here to help me out?"

"No, I . . . This is hard for me, too, Franny."

"Is it?"

"I was very close with your mother. I miss her."

"But she didn't tell you about me, right?"

"No. I'm sorry."

Franny looked out the greasy window. Some version of "White Christmas" was playing on the sound system. I shuddered at the thought of Christmas morning with the kids without Tom.

"I don't need your help," Franny said. "I can take care of myself. I've been doing it my whole life, you know?"

"I don't know. But I'd like to."

"Really?"

"Why is that such a surprise?"

"I haven't had much luck with people. Friends."

I covered her hand with mine. It was surprisingly soft. "I'd like to help change that, if you'll let me."

"How can you change it?"

"What if we gave ourselves a fresh start? I'm sure we both could use it."

A corner of her mouth lifted. "That sounds good."

I reached out my hand. "I'm Cecily, and I'm so happy to meet you."

Franny shook, firmer this time than she'd been at the funeral. "Nice to meet you, Cecily. I'm Franny Maycombe."

When I arrive at Joshua's house, Emily opens the door in tears.

"Daddy's marrying Franny! I don't want a new mommy!"

"What? I . . ."

I reach for her, but she turns on her heel and runs into the house. She's up the stairs before I can even get a word out. Julia barrels into my legs. One of her braids is coming undone.

"Aunt Cecily, it's horrible."

I drop down so we're at the same level. "What's horrible? Where's your father?"

"Upstairs. And Franny. Franny is horrible."

I feel the same sense of shock I felt the day I got Tom's texts, as if I'd stopped experiencing reality and stepped into some kind of altered state. Franny and Joshua? It can't be true.

"What did Franny do, honey?"

Julia wipes at her nose. "She made Daddy love her. But Daddy's only supposed to love Mommy. Even if she's gone. That's what he said. He said he would always love Mommy."

"Of course he'll always love Mommy. But sometimes, grown-ups love more than one person and . . ."

I stop myself. What am I saying? This isn't my situation to explain. I don't even know what's going on.

"Where's Franny?"

"She left."

"Why?"

"She and Daddy had a fight."

I feel light-headed. Where is Joshua?

I take Julia's hand and lead her into the living room. I pull her onto my lap, missing, for a moment, those days when I could do that with Henry or Cassie.

"Can you tell me the story from the beginning? As much as you remember."

Julia plops her thumb into her mouth but speaks anyway. "Last night, Daddy and Franny said that Daddy loved Franny and they were getting married."

"Are you sure?"

She just looks at me, slow tears running down her cheeks.

"Okay," I say. "And then what happened?"

"Em was mad. Real mad."

"What about you?"

"I didn't see that coming."

I want to laugh. Julia's always said the damnedest things, a sponge who absorbs all the language around her and spits it out at the oddest moments.

"Me, neither, honey. But when did Franny leave?"

"That happened today."

"Why?"

She shrugs. "Daddy was saying maybe it was a mistake."

"Getting married?"

"Because of Em. Because she was so sad."

"And Franny was angry?"

"Yes, but also sad. I wouldn't like it if someone said he was going to marry me and then said nuh-uh, not going to happen."

Who had this child been listening to? "What happened next?"

She leans her head back. "They told us to go back to bed."

"Wait, were you spying on them?"

She pulled her thumb out. "We snuck out of bed, but then they noticed us."

"That was naughty."

"That's what Franny said."

My stomach tightens. "Did she?"

"Yes, but then Em started crying again, and she said she was sorry, and we were all crying together, even Daddy. Em said she was sorry and that she would get used to it. She wants Daddy to be happy."

"What happened next?"

"We went to bed, but this morning, Daddy was making breakfast, and then Franny showed him some papers, and he got so mad. I was scared."

I hug her to me. "I'm sorry, darling. You don't have to tell me any more if you don't want to."

"It's okay."

I kiss the top of her head. "Let me go find Daddy, all right? You stay here?"

"Can I play in the basement?"

"Of course you can."

I watch her scuttle off. I take out my phone and make a call.

"This is Franny, leave a message."

"Franny, I'm at Joshua's house. Where are you; what's going on?"

I end the call and text her.

Where are you?

I watch the screen, waiting for a bubble to form, to show me that she's writing back. I see it after a moment. Then it disappears. Reappears. Appears again. Then, finally, a text.

Have you spoken to Joshua? Franny writes.

Not yet.

Tell him I'm sorry, okay?

Sorry for what? I'm going to call you.

I don't want to talk right now. Just talk to Joshua. He'll explain everything.

Why didn't you tell me what was going on?

The bubble appears again, leaves, appears. But no text comes.

Franny?

I wait and wait, but there's nothing.

I tuck my phone away and walk up the stairs. I can hear Emily crying in her room. I should go to her, but I need to find Joshua, I need to understand what's going on. How could he be marrying *Franny*? She's so different from Kaitlyn, and her daughter, and too young, and what could they possibly have in common?

I stop at the top of the stairs. I feel winded, panic gripping at my chest.

I lean against the wall. It's been years since I've been upstairs in this house, but not much has changed. The same pictures, the same hamper full of children's clothes at the end of the hall. One of the bedrooms was an office, but I assume it's where Franny's been staying since she moved in. Or is she sleeping with Joshua now? How did I let that slip by without noticing? Not that it was my job to monitor this house, this family, but yet, it kind of is. It was.

"Joshua?"

"In here."

I open the door to his bedroom. The blinds are drawn, the bed in disarray. I get a sudden image of Franny sleeping between these sheets, occupying the place Kaitlyn used to. I feel sick to my stomach.

Joshua's sitting at his desk, his back to me, his face half illuminated by the glow of the computer screen.

"Joshua, what the hell? You scared me half to death, and then when I get here Emily and Julia are freaking out, and they told me you and Franny are getting married. Is that true?"

"Yes. At least it was. I don't know anymore. I don't know anything anymore."

Joshua's shoulders start to tremble. I step forward and put my hands on them. He's still wearing the shirt he slept in, wrinkled and soft, and his hair's matted down. The last time I saw Joshua like this was in the first days after October tenth.

"Joshua, I'm at a loss here; can you please tell me what's happening?"

"Was Tom having an affair?"

My stomach knots again. "Why are you asking me that?"

"Is it true? Was he?"

"Yes, but I don't . . ."

He turns his chair around. His skin is pale and mottled.

"I found some e-mails. Or, I should say, Franny did. She showed them to me."

"Franny? How does Franny know about Tom? Why are we even talking about this?"

"Did he tell you about the affair?"

"No, I . . . I found out by accident."

"And do you know who he was sleeping with?"

"He didn't say. And then . . . Oh, no, Joshua. Whatever it is you're thinking, it's not true. It's not possible."

"I'm afraid it is, Cecily. You can read it for yourself."

He turns and pulls the screen toward us. It's open to a Gmail account, Kaitlyn's Gmail account. Joshua stands and guides me gently so I'm sitting in the chair.

I don't want to look, I don't want to look, at the end of everything, I don't want to know this. But my eyes are not mine to command, and so I read.

And now I know.

28

WINDING A SPRING

KATE

Riding the bus back from Montreal to Chicago was like winding her life back onto the coil she thought she'd escaped from.

Saying goodbye to the twins had been hard. Kate didn't tell them she was leaving. But Willie sensed something was off and started crying when she tried to put him to bed. Kate felt the tears spring into her own eyes. But she pried Willie's arms from around her neck and laid him back down in his bed. She soothed him as best as she could until he drifted off to sleep.

Then she went downstairs and packed up her things. She wrote a final post on IKWYDLS.com as she waited for Andrea and Rick to get home from their event. *I'm going back to make things right,* she wrote. *Wish me luck.* There was a flurry of replies, mostly against her returning. Kate found their caution comforting. Going against the grain felt right to her. Even when the friction was created by the liars and cheaters who populated this website.

Andrea and Rick arrived home around eleven. Kate sat on the edge of her bed and listened to them moving around. When she was sure they'd gone upstairs, she slipped out the back door with everything she owned on her back. The last thing she did was remove the stack of cash she'd stashed in the basement ceiling. This time she left a note. Not an explanation but a goodbye. A thank-you.

At the bus station she moved with purpose. She was afraid; she wanted to bolt in some other direction, but she couldn't. She'd been so selfish. This was the only way she could think of fixing any of it.

A hazy day on the bus. Jolts and jumps and fractured sleep. She felt the beginnings of a migraine coming on. The fingers of it gripping at her brain, pushing at her optic nerve. She took some pills she'd lifted from Andrea's medicine cabinet, something she used for anxiety. That put her into another blurring space, one where she didn't have a real grip on time or her emotions. Every bad choice she'd made in her life seemed front and center.

She tensed up further at the border. Had the connection finally been made between her two selves? She needn't have worried. The border guard came onto the bus, no scanner in sight, and barely looked at her passport. Within minutes, they were on their way.

And then she was back in Chicago. It was Halloween, night coming on early. She saw children in costumes, adults holding their hands as she should be holding her daughters'. At the bus station, she changed her money for US dollars and hailed a cab. She directed it to Evanston. Even before the cab pulled off I-94, everything was familiar. The smells. The lights. The way the houses looked against the night. Orange pumpkins and costumed children lugging bags heavy with candy.

It was lovely. Perfect. Why hadn't this been enough?

She paid the cabbie and stood outside the house. The cold bit at her nose. But that wasn't why she was shaking.

There wasn't a pumpkin outside, but the lights were on. She could imagine the activity inside; she'd seen it often enough. All she had to do was walk up the front steps like children were doing all around her, ring the bell, and none of this could be taken back. She'd cause more havoc, more hurt, more pain. The alternative was impossible to weigh.

Her feet made the decision for her. Her hand rose and pushed the bell.

The front door opened.

Cassie was standing there. "We're not— Omigod, omigod. Mom!"

"What is it, Cassie? And what did I tell you about—"

Cecily appeared. When she saw Kate, she turned white. Kate stepped forward to hold her up.

"Don't touch me!"

Kate recoiled. "I'm sorry, I'm so, so sorry."

"How can . . . ?"

A group of happy kids ran past the house, their parents calling after them to wait up.

Cecily stepped back. "You need to leave or come inside."

"What?"

"If you don't want the whole world to know you're alive, come inside right now."

Kate stepped inside. Cecily closed the door quickly behind

her. Kate was overwhelmed. There in the entranceway surrounded by boots and hooked coats, she felt dizzy. Cassie and Cecily stood there, echoes of each other, both casual in jeans and warm sweaters. Staring.

"Thank you—"

Cecily held up her hand. "Do not say that. God, I don't even know why I care. Why should I protect you? What the fuck, Kaitlyn? What the fuck?"

"I can explain."

"There's no way you can explain any of this."

"You're right. I probably can't."

"You're alive. My God. You're alive."

"I'm alive."

Cassie's eyes were wide, and she looked as if she was trying to speak. She leaned against her mother. Cecily put her arm around Cassie's shoulder. Her eyes narrowed at Kate.

"You ran away?"

"I ran away."

"Stop doing that."

"I'm sorry."

"Cassie, go upstairs."

"But Mom—"

"Go upstairs right now. Do not tell your brother who's here. Tell him to stay in his room. And do not text anyone or call anyone or do anything online."

"Mom—"

"Do it now, Cassie."

Cassie looked frightened by her mother's tone. She turned on her heel and ran up the stairs. A door slammed.

"How dare you?" Cecily spat out the words.

"I'm sorry."

"Stop saying that. You were my friend."

"I had to go, Cecily. I can't explain it; I just had to."

"Because of Tom?"

"What? Omigod, no. Not . . . You know about that?"

"I know about that. I know about that *now*."

Kate backed up until she hit the front door. "I'll go."

"You're not getting off that easily. You, what, ran away, let us all think you were dead, and now you're back? What the fuck is going on? Why are you here?"

"Franny Maycombe. She's the reason I came back."

"Seriously? I should've known you were capable of doing something like this when I found out you hid her from us. How could you do that, Kaitlyn? How could you not even tell me that you had a daughter? After everything I shared with you?"

"But I didn't. That's why I'm here. Franny's not my daughter."

"What?"

"I swear to God. I've never seen that woman in my life."

INTERVIEW TRANSCRIPT

TJ: Thanks for coming in again, Franny. It's been a couple weeks. How
      are you?

FM: I'm fine. I'm good, actually. Really good.

TJ: I'm glad to hear that.

FM: I've been thinking about our last conversation, you know.

TJ: You have?

FM: Yeah, like, a lot. And I just want to make it clear that my
      family—my adoptive family—they have nothing to do with this.
      Nothing to do with who I am today or what I'm about.

TJ: I find it interesting that you'd say that.

FM: I'm not sure what you mean.

TJ: Well, everyone's a product of their family, aren't they?

FM: I don't think so.

TJ: Why not?

FM: I think you can, you know, overcome your family. Like, there are people who had terrible childhoods, just the worst, but they're out in the world acting like normal people. They're not drug dealers or whatever. They have jobs and families and they're doing things. Normal things. So they didn't get caught by their circumstance.

TJ: Is that what you did?

FM: Maybe. I mean, I don't want you to think my adoptive parents were bad or anything. They didn't, like, abuse me. But like I said before, there was always this different thing about me in that house, like I was a guest who stayed too long, like I should be looking for somewhere else to live.

TJ: Are you sure about that?

FM: Of course I am. I mean, my sister even said that to me when I was a junior in high school. Like she expected me to move out right after graduation, even though she hadn't, because then our parents didn't have any responsibility for me anymore.

TJ: That sounds cruel.

FM: She was cruel. I'm telling you. That's why we don't talk anymore.

TJ: Yes, well, that's one of the things I wanted to talk to you about.

FM: What do you mean?

TJ: We've spoken to Sherrie.

FM: What? Why would you do that?

TJ: It's standard background procedure.

FM: What gives you the right?

TJ: You did, actually. When you signed the release to do the documentary, you gave us permission to speak to any member of your family who would agree to speak to us.

FM: No one told me about that clause.

TJ: You had the contract for two weeks. You were encouraged to speak to a lawyer, to have them review it.

FM: I couldn't afford to do that.

TJ: I'm sorry, you should've said.

FM: I wish you hadn't done that.

TJ: Spoken to Sherrie?

FM: Yes. She . . . She said bad things about me, didn't she?

TJ: I wouldn't say that, exactly—

FM: She's always been a liar. And she hates me. You know that, right? I told you. I just told you how mean she was to me.

TJ: That doesn't quite add up—

FM: I *knew* that if she had the chance, she'd find a way to screw this up for me.

TJ: Screw what up for you?

FM: My life. She just wants me to be miserable because she's miserable.

TJ: Again, I don't think that . . . Don't you want to know what she told me?

FM: It's just all going to be lies. She's a liar. She has been since we were kids. Always saying I was the one who hit her or took her toy or whatever. You name it. The names she would call me.

TJ: Yes, the subject of names did come up.

FM: What do you mean?

TJ: You tell me, Franny. Or should I say Eileen?

PART

CECILY

It took me six hours to get home on October tenth. When the immediate threat was cleared, they started running the trains, one at a time, packed to the gills as if we were in Tokyo. Police in riot gear checked each of us as we got on, searching through our purses, verifying IDs. It took forever and reminded me of a book I'd read years ago called *Jessica Z.*, about a young woman struggling to find her place in a world where acts of terror had become quotidian. Was this just the beginning, a complete shift in the way we had to live now, or was it simply a gas explosion as the rumors on the platform said?

When the doors to the train finally closed, I realized Teo was still with me. I hadn't thought about it as we shuffled through the line, but it was doubtful we were going to the same place.

"Is this your train?" I asked.

"Close enough."

"You didn't have to come with me."

"Sure I did."

Our arms were by our sides, our hands inches from touching. I laced my fingers through his. My hand had spent so much time in his that day, what did a few more minutes signify?

The train rattled past our changed city and on and on until it was out. It was a one-stop shop, the police officers told us on the purple line, running all the way to Linden, which meant we went right through downtown Evanston without stopping. It was unbearably hot and eerily quiet. No one was speaking; they were buried in their phones, hitting "Refresh" on their news feeds. I couldn't bring myself to look. I didn't want to know the details, how many dead, how many missing, who else I knew who wasn't coming home. I didn't want the confirmation that Tom was where I knew he was; his failure to answer any of the messages I'd sent him after Cassie's question was all the confirmation I needed. I kept my phone in my pocket, my eyes fixed on the back of the person standing in front of me, and tried not to think too much about what I'd have to face at home.

When we got to Linden, Joshua was there. He was standing in front of his minivan, one of a long line waiting like parents in a school pickup line. He was scanning the crowd, up on his tippy-toes, not wanting to miss anyone. I dropped Teo's hand and waved at him frantically.

"Joshua! Over here."

Our eyes locked for a moment, but then he continued his scan.

And that's when I knew. He wasn't there for me. He was there for Kaitlyn. Kaitlyn! She was as lost as Tom.

My knees buckled.

29

THE LEAST COMPLICATED

CECILY

Tom and I never spoke about the texts again. When I woke up the next morning in our hotel room, he was gone. He'd left a note—*out for a run, then coffee, I'm sorry*—and didn't return for several hours. When I could drag myself out of bed, I climbed into the large marble shower and stood there until it felt like I was drowning, as if every pore in my body was waterlogged, my skin turning into an angry prune. I still didn't know how to process what had happened, but I felt dirty, contaminated. I wanted to scour every inch of skin off my back, and my insides out, too.

As I scrubbed and scrubbed, I started to question everything that had happened in the last six months between us. All the times I'd cuddled up to Tom in bed. The times when we'd had sex. The small intimacies every couple has. Was it all tainted now?

Was six months enough? Should I go back a year? Two? How much of my life did I have to readjust? Tom didn't say, and I didn't ask. I didn't ask so many things. The lack of details was killing me, and yet I knew better than to make a list of particulars, because Tom would tell me, and then instead of speculation, I'd have facts. Somehow I knew the facts would be worse than anything I could imagine, even though I had a good imagination.

When I started envisaging Tom's tongue trailing over someone else's skin, I got out of the shower and wrapped myself in the oversize bathrobe like a hug. I kicked the blankets Tom had slept in into the corner. I didn't need any more reminders of him. I picked up my phone. There were messages from the kids with questions about missing soccer equipment, whether something was in the laundry. My mother asking if we were having a good time, Kaitlyn wondering if we could meet for lunch on Monday. I'm shocked at the gall of that now, knowing what I know, but then I was happy to hear from her. I almost called her to talk about what had happened because I needed someone else's voice in my head other than my own.

Tom brought back coffee, a bag full of freshly made bagels, and a container of fruit. We sat at the small table in our room in silence. He tried to speak, but I raised my finger to my lips and he fell silent. I couldn't eat, could only sip at my coffee, which tasted bitter and scalded my tongue. I felt as if I needed to hollow out my insides with a spoon, to remove every extraneous thing. My wedding band was tight on my finger. I twisted it off. Tom watched me do it, his eyes wide, wanting to ask if this was some greater symbol, if this was the end. But I silenced him again with a look, and then I brought out the laptop and rebooked our flights home. We dressed and packed quickly, and Tom took our luggage downstairs to check out while I did a last sweep of the room.

I stood in the doorway in my belted trench coat, looking at the ruin of the bed, the dirty windows that couldn't block out the iconic view. I shoved my hands into my pockets, balled into fists, and came up against the rough edges of a piece of paper. I pulled it out. It was the certificate Tom had given me the night before, the star he named after me, his big romantic gesture, which I would've been delighted with a few days ago but now felt like a cheap joke.

I tossed it in the trash.

I go upstairs, leaving Kaitlyn in the living room, and admonish Cassie again to stay in her room. "No texting, no outside communication," I say.

"But what's going on?" Cassie asks. "That's Aunt Kaitlyn, isn't it? How can she be here?"

I almost tell her to hush, Henry might hear, but what's the point? There's no way to keep this secret in my own house. Besides, things have been dicey with Cassie ever since I told her and Henry that things between her father and me were rocky before he died. "Not the best" was the euphemism I used when I explained why I was leery of the press, of people finding out our secrets. I didn't tell them about the affair or give them an explanation of why we were in trouble, just that we were. I told them we hadn't figured everything out yet, that we were still in the process of trying to figure things out when he died.

Cassie hadn't reacted when I'd told her, but two days later, she'd flown into a rage over a book she thought I'd moved in her room, and I knew what it was about.

"Aunt Kaitlyn?" Henry says, coming into Cassie's room. "She's alive? But does that mean . . . Dad's alive?"

"Oh no, I'm so sorry, honey. I don't . . . No, Dad's not alive."

Henry starts shaking. "But if Aunt Kaitlyn is, then he has to be, too. Their offices were on the same floor. And I read this thing on the Internet about how it was all some big hoax anyway, because if it had been a gas leak, then the building wouldn't have blown up that way and—"

"You're so stupid, Henry!"

"Cassie!"

"But it's true. Why do you even read that stuff?"

I put my arms around Henry. He feels cold, chilled. I rub my hands up and down his back, trying to warm him up. "Henry, Cassie, please. Not right now. I need to talk to Aunt Kaitlyn and find out what's going on. I promise I'll tell you as soon as I know, but it's very, very important that we don't tell anyone she's alive or here or anything like that, okay?"

"You'll tell us everything?" Cassie says. "Ha! Like you told us all about you and Dad fighting?"

"No, not like that. And this isn't a good time for this."

"You always say that. It's never a good time."

"Will you just give me this, Cassie? Please?"

"Why?"

That stops me. Why is it important to keep Kaitlyn's secret? Do I need another to add to the pile? But there's a reason she's at my house and not her own. And then there's what she just told me about

Franny, which, if true, is a whole other problem, one I can't even wrap my mind around.

"Because she hasn't had a chance to talk to her family yet, and they can't find out like this, that their mom's not dead. Imagine if Dad were still alive and you read about it on the Internet."

"But he *is* alive," Henry says. "He has to be."

"No, Henry. I'm so, so sorry, but he isn't. Remember? We saw him at the funeral home."

Henry's whole body is trembling now, either from remembering the awful sight of his father in a casket or the new, new reality that his father's still dead, maybe both. One of the "miracles" of October tenth—Tom's body had been intact, and his parents had insisted on an open casket. I was too tired to fight with them, so I caved. But when we'd walked into that tamped-down room and seen his waxy form in the coffin they'd picked out, I'd felt sick to my stomach. Cassie had run from the room, and Henry went so white I thought he'd faint. When we passed Tom's parents on the way out, I couldn't help but glare at them. Was this how they wanted to remember their son? If they knew the truth about him, would they feel any differently? But I already knew I could never tell them the truth, that Tom's secret was mine to keep now, even though death had parted us.

"But maybe . . . ," Henry says, then hangs his head in defeat. "He's really dead?"

"I'm afraid so."

He pulls away from me and slumps onto the edge of Cassie's bed. He curls into a fetal position. "This isn't fair!"

"I know, sweetheart. It isn't."

"But how is Aunt Kaitlyn alive?" Cassie asks. "We went to her funeral, too."

"I don't know. Let me go down and find out, okay?"

"Can I come with you?"

"That's not a good idea. Aunt Kaitlyn and I have some things we have to work out in private."

"Okay."

I sit down next to Henry and rub his back. He's shaking, emitting hiccupping cries I know are the end of his crying cycle. "How about you download that new game you wanted and play that?"

"For real?"

"Just don't kill too many bystanders, okay?"

"Seriously, Mom?" Cassie says. "That's your solution?"

"What do I have to bribe you with?"

"I don't have to be bribed. God, Mother."

My heart cracks. She's never called me "Mother" before. I feel an urgent need to call my own mother and apologize for every time I did that as a teenager.

"Just think of the girls. Kaitlyn's girls. Imagine if you were them?"

"I kind of *am* them."

"You're right. But you also know what I meant."

"Okay, okay. I already told you I wasn't going to say anything."

I stand and hug her quickly. "Thank you."

She shrugs away and slinks off. I give Henry another hug and ask him if he's going to be okay. When he says he will, I creep back down the stairs, passing our montage of family photographs. I purposively avoid looking at the one of all of us on vacation a few years ago. The person I've been thinking about since I got those texts has been hanging on my wall this whole time. She was in my house, right next to me, my confidante.

I hear a rushing sound in my ears. I sink to the stairs. I've had this feeling before, on the worst days, my own brand of panic attack. I place my head on my knees, wrap my arms around my head, and concentrate on breathing. *I will not call Kaitlyn for help. I will not call Kaitlyn for help.* I repeat those words to myself over and over until the feeling subsides. It takes only a few minutes, much less than it used to. In fact, it's been a long time since I've had one of these at all. I stare at the wall and think back over the last few weeks. I haven't had any anxiety since I left Linda's office a few weeks ago. Was she the cause of it? No. She was the deposit of my memories, the symbol of what was causing the anxiety in the first place.

I stand, straighten myself out, check my reflection in a photograph of Cassie and Henry and my mom from five years ago. I look pale but together.

No more putting this off.

Downstairs, Kaitlyn's sitting on the living room couch, watching the gas fireplace. There's only a small lamp on, and the way the shadows work, the weight she's lost, the difference in her hair color and cut—if I saw her on the street, I might not be sure it was her. I'd probably dismiss an across-the-street sighting, like I have the many times I've thought I've seen Tom, as a mind trick, my brain swapping out unfamiliar features with the known.

I walk into the room.

"Did you run away with Tom?"

Her head snaps around. She looks like a panicked animal caught on the road. "What? No. Tom is . . . Isn't Tom dead?"

"Yes, but then again, so are you."

"But Tom would never . . ."

"Tom would never what? Run away? Sleep with my friend? Betray his family?"

Kaitlyn flinches at each question.

"Tom would never run away. He loved you. He loved your kids."

"And you didn't?"

"Of course I love my kids; it's not like that."

"So what is it like, Kaitlyn? Please enlighten me."

She drops her head into her hands. The bones in her neck are sticking out of the unfamiliar argyle sweater she's wearing. "I don't know, I don't know. I've had a whole year to figure it out and I just don't know."

"That's not good enough."

"I know it isn't." She sits back up. The end of her nose is red. I feel violent, the need to reach out and smack someone, her.

See what you've done to me, Tom? You've turned me into a parody, a woman who might actually slap another woman just for the dramatic impact of it.

"So what, then?"

"Will you sit down, and I'll try to explain what I can? Please?"

I sit on the couch across from her and grab the blanket off the back. It's cashmere, soft and cozy. I need to be wrapped in the gentlest thing I can right now; another echo because this is exactly how I felt in that hotel room in New York. A coincidence or just one of life's little harmonies? Who cares, who cares?

"So what happened?" I say.

"Which part?"

"The Tom part."

"How do you know about the Tom part?"

"Coincidentally, I just found out."

"How?"

I measure my words. "Joshua told me."

"He knows?"

"He found some e-mails between you and Tom. Or Franny did."

"Franny did?"

All the color has bleached from Kaitlyn's face, and, like Henry at the funeral home, she looks like she might faint. I want to feel sympathy for her, but I'm having a hard time mustering the energy.

"I read that they . . . Are they engaged?"

"You saw that piece in *Vanity Fair*? Is that why you came home?" I saw the article after I learned about it from Joshua and the girls. It was all anyone was talking about these last two days.

"It's one of the reasons. What happened? How could . . . ?"

"Franny and Joshua have apparently grown quite close. She moved in a few months ago—to help with the girls, I thought—but it looks as if she's been worming her way into Joshua's heart. As your daughter. And then a couple of days ago, they had a fight after they told the girls they were getting married—"

Kaitlyn raises her hand to her mouth.

"Do you need the bathroom?"

As if the word prompted her, Kaitlyn gets up and runs to the powder room. I listen to her lift the toilet seat and choke up what sounds like her insides. I feel both cruel and satisfied. I never thought I was the vengeful type, but perhaps I am. Maybe this is what I've needed this whole time—my pound of flesh.

I wait a few minutes and then knock on the bathroom door.

"You coming out?" I ask.

"In a minute."

"I'm not going to do it, you know."

"Do what?"

"Hold your hair."

The door bursts open. Kaitlyn's crying and laughing at the same time.

"What are we going to do, Cecily? This is such a fucking mess."

"You think I know? This is your rodeo, Kaitlyn. We're all just along for the ride."

30

BACKFILL

KATE

Going back to work was both the best and worst thing Kate—Kaitlyn then—had ever done. The best because it opened her world back up. Turned the lights back on in her mind. Kept her out of the funk she could, and did, so easily slip into. Made her more patient with the girls when she got home. More patient with Joshua. She slept better. Felt better. She was better.

Was this what made her susceptible? Or was it the proximity?

She and Tom had carried on a mild flirtation for years. She didn't know when it started. It was part of the harmless background noise of her life. His eyes would meet hers sometimes at parties, as if they had a secret joke. They often laughed at the same things. Found the same things outrageous. Wanted to fight the same fights. And he always seemed attuned to her needs if they shared a meal. Her glass refilled at the right moment. The best slice of meat. Cecily was her friend, but she looked forward to those shared moments with Tom. They seemed brighter. More memorable.

It was a silly, harmless crush that neither of them did anything about. Kaitlyn had had them before and would have them again. One person can't fulfill every role in someone's life. Especially not after you've lost all sense of mystery about each other. That's what Kaitlyn always thought, anyway. That it made her feel better and that nothing would ever come of it.

Until, one day, something did.

The flirting had picked up once she'd gone to work for Tom. In fact, she'd been slightly concerned about it before she accepted the job. But they were friends. It was harmless. She needed the work. Two years of working together had flown by with real inside jokes this time, but limits, too. They didn't eat together. The door always stayed open if she was in his office. They never carpooled. Safe boundaries they'd put in place without talking about them. Without thought. Because that's what you say when you're acting subconsciously, isn't it? That some other part of you was in control the whole time, and you never knew it.

Then they'd had to stay up late working on a project leading up to the launch of some new software. The office had been alive with people. That atmosphere you only get when you mix stress, sleep deprivation, and the slightly off scent of take-out Chinese and pizza. They'd finished up around two in the morning, but Kaitlyn had volunteered to stay behind with Tom to help clear up the office. Kaitlyn had cleaned the break room, then sat down on the couch for a moment to rest. The next thing she knew it was morning. Her neck was stiff and Tom was shaking her gently. Someone had draped a blanket over her.

"Time to get up, sleepyhead," Tom said. His face was unshaven, his hair mussed. He looked tired but amused. Sexy in his rumpled shirt.

"What happened?"

"You fell asleep."

"Oh no. Joshua—"

"Don't worry. I texted him."

"Good. Thank you." She checked her watch. It was just after seven. The break room faced east. The sun was beaming in through the windows. "I should get home."

"I'll take you."

They gathered their things, then drove home in near silence, the traffic all the other way. The thrum of the tires on the pavement lulled Kaitlyn back to sleep. Tom nudged her again when they were at her front door. Joshua's car was gone. She must've just missed him and the girls on their way to school.

"Home sweet home."

"Yes," she said, looking at the solid brick, the sashed windows. She should do something about the flower garden. Her perennials were getting unruly.

"Take the day off," Tom said.

"Are you sure?"

"I'm going to."

"Well, all right, then."

"Thanks for keeping me company."

"Anytime."

Kaitlyn reached for her seat belt and came up against Tom's lips on her cheek, just left of her mouth. She pulled back.

"What was that for?"

"Thank you."

"I was only doing my job."

He shrugged. Kaitlyn felt uncomfortable, alert.

"I should get some sleep," she said.

"We both should."

Kaitlyn got out of the car and told herself not to look back. Not to be the girl who watched a man drive away. But what was she even thinking of? This was *Tom*. Her friend. Her friend's husband. It must be the exhaustion. It must be all in her head. She would rinse it out immediately with a good shower and be done with it.

Inside, her house was deeply quiet. The type of quiet it never was. She peeled the clothes from her body and climbed into the oldest, softest pajamas she could find. She fell quickly into a dead sleep. The buzzing of her phone woke her hours later. It was Joshua calling, checking in. She felt annoyed that he woke her, then muzzled the feeling. He was being thoughtful. She was still too tired to control her emotions. Feel the proper feelings. She thanked him for his concern. Made a joke about the office. Said she needed some more sleep. They hung up, and that's when she saw it. An e-mail from Tom labeled *You*.

She opened it.

You look adorable in the morning.

There was no more sleeping after that.

• • •

Kate wished she'd had more time in the bathroom to think out how to explain herself. She'd come to Cecily on instinct, unable to face her own house. Her own life. She'd had plenty of time, though. She could've worked this out on the bus ride. Instead, she'd stared out the window, her heart leaping around like a frog caught on a road. But she'd run out of road, and here she was. She felt as if the Kate persona she'd been living the last year had washed away, sliding down the drain of the sink she was standing at. She looked at herself in the mirror. She even looked like Kaitlyn again. She might as well accept it.

"How much do you want to know?" she said to Cecily when they were back in the living room. She wished she could ask Cecily for a drink. Something she'd avoided since her near blackout with the bottles of red wine in her hotel room that first week in Montreal. But there wasn't anything that could blunt this task. She had to face it head-on. Sober.

"About you and Tom? All of it. The minimum."

"I can't do both."

"I know. You know what? I wish I didn't know any of it."

"I wish there wasn't anything to know."

Cecily pulled one of the couch cushions into her lap. She wrapped her arms around it. "Do you mean that? How can you?"

The tone of Cecily's voice was a blow. Back when she'd been two things—Tom's and Cecily's—she'd built up some defenses. She'd had to. But they were all washed away now. By time. Knowledge. The pain in Cecily's voice.

"You have no reason to believe anything I'm saying," Kaitlyn said. "But I came to you. I was free and clear. I didn't need to come back. Does that count for something?"

"Maybe. Maybe it counts for a little."

"So what do you want to know?"

"I'm not ready to hear about the Tom stuff. Not now."

"Okay."

"Why are you here? What's the big plan?"

This Kaitlyn had given some thought to in the hours after she'd read that article about Franny in *Vanity Fair*. Had learned that she'd wormed her way into her family and was about to take her place. In those moments, she knew exactly what to do. Get to her family. Stop Franny.

"We need to find a way to let Joshua know Franny isn't who she says she is."

"Why do you care?"

"Seriously? How can you ask me that?"

"You ran out on him. You ran out on your *kids*."

Kaitlyn felt ashamed, but not as much as she ought to. This wasn't new information, after all. She'd been living with it for a long time. "I know what I did."

"They think you died, Kaitlyn. They've had to deal with that. Added to that, now there's Franny in the mix. And you're not dead. How are they going to process all of this?"

"You can't tell them I'm alive."

"I don't see how that's possible."

"They don't have to know. There must be a way. Please."

"What? I have to keep *your* secrets now? That's the big plan?"

"I don't have a plan. None of this was planned."

"I feel like we're going around in circles."

"We have to stop Franny. That's why I'm here. But I don't want to hurt anyone. I don't want to hurt anyone more than I already have."

Kaitlyn couldn't stand the pained expression on Cecily's face any longer. She broke eye contact and tried to focus on something else. The pictures on the mantel, the four of them together. Looking like the perfect family they weren't anymore. Because of her. Because of Tom. She should've deleted that first e-mail from him. She should've shut down any attempt to follow through. But instead she wrote back: *You don't look so bad yourself.*

And sealed her fate. Cecily's, too.

"How are we supposed to do that if you're not going to come forward?" Cecily asked. "I mean, why would anyone believe me? I haven't got any evidence."

"We'll have to get some, then. Investigate her. Look into her past. I've been reading a lot online, and I don't think anyone's done that yet."

A spark of hope crossed Cecily's face for the first time. "I might know someone who can help us with that."

INTERVIEW TRANSCRIPT

TJ: That's your real name, isn't it, Franny? Eileen. Eileen Warner.

FM: So what if it is?

TJ: Well, I'm interested in why you might have changed it, for one.

FM: Haven't you ever wanted to change something in your life? You know, start over, start fresh?

TJ: I'm sure it's a common feeling. But most people don't act on it.

FM: Well, I'm not most people.

TJ: Are you referring to something specific?

FM: What did she say?

TJ: Who?

FM: Her. Sherrie. What else did she say when you spoke to her?

TJ: She mentioned you'd been in some trouble.

FM: Typical. Tell me something, is this how the rest of this interview's going to go?

TJ: How do you mean?

FM: Are you going to pull out pieces of information one by one and spring them on me? Do you think I'm going to sit through that?

TJ: You don't have to do anything you don't want to.

FM: That is such a joke.

TJ: I feel as if we're having two conversations here.

FM: Now you know how I feel, right? When did you speak to her? How long have you been letting me sit here making a fool of myself? Since the first time? Since the beginning?

TJ: Calm down, please.

FM: I *hate* it when people say that to me. I am calm, okay? I'm allowed to raise my voice when something upsetting is happening to me. I'm allowed.

TJ: Do you want to end the session?

FM: No, I want to know what else you know about me. All of it.

TJ: You know that's not how this works.

FM: Well, none of this is working out the way it was supposed to, is it?

TJ: How about . . . What if you just told me your story in your own way? Without my prompting you or anything. Just tell me whatever you want to tell me.

FM: Why should I do that?

TJ: You might find it helpful to unburden yourself.

FM: Like therapy?

TJ: It doesn't have to be like that. And I'm not a therapist.

FM: Then what would be the point?

TJ: You'll have to decide that for yourself. But I've found, doing this all these years, that often there's a certain kind of catharsis in telling someone your story.

FM: And if I do that . . . what? You get your big scoop, right? And I'm . . . I just go back where I came from like none of this ever happened.

TJ: It doesn't have to be like that.

FM: Oh, sure, right. You don't know what's going to happen. No one does.

TJ: Why don't you tell me, and then we'll see?

FM: Just tell you the truth? The truth, the whole truth, and nothing but the truth?

TJ: This isn't a court of law.

FM: Maybe not. But I'm going to be judged anyway, aren't I?

31

THE FRIEND OF MY ENEMY

CECILY

"Everything I tell you is confidential, right?"

"Of course. Why do you ask?"

I'm back in therapy, back in the confines of Linda's office, the tie I thought I cut turning out to be just another loose end to get tangled in.

"Because I have to tell you something I can't tell anyone, so I have to know it's safe."

"I have to keep confidentiality unless I think you're a threat to yourself or others. Are you?"

I think of the flashes of red rage I've felt off and on since Kaitlyn

walked back into my life. But if I didn't strike her last night, I'm unlikely to do it now.

"No, it's nothing like that."

"Is it illegal?"

"That's a good question. If you fake your own death, is that illegal?"

"Is this a hypothetical discussion or something you're planning?"

"What? Oh no, no, it's not about me."

"But it is about someone."

"Maybe. I'm still fact gathering here."

Linda shakes her head. "Well, I'm not a lawyer, but theoreti-
cally, if you faked your death to get an advantage, insurance money,
say, then yes, I think it would be illegal."

"What if it was just to get away? Not for financial reasons. Not
directly, anyway, and I don't know how this person could've known
about that anyway . . ."

"Cecily, why don't you simply tell me who you're talking about,
and we can take it from there?"

"And you'll keep whatever I tell you to yourself?"

"Yes."

I lean back on the couch, unleashing a trace of the previous oc-
cupant's perfume. I don't recognize it, but it smells expensive. I've
smelled it before, and my mind wanders to who it might be. Do I
know her? Linda specializes in people in highly confidential positions. She has separate in and out doors so patients don't run into
one another in the lobby. I never thought I'd need that kind of privacy, but I'm happy for it now.

I force the words out. "Kaitlyn's alive."

"Kaitlyn Ring?"

"Yes."

"Are you certain?"

Linda's looking at me in a way she hasn't before. As if I might be crazy. It didn't occur to me that this might be an issue, that I'd be the one treated with suspicion.

"I've spoken to her," I say. "So yes."

"How is that possible?"

"If what she says is true, and I'm adding a big 'if' here, she was having some kind of panic attack a few moments before the explosion, so she left the building. That's why she was at the elevators a few minutes before . . . I don't know if I ever told you that part?"

"I don't think so."

"Well, I probably shouldn't be telling you this, either, because it's Initiative business, but anyway, you said it was confidential, so . . ."

"Take a breath, Cecily."

I inhale deeply.

"Take two."

I do it again. In and out slowly like Linda showed me early on in our sessions when everything would come spilling out of me in a manic stream.

"Better?"

"Yes, thanks."

"So she was leaving the building, and then what?"

"She's not sure. Everything blew up and she came to a block away. She doesn't know how she ended up there—she thinks she was thrown by the blast; it's super-unclear—but the next thing she knew she was buying a bus ticket for Montreal. That's where she's been all this time. Montreal. Looking after someone else's children! Can you believe that?"

"This is a bit hard to absorb, I'll admit."

"Right?"

"How did you learn all this?"

"She showed up at my house last night."

"She's back?"

I nod. "She read that story in *Vanity Fair* about Franny. I don't know if you saw it, but Franny's engaged to Joshua."

"Yes, I did see that."

"I'm sure you'd have a field day with that one. Man gets engaged to his wife's secret daughter. Only she's not her daughter."

"What?"

"Apparently, Franny's a fraud."

"This is a lot of information to absorb, even for me," Linda says. "How are you doing?"

"I'm a fucking mess. But I haven't even gotten to the best part yet."

"There's a best part?"

"Yeah, good point. It's probably the worst part. She's the woman."

"The woman?"

"The other woman. The woman who was sleeping with my husband. It's Kaitlyn. It was Kaitlyn this whole time."

Saying it out loud rips something apart inside me, and now I'm crying like I haven't since my early sessions. Hard-core crying that will end in hiccups, like Henry.

When I finally made it back upstairs last night, Henry had fallen asleep cradling his DS, and Cassie was reading the new Veronica Roth book. I'd said a quick good night and told her I'd fill them in in the morning but that the information ban was still in place. Then I'd texted Linda that it was an emergency, and could she please fit me in?

"That's disappointing news," Linda says. "I'm sure."

"Disappointing? That's all you've got to say? I find out my life is actually some Lifetime movie plot and that's 'disappointing'?"

"Perhaps that wasn't the best choice of words, but you seem very angry with me right now."

"Maybe I am."

"Why?"

"Because I wasn't prepared for this. What have I been doing here all this time if something like this can just blindside me and send me back where I was a year ago?"

"Are you back where you were a year ago?"

"Of course I am. Look at me. I'm a mess."

"I don't see a mess."

"You don't?"

"I see a woman who's survived some big shocks only to have several more thrown at her. So it's no surprise that you feel off-kilter today. It would be more surprising if you didn't."

My shoulders start to shake. "How could she do this? How could she do this to me?"

"She must've been very sad. Very confused."

"I'm thinking more that she's some kind of sociopath."

Linda gives me a half smile. "That damn book."

"What?"

"*The Sociopath Next Door*," Linda says. "Everyone thinks they can diagnose a serious clinical condition now."

"But am I wrong? Isn't it totally crazy what she did?"

"I don't know Kaitlyn, so I can't say. But you've told me before that she suffered from clinical depression, and affairs are a common side effect, shall we say, of depression."

"They are?"

"It's a way of feeling something, when everything else feels like nothing."

"So I'm just a side effect? My family's a side effect?"

"Of course not. I'm simply providing some context for her behavior."

"It's totally fucked up."

"You could also say that." Linda smiles at me. "Cecily, I can't begin to imagine what you must be feeling right now. Hate, regret, anger, confusion I'm sure are all a part of it, but I sense there's something more. Something more immediate that's pulling at you."

"She wants me to help her."

"Help her how?"

"Help her with her plan to expose Franny."

Linda looks at her hands. For a woman who presents as so calm, so in control, they're a wreck. Bitten nails, ragged cuticles.

"Does she need your help? Couldn't she simply come forward and expose Franny?"

"But then she'd be exposed, too. And the girls and Joshua would know what she did."

"Which is worse than what they think now?"

"Yes."

"That's a tough position she's put you in."

"It's a ridiculous position to be in."

"But you've made your choice, I think. That's why you're telling me instead of speaking to the press. Or simply telling Joshua yourself."

"I couldn't do that. Am I wrong?"

"What does your heart tell you?"

"It feels like it isn't working properly."

"I think your heart is working fine."

"Sure, right."

"Look at the love you're displaying now, Cecily. For Joshua, for his children, even for Kaitlyn. It may come at a cost, but you should be proud of that heart."

I know her words are a compliment, something that should warm me. But I don't feel warm.

I feel cold and sick, sick in my heart.

On my way downtown, after I beg off work, I try Franny again. The call goes right to voice mail. I try again, then leave her a message. *I'd appreciate it if you'd call me*, I text. *It's important.* I wait for the bubble to appear, but the screen stays blank. Perhaps she's turned it off. Or maybe she's reconciled with Joshua and doesn't want me to know. I start to dial his familiar digits, then stop. I can't talk to Joshua right now, not with Kaitlyn hiding in my basement, and I have no idea what to say to him or how I'll react when I hear his trusting voice.

I'm heading downtown to meet Teo. When I texted him from the therapist's parking lot, I wasn't sure he'd agree to meet me. Not after the way we left things last time. But I have a lure, one I was fairly certain he wouldn't be able to resist, and I was, sadly, right. I use it right off, not wanting to find out if my own request would be sufficient. I can't take any more rejection right now, not even that of someone who's rejected me already.

When I get to the coffee shop around the corner from the Compensation Initiative, Teo's already sitting at a table, though I'm ten minutes early. He's wearing his trademark outfit, that smooth path he's created through life.

He stands when I get to our table.

"Let me help you with that."

He takes my coat and hangs it on a hook on the wall, then returns with a large cup of coffee for me.

"You take it black, right?"

"Yes, thank you."

"How've you been?"

"Fine."

I take a sip. It's too hot and scalds my tongue, which seems about right for today.

Teo fiddles nervously with his napkin. He has a muffin in front of him, carrot, I think, but he hasn't taken a bite.

"How are things with you?" I ask, feeling, like I did weeks ago, as if we're in some well-mannered drama where we should be wearing period costumes.

"Fine. Busy."

"How's the documentary coming?"

"Chugging along. Obviously the news about Franny and Joshua is going to put a different spin on things."

If only he knew.

"You didn't see that coming?" I say, thinking of Julia.

"Frankly, no. She was still calling him Mr. Ring half the time in her sessions with me. And he'd skipped our last few appointments claiming he had work conflicts, which, in retrospect, I should've realized meant more than that he didn't want to talk to me."

He sounds frustrated, defeated.

"Do you ever think about giving it up?"

"What? Filmmaking?"

"Documentaries. I remember reading once about how you can spend years of your life on something and in the end, there's no story there."

"That can happen."

"Not in this case, though."

"If anything, there's too much story."

"Is that even possible?"

He shrugs. "It can be hard to keep three narrative threads balanced. And right now, I have two threads mixing, and though I have no idea what it is you're about to tell me, I suspect things are going to get more complicated from here."

"Oh, the tangled webs we weave."

"Said the spider to the fly."

"Interesting choice of response."

"Nah, I just couldn't remember the rest of that line."

"Somehow, I highly doubt that."

I try another sip of coffee. It's cool enough, but I can't taste if it's good or bad given my scalded tongue. When did every little thing in my life start feeling like a metaphor?

"Am I right?" Teo asks.

"About what?"

"About why you wanted to meet."

"Yes."

"So what is it?"

"I need to establish some ground rules first."

He leans back. "Such as?"

"I'm going to tell you something, but you're going to have to take it on faith that what I'm saying is true. I'm not going to be able to tell you how I know it, and if you try to find out, I'll get your funding pulled."

"Whoa, wait. What?"

"I want you to know how serious I am."

"If I tell you I'm not going to do something, you can trust me."

"Can I?"

"Of course you can. What have I ever done to make you think you couldn't?"

"Oh, I don't know. Make me think you like me, ask me out, then tell me you can't see me anymore the second it might come out that we're dating. Or whatever the hell we were doing."

"That's not what happened."

"It's exactly what happened."

He looks at his hands. "Okay, factually, yes, maybe. But you're speaking as if I meant to hurt you, and I didn't."

"Maybe not, but you did."

"I'm sorry."

"Yeah, well, join the club."

Neither of us speaks for several moments. I'm doubting the wisdom of coming here, asking for his help. But I wanted to see him again and not just in the confines of an interview.

"Is that the only condition?" Teo asks eventually.

"I'll also need your help."

"How so?"

"What I'm going to tell you needs to be investigated. It needs to be independently confirmed. I don't know how to do that, but I think you do."

"And it's related to the documentary?"

"Yes."

"To Franny?"

"Why do you think that?"

"She seems the most likely candidate. I'll do it. But I want something in return."

"What?"

"One more interview with you. You've been holding back, I'm not sure what, but something. And part of the reason I did what I did was that if I were doing my job properly, I'd be looking into what that is."

"You want to investigate me?"

"No, I don't. That's the problem. I'm more interested in preserving your privacy than in getting to the nitty-gritty. And I shouldn't be. Not if I want to make the film I think I can."

"So that's why."

"Yes. In part."

"What would I have to do?"

"One more interview, like I said. But you tell me what it is you don't want me to know."

"And, assuming there is something, you'll include it in the documentary?"

"That depends on what it is, I guess. But probably. That's the idea."

"I'm going to have to think about that."

"I understand. So no agreement today?"

"I guess not."

He picks a piece off the top of his muffin. "I don't suppose you could give me a preview of what this is all about?"

"Nope."

"It was worth a try. But you have to know the suspense is killing me."

32

THE BIG DIG

KAITLYN

When Kaitlyn woke up in another unfamiliar bed in another basement, she thought she was dreaming. It was later than she usually slept, almost eight. She felt a moment of panic. Had she forgotten to set her alarm? Were the twins wandering around the house unsupervised? No, wait. This wasn't Westmount. And Andrea would've woken her up anyway, if that were the life she was still in. No, she was in Chicago. In Cecily's house. Told to stay in the basement until further notice.

Cecily and Tom had renovated it several years back in anticipation of Cecily's mom moving in. Only she hadn't. Tom had been annoyed at the waste of money. Which Kaitlyn shouldn't know.

Because Tom was the one who told her. Any knowledge she had from Tom about his life with Cecily was contraband. Something to be cast off, forgotten. It was a nice basement, though.

Kaitlyn went to the bathroom. When she came out, Cassie was sitting on her bed.

"You probably shouldn't be down here."

"Probably not. But Mom didn't say that."

"Where is your mom?"

"She had to go out."

"Work?"

Cassie shrugged. She was taller and slimmer than the last time Kaitlyn had seen her. She had a dancer's body, though she'd never danced.

"Why aren't you in school?"

"In-service day."

"Ah."

"Where's your brother?"

"Mom dropped him off at a friend's. It's just the two of us."

Kaitlyn felt strangely nervous. She couldn't recall ever spending time alone with Cassie before. Cassie was so much older than her own girls. And though she remembered being fifteen, she didn't know how to talk to a fifteen-year-old today.

Cassie patted the bed next to her. "I brought you some clothes to change into."

"Thanks, but I have some of my own things."

"Did you get them in Montreal or take them with you?"

"I bought them in Montreal."

"So you didn't, like, plan to leave?"

"Why would you think that?"

Cassie pulled at the end of one of her braids. "I just remember, sometimes, you'd stare off into space, and it took a few times for you to hear people calling your name. And I was thinking this morning that maybe you were planning on leaving, like that was something you thought about a lot because you seemed unhappy before."

"You're a pretty observant kid."

"You look a lot like these girls in my school, especially this one girl, Charice, who tried to kill herself last year. Only they told us that she was sick, like with some kind of disease or something, but her best friend told everyone what happened, and she was so embarrassed when she came back to school."

"I never wanted to kill myself."

"That's good. But life kind of did that for you, I think."

"I'm not sure I can have this conversation without coffee."

"There's a machine upstairs. I know how to use it, but you can't tell Mom."

"I can keep a secret."

"I'm not finding anything in Madison," Cassie said hours later.

"Madison?" Cecily asked as she walked into the kitchen, bringing the cold inside with her. "What's in Madison?"

"That's where Franny's from. Or where she says she's from, anyway."

Cecily gave Kaitlyn a sharp look. "You're investigating Franny with my daughter?"

"It was my idea, Mom," Cassie said. "I want to help."

"What did you tell her?" Cecily asked Kaitlyn.

"That I was living in Montreal, and that I came back because of what Franny's doing."

"What else could she have told me?" Cassie asked.

"Nothing, honey."

"You promised there wouldn't be any more secrets."

"I know, but some things aren't about us. Some things aren't things we should know."

She turned away from the screen. "Like what?"

"Like grown-up things I wish I didn't even know myself."

"This is so unfair."

"Probably. But trust me—you don't want to know this."

Cassie looked at Kaitlyn.

Kaitlyn felt as if she was being inspected.

"Is that true, Aunt Kaitlyn?"

"Definitely true."

Cecily dropped a grocery bag onto the kitchen counter and began unpacking its contents. "Did you find anything?"

"Not yet," Cassie said. "Franny doesn't have Facebook or Insta or Snapchat or anything. Like, no social media *at all*."

"I'm not surprised."

"Also, I did a bunch of Google searches and even did a Google Image search, and, like, her picture isn't online anywhere except for in that article."

"What's a Google Image search?"

"You can take a photograph and search online records for something that resembles it," Kaitlyn explained. "Or so Cassie taught me."

"Good thinking, Cass."

"Thanks, but nothing, nothing, nothing. Then I remembered

that she said a couple times that she came from Madison, so I looked up. Did you know that's in Wisconsin?"

"I did."

"I haven't ever been there, have I?"

"Nope."

"I didn't think so. We did go to Wyoming, though."

"Yes. That's where we used to go skiing."

"That was so fun. Could we go again this year?"

"Maybe."

Kaitlyn watched the easy banter between Cecily and Cassie and felt jealous. Cecily had always been such a natural mother. Making it look easy, too easy. She knew part of it was an illusion, but not all.

"So," Cecily said. "Nothing in Madison?"

"No."

"Did you try the local paper? Maybe they have archives that aren't indexed?"

"Good idea."

Kaitlyn took over the computer from Cassie. As Cecily and Cassie put food away and then got started on lunch, she searched for variations on local paper names. *The Madison Record. The Madison Free Press.* She found a site that listed all the local papers in Wisconsin, which brought her to *The Capital Times.* She tried several different searches, but nothing came up. She looked around but couldn't find a good archive function, either. She flipped through various stories, but there wasn't anything. Going through them all would take forever.

"Maybe we should hire a private detective," Kaitlyn said.

Cecily looked up from where she was making a salad. "No luck?"

"None. Where did Cassie go?"

"Up to her room."

Kaitlyn hadn't noticed her leave. "She's a great kid, Cecily."

"I know."

Kaitlyn looked down at the screen. At her fruitless search results. "She's not anywhere. It's like she doesn't even exist. Now there's a thought."

"What?"

"Maybe she doesn't. Maybe she made herself up. Or changed her name, at least."

"That could explain a lot." Cecily pulled a bottle of white wine out of the fridge and poured two large glasses. "I wouldn't normally drink in the middle of the day, but I'm ready."

"For what?"

"For the story. At least part of it, anyway."

She held out a glass to Kaitlyn. Kaitlyn rose from the computer and took it. The cold Chablis tasted like her past. So many memories of drinking this same wine, in this same room. Probably from this same glass.

"Which part?"

"Did you ever sleep with Tom here? In our house?"

"What?"

"It's one of the things that's been bugging me ever since I found out. Did he actually bring that whore into my house? And now I know it's you, and obviously you've been in my house. So please tell me you did not fuck my husband in my own house. Give me that at least."

"Of course not. Oh my God, no. We never . . . I never slept with him anywhere."

"Don't get technical. You know what I mean."

"No, I don't."

"Come on. I read your e-mails. And that text he sent to me by mistake. You guys were fucking all over the place."

Kaitlyn felt sick to her stomach. Those e-mails. She'd been addicted to them. Reading them, writing them, had made her wet and given her vivid, lurid dreams. Their words had come to her at the oddest moments. But they'd never been more than words.

"No, never. I . . . God, I don't know how to explain this, but all we ever did was write to each other. Which was horrible, awful. We were awful. Terrible. But it never went any further than that. I swear."

"Please. All those late nights at the office. All that time you spent together and you never so much as kissed?"

"Once. We kissed once. At the office Christmas party when we were both drunk. That's it."

"So all of that was just, what, fantasy?"

"Yes."

"Jesus fucking Christ."

"I'm so sorry, Cecily. So awfully sorry. It happened gradually, and by the time I admitted to myself what was going on, it was too late. It was like a drug. Those e-mails actually made me feel high. But I told Tom early on that it couldn't ever be more than that. That he couldn't ever even speak to me about it out loud."

"But you kissed. At the Christmas party, you kissed?"

"Yes. When that happened, I told him we had to stop."

"And it was months later when I found out. So this was still going on then?"

"Less frequently, but yes. Yes, sometimes we'd backslide. It had been months, but the night before, we'd worked late together . . ."

"This is such bullshit. Will told me. He told me Tom left the office that night when you guys were working late. And there was a hotel bill at the Langham. He knew Tom was seeing someone, but he wouldn't tell me who it was. Which makes total sense now, of course. As does his look of pity when we were talking about it."

"We did leave together that night, but nothing happened, I swear. I mean, not nothing. We . . ." Kaitlyn thought back. She remembered the drinks they'd had in the hotel's bar. "We went to a bar and we drank and we . . . God, this sounds so stupid and twisted, but we sat there and sent messages to each other."

"I'm supposed to believe that?"

"Why would I make this up? You already thought the worst of me."

"This might actually be worse."

"How?"

"Because you sat next to me and held me while I told you all about what I thought had happened, and you never corrected me. You never let me know that it wasn't as bad as I thought."

"I couldn't have done that. What could I have said?"

"You could've asked Tom to tell me."

"I talked Tom out of telling you."

"You what?"

"He realized he'd sent that text to you instead of me right away. He wanted to call you and tell you everything. I walked into his office when he was dialing your number. He told me what had happened. I told him not to do it. That if there was a way that he could keep you from knowing what he'd been doing, what we'd been doing—"

"You plotted with my husband against me?"

"That one time. Yes. But other than that, we never talked about you. That was a rule. No talking about our families."

Cecily drained half her glass. "I think I've heard enough."

"I'm sorry."

"I don't get it. I don't get how you could do that to me after everything I did for you."

"I'm sure there isn't anything I could tell you that would make this any better."

"You could try, though."

Kaitlyn pushed her glass away. She didn't feel like she deserved its comfort. "Maybe I should go."

"What about Franny?"

"I'll figure something out."

"You're going to run away again, aren't you?"

"I'd like to say I won't, but I don't seem to be in control of what I do these days. Not reliably."

"Another impossible choice."

"What's that?"

"You keep presenting me with these terrible decisions. Take you into my home or hurt your family. Help you expose Franny or hurt your family. Let you leave or hurt your family."

"You're right. I'm horrible."

"Don't do that. Don't agree with me."

"I'm going to go."

"No. You have to finish what you came here to do. And I'm going to help you."

"You don't have to."

Cecily looked grim. "Yeah, I do. Besides, it's the only way I can guarantee that you go away and never come back again."

"Is that what's going to happen?"

"If I help you, then yes. Do we have a deal?"

Kaitlyn struggled for a moment. Was she actually going to agree to never see her children again? But hadn't that been the plan all along? Wasn't that why she hadn't gone right to Joshua? She wasn't going to see her girls again. She'd known that back in the bus station a year ago. At least she could save them from a worse mother than her.

"Deal."

INTERVIEW TRANSCRIPT

TJ: Go ahead, Franny. In your own words.

FM: Well, it's like Sherrie told you. I got into some trouble at home, you know?

TJ: What kind of trouble?

FM: Just stupid things that girls do sometimes. Like wanting to be tougher than the boys to get their attention. I started making up these stories, at first, about how badass I was. I stole drinks from my parents' liquor cabinet. I lifted this necklace from the store. I snuck out late at night, and they didn't even know I was gone. But I could tell they didn't believe me, so I had to show them, right? I had to prove it.

TJ: Why?

FM: It sounds dumb, but I felt like I had to, okay? Like no one was going to accept me for who I was if I didn't have some extra tricks up my sleeve. So I started doing stuff. Stealing liquor. Taking stupid things from stores. Sneaking out of the house and going to hang with the guys in this parking lot they all hung out in. I became the cool girl, the girl who could bring the good stuff no one else could get.

TJ: That sounds dangerous.

FM: It wasn't, until it was, you know? Like this one time, I was convincing this older guy, like maybe twenty-five, to buy me a bottle at Vic Pierce, this liquor store, and he was acting all nice, but then he expected me to do something for it. I grabbed the bottle, and he ran after me, but I was yelling at him, "I'm fourteen! My dad's a cop! I'm fourteen!" And he let me go.
[Laughter]

TJ: What's funny about that?

FM: I was sixteen, and my dad wasn't a cop.

TJ: Still, that doesn't sound like a funny story.

FM: Nothing's funny when it's happening. But when it's over, it can be sometimes.

TJ: Perhaps.

FM: Anyway, it was all mostly fun until my parents realized what I was doing and sent me to this teenager boot camp thing.

TJ: What's that?

FM: You know, like one of the therapy places where they basically kidnap you and take you out into the wilderness until you straighten up and fly right.

TJ: What was that like?

FM: It was hell. Nothing funny about it at all. They made us get up at six and do drills and clean the latrines. And all that shit you see in the movies about people yelling in your face and making you climb walls and stuff? That's exactly what it was like. Only worse. Because I was sixteen years old, and I hadn't done anything to deserve it. Like, there were girls I knew who were doing way worse things than me.

TJ: I'm sure your parents just wanted to help you.

FM: Yeah, but that's an extreme way of doing it. And it doesn't work, you know. There's no science behind those programs at all. You're not more or less likely to succeed if you attend one.

TJ: I've heard that.

FM: I looked it up. After I got out of there and I had to do summer school to make up for the classes I missed. I researched these places, and I put together this big file to show my parents it doesn't work. It can even make things worse.

TJ: What did they say?

FM: All the stuff you'd expect. They were sorry. They didn't know what to do. Wah, wah, wah. And then they died. My sister told you about that, right? I bet she did.

TJ: She did.

FM: She's the one who went to the police, you know. Can you believe it? She always had it in for me.

33

MY TURN

CECILY

When Tom and I got back from New York, we didn't speak about what had happened. I'm not sure why. It wasn't as if we came to an agreement or anything, only every time he tried to bring it up, I'd stop him. I couldn't stand to hear about it. I almost couldn't stand to be around him. So we made up some excuse to the kids about why we'd come home a day early, and then I concocted another story about how Tom had to go on a long business trip. Tom got the message and packed a bag and went to live in a hotel near his office.

He stayed in that hotel for two weeks. Two weeks of nights where I cried myself to sleep and missed his body in the bed next to me and his help with the kids, and where I tried not to think about the fact that she was probably there with him every night, though he swore he'd broken things off and that he was just going to "think."

Like you're in a time-out, I wrote. I couldn't stand speaking to him on the phone, so we had taken to exchanging e-mails.

Maybe that's not a bad analogy, Tom wrote back. *I haven't been thinking much lately about what I've been doing. Maybe it's time.*

And then I would go cry in the bathroom, worried the kids would hear me or see my reddened eyes. Before, they always seemed so oblivious to us, lost in their own worlds. But now, suddenly, they were both asking lots of questions about where was Dad and how come this trip was longer than the others and Dad would've loved this episode of whatever TV show we were watching.

It was torture, like I was trapped in someone else's dream, and until they woke up, there was no escape for me. I have never felt so out of control in my entire life.

Talking to Kaitlyn helped. She was the one who told me it was okay to hate him. She was the one who told me it was okay to leave him. She was the one who told me that whatever I decided, to stay or to go, she'd support me. She was on Team Cecily, and Tom could go fuck himself.

That always made me laugh. "Tom can go fuck himself." She always said it so emphatically. Was that all an act? Or was she mad at Tom, too, mad for letting whatever there was between them turn into deceit and sneaking around and . . . I don't want to know.

When I told Kaitlyn I was letting Tom move back home for a trial run, she brought over two bottles of our favorite wine, and we sat up till midnight drinking it.

"Am I an idiot to be letting him come back?" I asked.

"'Course not. He's your husband. The father of your children. And you love him."

"But do I? Do I love him? Or am I just so used to having him around that it feels like love?"

Kaitlyn bit the rim of her glass. "I think you'd know the difference."

"Maybe. I just hate him right now."

"I know."

"What's he like at work?"

"I haven't been talking to him."

"But do people know? Does anyone suspect?"

"I haven't heard anyone say anything."

"But they wouldn't to you, would they? They know we're friends."

Kaitlyn poured herself another glass, emptying the bottle. "I should've brought three."

"I'm going to be so sick tomorrow."

"Drink lots of water. Take some aspirin. Or Tylenol. Or whatever."

"We're so drunk."

Kaitlyn laughed. "We're not drunk enough."

I agreed with her and went to find another bottle in the fridge, and we drank on, and on, until the wine made me turn nasty, bitter, a person I didn't like or recognize living inside me, speaking through me about what I'd like to do to the woman who'd slept with my husband. Kaitlyn tried to reason with me, to talk me down. She reminded me that Tom was the one who'd hurt me, who'd broken his promises. He was the one who I should be directing my righteous anger at.

Even though she was right, I couldn't help feeling a surge of hatred toward this unknown person who'd come into my perfectly okay life and turned it into a mess. And all the while she was sitting across from me, or rubbing my back, filling my glass, supporting me. I can have some sympathy for the cognitive dissonance she must've been living through. She was right that Tom was the one I had to decide if I could forgive and move on with, that this other woman, whoever she was, was nothing to that decision.

But I can't forgive the act in the first place. Whatever it was between them, that betrayal isn't something I can move past. Just like I couldn't move past it with Tom.

"Okay, I'll do it," I tell Teo the next morning, back in the coffee shop. We're sitting at the same table with the same drinks before us, and of course Teo's wearing the same thing, or its sibling.

"That's great."

"But I want you to tell me something first. How did you know I was holding back? Was it just a good guess, or do you actually know something you haven't been telling me?"

Teo takes a bite of his muffin. "I know some things."

"Like what?"

"Tell me what you wanted to tell me yesterday, and I'll tell you everything I know."

"This is like the prisoner's dilemma."

"How so?"

"Neither of us trusts the other, even though acting together is clearly in our best interests."

He smiles at me. I feel a tug at my heart, but I try to ignore it.

This man's already left me behind once. I don't need to be chasing after him.

"You're right," Teo says. "Though I'm not sure why that is."

"I have every reason not to trust you. I'm not sure why you don't trust me."

"It's this narrator thing. I have to bring a level of distrust to my subjects. You can get caught out if you don't."

"How so?"

"It happened to me on my first film. I was hired to do a documentary about a historic football team that was going for its twenty-fifth championship. It had all the elements you'd want. Kids from two neighborhoods, so all the racial tension and overcoming circumstances and stuff, but the twist was that in this case, the black kids came from the more affluent neighborhood and the white kids were the ones being bused in to keep up the diversity. The quarterback's dad had been the quarterback when they'd won the first championship. The coach was about to retire. It was all teed up."

"So what happened?"

"It was bullshit. After the documentary came out, a reporter did this hatchet job about how I'd been snowed. Half the team was taking steroids, and I never knew. And the coach had this deal with the rival team to let them win. The whole thing was corrupt, and I'd made this puff-piece promo film. It nearly cost me my career. It took five years before someone would finance one of my films again. And even then, my reputation's never fully recovered."

"Is that why you were shooting a commercial on October tenth?"

"One of the reasons. Not that documentary filmmakers usually lead glamorous lives."

"And that's why you sold my picture? You needed the money."

"I did."

"You should've said something."

"Perhaps. But maybe you've noticed? I'm not big on sharing."

"No, I haven't noticed that at all."

We smile at each other, and a shadow lifts.

"Franny isn't Kaitlyn's daughter," I say. "That's what I came to tell you yesterday. She's a fraud."

"Yeah, I thought so."

"What?"

He raises an eyebrow. "You think I'm going to get caught out like that again?"

"How did you know?"

"I have a very good investigator I work with now. And Franny didn't cover her tracks all that well. For starters, Franny Maycombe's not her real name."

"That makes sense. We . . . I looked for her online and couldn't find any trace of her. It occurred to me that she'd probably changed her name along the way."

"But what made you start looking in the first place?"

"Nuh-uh. I told you that was off-limits, remember?"

"Can you at least tell me if it's something that would ruin me if it came out?"

"I don't think so. I don't think anyone would assume you should've known this."

Teo doesn't look like he believes me, and I suspect he'll be making a call to his investigator when we finish up. I'm going to have to move Kaitlyn. It's already dangerous enough having her in my house.

"But I can't tell you either way, and I hope you leave it at that, okay?"

"I'll try. You mentioned wanting my help with something."

"We need to expose Franny."

"Why?"

"Because she's supposed to marry Joshua, and those kids have been through enough."

"Why don't you simply tell him?"

"Why would he believe me? I don't have any proof. He'll just think I'm upset about . . . Wait, what is it you know about me? All's fair."

"In love and war? Which one is this?"

"You tell me what you know, and maybe I'll clarify that."

He reaches into his messenger bag and pulls out a file folder. Unlike the ones from the Compensation Committee meetings, this one's plain blue, purchased at a dollar store. He flips it open. Inside is a credit card statement. He points to an item that's highlighted in yellow.

"What were you consulting a divorce lawyer for?"

34

CORNER PIECE

KAITLYN

Kaitlyn had received the first e-mail from Franny when she was pregnant with Emily. Only Franny was calling herself Eileen then. Eileen Warner.

Kaitlyn was working at an architectural firm that did midlevel housing projects. She'd been carrying her pregnancy around like a secret. Knowing that when she announced it, everything at work would change. Not overtly but gradually. Her bosses were old-school men, even the women. They'd come up hard, not seeing their families. Parenting was the responsibility of their stay-at-home wives or nannies. Maternity leave was for sissies. They'd pretend to be happy for her, but they'd be plotting her exit. And she loved her job. The late-night camaraderie. The site visits. The sense of knowing she'd contributed to something tangible in the world, someone's dream come true.

Kaitlyn almost hadn't opened the e-mail. They'd been getting a lot of spam at the time, and it had an odd subject line: *Inquiry*. The content wasn't much less mysterious. She felt certain as she read it that she was going to be asked to wire money to a Nigerian bank account. Rambling lines about a search. A discovery. Kaitlyn read the words but couldn't grasp the meaning. And then, there it was: *I think you're my mother*.

An odd sound escaped her before she could stop it. The woman in the cubby next to her looked up.

"You okay?"

"I'm fine. I just got the strangest e-mail."

"Delete it."

Mary was always full of such practical advice. It was like having a mother in the office.

Kaitlyn had looked at the e-mail again. Could she simply delete it? Would that be cruel? It would be better to write her back, and tell her she'd made a mistake. But something about the e-mail made Kaitlyn uneasy. She wasn't sure what it was. Had she detected a threat in there? She read it again. It seemed less confused this time. Suffused with emotion, as one would expect. She'd had trouble concentrating since the pregnancy began. Pregnancy brain, she'd heard it referred to. All those extra hormones rushing around her body. Turning her brain back into a teenager's. There wasn't anything to fear here. Only a girl in pain.

So she wrote back. *I'm so sorry to tell you this, but I'm not your mother. I wish you the best of luck with your search.*

She should've listened to Mary.

• • •

Back in Cecily's basement, Kaitlyn couldn't sleep. It was one thing being thousands of miles away from her family. But knowing they were only a few streets away, that was a different challenge. Cecily had explained to her that Kaitlyn would have to go in the morning. She wasn't sure where, but she'd figure something out. The help she'd enlisted couldn't be entirely trusted, Cecily had said.

"So I took a risk."

"You could've asked me first," Kaitlyn said.

"I believe the words you meant to say were 'thank you.'"

Kaitlyn wanted to bite back but didn't. This was how things had to be now. She had to take it. Whatever there was, she had to swallow it and say thank you. Because she'd chosen this. The leaving and the coming back. She'd been free and clear. Even in her own life, she could've made different choices. Every step she'd taken had led her here. There was no point in wishing things were different. There would only be more of the same.

"Thank you."

Cecily had suggested they go to bed. Figure things out in the morning. Kaitlyn agreed, thanked her again. Went to the basement to pack up her meager belongings. Assumed the familiar position of staring at the ceiling.

But her daughters called to her like a siren's song. She could almost smell them in the room with her. That mix of baby powder and tearless shampoo that was all their own. She couldn't do this. Be this close to them and not see them.

Kaitlyn crept from bed and dressed in the darkest clothes she had. She pulled on her coat and tucked her hair up into her hat.

Wrapped a scarf around her face. She left by the basement exit after disabling the alarm. Cecily hadn't changed the passcode in years. She hugged the side of the house, letting the wind whip against her. Winter in Montreal was cold, but not like this. That sharp bite of damp that penetrated whatever you wore. Her bones hurt. But she wasn't going to turn back now.

There was a car parked in front of Cecily's house with two figures in it. There was a flash of light, an incoming text. Kaitlyn could see Cassie and a man. No, a boy. Cassie was kissing a boy. Kaitlyn watched for a moment, wondering if Cecily knew. Whether she should interrupt them, though that would be foolish. It was fine. Innocent. Just kissing.

Kaitlyn turned away and walked in the opposite direction toward Church Street. She still remembered her one and only kiss with Tom with frightening precision. Two years ago, give or take a month. The office Christmas party. A few months into their e-mail exchanges. Things had progressed slowly, but in the past few weeks, they'd become graphic. Detailed. Tom had been worried the IT guy might find them, so they'd switched to Gmail. That must've been the account Franny found. How, Kaitlyn had no idea. Had she written her from that account once by accident? Had she somehow stayed signed in on an errant laptop?

It was snowing. She'd had too much to drink and had been avoiding Tom. His e-mails stalked her around the party. She shook her head at him when they made eye contact. Made a show of turning her phone off. Tried to dance to some silly song with some of her coworkers. When it was time to go, he suggested they take a cab together. She knew it was a bad idea. Knew her defenses were down.

That if he tried something, she wouldn't be able to resist. But he read her mind and told her not to worry. And she trusted him. She had to, didn't she? She'd placed her whole life in his hands.

The roads had been slippery. The cabdriver drove slowly. At some point, Kaitlyn found her fingers entwined with Tom's. His hand was rough, chapped from winter. He traced a small circle over and over on the back of hers with his thumb. Even that small point of contact felt dangerous.

A few blocks from her house, the cab swerved on the ice. She was thrown against Tom. Into his arms. She closed her eyes and let it happen. His lips on hers. Hungry, but gentler than she'd expected. Slower. An agonizing kiss that they ended as the cab pulled up to her house.

She'd wanted to cry, but instead she'd leaned against his ear and said, "I can't anymore," then bolted before he could say anything. When she got inside, she'd left her purse on the floor, resisting the temptation to turn her phone on and wait for the message that was sure to come.

Kaitlyn passed the high school, turned right, and now she was outside her house. Remembering still how that kiss stayed with her for days. Weeks. The dreams it provoked. What would've changed, she wondered, if she'd given in? If they'd done all those things they'd written about? In the end, both their marriages had ended.

What if, if, if?

It was after ten. Only a few lights were on in the house. The living room. The den. She could see the flicker of the television through the windows. The lights were all off upstairs. Of course. What was she thinking? That her daughters would come conveniently to the front windows, perfectly lit for secret viewing? Called there by her presence? Those sorts of things didn't happen in reality. Even in her alternative reality.

Kaitlyn crossed the street. Her boots were silent on the pavement. She walked up her driveway, then hugged the house the way she'd hugged Cecily's. She approached the side window to the den. The curtains were pulled back. Joshua never closed the curtains. It was always Kaitlyn who'd closed out the light. Closed out life. She'd had it all in front of her, but she hadn't wanted it. Or couldn't reach for it. It amounted to the same thing. She felt like a visitor in her own life, a guest who'd stayed too long.

Joshua was sitting alone on the couch. An episode of *Ray Donovan* was playing. They'd started watching it together a few months before Kaitlyn left. Kaitlyn found parts of it too violent. Another casualty of parenthood. Things she used to be able to tolerate easily became hard to watch.

Kaitlyn leaned in. She caught a few lines of dialogue. It was from the pilot. He was cycling back to the beginning. Was he thinking of her? Wondering if the e-mails she wrote while she sat next to him were the ones he'd read the other day? Matching up the time stamps with events in their life?

She'd meant to erase all those e-mails. Delete that account. She'd almost made it, too. But she felt like she needed evidence. That it wasn't all in her head. That what they'd had existed. She wasn't sure why. So she kept one or two threads. Had kept the account alive. She knew she'd never read them again. And in this last year, to the extent she thought about it at all, she assumed time would do for her what she couldn't bring herself to do. Erase the traces. Put their messages in the trash where they belonged.

A shadow shifted in the room, and there was Franny. Or Eileen.

She never did find out her real name. She sucked in a cold breath. It was strange to see her in her house. Sitting in her old place. The look of tenderness that crossed Joshua's face made her question her plan. They'd clearly made up. He deserved to be happy. But the girls. Franny would raise the girls. She was a . . . She wasn't sure of the diagnosis, but it wasn't right. *She* wasn't right. Kaitlyn had left in part to take her own diseased mind away from her daughters. She couldn't be replaced by someone far worse.

Joshua leaned over and kissed Franny. And there it was. The moment she'd also come looking for.

Her life, through the looking glass.

INTERVIEW TRANSCRIPT

TJ: What did Sherrie tell the police?

FM: That I killed my parents, of course. Don't look so shocked. She told you all this already, right?

TJ: Not exactly.

FM: Hmm. That's interesting. Anyway, I didn't do it.

TJ: Why would she say you did?

FM: Because, it's like I told you. She has it in for me. Always has.

TJ: But why would the police take that claim seriously, then?

FM: Because the brakes on my parents' car failed. So maybe they could've been tampered with or something. And I was the bad seed, right? I'd been to that boot camp thing and arrested a few times.

TJ: How far did the investigation go?

FM: Far enough. The police questioned me for hours. I was under investigation.

TJ: Were your parents' brakes tampered with?

FM: No! The brake light had been on in my dad's car for weeks. He was so stingy, he didn't want to get "taken for a ride" by the mechanic.

TJ: Just a car accident, then.

FM: Yeah, but then I'm forever the "suspect," you know? And Madison's not that big a town. Everywhere I went, *everywhere*, people were looking at me funny.

TJ: So you left?

FM: Yeah, that's right. I was sick of being that person. Living in that narrative.

TJ: Which narrative?

FM: Me as the bad guy. The antagonist. That's what I am, right? You know those "learn to write screenplays" ads you always see on Facebook or whatever, with famous writers? I took one of those classes once. Anyway, it talked about how every piece has to have a villain, an antagonist, and I saw your board, the one you have up in the other room, and it's obvious that's who I am in this story.

TJ: Maybe we make our own place in stories.

FM: In your own story, sure. I agree with that. But I'm not in my story. I'm in yours.

35

NIGHT MUSIC

CECILY

The last thing I want to do is go to a church and watch a kids' Irish dancing show, but I'd promised Sara weeks ago that I'd attend her son Ben's recital with her, and she's done so much for me this year I don't feel like I can back out. Besides, if anyone's looking, I should stick to my routine and show up where I'm expected. These are new thoughts. Before, I never ascribed any real credit to those who might look into my background. But after this afternoon, I can't feel that way anymore. I know better now.

A half inch of snow fell this afternoon when I was meeting with Teo. The driving's dicey, and the entranceway to the church basement is scattered with boots. I add mine to the collection, hang my black coat on a wire hanger next to six others, and pay for my ticket. I pay another ten dollars to enter the wine raffle because: wine. Then I take a program and search the room. Sara's sitting midway up, glaring across the aisle at her ex-mother-in-law.

Sara and Bill's divorce a couple years ago was awful, an example that gave me pause even as my own marriage was collapsing around me. I understood her acrimony, but his family's wholehearted decision to blame her and turn their backs on her was a puzzle. My own mother might hate Tom, but she'd never have spoken badly about him to the children even if he'd lived. Bill's mother, on the other hand, regularly denigrated Sara, saying such charming things as, "Your mother should be a personal shopper; she's so good at spending other people's money," and actively encouraged Bill's paranoia that Sara might take the kids and run away.

"What's the witch done now?" I ask as I sit next to her. She's wearing her hair in a ballet bun, which suits the clean lines of her face.

"She tried to keep me from coming tonight. Said it was Bill's night with the kids, and I wasn't welcome. As if I'm somehow a bad mother for wanting to come to my son's dance recital in a public venue. What the fuck?"

"She's evil."

"And to think I used to like her."

"I always thought she was batshit crazy myself."

She laughs. "Thank God for you."

I open the program. "What's on the bill tonight? *Lord of the Dance?*"

"Probably."

"And the alcohol is where, exactly?"

Sara looks sheepish. "Did I say there'd be alcohol?"

"Pretty sure you did."

"Do super-fattening cookies count?"

I sigh. I could use a drink. "They're at least going to be wearing cute costumes, aren't they?"

"I can guarantee that."

"Phew."

We lean back in our chairs, those wooden hard-backed kind I don't think they even make anymore.

"Where have you been for the last couple days?" Sara asks. "Feels like forever since we talked."

"It's been busy with the new job and . . . everything." I wish I could tell Sara what's going on. I need someone to talk through all this with like a girlfriend, not just a therapist like Linda, and the only person I have is the person who screwed it all up in the first place.

"That Franny news is crazy. Have you spoken to her? Or Joshua?"

"Franny, no. Joshua, briefly." I hesitate, then fill her in quickly on what Joshua found, the e-mails between Kaitlyn and Tom. Surely this much is safe to share.

"Oh my God," Sara says several times while I'm speaking and one more time when I'm finished.

"I think I used some more colorful words."

"That is . . . I don't even know what that is."

I look down at my program. There is, in fact, going to be a *Lord of the Dance* starring her son.

"I'm having trouble processing this," Sara says.

"Join the club."

"She always seemed so innocent."

"Did she?"

"I thought she was a prude. Remember that time when I was telling the story about"—she lowers her voice—"my one-night stand with that guy from yoga?"

"You guys never got along, though."

"And now I know why."

"You think you saw something in her I didn't?"

"You don't?"

The Irish-dancing teacher takes the stage. She's in her seventies but still has the upright carriage of a dancer. She's wearing a floaty hippie dress, and she thanks us all for being here through a tinny microphone. This is their most important fund-raiser of the year, and they have lots of dancers to send to the Irish-dancing competition in Dublin. Please eat a lot of cookies. Ha-ha-ha. She leaves the stage, and the curtains part. Four tiny girls and Sara's son Ben are standing in the middle of the barren stage in glittering green costumes. They're adorable.

"I haven't even told you the best part," I hear myself say.

"What did you say?"

"I haven't . . ." The music blares, and the kids start to clomp their feet on the floor. They're off the beat but impressive nonetheless for six-year-olds.

"I've got to record this," Sara says, getting up with her phone.

She walks to the stage. I watch her ex, Bill, who I used to be friends with. When things turned nasty, Tom and I ended up taking sides. But when they'd first broken up, Bill had moved into the mother-in-law's suite they'd installed above their garage. He'd slip into the house every morning to be there for the kids at breakfast. It was that act that kept me from hating him. I've told Bill this, too, but that doesn't keep him from glaring at me as he walks past my seat. Hate is such a weird emotion, and contagious, apparently.

The music ends as the kids clack their final clack. Ben raises his hands above his head in victory as the girls crouch around him looking up in adoration, and I shudder at the stereotypes that are being inbred so young.

Sara returns to her seat. Only twelve more numbers to go.

"Ben looks like Bill," I say.

"He does."

"Is that hard?"

"Is it hard for you when the kids look like Tom?"

"Sometimes." A tear slips out, and Sara pats my hand gently.

"I feel like this conversation might need more alcohol than this church basement can provide," she says.

"You have no idea."

"What were you saying before? What's the part I don't know?"

"I'm not sure you'd even believe me if I told you."

"Try me."

The music starts again as some older girls with their hair in ringlets take the stage. Their costumes are stiff with embroidery. Sara's told me how much those costumes cost, and she'd thanked her lucky stars she had only sons.

"Not here," I say.

"Come by later? I think there are still some good bottles in the wine fridge above the garage. I think Bill was hiding them from me when he was living up there."

A light bulb goes off. Maybe Sara can solve two problems at once.

"I'll try but . . . This might sound crazy, but can I borrow that room above your garage?"

"Why?"

"I need to hide something there."

Several hours later, I'm up in my room, going through my nightly routine. As I lather my face in the same cream I've used for twenty years, I eye Tom's toothpaste lying on the counter. His toothbrush is still in its holder, charged up for its next use. His comb and brush and razor are all here, too, keeping me company like they do every night. Why am I holding on to these things? I always told myself it was for the children, so they wouldn't know or guess how things were between us. But maybe I was the one who couldn't accept it.

I pull the garbage can from under the sink and sweep my arm across the counter, collecting toothpaste, toothbrush, etc., all the things Tom left behind. It makes a satisfying *clang* as it hits the sides of the metal container. I open the medicine cabinet and empty that, too, of the expired medications and the special dental floss he used. I should dispose of this properly, in a safe manner, but right now putting it in the trash is what I need to do.

I finish up the bathroom—dandruff shampoo, be gone!—and walk to our closet. I open the doors, and my energy dissipates. A lifetime of Tom's clothes stares back at me. This is hours of work. I should let the kids participate, deciding what they want to keep, if anything, and make a thing of it, a ceremony. Or maybe I'll tell them to pick one thing to remember him by and then call a charity to come and pick it all up. Some of these suits might be worth something to a charity shop.

I hear a car door slam. I look out the window. It's Cassie, running up the front walk as a car drives away. I check the clock. It's after ten, way past curfew even if she'd asked me if she could go out. I listen to her shuffle up the stairs.

"Cass," I say, "come in here."

She walks into my bedroom looking sheepish. "Sorry, Mom."

"Did you sneak out?"

"Just to right outside. So technically, I didn't even leave the property."

"Technically?"

"Okay, I totally did. But Kevin wanted to talk."

Her eyes are bright, and she's wearing lip gloss that's partially faded away. I know that look, the look of a girl who's been kissed.

"Oh, honey."

"I'm sorry, Mom. It wasn't a big deal, and I would've asked you, but I thought you might say no and . . ." She sits down on the edge of the bed. She touches her lips with her fingertips. "He kissed me."

I stifle the urge to call this boy's mother and tell her to keep her son away from my child. Tom. These are the times I need Tom. This is why I let him move back in, because doing this without him, watching them grow up and change and experience all the firsts they still have to experience is too much for me to do alone.

"Was it nice?" I ask, trying to keep my voice even.

"You're not freaked out?"

"Of course I'm freaked out. I want to strangle this kid. I'm trying to be the cool mom. How'm I doing?"

She stands up and trips into my arms. "You're doing great."

She buries her head in my shoulder. We're the same height now, and sometimes when I look at her it's like flipping through one of the photograph albums my mother curated so lovingly. My first kiss was from a boy named David. He stole it at a school dance.

"I miss Dad."

"Me, too, honey. Me, too."

"You do?"

"Of course."

"Even though—" She stops herself. She doesn't have the right words yet to express what was going on with her father and me, even the little she knows, and I'm not about to tell her what happened between him and Kaitlyn.

Can what Kaitlyn said be true? That they had a digital relationship that never went beyond one stolen kiss? And even if it is, is it better that Tom let me think the worst of him? Or did he know that even if he'd told me the truth, it was too much to forgive? That the fact that he'd participated in it at all, had sought it out, showed him something in us that was broken that he didn't want to take the time to fix? Though he did try to tell me. He did, and I didn't want to hear it. He could've tried harder, he could've persisted, but he let it go when I asked him to. Whose fault is that?

"Even though, nothing," I say. "I'll always love your father. No matter what happened between us. I spent more of my life with him than without him. And he gave me you and your brother. I can't imagine what my life would've been like without him."

"But then you had to learn."

"We all did. But we're doing okay, aren't we? You got kissed today. Things can't be so bad."

She smiles. "Do you think that means he likes me?"

"I sure hope so."

She pulls away, confused. I watch the insecurity of a dating girl flit across her face. This little twerp has already hurt her, and there's nothing I can do about it but stand back and watch.

"What about Teo?" Cassie asks.

"What about him?"

"I heard you and Aunt Kaitlyn talking about him. Is he going to help you?"

"You shouldn't be listening in on conversations."

"How would I ever learn anything, then?"

"You could ask."

"And you'll tell me?"

"Yes. I told you before, if I can answer, I will."

"So tell me."

I pat the bed, and she sits down with me. "Teo's going to help us figure out who Franny is. She's been lying and tricking people, and we want to put a stop to that."

"To get money? Is that why she did it?"

Was that what this was all about? A payday for Franny? But if so, why would she marry Joshua? She could just file her claim and be done with it. Take her money and run back to wherever it was she came from. Sticking around didn't seem like Franny. But then again, I clearly don't know Franny at all. I know someone she invented to get access. She'd felt familiar because she'd told me what I wanted to hear. Like all good confidence men, she knew how to extract the information she wanted, then turn it back on the source so it felt like they knew things they didn't.

"I don't know. Maybe we'll find out someday."

"Is Uncle Joshua going to be embarrassed?"

"Why?"

"When everyone finds out about Franny? Because now everyone

knows they were supposed to get married, because of that article, and then everyone will know he was tricked."

"I hope he's not embarrassed. She tricked everyone, not just him."

"Will you call the police?"

Another step I haven't thought of. Do I want to see Franny punished? No, I don't. What she did was wrong, but there was good in it, too. Look how hard she worked to get Joshua and the girls their compensation money, even though it had been her rule that made it hard for them to get it in the first place. What was that about, I wonder? Why was she so insistent about a DNA connection? Was it merely to draw attention away from herself, to name the thing people might think she was—a fraud—so she was the one who said it first?

"I'm not sure. That depends on what we find out, I guess."

"But if someone lies to get money, then that's fraud, isn't it? They should go to jail."

I shiver. "She hasn't gotten any money yet."

"People who do bad things should be punished. That's what Dad always used to say."

"He did, didn't he?" I stroke Cassie's hair. "So tell me more about this boy."

36

SOMETHING, SOMEWHERE
IN THE MIDDLE

KAITLYN

The second e-mail from Eileen arrived a year later. Kaitlyn was on maternity leave then, or that's what she was telling people. Her post-partum depression was keeping her from returning to work. Worse than any depression she'd ever felt before. Her days were a foggy mix of sleep and caring for Emily when she was able to. Joshua had hired a nurse to be there during the day. Kaitlyn felt ashamed that she needed help. In truth, the nurse was there for both of them. They both needed caring for.

Despite everything, Emily was thriving. A bouncing, happy baby girl with ringlets in her hair. She cooed and sighed and smiled.

Everyone was always telling them they should take her to an agent. That her baby belonged in catalogs, in commercials. As if it were a compliment that people thought her baby was attractive enough to sell things.

Kaitlyn knew she should be happy. But instead she was bitter. Bitter motherhood didn't feel like a blessing but a curse. That the weight she'd gained wouldn't leave even though she was barely eating. That Joshua thought he could farm out his care of her and their daughter to someone more competent. It all felt horribly unfair. What had she done to deserve this? She'd made mistakes in her life, but hadn't everyone? All she wanted was a fresh start. A peaceful three months at home with her baby. Was that too much to ask?

To keep up the pretense that she might return to work someday soon, Kaitlyn was still checking her work e-mail. It was fall, and the leaves were changing. That's how Eileen started her e-mail: *It's fall. The leaves are changing. Another year's gone by, and I still haven't found my mother. Only, I think I did find her. I think it's you. Will you please, please contact me? Will you please get in touch? I'm so sad.*

It was these last words that got to Kaitlyn. She was so sad, too. Maybe there was something she could do to help this girl. Let her know that someone cared about her struggle. Give her someone to talk to.

Kaitlyn wrote back.

Cecily woke Kaitlyn before it was light out.

"What's going on?" Kaitlyn asked. "What time is it?"

"It's six."

Kaitlyn rolled over and rubbed her eyes. Cecily was a shadowy form above her.

"We need to move you to somewhere safer," Cecily said.

"You think that's necessary?"

"My friend Teo, the documentary filmmaker I told you about, has agreed to help us. But the way he's going to do that is by hiring a private detective, and I'm going to have to meet with him today. Do you want to be in the house while a PI is sniffing around?"

"That doesn't sound like the best idea."

"Right?"

Cecily snapped on the light. Kaitlyn shut her eyes, flashing back to when she still lived in her childhood home. Her mother used to do this. Pry Kaitlyn from the safety of her bed. Make her face the world when all she wanted to do was wallow in the dark.

"Up you get."

Kaitlyn threw the covers back. She'd slept in her clothes. She hadn't had the energy to change when she'd gotten back from spying on Joshua and Franny.

"Did you sleep in that?"

"Obviously."

Cecily sighed. "Are you okay?"

"I'm fine. I can be ready in five minutes. Where are we going?"

"Sara's house."

"What? You told her?"

"I had to tell someone. And she has that apartment over her garage, so it seemed perfect."

Sara had always hated Kaitlyn. Kaitlyn confronted her about it once. Sara said she was "crazy." But Kaitlyn wasn't. She knew jealousy when she saw it. "What about just putting me up in a cheap hotel somewhere?"

Cecily crossed her arms. "But how would you eat? And what if someone was following me and saw you when I went to see you? That happens sometimes because of that stupid photograph. I assume you've seen it?"

Kaitlyn got out of bed. She felt rumpled. "I'm sorry I wasn't there for you that day. And very grateful you never made it to that meeting with Tom."

"I can agree with the second part."

Kaitlyn bit her lip. "Don't worry—I'll be gone for good in a few days."

"Yeah, you will."

INTERVIEW TRANSCRIPT

TJ: What happened next, Franny? When did you leave Madison?

FM: About six months after my parents died.

TJ: What then?

FM: I became a wanderer. After a while, I realized that what I was looking for was my mother. My real mother. Kaitlyn. The rest isn't that much different from what I told you before.

TJ: Are you sure?

FM: Of course I am.

TJ: Sherrie said you weren't adopted.

FM: She didn't know.

TJ: How's that possible?

FM: Our parents never told her. I asked them not to.

TJ: Why?

FM: Because I felt like enough of an outsider already. My sister would've used it against me every day if she knew the truth.

TJ: My investigator can't find any record of your adoption.

FM: He must not be a very good investigator, then.

TJ: He's the best.

FM: Clearly not. I *was* adopted, okay? And Kaitlyn was my mother. I can prove it.

TJ: How?

FM: Because our DNA matched. That's how we knew the mug was Kaitlyn's. That protocol I put in place, it requires a DNA match to qualify for compensation. And I qualified because we found that match using my DNA.

TJ: Can you show me the test results?

FM: They're supposed to be confidential for Initiative use only.

TJ: But you can get them anyway, can't you?

FM: Well, yes, probably. If Cecily agrees. If we both ask, we can probably get them to agree to release them to you.

TJ: Will you ask her?

FM: Maybe you should.

TJ: How come?

FM: Cecily's not too happy with me right now because of Joshua. And also because of some other stuff I found out.

TJ: Such as?

FM: It's private.

TJ: Have you spoken to Cecily recently?

FM: She's called a bunch of times, but I was keeping clear of her for a bit, you know? Trying to give her a chance to calm down. Because I get it that it's a bit surprising what's going on. But Joshua was so kind to me through all this. We kind of healed each other. And now we're going to be a real family, just like I always wanted.

37

MAYBE, MAYBE SOMEDAY

CECILY

I went to see the divorce lawyer in the weeks when Tom was living in the businessman's hotel downtown. I wanted to know how it could go, what my rights were, how the money would be worked out. Sara suggested I go to a shark, a barracuda, one of the lawyers who sees your ex as so much chum in the water. She regretted she hadn't done that, wishing she'd made Bill twist and turn legally, given how he's treated her. But I knew myself. I didn't have predator instincts. I didn't want to see Tom twist and turn and have to twist and turn along with him. I didn't want to go to court—the thought of it terrified me—and so I knew that if we did this, if I did this, and we were going to be over, officially, then it would have to be some kind of mediated solution.

Just sitting there in a lawyer's office felt so alien to me, even though she handled the meeting with a practiced hand. She had a box of Kleenex ready and a yellow legal pad to fill up with my familiar story. How many variations of the same thing had she heard? Hundreds? A thousand? It was dizzying to think about. Tom and I weren't just some statistic. We were each other's history, a family, parents. Whatever she wrote down about us would never be the whole story, even if she could predict every detail. Was this how we were supposed to end? In court documents that would bear only our initials so they remained private? Our children referred to as C. and H.? Our furniture appraised and divided equally?

But what alternative did I have? Let Tom off the hook? Let him move back in and sleep next to him for the rest of my life knowing what I knew? Could I forgive him, did I even want to make the effort? What chance did we have when I couldn't trust anything he said?

The questions in my head were louder than the answers the lawyer was providing to the ones I asked out loud.

I met Tom for lunch after the meeting. It was the first time I'd seen him since he'd left, the first time we'd spoken in person. When we'd made the appointment, I wasn't even sure I could go through with it. Walking into the restaurant, I felt dizzy. Then I spotted Tom, and I relaxed. He was sitting near the window, a drink on the table, and he looked like shit. His face was puffy, and he needed a haircut. He'd put on weight, and the buttons on his shirt were straining a bit. It made him more approachable to see him so obviously miserable.

I'd been imagining him reveling in his newfound freedom. Instead, it looked as if he'd spent the last two weeks drinking and stress eating.

He rose as I came to the table, then kissed me quickly on the cheek.

"Hi. You look great."

"Thanks."

"Thank you for meeting me."

We sat down. A waiter came over with a glass of white wine. Even though it was barely past noon, I was grateful for the drink.

"What do you want, Tom?" I blurted.

He looked startled but determined; his eyes fixed on mine. "I want to come home."

"Just like that?"

"I miss you. I miss the kids. I know I fucked up, but I'll do whatever it takes to make things better. Counseling. Sleeping in the basement. Whatever you need me to do."

"Is there a time machine in the basement I don't know about?"

"I wish there were, Lily. I wish I could go back and change everything about this."

"You just wish you hadn't gotten caught."

"That's not true. I swear."

"How can I trust you?"

"I want to regain your trust. So whatever conditions you want to impose. Whatever you want to know, just ask and I'll tell you." He pulled out his phone and handed it to me. "I'll give you the pass code, and you can check it whenever you want."

I dropped it on the table. I felt dirty just holding it. "Are . . . Are your texts with her still on this?"

"I deleted them. I deleted everything."

"So I can't know everything, then."

He went pale. "I'll tell you whatever you want if you want me to, though there isn't that much to tell. But maybe . . . I know you, Lily. You don't want to know the details. You'll just turn them over and over in your mind and wonder if I've told you everything. I betrayed you and our family. I'm so ashamed of having done that—you have no idea. But let me bear the burden of it, okay? The details aren't what's going to heal us."

Tom started to cry.

"Please stop," I said.

"I'm sorry." He wiped at his eyes with his napkin.

"Don't make me feel sorry for you."

"I don't want that. I don't want that at all. Please, Cecily, can we please just try? I'm on my knees here."

"Maybe you should be."

He pushed his chair back.

"What are you doing?"

"Getting down on my knees."

"What?" I looked around. Half the restaurant was watching us. "People are looking."

"I don't care."

"I care, you idiot."

He stopped, got back in his chair. "I wanted to show you how serious I am."

"Okay, I get it. You're serious."

"Will you give me a chance? Please?"

I thought back to what the lawyer told me. That coming to see her didn't have to mean my marriage was over. That there was nothing final about talking to her, that information never hurt anyone.

I should be absolutely sure about what I wanted before I made the decision to file papers. And that was the problem; I wasn't absolutely sure about anything. All this was so new and shocking and unexpected. I hadn't even thought my marriage was in trouble before I read that text. Maybe that made me an idiot, but it also meant that if I wanted, maybe there was something left for me to save.

"I can give you a chance."

I work my shift in a daze, checking my phone constantly to make sure Kaitlyn stays put and to see if there's any news from Teo. It rings only once, but it's my mom.

"Hi, Mom."

I signal to a waiter to take my place at the podium, walking down the hall to the bathroom, where it's quieter.

"Honey, I'm so glad you answered. I haven't heard from you for days."

"I texted you this morning."

"A text. That's not communication. And I thought you were coming over on Halloween?"

Halloween. That feels like weeks ago.

"I'm sorry. We got distracted. Was it hard?"

"It was fun, actually. Your dad would've been proud of me."

"I'm sure he would. I know I am."

"So, where have you been?"

"Cecily?"

I turn around. The waiter who replaced me is standing there, looking anxious.

"Mom, can I call you back later? It's busy here."

"Of course. But, Cecily?"

"Yes?"

"Take care of yourself, okay?"

I hang up, staring at the phone. Does my mother know what's going on? How could she? No, it's just momtuition; I have it myself sometimes with the kids. I put the phone away and go back to work.

Finally, around five, Teo texts me that they're ready, and I suggest they meet me at six thirty. I call Cassie and ask her to take Henry out to dinner and a movie so we can have the house to ourselves. Cassie asks if Kevin can go with them, and I agree. If I could send Henry as a chaperone on all her dates, I would.

Teo's car pulls up at the same time as mine. I don't know what I was expecting his investigator to look like—some variant of Humphrey Bogart, perhaps—but Joe Connor is a short, small man with round glasses and a bald head, no fedora in sight. Being unassuming is probably a good thing in his line of work.

I direct them where to put their hats and coats and go to the kitchen to put on a pot of coffee. I feel chilled to the bone, though the house is warm. Teo and Joe sit at the kitchen island while I hover.

"What did you find?"

Joe pulls a blue file out of his bag like the one Teo had the other day. He opens it. An arrest photo of Franny is sitting on top. I take the piece of paper: Eileen Warner, eighteen, arrested on suspicion of murder.

"Murder? She's a murderer?"

"They never laid charges."

"Who was she accused of killing?"

"Her parents."

"Jesus."

"Her sister turned her in. Said she'd seen her tampering with the car the day before the accident that killed them. The brakes failed, and they drove into a ditch."

I feel even colder. "How come she got off?"

"They couldn't find any signs of tampering with the brakes, and there was a long history of animosity between Eileen and her sister. No evidence of a crime plus unreliable witness means no prosecution."

"But did she do it?"

Joe swings his head back and forth. "She might've done. I spoke to her sister. She's convincing. Says that she and Eileen actually got along all right growing up. But then Eileen started hanging with the wrong crowd, ended up in some kind of juvenile detention program, mixed up in drugs and petty larceny. When she got out of the program, she was very angry with her parents. Telling them they'd ruined her life and whatnot. Then Sherrie saw her working on the car, and the next day her parents are dead."

"Is there . . . Should we be reporting this to someone?"

"Probably no point in that. I didn't find any more proof than what the police had at the time. Absent a confession, it's highly unlikely they'd reopen the investigation."

"Well, what about that? Why don't we get her to confess?"

Joe takes off his glasses and polishes them with the end of his shirt. "You've been watching too much TV."

"I have?"

"If you think I'm going to be able to get her to confess in a way that will stand up in court, you surely have."

"There's no point in getting a confession that can't be used," Teo says. "And we could end up the ones in trouble. Besides, that wasn't the point of all this. We wanted to find enough to persuade her to leave Joshua, right? This, and the other things we've found, should do the trick."

"What else did you find?"

"The name change," Joe says. "And her sister says she wasn't adopted. I looked into it, and she's right. No adoption records anywhere in Wisconsin by her parents. And they had lived there since before Eileen was born."

"Couldn't they have come to Illinois to adopt?"

"They could've, but I checked the records here, too."

"Aren't those records sealed?"

"Some are and some aren't."

He looks blasé. If I press him about where he got his information, I'm sure he'll give me some variation of "I have my methods."

"Why are you surprised?" Teo says. "You were the one who told me that she wasn't Kaitlyn's daughter."

"I know, it's just . . . My source isn't the most reliable person."

"How so?"

"Let's leave it at that, okay?"

Joe looks curious. Too curious.

"Right, Teo? We had a deal."

"We do—don't worry. Joe's not going to go investigating without getting paid, right, buddy?"

"True enough."

"So how do we do this?" I ask. "How do we convince her to leave? She's not even returning my calls or texts right now, and I'm not sure where she is."

"She's back with Mr. Ring," Joe says. "They reconciled, apparently."

I feel stunned, though I'm not sure why. Joshua doesn't know what I know. They got into a fight because he was hurt about Kaitlyn and Tom.

"Well," I say. "That makes it easier, I guess. Poor Joshua."

"I thought I'd ask her to come in for a final interview," Teo says. "Kill two birds with one stone, so to speak."

"Is she talking to you?"

"Nope."

"So how do we make that happen?"

Teo hesitates. "What if you speak to Joshua?"

"And say what? Your fiancée's a complete fraud, and Teo would like to confront her with the information so you have a better ending for your documentary?"

Teo smiles. "You'll make it sound much better than that. Besides, you're going to have to speak to him about it at some point, aren't you?"

The reality of it all hits me. Because Teo's right, I'm going to have to speak to Joshua about all of this. This and the other things we left hanging when Franny found those e-mails. But how can I do this to Joshua? He's had enough loss already. And maybe his and Kaitlyn's relationship wasn't great, I could always see that, and she was unhappy, but he's a great dad and has managed a tough situation well. On the other hand, I can't let Kaitlyn's girls be raised by someone like Franny. What I know already is enough, and nothing Joe found makes it any better, even if she didn't kill her parents.

"Yes, you're right. But I'm not looking forward to it."

"I don't blame you."

"Can I have that file?"

Joe looks at Teo, who shakes his head. "Sorry, ma'am, but this here is my confidential work product. If it goes out of my hands, then I could be compromising myself and the people who helped me get it."

"How am I supposed to convince Joshua, then? If someone told me this kind of stuff about my husband, I probably wouldn't believe them unless I had the evidence. Unless I could see for myself that it was true."

"I have an idea," Teo says. "But you're probably not going to like it."

He tells me what it is, and he's right. I don't like it, but it's going to be effective, I think: kill another two birds, or three in this case.

It's just sad that there are so many birds that need killing in the first place.

Joe leaves, and I text Joshua and ask him to meet me for coffee — alone, I emphasize. He dithers a bit but then agrees to meet me after the kids are in bed. *Franny can watch them*, he writes, his way of letting me know she's back.

"It's all set," I say to Teo.

"Good. Thanks for doing that."

"I haven't convinced him to do anything yet."

"I have faith in you."

I sink onto the couch. "I have no idea why. I've been a complete mess the entire time you've known me."

He sits down on the coffee table in front of me. Our knees are almost touching. He looks tired and stressed. This isn't easy for anyone.

"You're not a mess," he says. "You're great."

"If you could see the inside of my brain right now, I doubt you'd think that."

"I'd love to see the inside of your brain."

"I'll bet. The better to document me."

"That's not what I meant."

He's looking at me so intently, as if he's become the camera, recording my every move. I cover my face with my hands. I'm so sick of being observed, of being seen. Before, I was invisible, a star only in my own life. We could all use a trip to the past.

"This is the problem with us," I say.

"What's that?"

"It's not just the trust thing we were talking about the other day. It's this film. It's always going to be between us."

"I'll be finished with it soon."

"But it won't be finished with me. It's going to come out, and for your sake, I hope it's a big success, but for me, I wish that no one would ever see it."

"Why did you agree to participate, then?"

"You're very persuasive."

"I'm not that persuasive. Come on, I'm not recording this; just tell me."

I look at my hands. I'm still wearing my wedding ring. I put it back on my finger on the way home from New York and never took it off again. "I felt guilty, I think. Guilty I survived, guilty I got that check. Guilty I wasn't the grieving widow everyone thought I was. And I had this silly idea that maybe it would bring closure to the whole thing. That once everything was down on tape, I could move on, and everyone else could, too. I could go back to being who I was before."

"That makes sense."

"Does it?"

"Of course it does. But you don't have to feel guilty, Cecily. I'm sure you're not the only one whose marriage was in trouble and whose spouse died that day."

He doesn't know how right he is.

"That's probably true."

We stare at each other for a moment until the heat rises in my cheeks.

"You know what I see?" Teo says. "What I'm going to show in my film?"

"What?"

"Someone who never understood how strong she was. Think of all the amazing things you've done this year. You're a symbol to so many people of what survival can look like. How you can turn tragedy into something positive not just for yourself but for others, too." He leans in as he talks, closing the space between us. "And that's why I wanted you in my film. You're the hero, Cecily, whether it feels like it or not."

"I wish I could see myself that way."

"What's holding you back?"

"The truth."

"What's the truth?"

I sit up, and now our faces are so close I can smell the coffee Teo's been drinking.

"I had a crush on you," I say.

"Had? What happened to it?"

"You know what happened."

He frowns. "I killed it."

"You did."

"That's too bad."

"Is it?"

"Yes, because my crush is still alive and well."

He comes closer, and I can feel the kiss before it starts. A real kiss this time, not some hurried thing on a street corner. Soft lips, his tongue in my mouth, his hands on my hips pulling me toward him.

I want this, I want this, I want him. But then I stop.

"We can't."

He rests his forehead on mine. "Are you sure?"

"You're the one who put the brakes on. Nothing's changed, has it?"

"No." He kisses my forehead and stands. "I should probably go."

"I have to meet Joshua soon."

"Right. Let me know how that goes?"

I stand, and we walk to the front door. "I will."

He puts on his coat, then strokes the side of my face. "I wish things were different."

"We all do."

I open the front door and watch him walk to his car. He gives me a wave as he drives past the house, and I can't help but wish I'd made a different decision. But then again, do I need another man in my life who has doubts about whether we should be together? I deserve to be someone's first choice.

I deserve to be someone's sun.

38

I SPY WITH MY LITTLE EYE

KAITLYN

There was something about hiding above a garage that belonged to someone who'd never liked her that made Kaitlyn feel more like a fugitive than she had all year. She didn't trust Sara not to blow the lid off this whole thing. The look of disgust she'd given her when she let them in hadn't helped. Kaitlyn didn't need those kinds of looks from others. She was disgusted enough with herself. And all it meant was that staying there felt dangerous. She might be discovered at any moment. A SWAT team on the stairs. A door kicked in. Then cuffs. Being booked and photographed. A cell with a bad mattress and a scary roommate.

Child abandonment. That's what she'd done. She'd looked it

up once. It was a Class 4 felony in Illinois. She didn't know what that meant, but she knew felonies were generally something to be avoided. They probably wouldn't put her in jail, but given how she'd gone about it, they might want to make an example of her.

She'd also Googled "is faking your own death illegal?" The search auto-filled; someone before her, many people, in fact, had asked the same question. Even though she'd done it in another anonymous Internet café, she'd gotten nervous. Was there some alarm that went off in Skynet if you Googled child abandonment and faking your own death? If there wasn't, there should be.

Pseudocide. That's what faking your own death was called. It wasn't illegal, but according to an article she'd read, it generally required so many other frauds to pull it off that you were bound to make it illegal. Kaitlyn didn't think she'd done any of those things. She hadn't created a false identity. She'd gone back to who she was before she was married. She hadn't involved anyone else, so it wasn't a conspiracy. Or filed for insurance or run out on loan payments. Though maybe she had. Joshua had to pay the mortgage by himself now. And she owed support to her kids.

She had to face it. She was a criminal. If she was caught, bad things would happen. She had to stay uncaught. In a day or two, when all this was taken care of, she could leave again. Go back to Canada. Maybe Andrea would even take her back. If not, there were enough families in need of her services. It was a way to make up for abandoning her own children. Being a surrogate mother.

Eileen had felt abandoned. That's what she wrote to her in the first in a long series of rambling e-mails. Her whole life, she felt as if she didn't fit in. That missing biology was a main character in her life. One she couldn't get past. That's why she was so desperate to find her mother.

Kaitlyn was sympathetic at first. How could she not be? And it made her feel useful. Like she was helping Eileen get better. Providing her an outlet. A sympathetic ear. It helped Kaitlyn put some things in perspective, too. Her own life wasn't that bad. She should try to appreciate it more. Maybe her family, motherhood, hadn't worked out as she'd hoped. But that didn't mean it was all bad. That it couldn't improve. If telling someone her problems helped Eileen, then it could help her, too. She went to see a counselor. She got medication. The clouds lifted.

Then Eileen had written: *You're my mother, aren't you?*

No, Eileen, Kaitlyn had written back. *I'm sorry, but I'm not.*

But I feel so close to you, you know? I feel that tie I was missing, that bond. It's you. I know it's you. Please can we meet so we can verify?

Verify how?

A DNA test.

I'm not your mother.

But I have the record. My birth certificate from the hospital.

Eileen didn't seem to have understood her. She could get like this sometimes, a dog with a bone. Denials wouldn't dissuade her.

I'm not doing a DNA test, Eileen. Subject's closed.

But no subject was ever closed with Eileen. It might recede for a while, but it was bound to come back. And since she wasn't going to do a DNA test, it would become a loop. One they'd spin around over and over until Kaitlyn was sick.

Kaitlyn had tried to help her, but there wasn't any way out.

A few weeks later, when Kaitlyn's boss asked her some pointed questions about whether she was ever going to come back to work, she took the plunge and said no. A few weeks after that, her work e-mail account was shut down.

She didn't tell Eileen.

INTERVIEW TRANSCRIPT

TJ: There seem to be some inconsistencies in your story, Franny.

FM: Oh yeah? Such as?

TJ: Sherrie said that you often asked if you were adopted as a child, but your parents consistently denied it.

FM: I told you. I asked them not to tell her.

TJ: If you didn't want your sister knowing you were adopted, it doesn't make any sense that you'd bring up the possibility with your parents when she was around.

FM: I was a kid. I said stupid things. Maybe I was testing them, you know? Seeing if they'd respect my wishes.

TJ: Then there's the stint in juvenile detention you failed to mention.

FM: I told you—I did some stupid shit, stealing and such. I went to juvie for a couple months. What does that prove?

TJ: Nothing in and of itself, though I do find it revealing that you didn't tell me about it.

FM: I told you the big stuff. The relevant stuff.

TJ: And you spent time in a mental health facility.

FM: I suffer from depression sometimes. I'm not crazy. There's lots of reasons people go to those places. They helped me get better. I take my medication and I'm mindful or whatever, and I don't have those low moments anymore.

TJ: But it's another thing you didn't tell me.

FM: Why would I tell anyone that? You try telling people you spent time in a funny farm, and they're all thinking it's that *Cuckoo's Nest* book, you know? Like I was talking to walls or wearing tinfoil on my head. It wasn't like that. It was peaceful. Restful.

TJ: You told me you got a copy of your birth certificate and your birth mother called you Marigold. Is that right?

FM: Yes.

TJ: Well, I have a copy of your birth certificate right here. Eileen Marissa Warner. Born on October 10, 1994. That's your birthday, isn't it?

FM: Yes.

TJ: Strange coincidence about the date.

FM: I guess. I never thought about it.

TJ: I find that hard to believe.

FM: I never cared about my birthday. Why are people so fixated on getting older and celebrating that? It seems stupid to me. And then my mother died on my birthday, and it just made it that much worse. So I didn't mention it.

TJ: I looked back at the paperwork you filled out when you signed the waiver to participate in this film, and you put a different birth date down.

FM: It was this thing I did when I changed my name. I gave myself a new birthday, so I was starting over completely.

TJ: I see. Coming back to your birth certificate . . . It clearly doesn't say your name is Marigold.

FM: That's the one with my adoptive parents on it, right?

TJ: Yes.

FM: It's not my real birth certificate. They give you a new one after you get adopted.

TJ: I see. Do you have this other birth certificate?

FM: Not on me. I don't carry things like that around.

TJ: If you could send me a copy when you have a chance, I'd appreciate it.

FM: Sure, I'll do that. Are we done here?

TJ: There's one more thing I'd like to discuss. Why did you insist on having DNA matches to the wreckage for families to get compensation?

FM: I told you. To keep people from defrauding the fund.

TJ: It wasn't to distract away from your own fraud?

FM: What? I'm not a fraud.

TJ: You're sure about that?

FM: Of course I am.

TJ: Because I do have a copy of your DNA test.

FM: Why didn't you say so before?

TJ: I was giving you a chance to tell your own story.

FM: Uh-huh.

TJ: As I'm sure you're aware, your DNA didn't match to anything in the site. They used Kaitlyn's daughter Emily's DNA to match to her mug.

FM: No, that's not right. There was a match—there was.

TJ: I have the results right here. Would you like to see them?

[Pause]

FM: All this shows is that they forgot to test both samples when they found the mug . . . That doesn't prove anything.

TJ: Well, yes, that's technically true, but . . . We could run the test again. Would you agree to do that?

FM: You can run whatever tests you like. The lab has my DNA sample. They'll tell you. They'll tell you Kaitlyn Ring's my biological mother.

TJ: All right, Franny. Please calm down.

FM: Don't say that to me.

TJ: I'm sorry.

FM: We talked about that. I told you I hate that. I told you.

TJ: Are you okay? Do you need me to call someone?

FM: *[Muttering]* Stupid, stupid girl.

TJ: Franny?

FM: Are we done?

TJ: Yes, of course. I can't keep you here.

FM: This is such bullshit. And you know what? I revoke my consent. I take it back, okay? You don't have the right to use any of this.

TJ: The release doesn't work like that. It's irrevocable.

FM: We'll see about that. *[Shuffling sounds]* I can't get this thing off . . . No, don't touch me; I'll do it myself.

TJ: Franny, I—

FM: Forget it, okay? Just forget it. You want to bring me down. My whole life, everyone's wanted to bring me down. But you'll see. You'll see. I always end up on top in the end.

39

WRAP-UP

CECILY

"I'm sorry you had to see that," I say to Joshua. We're standing in the production room off the boardroom, where Teo's been conducting his interview with Franny. It's not equipped with two-way mirrors — this isn't a police station — but there's a monitor, and we've seen the entire thing.

Joshua's jaw is rigid. At one point, he was clenching his fists so hard I thought he might punch something. "It's fine. Fine."

"You didn't believe what I was telling you, and I couldn't think of another way to show you."

"I get it."

I feel terrible, but as I suspected, when I met Joshua last night for coffee, he didn't want to hear anything negative about Franny. I didn't even get into the details. Instead, I told him I didn't think Franny was who she said she was, and that Teo needed them both to come in for a final interview now that they'd decided to get married.

"I'm not sure either of us wants to participate in this anymore," Joshua had said.

"I know exactly how you feel."

"Then why are you trying to push me to do it? Push us?"

"We made a promise, and if we back out, then Teo won't have a film. That's a year of his life down the drain. It might end his career."

Joshua swirled the coffee around in his cup. "I would've thought you'd want his career over, given everything he's done to you."

"He was just doing his job. None of this is his fault."

"Isn't it?"

His phone was sitting on the table, and it buzzed with an incoming e-mail. He checked it, then pushed his phone aside. "I still can't believe what I read . . . Tom and Kaitlyn. It was like it was two different people who were writing those messages."

"I feel the same way, but maybe . . . I know this sounds crazy, naive, even, but maybe it was just words. Maybe they weren't doing those things in real life."

"Why would you say that?"

"The way it was written. It seemed like fantasy. Not . . . active, not describing something that had actually occurred, just something they'd thought about doing."

A pained expression crossed his face. I felt bad for making him even think about what we'd read.

"I guess that's possible. Still, doesn't make it right."

"Nothing's right."

"And you never had any idea? You two being so close and all?"

"Never. She was clearly very good at hiding things. As was Tom."

He shook his head. "Not so good. I kind of knew she had a crush on him."

"You did?"

"Sure. She had one for years."

I stared into my own cup. "I never knew."

"You didn't know what Kaitlyn looked like when she was in love."

"Oh, Joshua."

"It's all right. I figured it was harmless. Twenty years is a long time to be together without ever having feelings for another person. I never thought she'd act on it."

"That's the most surprising part."

"You're not surprised about Tom?"

"Of course, but not in the way you'd think. I knew Tom had an affair six months before he died. And that shocked me, but it wasn't unfathomable. I could understand it intellectually."

"But the Kaitlyn part? You must be surprised about that."

"Yes, I was shocked. You saw. I still have trouble believing it, to be honest. But tell me—how did Franny find those e-mails?"

"They were on Kaitlyn's laptop. It was still signed in to that account. She feels bad for snooping, but once she found the e-mails, she felt she had to tell me about them."

"I wish she'd kept them to herself."

"It wasn't her secret to keep."

"I guess."

"What did you mean before when you said you didn't think she could be trusted? Is that why?"

"Partly."

"What else, then?"

"Well, getting engaged to you is something."

"But I'm the one who did that."

"Are you, Joshua?" I covered his hand with mine. His wedding ring was missing, the skin where it used to be white and puckered. "Franny had no part to play at all?"

"Of course she did. But it was a mutual thing."

"Her mother's husband?"

"I know it sounds wrong, but you can't help it when feelings develop, can you? Look at you and Teo."

"What about us?"

"Not very professional, is it, for him to be dating one of the subjects of his film."

I withdrew my hand. How did he know about that? He must've recognized Teo in that photograph. "We're not dating. And even if we were, I hardly think it's the same. Franny's twenty-five years younger, and you think she's your wife's daughter. You only just met her, and now here you are, ready to commit your life to her?"

"What do you mean, I *think* she's Kaitlyn's daughter? Isn't she?"

I wanted to tell him then and there in the coffee shop about everything, but if I did, I knew he'd confront Franny about it, and then she'd never show up for the interview. And Franny has this way of convincing you about things, of working her way into a person. She'd done it to me, and she'd clearly done it to Joshua. I had no faith that he'd be able to resist her charms, see past her explanations. And I'd been right. Even when confronted with the truth in her interview with Teo, she'd held fast to her story and had come up with excuses. She'd almost convinced me she was innocent.

"I misspoke. And please don't speak to Franny about this, okay? I'm trying to look out for you and the girls."

"Is that why you want us to do that interview so much? Because it's the best thing for me and the girls?"

"Yes, actually."

"Come on."

"You'll have to trust me, Joshua. Please. Come and do your interview tomorrow. Bring Franny. I promise you it'll be a good thing in the end."

He'd agreed to come and had texted me this morning that Franny had agreed as well. We'd spent the last two hours watching Teo on the monitor as he got Franny to commit to one version of her story and then slowly picked it apart. Joshua had been angry, wanting to stop the proceedings, but I held him back. As her story started to unravel, he sat there, his shoulders falling, a look of shock that was becoming too familiar to me on his face.

"Are you going to be okay?" I say to Joshua now. "Do you want me to take you home?"

"I can manage it on my own, thanks."

"What are you going to do?"

"About what?"

"About Franny."

"That's between her and me."

"You're not . . . You can't continue to be with her after this?"

"That's none of your business."

"But she's not well. She's . . . She lied to you from the beginning, Joshua. She lied and manipulated and cheated and . . ."

"Maybe she did. Maybe she didn't."

"How can you say that? You saw what I saw."

Joshua looks wild-eyed, undone. I've never seen him like this. "What did I see? A clever man trying to make a sensational end to his film, that's what. Taking advantage of a vulnerable girl who's had enough terrible things happen." He stands, swaying slightly, then steadies himself against the wall. "Franny will be able to explain all of this; we need to give her a chance."

"I—"

"I gave you a chance. I came down here and subjected Franny to this. Now I want to take her home and discuss this with her privately."

He pushes past me and out into the hall. He walks into the room next door, where Franny's crying and struggling to get into her coat. Joshua takes her into his arms.

"It's going to be okay, darling."

"Joshua, Joshua, I didn't . . ."

"Hush now, it's okay. Don't say anything more. We'll discuss all this at home."

Teo meets my eyes. He shakes his head. I shake mine back at him.

"Needless to say," Joshua says to Teo, "I won't be sitting for an interview."

"I understand."

"And we'll be speaking to our lawyer to see what recourses we have."

"That's your right, of course."

"You've done a terrible thing here."

"I don't see it that way."

"Of course you don't."

"Just leave it, Teo," I say. "He's not going to listen to you."

Franny looks up at me from where she's been hiding her face in Joshua's shoulder. "I thought you were my friend."

"Friends don't lie about who they are."

"You're such a hypocrite. You've been lying this whole time, too. I saw. I saw in Kaitlyn's e-mails."

Joshua pats her on the shoulder. "Let's leave that now, Franny, all right? Let's go home."

"Yes, sorry. Of course I want to go home with you."

"Good."

He takes her by the hand and leads her out of the room. When we're alone, I say to Teo, "Can you believe that?"

"I'm not that surprised, honestly. Franny's very good at what she does. She has an explanation for everything."

"She can't explain away DNA."

"Sure she can. She'll just say the lab screwed up the results, that they mixed up the samples. It happens all the time."

"Does it?"

"Not often, no," he says. "But all she needs is a wedge of doubt to work with."

"So this was all wasted effort."

"I don't think so. Joshua knows the truth now. What he chooses to do with that information is another thing."

"I feel like shit."

"Why? You were only trying to help him."

"Is that what I was doing?"

He stands in front of me and takes me by the elbows. "You're much too hard on yourself."

"Isn't that always the way with heroes? Never content with the people they've saved, always concentrating on the ones they lost?"

His shoulders rise up and down. "Life's complicated. There are no easy, binary inputs. You can't expect a particular result where people are concerned."

"It would be so much easier if you could."

"Ain't that the truth."

"So what now?"

His hands move up my arms. "I finish the film. And then, hopefully, you'll go out with me again."

"Still on that, are we?"

"Is that okay?"

"Yes," I say. "But there's something I have to do first."

"What's that?"

"Confess."

I stop my car in Sara's driveway with a heavy heart. Today hasn't gone according to plan, and I feel that I've let Kaitlyn down somehow. Not that I owed her anything, but I don't like failure. No one does, but these issues with Franny felt like something manageable, something salvageable from this horrendous year. I could check off this box and then move on with my life.

I climb the back stairs and knock on the door. Kaitlyn opens it. She's wearing her coat. Her backpack's on the floor, the room clean of her meager possessions.

"Were you even going to wait for me to come back?"

"Of course. But there's a bus leaving in a few hours. I want to catch it."

"Where to this time?"

"Better if you don't know, probably."

"Probably."

Kaitlyn scrapes her hair back and fastens it with a hair tie. She pulls her hat over it. She could be anyone now, any woman in her midforties. It's not just her looks, it's the way she carries herself. She truly has become someone I don't know.

"How did it go?" Kaitlyn asks. "What did Joshua say?"

"We laid it all out, and Franny tried to explain everything away."

"Of course she did. But she can't."

"I'm not sure it was that simple for Joshua."

"What do you mean?"

"He didn't know what to think. He wanted to talk it out with Franny."

"He *what*?"

"They left together."

"He took her back to my house? To be with my kids?"

"For now. I'm sure that when this all sinks in . . ."

Kaitlyn wrapped her arms around herself. "No, you don't know her. You don't know her like I do."

"What are you talking about . . . ? Wait, what? You know Franny? You've met her?"

"We used to . . . correspond."

"When?"

"Years ago. She contacted me when I was pregnant with Emily. She thought I was her mother. She seemed so lost. So I wrote her back. I tried to help her. And for a while, I thought I was. But then she changed, things changed, and . . ."

"And what, Kaitlyn? Jesus Christ. Why didn't you tell me this in the beginning?"

"Because I'm not proud of what I did, and you already thought badly enough of me."

"What did you do?"

"I disappeared. She was getting aggressive about us meeting, wanting me to take a DNA test, all kinds of crazy things. So I cut her off. I changed my e-mail address and didn't tell her. I think I'm the reason she ended up in that mental institution. I think she tried to kill herself after I rejected her."

"But if she was convinced you were her mother, and you're not, then you were probably right to do that."

"I wanted to help her. But I had my own issues to deal with and the baby, and she was a lot of work. Very needy. I could've tried to get her help. I shouldn't have disappeared on her. But that's my MO, isn't it? The disappearing mother. Franny was just the test run."

"I can't believe I'm saying this, but I don't think you can blame yourself for this one."

"I'm the reason Franny's here, doing this. If I'd handled it better, she wouldn't have moved in on my family to exact some kind of revenge."

"You can't know that."

"She couldn't have done it if I hadn't run away."

"That's true. But she's ill. You're not responsible for that."

Kaitlyn closes her eyes, going to her own private space. I watch her. She opens her eyes again. She seems more focused.

"I can't believe Joshua. What's wrong with him?"

"He's hurt and confused."

"My fault again."

"Yes."

She smiles wryly. "I should get going."

"Okay."

"Thanks for helping me."

"I was trying to help Joshua and the girls."

"Fair enough. But thank you just the same." She walks past me to the door. "I'm truly sorry. I hope you know that."

"Will you keep in touch?"

"You want that?"

"I want to know that you're alive. That you're okay."

"I'll try."

"The girls will be all right."

"I'm going to make sure of that."

Kaitlyn opens the door and walks out of the apartment. I follow her.

"Wait, what do you mean? What are you going to do?"

"What I should've done in the first place."

She hurries down the stairs. I almost call her name, but then I stop myself; there are people on the street, people who might recognize her. And what can I do anyway? I can't control Kaitlyn any more than I could control Joshua. I've done enough.

For once in my life, I've done too much.

INTERVIEW TRANSCRIPT

Subject: Cecily Grayson (CG). Conducted by: Teo Jackson (TJ).

TJ: Are you ready?

CG: Ready to spill my big secret?

TJ: I'm here to listen to whatever you want to tell me.

CG: I don't mean to be dramatic. Probably in the grand scheme of things, my secret's not that big, but it could have important consequences for me.

TJ: I understand.

CG: You asked me the other day about the fact that I'd visited a divorce attorney. I told you Tom and I were having trouble in our marriage and that I'd gone to see a divorce attorney to explore my options. That's not the whole truth. The truth is, that was only at first. I'd found out some things about my husband, some things that made it hard for me to trust him again. He left for a while. That's when I went to see the divorce attorney.

TJ: But you didn't file for divorce?

CG: Not then. I let him move back home. But something was broken between us. He tried hard, he wanted things to work, but I didn't feel safe with him anymore. I didn't feel like I should.

TJ: I'm sorry to hear that.

CG: It's all right. Anyway, I told him I wanted a divorce. He fought me on it. He wanted to try to work things out, to stay together for the kids, to give it longer than I wanted to. But I couldn't see my feelings changing. I wasn't getting over it. I was just getting more and more angry each day. I was so consumed by it, it felt like a sickness. A cancer. It was killing me.

TJ: What did you do?

CG: He agreed to move forward with the divorce. There was a law firm in his building that did their corporate work that also had a divorce attorney on staff. We negotiated how it would work, and they got everything ready for us to sign so we could file. We worked everything out, but we hadn't told the kids. Tom asked for that. That we not tell them until we were ready to file. I think he was hoping I'd change my mind.

TJ: Then what happened?

CG: October tenth. I was going to his office because we were going to sign the documents, and that would've been it once the judge signed off.

TJ: But instead, he died?

CG: And you took my picture, and all of a sudden I was this person, this "widow," this symbol. And there was the money.

TJ: What about the money?

CG: If the divorce were final, I never would've gotten any money. But it wasn't. Tom and I were in financial trouble. We were going to have to sell the house and move into separate apartments, and even then it would've been a stretch, even with my going back to work. And I couldn't use the money the kids got to clean up my problems. That went into a trust for them until they're twenty-one. So I didn't tell anyone. I took the money when I didn't deserve it. I'm a complete fraud.

TJ: But you were still married.

CG: Technically, by a matter of inches. But I didn't want to be. I didn't want anything to do with him. But everything I have, any security I have, is because he died. And this image people have of me, it's false, a lie. I always say how much I hate it, but I've gone along with all of it. The attention, the press. I told myself it was a way to make it up, to be the person people wanted me to be. But I think I enjoyed the attention, deep down. I liked the perks. I'm a terrible person.

TJ: I don't think so.

CG: You're not the most objective audience.

TJ: That might be true, but you did do all the things people asked you to. You helped people. You had to take care of your family, your kids, their future. You were doing what you needed to survive.

CG: Is that the story you're going to tell now? With this footage?

TJ: I'm not sure. I'll see how it plays out in the editing room.

CG: You should leave me on the cutting room floor. Or make me into the villain. There's a good twist for you; the Poster Child actually belongs on a Most Wanted poster.

TJ: I don't think you did anything illegal.

CG: Only morally bankrupt. Added to that, I wanted this to happen.

TJ: What?

CG: For Tom to die. I wanted Tom to die.

TJ: But you're not responsible for the explosion.

CG: I know that objectively. But . . . my therapist doesn't like it when I say this, but sometimes it feels like I willed the explosion to happen. Sometimes I wonder if I was late that day because I was saving myself.

TJ: Maybe you *were* saving yourself.

CG: How?

TJ: You were reluctant to end your marriage. Maybe that's why you were late. Maybe you wanted to save things with him after all.

CG: I never thought of it like that. I was late that day because I didn't want to get divorced.

TJ: How does that sound? True?

CG: It feels like it might be true.

TJ: So you are a widow.

CG: I am a widow.

TJ: You deserved the money.

CG: Are you trying to hypnotize me? Getting me to repeat after you?

TJ: I don't think so.

CG: I deserved the money. Maybe, maybe that's right.

TJ: Thank you for telling me this, Cecily.

CG: What do you think's going to happen now?

TJ: I don't know the future. I only curate the past.

40

ONE ENDING

CECILY

When I get home, Cassie and Henry are making dinner.

"What's all this?"

"Cassie's making me cook."

"God, Henry. Am not."

"I'm in the kitchen, aren't I?"

"It was your idea, dummy."

"Kids, kids. Please. It's been a long day. What's on the menu?"

"Spaghetti and meat sauce."

"My favorite."

Cassie smiles at this. "Henry's making his garlic bread, too. And I made a Caesar salad."

"What did I do to end up with such wonderful children?" I sit at the kitchen counter and watch them work. Cassie takes a bottle of wine out of the fridge and pours me a glass. "Is there a dead body in the garage or something?"

"Mom! Why would you say that?"

"I feel like I'm being buttered up for something."

"Can't we just do something nice for you sometimes?"

I take a sip of wine. It reminds me of Kaitlyn, but that's not necessarily a bad thing. Or not only a bad thing. It's confusing. "Of course you can. I'm just naturally suspicious, I guess."

"Humph," Cassie says. "How did it go today?"

"Not as expected."

"What does that mean?"

I hesitate, but I can see Cassie winding up to give me her you-said-no-more-lies speech, so I tell them that we told Joshua that Franny isn't who she says she is as the kitchen starts to fill with the wonderful smell of garlic bread. Henry seems nonplussed—all of this is very much grown-up stuff and he still sometimes wears footie pajamas—but Cassie looks upset.

"We need to talk to Uncle Joshua. Tell him he's making a big mistake."

"It's his mistake to make."

"But what about the girls?"

"He's their father. He'll always protect them."

She seems unconvinced. She looks so much older, standing there in her apron, stirring the sauce. I feel like a kid, sitting on the other side of the counter, waiting for my dinner, but there's a peace to it, too. We did this. I did this—survived the year, kept my family intact, and myself. It feels like all this has finally chased my anxiety away. I can feel its absence more than anything, and this makes me hopeful. Maybe it will leave forever, like Tom, only a memory. If not, then I can handle it. I've survived the worst of it. I can survive any aftershocks that come my way.

"I feel so bad for those girls," Cassie says. "To have to live with Franny?"

"Let the dust settle. I have a feeling Joshua will come to his senses."

"I hope so. So what now, Aunt Kaitlyn just leaves, and no one knows she's alive?"

"Are you okay with that? Both of you? It's not fair of me to ask you to keep this secret if you don't want to."

Cassie puts an entire package of spaghetti into a pot of boiling water with a pinch of salt. "I think we should keep it. Some things are better as secrets. People can be hurt by the truth."

"I agree. But not between us."

"There are some things I'm not going to tell you."

"I know. But nothing important, okay?"

"Okay, Mom."

I know she's appeasing me, but I decide to lean into that. I've faced enough harsh truths in the last little while.

"What about you, Henry? Do you want to tell about Kaitlyn?"

He opens the oven to check on his bread. "I don't think so."

"It's a big secret to keep."

He puts the loaf in front of me. It takes an act of will not to rip open the tinfoil and down the entire thing. I didn't eat much today, and it's catching up to me.

"It's like what Cassie said. The truth would hurt Emily and

Julia, and Uncle Josh, too. And she's not coming back, right? She's leaving."

"She's leaving."

"I say we don't tell."

"But what if they were you? What if Dad was alive, but he'd run away from us? Would you want to know?"

He shifts back and forth on his feet, maybe trying not to cry. "That would be an awful thing for Dad to do."

"Yes."

"I don't think I'd want to know. But he didn't do that, right, Mom? He's dead."

"Yes, honey. I'm sorry."

"Okay. I just wanted to make sure."

He opens the foil, and a head of steam billows out.

"That smells amazing. Let's eat."

Cassie looks at the clock. "We're waiting for one more person."

"Who's that?"

"That's me," Teo says, walking into the kitchen.

"What are you doing here?"

"Surprise!" the kids say together. "We invited him!"

"How did you get in?"

"I left the front door unlocked," Cassie says. She walks over to me and gives me a hug. "Be happy, Mom."

My throat tightens. "I'm happy."

"Be happier, then." She pulls away. "Time for dinner. Everyone sit down."

I can't help but smile at my bossy daughter, doing her best impression of me. I pick up my wineglass and walk into the living room.

Teo follows.

"If you want me to go, I will."

"I don't want you to go."

"Good."

He brushes my cheek with his lips, then pulls away as Cassie and Henry carry the food into the dining room. We gather around the table. Instead of sitting in Tom's place, Teo pulls a chair around to Henry's side, winking at me as he sits down.

"Should we give some gratitude?" Cassie asks.

"Good idea. Hands, everyone."

I reach out and take each of my children's hands. Henry holds Teo's, and Cassie reaches across the table to take his other hand.

"I'm grateful I didn't get grounded when I snuck out of the house the other night," Cassie says.

"What?" Henry says. "Aw, Mom, that's not fair."

"Hush, Henry. Your turn."

"I'm grateful Mom is buying me the new *Dead Space 3*."

"Not a chance, kid."

"I'm grateful to be here, among friends, eating good food," Teo says.

"You haven't tasted it yet."

"Mom!"

"I'm grateful for all of you. Even for the surprise dinner guest."

"Let's eat," Henry says.

Cassie starts dishing out the pasta, and Henry passes the garlic bread. I look around the room at these people I love, or hope to love. They are so much more important than the things I filled this house with. They're what I carry with me everywhere, no matter where we might end up. I have these things because I wasn't in the building that day.

I wasn't in the building that day because I was late.

Whether it was the universe looking out for me or just a happenstance of my personality, I'm most grateful for that of all.

41

ANOTHER ENDING

KAITLYN

When Kaitlyn left her hiding place, running away from Cecily, she knew what she had to do. It was a big risk, but she had no other choice.

She pulled out her phone, the one she'd bought in Montreal, and sent a message to an address she couldn't forget. Then she went to wait.

She picked a seedy bar near the bus station. A bar no one she knew would dare to be seen in. It had been the scene of at least three shootings last time Kaitlyn checked. The bouncer gave her the eye when she walked in, questioning her choice of drinking establishment. She was the only woman in the place besides the waitresses and the prostitute sitting at the bar.

She ordered a beer and took a table facing the door. The table was littered with peanut shells and stale popcorn. A small part of her wondered if this was where she'd be caught. If she'd miscalculated, and the front door would bang open to reveal the police. Full of noise and threats to *stay down!* But she was sure she'd judged properly. As she told Cecily, she knew Franny, Eileen, whoever she was.

After she'd changed her e-mail, there'd been radio silence for years. In that time, Kaitlyn had pieced her life back together. She'd had Julia, gone through another round of postpartum, become friends with Cecily. She'd let her guard down was what she'd done. So much so that when she'd gone back to work, she hadn't even thought about the fact that Eileen might find her. That she should ask to be left off the company website.

That had been a mistake. A month after she started working at Tom's company, Eileen had contacted Kaitlyn on her work e-mail. She called herself Franny, but Kaitlyn knew exactly who she was. It was like being caught in that movie *Groundhog Day*. Everyone else, including Franny, seemed to have amnesia. No one even noticed the feedback loop. Only Kaitlyn knew what was going on. That she'd been through all this before.

At first Kaitlyn wondered if Franny was playing a prank. There was probably some slang she hadn't learned that described what it was. "Catfishing" or "cyberstalking" or something like that. Kaitlyn told Franny she knew who she was and that they'd been through this. *Stop writing me.* But Franny persisted. They were two ships passing in the night. Kaitlyn would write something like: *I'm not your mother. Stop writing me.* And Franny would respond with: *I've missed you so much, too. I can't wait for us to meet in person.*

It was infuriating. She tried blocking Franny's e-mail, but she'd just opened another account and written her again. She tried not answering, but then Franny's tone turned threatening. She couldn't wait to meet her stepfather and sisters, she said. Then she'd name some location the family had all been to the week before as a good meeting place. In a desperate moment, Kaitlyn even called the police, but the bored dispatcher didn't give her much hope of relief. She took Kaitlyn's details down and said a detective would call. But when he did, weeks later, and Kaitlyn described what was going on, he said there wasn't much they could do. If this woman hadn't made any threats, she'd be better off just ignoring her until she went away.

So Kaitlyn did what he said. When a new e-mail from Franny came in, she deleted it without reading it. She never answered. She didn't even block her because that might be seen as some point of connection, a conversation.

In the weeks before October tenth, Kaitlyn had a lot on her mind. Mostly to do with Cecily and Tom, and the fact that they were getting divorced. Cecily was torn up about it, but Kaitlyn thought only of the relief it might bring. Maybe she should get divorced, too. Not to marry Tom, that wasn't what she wanted. But to make some major changes in her life. To come clean with someone, herself, at least. And the thought of having some time to herself, the weeks when Joshua would have the girls . . . That was appealing. Too appealing. She began to fantasize about it as she used to do about Tom's messages.

She'd sat at her desk that morning waiting, waiting. Knowing the meeting between Tom and Cecily was going to begin at ten a few floors above her. Then the e-mails started. Constant, relentless. She wanted it to stop. She'd gotten up from her desk and almost run to the elevator. She barely remembered the ride down, the exit into the lobby. Then the explosion. Then she was out in the street, running again. She'd been running ever since.

Franny entered the bar, a scarf tied around her head and big glasses over her eyes. Kaitlyn cursed to herself. Always the drama queen, needing attention wherever she went. Franny was the one who was going to get them caught. She should've met her in the park and brained her with a rock. And good riddance.

The violence of this thought surprised her. She wondered if she could pull it off. But that would be too easy for Franny. She hit a button on her phone and turned it over so it was facedown on the table as Franny sat.

"I can't believe this," Franny said. "You're alive."

"I'm alive."

"But why, Mom? How?"

"Stop calling me that."

Kaitlyn knew she shouldn't let Franny get to her, but she couldn't help it.

"You said I could call you that."

"I never . . . Never mind. Thank you for coming."

"I can't believe it. You're here. We're going to be together."

"I'm here."

"This is so great. It's what I've always wanted."

"What about Joshua?"

"What about him?"

"If I'm alive, you can't marry him."

A smile crossed Franny's face that Kaitlyn could only describe as creepy. "That'll work out. Joshua's such a sweetie."

"You're unbelievable."

"That's not a nice thing to say."

"I'm not feeling very nice right now. So, how did you do it?"

"Do what?"

"The explosion. I can't work it out."

The smile dropped from Franny's face. She looked around her. She seemed scared.

"No one's here," Kaitlyn said. "It's just you and me. How'd you do it?"

"I didn't do anything."

"Oh, come on. October tenth at 10:00 a.m.? October tenth is your birthday, and you used to write me at 10:00 a.m. every day. I should've seen it right away, but I had my own . . . I was distracted. I know you did it. I just want to know how."

"Don't you want to know why?"

"I've got the why. It's me. Some form of punishment because you felt rejected."

"You did reject me. Over and over again, my whole life."

"For the last time, Franny, or Eileen, or whoever the hell you are, I'm not your mother."

"You are. I had a DNA test done."

"No, you didn't. I never gave you my DNA."

"Yes you did."

Kaitlyn was back in the terrible merry-go-round. What was there to say to this girl?

"When? How?"

"Okay, fine. So I took a glass you left at a restaurant, okay? So what. It's the results that count."

"You what?"

"You kept lying and lying. What choice did I have? You're my mother."

Kaitlyn closed her eyes. When had she lost control of this conversation? This wasn't going to work. Threats never worked with Franny. She knew. She'd tried. There was only one choice.

She opened her eyes and did her best to smile.

"Okay, Franny. You win."

"You admit it? You admit you're my mother."

"Yes."

"Why are you admitting this now? After all this time?"

"Because I'm tired. I'm tired of denying it. Of running."

Franny started to cry. "I can't believe it. It's happening, it's finally happening."

Kaitlyn reached across the table. She felt sick to her stomach as she stroked the back of Franny's hand.

"I'm sorry I lied to you."

"Why did you?"

"I'll tell you everything, okay? But I need you to be honest with me. I need you to tell me how you blew up the building."

"Why do you want to know?"

"Because I want to be close to you. But there can't be any secrets between us for that to happen. So tell me. I want to understand."

Franny was shaking her head, but Kaitlyn could feel her tipping. She leaned forward.

"It's pretty amazing that you got away with it. I'm impressed."

"You are?"

"Of course I am. You must be very, very smart."

"Everyone thinks I'm stupid."

"I've never thought that. So tell me, Franny. Tell me, sweetheart . . . How did you do it?"

Franny smiled the slowest smile Kaitlyn had ever seen. "It was easy. People are stupid, you know? And they underestimate people. They underestimate people like me all the time."

"I'll bet they do."

Franny's smile spread. She was enjoying this. "I was working at Peoples Gas as a secretary."

"You were living in Chicago?"

"I moved here two years ago."

"That's how you were following us around so easily?"

"That's right."

"And what happened at work?"

"All I was hearing about was how bad the pipes were. How one might blow at any moment and God forbid because it could bring down a whole building. And one day this guy, this technician, Carl, who was a bit sweet on me, showed me a map of where the worst pipes were. And he pointed to one, and it was like a sign or something. It was right under your building."

Kaitlyn shivered. "And then what?"

"I asked him, all casual like, how could it happen? What could make something blow up? He told me it would only take a small hole in the pipe. Something that could easily go overlooked, especially if one of the sensors was out, which they were all the time. The gas would accumulate, and if it didn't get repaired quickly, all it would take is a spark to blow the whole thing up."

"How did you get in the tunnel?"

"That was easy, too. All the maps were there, and I swiped a security pass when a worker came in one day. I just had to be patient."

"And that morning you went down and made a hole in the pipe?"

"Yes, and I turned off the sensor so no one would know there was a leak."

"That was clever. What created the spark?"

"I found this thing on the Internet about how to rig a trash can to burst into flames on a delay . . . I put that in a maintenance closet where I knew one of the vents led down to the tunnels. The timing worked out even better than I expected."

Franny smiled that smile again. The room turned cold. Kaitlyn leaned back in her chair. All she wanted to do was get up and run, but she had one last thing to do.

"I want you to leave town," Kaitlyn said.

"You want to go somewhere together?"

"No."

"What? I thought . . ." The color fled from Franny's face. "You tricked me, didn't you? You still don't care."

"Yes, I tricked you."

"Well, I'm not leaving."

"Yes you will."

"Why should I?"

Kaitlyn turned over the phone. The record function was on, blinking red. "Because if you don't, this recording's going to the police."

"What? You wouldn't do that . . . You'd be caught, too."

"I'll take my chances. You'll leave tonight. Now."

"No, I have to go say goodbye."

"You're leaving in thirty minutes. I even bought you a ticket. You can e-mail them once you get there. Joshua will be relieved. Trust me."

"He chose me, you know. I didn't even have to work that hard."

Kaitlyn hit the button to end the recording. Franny tried to grab it from her, but Kaitlyn was too quick. She pocketed the phone.

"Don't bother. See that guy at the door? I paid him five hundred dollars to watch out for me. If you try anything, he will be on you so fast." She pushed a bus ticket across the table. "Take the ticket, Franny. Eileen. Go home."

Franny looked at the location. Madison.

"I don't want to go back there."

"I don't care. You can leave and go somewhere else if you want. You just have to promise not to come back to Chicago."

"How will you know if I do?"

"I have something set up."

It didn't take Franny long to get there. "Cecily."

Kaitlyn didn't say anything.

"I made sure Joshua knew what you did with Tom. I knew he'd tell Cecily," Franny said.

"Thanks for that."

They glared at each other. Kaitlyn had a sickening thought that she and Franny weren't so different after all. And wasn't the explosion at least partly her fault? If she'd handled Franny properly, maybe none of this would have happened. They'd both spend the rest of their lives in purgatory. It wasn't enough to pay for her own sins, but it was something.

"You'd better get going, Franny. You wouldn't want to miss your bus."

Franny's eyes darted around the room, looking for an exit.

"There's no way out. Take the ticket. Go to Madison. Then go where you want. Start over for good this time. And get some help. Forget about me. Forget about my family."

"I can't ever forget about you."

Kaitlyn suspected the feeling was mutual, but she didn't want to think about that right now.

"Let's go. Stand up."

Franny followed her instructions. Kaitlyn left some money on the table for her drink, then tapped Franny between her shoulder blades, leading her out of the bar. They crossed the street, Kaitlyn with a firm grip on Franny's arm. She took her to her bus stop. She waited with her until it was time to get on. They didn't say goodbye.

There was nothing left to say.

SOON AFTER GIVING HER LAST INTERVIEW TO THE
PRODUCTION CREW, FRANNY MAYCOMBE DISAPPEARED.

SHE NEVER PROVIDED THEM WITH A
COPY OF HER BIRTH CERTIFICATE.

A MONTH AFTER FILMING FINISHED, THE PRODUCTION
OFFICE RECEIVED AN ANONYMOUS ENVELOPE.

IT CONTAINED PARTS OF A RECORDING WHERE
SOMEONE IDENTIFIED AS FRANNY MAYCOMBE
IS HEARD CONFESSING TO DELIBERATELY
SETTING OFF THE EXPLOSION ON OCTOBER
TENTH THAT KILLED 513 PEOPLE.

THE PRODUCTION COMPANY TURNED OVER
THE RECORDING TO THE POLICE.

THEY'RE CURRENTLY INVESTIGATING
THE PROVENANCE OF THE TAPE.

THEY NOW BELIEVE THAT THE TRIPLE TEN TRAGEDY
WASN'T AN ACCIDENT BUT A DELIBERATE ACT.

FRANNY MAYCOMBE IS THE PRIME SUSPECT.

HER CURRENT WHEREABOUTS ARE UNKNOWN.

EPILOGUE

ANONYMOUS POST FROM
IKNOWWHATYOUDIDLASTSUMMER.COM

I have a secret.

Twenty-four years ago, I gave a baby up for adoption.

When I was eighteen years old, I won a contest to intern at a famous magazine in Europe. I was so surprised I won that it took me weeks to tell my parents. I'd lie in bed and stare and stare at the envelope, the letter. I read everything I could about the city. I bought tapes and learned the language. Actually learned it, not just the way you do in school. I loved the way it rolled off my tongue. The way it tasted.

My parents were strict, and I was a bit wild. I thought I was carefree, that they were too cautious. But I can see their point of view now. I was reckless. The kid who'd walk along the edge of the seawall. The one who didn't listen when her parents told her to step away from the ledge. I scraped knees, broke a wrist, got a mild concussion. They'd frown while I laughed. The pain was worth the experience.

So this, I knew this, even though I was eighteen, would be a problem. I needed to show my parents I could be trusted. That nothing would happen to me. That I'd be safe.

Somehow I did. They hemmed and hawed. I begged and pleaded and promised.

And then they let me go.

I met him the third day I was there. I see the cliché now. An older man, my boss, married. The heedless, naive girl from North America. After, when it was over, I realized he'd manipulated it all from before I arrived. That he'd chosen me because he saw something in my essay. My photograph. Something pliable. Something broken that he could exploit rather than fix. That even the flowers he'd given me—marigolds—were part of the information he'd gleaned from my application. Was he a sociopath? Given everything, I've wondered. But then? I thought he was charming. Smart. The man for me forever.

Until the stick turned blue two months into the New Year.

Then he was cold, distant. More clichés upon clichés. I would have an abortion. He would pay, grudgingly it seemed. Of course he wouldn't leave his wife. Had I done this on purpose?

It was nasty. I was afraid. I didn't know how to tell my parents. I couldn't bring myself to end the connection I had to him. I loved him.

I loved him.

I found a place to go. My parents weren't expecting me back until the summer. I called them once a week with updates, fake stories. Even to me, my life sounded fabulous.

Then, in small towns, there were still places for girls like me. The nuns who worked at the place I went to were kind but censorious. As I grew larger and larger through the spring, I felt as if I was being crushed under the weight of their judgment. I craved my own language, food, city. I wanted to nest.

I wanted to go home.

That was impossible, but I found a place to go that was near enough. A sister organization the nuns approved of. I told my parents I'd been asked to stay on. The university would defer another year, and I could start my courses by correspondence. I made it seem as if it was their choice, and they agreed. They missed me, though. I said I'd call more often.

I flew home in my eighth month, the end of a hot August, passengers staring. I looked so young. A baby having a baby. I remember my hair sticking to my neck. How I could never get cool. How often I had to pee.

The nuns met me at the airport, drove me to Wisconsin. I barely remember anything of the drive, flat land flashing by. Then weeks staring out the window, feeling as if I was forcing myself to eat. Then pain. They never tell you about the pain. A conspiracy of women. I even found myself doing it, so much later, when I was pregnant with my daughter. I must've been exaggerating. It couldn't be that bad.

It was. And then it was over, and I was holding this alien thing. I thought I'd love it. Her. I thought I'd love her because she was a part of him. Instead, I turned my face away. I couldn't face this, not now, and so the choice was made for me. Forms were signed. The baby was whisked away. I went back to the nuns until the weight had slipped from my body.

The last month I was there, I read every issue of the magazine I was supposed to have contributed to. I made my weekly calls to my parents. I tried not to think of what I'd done. I surprised them the day before Christmas. Twinkling lights and a sprinkle of snow. My parents were delighted. I was so skinny, though—was everything all right? I nodded and brightened my smile and let my mother take me shopping for the college I would finally start in January.

At night I cried. Then I taught myself how to forget. Her smell, her face. I erased each memory one by one by one. The memories of him were the hardest. His laugh, the way he held me. The cold look in his eyes when I told him. But I did it. I did it.

I went to college. Every fall, around her birthday, the one day I couldn't forget, a dark cloud descended. The fall blahs, I used to say, and take my medication. The clouds would lift, but I was a different person. Cautious. Lacking trust. Looking for security.

The man I married matched the new me. Or so I thought. I fashioned a life. The years rolled away. I wasn't happy, but I was managing.

Then she came back. My daughter, the one I'd abandoned. She wrote to me. She wrote to me, and I was terrified. She wrote to me, and I was sad. She wrote to me, and I told her I wasn't her mother. That she had the wrong person. That I never gave a baby up for adoption.

So many lies.

ACKNOWLEDGMENTS

This book came tougher than some. Keeping me company along the way were:

My sister and first reader, Cam.

My friends on the roller coaster, especially Tasha, Janet, Tanya, Stephanie, Lindsay, Christie, and Candice.

Wait, I have male friends, too: my patient and supportive husband, David; Eric; Presseau; Adrian; and Dan.

My writerly peeps; my agent, Abigail Koons, and the whole Park Literary team; my editor at Lake Union, Jodi Warshaw, and the great author team there; Danielle Marshall and publicists Dennelle Catlett and Kathleen Zrelak; my new team at S&S Canada, Laurie Grassi,

Nita Pronovost, and Kevin Hanson. And Paul Benjamin. Thank you all for believing in me and my writing.

The other writers in my life, especially Therese Walsh, Liz Fenton and Lisa Steinke, Heather Webb, Barbara Claypole White, Kathleen McCleary, Bruce Holsinger, those in the Fiction Writers Co-op, and Shawn Klomparens. You read, you listened, you gave great feedback. This book, and my life, would be less without you.

My readers, who I am so grateful for.

And Sara: who this book is for. She knows why.

This book was written principally in Montreal, Canada; Jackson Hole, Wyoming; and Puerto Vallarta, Mexico. February 25, 2016, to January 1, 2017.

THE

GOOD
LIAR

CATHERINE McKENZIE

A READING GROUP GUIDE

BOOK CLUB QUESTIONS

1. Few people knew about the impending divorce between Cecily and Tom. What do you think about Cecily's motives for keeping it a secret?

2. Do you think Cecily's anger toward Tom even after his death is a way for her to avoid dealing with her grief and feelings of guilt, or is what he did so awful?

3. What would Cecily have to gain or lose by forgiving Tom?

4. Do you think Cecily is right to eventually tell Cassie and Henry about the difficulties in her marriage?

5. Cecily was supposed to be in the building at the time of the explosion but wasn't. What role do you think fate played in that situation? How might Cecily and other characters have acted at various times if their beliefs about fate or coincidence were different?

6. Cecily feels too guilty about hiding the trouble in her marriage to see that she's been a hero to many after the tragedy, while Kaitlyn believes herself to be a "bad mother," even though she's a good nanny. Why do you think some people have trouble seeing the good parts of themselves and focus only on their faults?

7. What do you think of Kate/Kaitlyn's choice to run away from her family?

8. How much regret do you think Kaitlyn has about her actions in life? Do you believe she does love her children? How differently do you think you'd feel about it if the character were a man?

9. Kaitlyn risked exposure by returning to Chicago to save her family from Franny, but then she chose to leave again. Why? Do you think she made the right choice the second time?

10. Why do you think that Franny acts the way she does? What does that reveal about her? What is she hoping to accomplish?
11. Why are people so suspicious of Franny and her motives? What might she have done differently to alleviate those fears?
12. Why do you think Kaitlyn refuses to acknowledge Franny? How much of a role does that play in Franny's actions, and in Kaitlyn's own?
13. Has there ever been a time in your life when you were tempted to run away from everything?

This is your eighth novel. What was the inspiration for this one?
I have had the idea for part of this novel kicking around in my brain for years: What would happen if someone used a national tragedy to run away from her life? I wasn't sure there was enough of a story there, so I parked it. Then I heard various stories about people faking their way into tragedies, which I also thought was fascinating. And then, finally, I heard a story about a 9/11 widow whose divorce was about to be finalized right before the towers fell. The three ideas fused together and became *The Good Liar.*

What interests you most—characters or plot?
I always start with plot—the big question or premise the book will be about. In this case, it was an image of a woman running away from a tragedy, a woman running toward the same tragedy, and one stuck in the middle of it. Once I have the premise, I think more about the plot. What's the beginning, middle, and end? Where does this premise go? When I have that, I wait for the voice of the main character to show up. I do this by thinking about that person: who are they, how are they trapped in this situation, et cetera. When I hear that voice, I start writing.

This story is about lies on so many levels: Tom's affair, Kaitlyn's dishonesty throughout her marriage, Franny's deception surrounding her background, Cecily's lies to herself and others about

her feelings for Teo. **What is it about deception that you find so fascinating?**

I think there is a lot of withholding in life, and even more so in books. When you are writing suspense, there are — in my view — two ways to go about it. You can create tension and fear through external forces (What was that noise in the basement?) or you can do it through having your characters be unreliable (which is another word for liars). I've never been a fan of external fears (I hate horror movies — I don't enjoy being visually scared or the gore involved), so I tend to gravitate toward character-driven suspense.

When you're writing, do you always know how a story is going to end?

Generally. Sometimes the fine details change, or, as in this case, I added an epilogue that I hadn't envisioned specifically, but for which I subconsciously left bread crumbs throughout the book that I picked up in that chapter.

Do your characters, and how they grow and develop as you're writing a story, ever make you veer off course as far as plot goes?

I'm sure this happens, though maybe more on a subconscious level than an overt one. I don't recall specific instances of me having to change a significant plot point because of the way a character is "acting." I'm more likely to adapt the way a character is acting to the plot.

What character in this book did you most identify with and why?

That's a tough one! To write believable characters you have to get into their skin to a certain extent, and understand their point of view.

I would say I understand part of each of their characters: Cecily's need to please; Franny's wish to be loved; and Kate's desire to *run*.

You practice law in Montreal. How do you manage to find the time to fit in writing, and how do you think your work as a litigator complements your work as a writer?

As a lawyer you need to be organized and efficient, and both of these characteristics help my writing and give me the time to do it. I mostly write on the weekends and vacations these days. The first third of this book (rough draft) was mostly written in a week while I was skiing in Jackson Hole, Wyoming. The last third in two weeks while I was on Christmas vacation in Puerto Vallarta, Mexico. The middle took all the time in between.

What is the greatest influence on your writing?

Reading and watching great books and television shows. Being surrounded by great writing is key. For instance, shows like *Gilmore Girls*, *Felicity*, *The West Wing*, and of course *The Wire* are great places to learn characterization and dialogue. Early favorite books of mine include the Anne of Green Gables books, the Little House on the Prairie series, and the works of Frances Hodgson Burnett. I spent my teen years reading Stephen King and murder mysteries like Agatha Christie and Rex Stout. I found Jane Austen in my early twenties. And now I have individual love affairs with books like *The Fault in Our Stars*, *The Night Circus*, and *The Time Traveler's Wife*.

ABOUT THE AUTHOR

© JASON MOTT

CATHERINE McKENZIE's novels—*Fractured, Smoke, Hidden, Forgotten, Arranged,* and *Spin*—are all bestsellers and have been translated into numerous languages. Catherine practices law in Montreal, where she was born and raised. Visit her online at www.catherinemckenzie.com, on Facebook at www.facebook.com/catherinemckenzieauthor, and on Twitter or Instagram at @CEMcKenzie1.